The Reapers MC, Ravenswood Series

Reaper Released

Book Two

Harley Raige

Copyright © 2023 Harley Raige
All rights reserved.

No part of this book may be reproduced or transmitted in any form, or by any electronic or mechanical means, including photocopying, recording, or by any information storage and retrieval systems, without written permission from the author, except for the use of brief quotations in a book review.
For permissions contact: harleyraige@gmail.com

This is a work of fiction. Names, characters, organisations, and incidents are either products of the author's slightly deranged, mildly twisted imagination or used fictitiously. Any resemblance to actual persons, living or dead, is purely coincidental.
Edited by www.fiverr.com/immygrace

For updates on my upcoming releases, please follow me on
www.tiktok.com/@harleyraige

www.instagram.com/harleyraige

www.facebook.com/harleyraige
Join our group at
www.facebook.com/groups/the.rebels.of.raige

Become a Rebel of Raige and join the Rebellion!

Authors Note

The author is British, this story does contain British spellings and phrases. This book also contains possible triggers, including but not limited to kidnapping and murder. It also contains explicit sexual situations, strong violence, taboo subjects, a shit tonne of offensive language and mature topics, some dark content, plus F/M.
18+

Dedication

Mum,
Thankyou for everything you do, you are my rock.
Love Forever and Always.
This ones for you!

Contents:

Reaper Released
Authors Note
Dedication
Contents:

Scar	1
Ray	11
Steel	21
Ray	36
Ray	42
Ray	59
Ray	68
Ray	74
Ray	84
Ray	118
Steel	132
Ray	137
Scar	149
Steel	154
Ray	159
Ray	188
Ray	207
Steel	221
Ray	224
Ray	315
Ray	320
Catalina	325
Ray	331
Ray	372

Acknowledgements 389
Books by Harley Raige 390

Scar

I'm in a state of panic, but then my sister's words ring through my head, and I pull out my phone. After explaining what has happened, Uncle Bernie tells me to go straight to Ares's office and stay there till he gets here. It will be a few hours as he's out of state, but I must make sure I'm not seen by anyone other than Ares.

Ducking out of the van, I run around the whole back of the clubhouse and in the far back door, up the stairs and not even knocking, I run straight into his office. Well I say run but my screaming ribs say different.

"Shit, princess, what the fuck?" With the panic on his face when he sees me, and the panic on mine, he takes in the tears rolling down my face. I slam the door shut behind me but gasp when I see Viking, Tank, Dice, Priest and Blade all standing there, staring at me.

"Fuck!" I sob. "No one can see me. No one can know they didn't take me!"

"Princess, I need you to calm down, okay? You're

not making any sense. Guys, can you give us a minute?" The guys make a move to leave, but I step against the door.

"No! No one can leave this room till Uncle Bernie gets here. No one can know I'm still here. You need to keep me here, and they need to stay. They can't go. No. One. Can. Know!"

Viking steps forward and places his hand on my arm. "Scar?" he says gently. "What's going on?" I turn and lock the door, then breathe out the breath I'd been holding since the second Ray had been taken.

"They took Ray. Two guys came and took her. They were looking for me… Said Shay had sent them, then they thought she was me and took her. I hid from them and called Uncle Bernie, and he said to come to your office and don't let anyone see me, but you've seen me, so you can't go! You need to stay! You have to!"

"Scar, give me your phone. I need to call your Uncle Bernie, okay?"

I nod and give him the phone, opening it for him and passing it over. While Ares talks to Uncle Bernie, the guys sit me down on the sofa and get me a drink.

Viking pulls me into a hug and holds me there. "Don't worry, babe, we will get her back, okay?"

I sob into his shirt as I nod, but he just rubs up and down my back while he holds me tight. After Ares gets off the phone, he sends a message to the whole club.

When the guys' phones bling, they look, and I see "911."

"What does that mean?" I ask.

Ares explains that it's to get everyone back here immediately, and it's sent to the whole club. As far as anyone is concerned, it will be me who has been taken, so we have to keep me out of sight. Ares has put a call out to all the members out on jobs. And now we have to wait for Uncle Bernie to arrive.

There's a loud knock on the door. Ares asks who it is, and Dozer replies, so he's let in, too, fuck's sake. At this rate, the whole club will be in this office. Once they explain everything to him, he pulls me into a hug. "Hey, she's a badass motherfucker, don't worry. They will soon bring her back when she starts being... ya know, her usual self."

I huff a humourless laugh. I know he's trying to be funny, but I actually think he's right. Ray isn't the kind of girl who just gets kidnapped and plays along nicely. She's gonna fuck shit up, and maybe end up dead.

I must pace that office for a good hour at least. The boys are practically going stir-crazy. Dice has been sitting at Ares's desk, hacking into security footage, trying to follow the van and find out who has taken her. About two hours after she's gone, there's a knock at the door. Stepping back, I hide behind the guys.

I hear a deep gravelly voice I don't recognise. "Ares, what's going on, brother?" Ares makes his way opening the door, and a god-honest mammoth of a man walks in.

"Fuck, Steel, thank god you're here!" Clapping him on the back, he leads him into the office and locks the door again.

"No. No. No. No. No! What the fuck? No one can know I'm here, fuck! Fuck!"

"Calm down, princess. Steel is my best friend. My Enforcer. I trust him like I trust the others in this room. This is my entire inner circle. I trust them with my life, okay?"

I nod, but this is Ray's life. What about hers? Should I trust them with that? I let out a shaky breath. What else can I do? Thirty minutes later, there's another knock.

A young male voice comes through the door. It might be Roach. "Pres… Sorry to bother you. There's a guy out here saying he needs to see you… He says he's called Bernie."

"I'm coming. I'm gonna go grab him, princess, okay, then I'll bring him back here." He turns to Steel. "Protect her for me, Brother. I won't be long, don't let anyone else in this room!"

"Don't worry, Brother. I'll guard her with my life. You know that!" I don't know who this guy is, but he's fucking scary. He has the shiniest blacker than black hair in a faux hawk, a deep scar that runs from his right eyebrow, down through most of his eyelid, and down onto his cheek. His voice sounds like he eats gravel for breakfast and washes it down with razor blades. He must be about six foot four, and he has grey eyes that look like liquid metal. They almost swirl as I look at him. He's even bigger than Viking. He's solid muscle, his black T-shirt straining against them. He walks over to the Fucked Up Five, and they all speak under their breaths while Dozer sits with me, rubbing my arm.

"Did you know about the lodge?" Dozer breaks me from my inner panic.

"Lodge?"

"Did Ray tell you about our… fight?"

"Fight?"

Blowing out a breath he informs me. "We had a fight at the lodge about you guys leaving. She punched me and knocked me on my ass. So I grabbed her and threw her in the lake up there, and she managed to drag me in too. We've not really spoken since."

"Oh," is all I can muster to that, and knowing Ray, that's only the half of it.

"Well, I went up there this weekend, and I'm pretty sure she must have been going up there all week. She's repaired and painted nearly everything. The whole time I was ignoring her at work, angry 'cos you guys were gonna fucking leave, and she's up there fixing up my lodge so it's almost ready to move in. There's only the bathroom to tile, and it's done!"

"She will be pissed she didn't get to finish it before we leave! Once she starts something, she's a force of nature!" A slight sob sneaks out as Dozer pulls me in tighter. "I can't lose her, Dozer. She's all I've got!" I lean into him and just sob as he rubs his hands gently up and down my back.

"She's gonna be okay. I can't lose her either, especially knowing how I've treated her this week, but what she's been doing for me… I know she did it because I won't have the time once she's gone." I can feel him shaking his head against the top of mine as he continues to rub my back.

There's another knock at the door, and Ares's voice rings through it. Steel lets him and Uncle Bernie in and locks the door again. I run straight into Uncle Bernie's arms and break down, again.

After he has calmed me down, and checked over my injuries, he explains that if Ray phones, we need to make sure we pretend she's me, and that Uncle Bernie needs to speak to her. Ares explains how he has all the boys waiting in the clubhouse and is calling Church as soon as we know something.

RING. RING. RING. I shit myself and dive up off the sofa. It's Ares's mobile.

"Withheld number," he murmurs.

"Remember, it's Scar you're asking about, and we need to talk to her if possible," Uncle Bernie says and Ares nods.

"Hello?"

"Hello, Ares?" a computer voice comes down the phone.

"Who is this?"

"Not important! We have your girlfriend and if you want to see her alive again, you will pay what we ask."

"What do you want?"

"Two million, untraceable, delivered at a specified location on Friday afternoon."

"Friday afternoon? It's Monday now. That's too long. I want her back now, let me talk to her!"

Then a sobbing voice comes over the speaker. "Babe, is that you? It's me, Scar!"

"Hey, princess, you okay?" Ares asks her, she doesn't sound right, she's crying and whimpering. That doesn't sound like Ray.

"Babe, I need to speak to Uncle Bernie. Can you get him a message?"

Bernie buts in. "I'm here, Scar. You good?"

More sobbing, then, "Uncle Bernie, I need you to look after the kids. Give the boys their medication. Jay needs his normal tablets three times a day. Don't let him have pizza he's allergic." More sniffles. "Travis needs the big tablets, they're one a day. There are also some little blue ones, but don't worry about those.

"Keep an eye on the chickens, there's a fox hanging around, maybe two, okay? The boys will be devastated if anything happens to them. I'm okay, I'm not hurt. I will be back before you know it. Tell my sister K.F.D.! I love you!"

Then there is what sounds like a slapping sound, a gasp and more crying. We're all looking around at each other, but Uncle Bernie's smiling like a fucking psycho.

"Let me know when and where. I will have your money!" Ares says as the line goes dead.

"What the fuck was that?" Viking spits out.

"That's not the Ray we know. She wouldn't crack like that. That's not right. There's something wrong. They must have done something fucking terrible. I'm gonna murder them all."

Tank starts pacing, fisting his hair.

Blade put his arm on his shoulder. "Hey, we'll get her back, okay?"

Uncle Bernie clears his throat and waits for all the attention to be on him. Everyone's staring daggers with their arms folded across their chests, and Bernie's smiling, fucking smiling.

"How much do you guys know about Ray?"

The Fucked Up Five look around at each other, nodding. "We've just been away with Ray for the weekend. She told us… enough," Tank says.

"We've seen the tattoo!" Viking points to his back.

Priest adds, "She told us enough of the story!"

Ares looks confused. "What the fuck are you talking about? What tattoo? What story?"

Bernie starts with, "Right, it's not my story to tell. I'm sure when she gets back she'll fill you all in. Until then, all you need to know is Ray isn't like other girls… She had an… *unconventional* upbringing… Me, her dad and her three other pas, we raised her differently.

"Ray has certain skills. What you heard then was an act for their benefit. So she told me she's under constant armed guard by between three to five men. There's a boss who's around most of the time and a few that are around sporadically, but they're not an issue. She's there of her own free will. She can escape, and she will once she's got the information she needs, she's not hurt.

"There's a rat in this club, maybe two. That must be how they got to her in the first place, so if they phone back, just agree to whatever, because she will be back Friday before the so-called drop-off.

"Scar, you heard the last bit, so you know what she means by that." I nod, but don't elaborate. "I need to get Scar out of here, and you need to set up some kind of hunt without letting the guys know they're not looking for Scar. They need to think it's her they're looking for!"

"Fucking hell, this is messed up. How the fuck do we get Scar out of here without anyone knowing?" Ares asks, pacing along the edge of the desk.

"Hey, Brother!" Steel growls, his voice vibrating through my chest, giving me an uneasy feeling. It's almost like being stood too close to a loudspeaker. It vibrates through every cell of my body. "We've got this, okay? Dozer, can you and Viking go to my room? At the foot of my bed is a foot locker. Dump everything out of it onto the bed, and bring it back here. I think Scar will fit into it, and we will carry her right out to Bernie's truck. You do have a truck, right, Bernie?"

"Yes, son, I have a truck!" Bernie smirks and Steel smiles back, although it doesn't meet his eyes.

Ares glances around the room. "Only use our encrypted chat log. Dice, can you add Bernie to it? Guys, get the box. Let's get Scar out of here. Can you all give us a minute?" All the guys and Bernie move out of the room. Ares sends a text to the whole club.

Pres: Church! Thirty minutes!

Ares pulls me into a hug. "Stay safe. Stay with Bernie, okay? I will burn the world down if anyone hurts you or your sister. When she gets back, we need to have a talk, okay?"

I nod, and a little whimper comes out. "Ares... Fuck, I'm scared. What if she doesn't make it? What if something bad happens? What if they find out it's not me they have and they kill her? I can't lose her."

"Let's hope Bernie's right, and Ray's as capable as he seems to think she is, and is just biding her time to gather whatever information she thinks she needs. But while there's a rat around here, I need you gone, okay? I need you fucking safe. I will break if anything else happens to you!" He kisses me like it might be our last. When the knock comes at the door, the guys come back in with the foot locker and I lower myself inside.

"Bernie's already outside bringing his truck to the front doors. We're gonna load you onto the bed of it and strap the box down, okay?" Steel's looking at me like I need to trust him. I hope I can. I know the other guys a little and know that Ray trusts them all, but Steel? I haven't seen him before today, and that makes me uneasy. I'm not in a position to be picky. I nod. I have to trust Ares knows who to trust.

They take me outside and strap the box down in the back of the truck, and Uncle Bernie drives away. He doesn't stop till he drives in his garage and lets me out of the box.

I can't stop crying. "Uncle Bernie, this is all my fault. What the hell am I gonna do?"

"Hey, don't worry. You know better than anyone what Ray is capable of. Anyway, I thought you could use some company." As we walk into the house, Demi runs at me and we both sob. Bran scoops us both into his arms and tells us not to worry. This is Ray, after all.

Ray

After I'm unceremoniously tied up and shoved in the van, the binds on my wrist feel like they've been tied by a blind two-year-old. They haven't bothered blindfolding me, so they are either really stupid, or they fully intend on killing me. Well, trying, at least. We drive for only about twenty minutes, and we've gone past the campsite I just stayed at with the boys, but not by much, so I know vaguely where I am.

We come to a stop. I'm led from the van into a barn. There's a chair near the centre, and they take me past it. There's a hook overhead, and they hang my arms from it, tiptoes touching the floor. Looking around the room, there's an old tractor in the corner, various old farm tools like a pickaxe, spade, a pitch fork, and random hooks and various lengths of rope. There's a barrel of something in one of the corners, and a couple of jerry cans. Maybe they will have fuel in. There's so much here I can use.

It's obvious the guys who have taken me have been working with Shay. I know from the garage she was Boyband's ex, the one who trashed his bike.

Reading between the lines, her and Scar had a run in while I was away, so number one on my mental kill list is definitely Shay. These guys are Mexican, and although I won't say I'm 100 percent fluent, I do know more than most, so I'm able to listen in, because they haven't bothered to check if I actually know Spanish.

I keep up the sniffles and sobbing while they are near and listen to every word. They've given me some water, and they called Ares earlier, and I managed to give them a cryptic message that I knew Pa Bernie would understand. We used to see how much information we could tell each other without the others cottoning on, so we came up with our own system. Hopefully I remembered it properly, as it's been a while since we've used it.

I know they will keep Scar safe, so now I have to play my part. I'm going for the idea that these guys are stupid, because they have just let slip that the guy running the show, Miguel Lopez, is one of the higher-ups in the Castillo Cartel, and they are going to double cross the leader Carmen Castillo and take over the cartel. She also has a daughter, Catalina, who's around fifteen, who the sick fuck's gonna marry. I mean, the bastard has to be in his forties.

Turns out he's fucking Shay, and she's fucking Boyband and sharing the club's secrets. Then they are gonna frame the club for wiping out the Castillos. Well, we'll see about that.

I just keep sniffling and listening and hoping that fucking Shay doesn't turn up or the bitch will ruin everything. One of the guys slaps me around a bit while spouting trash that they don't think I understand,

and it's taking all I have to just take it and whimper, but I'm actually doing my own head in, fucking hell! I just need a little more and then I can kill them.

Through the day they hang me from the hook, and through the night they tie me to a cot, next to one of the main support beams.

I've been working on a plan. It's only Wednesday, and I need to get out of here by Friday morning at the latest, so I'm just keeping my ear to the ground and crying when they slap me. It's kind of awful. Jose hits like a fucking girl, preferring to slap rather than punch my face, so while it stings, there isn't any damage as such. He does like to punch me in the stomach quite often whenever he passes me by, but I have to pretend it hurts more than it actually does.

Franco often gets a little handsy, grabbing me around the jaw and snarling in my face while groping my tits and arse. I bite the inside of my mouth and try not to headbutt the twat, but I'm gonna kill that fucker so good, that piece of shit's gonna die. I know I'm gonna be left with bruising from his rough groping and he's gonna pay with his motherfucking life.

Hugo's a different story, never touching, but his penetrating gaze follows my every move. He seems to get hard watching the others do what they do, but stoically stands there all the same. Occasionally I catch him licking his lips or adjusting his junk, but always from at least six feet away.

After finding out a few more juicy bits of gossip, Franco lets slip that they are actually planning on selling me after they get the ransom. They are gonna double cross the club. They have been working with another club up the coast, the Hellhounds of Havenbrook. Once they overthrow the head of the Castillo Cartel, they are getting into the human trafficking business, and little ole me, I'm gonna kick start their little empire. But they have also let slip in front of me dates and places of other... let's say less than legal activities, which I'm gonna make the Hellhounds pay dearly for. If there's one thing I can't stand, it's human trafficking. I think I just found a hobby, and I'm gonna destroy everyone involved.

After more of the same, more secrets spilled, a few more smacks around and plenty more groping, I'm ready to get the fuck out of here. Fucking amateurs haven't even checked me properly, too busy groping me. They are gonna lose their lives for this.

It's the middle of the night, early hours Friday morning. I reach down and slide my knife out of my boot, slicing through the rope and checking my watch. It's 2.30 a.m. Franco will be in the van asleep. Jose's on guard duty at the front, and Hugo's at the back, which means they're asleep by the doors. Fucking dicks!

Miguel won't be here till around eight, and he will have Dumb and Dumber with him. I haven't even bothered to learn their names. From what I can make out, they're Hellhounds, and they aren't very bright. Grabbing a few lengths of rope, I make two nooses, sliding my socks off and my boots back on. I slide my socks over my hands. Hopefully that'll help with the rope burn.

Throwing the ropes up into the hay loft with my blade in my hand, I sneak to the back side of the barn to where Hugo will be and climb up into the hay loft, sliding out of the door at the back. He's below me, sitting on the floor, back to the barn, asleep with his head lolling forward. There's what looks to be an AR15 laid half on his lap half on the floor with his hands palms up beside him. Time to hook a fucking duck!

I will only get one chance, and I need to snatch him up quickly so he can't shout, or worse, grab for the rifle. Opening up the noose, I tie the other end round my waist. My plan is to hook him, then jump under the hay loft back into the barn, using my body weight to yank him up, spragging myself under the underside of the hay loft, hopefully giving me enough leverage. Here goes nothing.

I dangle the rope out the hay loft. It takes a few attempts to get it to land over his head. I pull it gently so It snags under his chin. I take some of the slack from the rope, wrapping it around my back and around my arm, taking a deep breath and taking a quick few steps back, while dragging on the rope, heaving the weight of Hugo off the floor.

Hearing a startled strangled cry before feeling the struggling, I lean back out of the hay loft, spragging my feet underneath the ledge and pushing so I'm standing upside down. I stretch out to my full height. If he has a knife and can get to it, this will go horribly wrong for me, so I hang on for dear life, and when the scraping of boots stops on the wood and the faint gasping sounds stop, I wait a tad longer.

I still stay there until I think I might pass out before easing slowly off and using his weight to pull me back into the hay loft. I tie the rope off and cut myself free before sliding down the rope and Hugo's limp body.

I snatch up the AR15 and slide the knife back out of my boot. My trusty Emerson Karambit. I fucking love this knife. I sneak around the side of the barn to the van. I have a couple of lengths of rope with me. I need to disable Jose and Franco before Miguel, Goon One and Goon Two turn up.

Checking on the van, Franco's spark out, so I creep around to Jose and slide up beside him, reaching a hand over his mouth. I stab him in the neck. I want to make it slow and painful, but I can't afford to. I need to make this quick and clean and get the job done. Watching the life drain out of him, I drag a hay bale over and shove it on top of him to hide the blood. Heading around to the van, I check the time. It's nearing four.

I know cracking the door will startle him, so I have to be fast. I crack the van door and slide it back. Franco lurches up as he gets to the opening. I dive in as he swings at me. I hiss as there's a pain in my right thigh, but I just stab wildly at him, directing my blade at his chest. He falls back, clutching at the wounds. I reach up and stab him in the neck. He gasps at me while I grin down at him. I stab once more for good measure before he stops struggling.

I look down, and there's a gash on my right thigh. Motherfucker. He has a Swiss Army knife in his hand. Well, fuck you, Franco. You missed out on the horrible death I had in mind for you, but tough, you're dead now, anyway.

I cut a strip of fabric from the bottom of my shirt and tie it around my leg. I tie some of the rope around Jose's body and attach him to the van. Work smarter, not harder, am I right? I start the van up and drive it inside the barn, where I drag Jose's body with me. Checking my watch again, it's nearly 6.30 a.m., so tossing Franco out of the van and dragging his dead arse out of the way, I cover the blood in the van with the blanket Franco was using. I drive the van back out to where it was and leave the keys in the ignition for my getaway, grabbing some granola bars from the glove box and a couple of bottles of water. I gather all the weapons I can find before heading back inside.

Chilling and regaining my strength, I have the AR15 from Hugo, the Swiss Army knife from Franco, a Glock I found in the glove box, a hunting knife and a Beretta from Jose. I also nicked Jose, Hugo and Franco's phones. I removed the face IDs from them, so I can open them without a password or facial recognition. I switched them all off, removed the batteries and stuffed them in the glove box. So now I just wait. I need to chill out and regain some energy, snacking on the bars and water out of the van. I sit up in the hay loft and wait, and wait, and wait some more.

This won't be the bloody death I wanted them all to have, but dead is dead. It doesn't matter how brutal or fancy you make it. Watching the time slip by is all I can do for now.

At 7.55 a.m., I hear Miguel pull up and Dickhead One and Dickhead Two pull up on their bikes. I jump out of the hay loft and slide around the front, watching

Miguel pacing backwards and forwards on the phone near the van

"Fuck, Shay… I don't give a shit… The deal's done… She will be sold… I don't care what you want… No, you don't get to kill her, she's gonna make me a fortune… Who do you think you're talking to?" The line must have gone dead.

Ah, trouble in paradise. That makes me smile! I head back inside as I want to contain the mess to the barn. I wait with the gun in the shadows. I have used some of the straw to make up a lump in the bed and slipped the scratchy blanket they left me around it. It won't fool anyone close up, but from the doorway where I'm hiding, you can't tell it isn't a person.

Dumb and Dumber enter first. Dumber has his gun drawn, so he's my priority. Dumb still has his holstered. Miguel flanks them as he walks in. I pistol whip him and knock him out. I need him alive. As he drops, Dumber swings round and lets out a shot just as I return one. His hits me in the stomach, and mine hits him between the eyes. He crumples to the floor. Dumb is only just drawing his weapon so as I shoot, I take out his knee cap, dropping him to his knees. I storm over, and he tries to shoot again, clipping my left bicep. I shoot him in the chest and he crumples backwards onto the floor.

Walking over, I let off a couple of rounds between the eyes to be safe, then head over to Miguel. I bind him good, like a Christmas fucking ham, and bring the van round, throwing him hog-tied in the back. I fish everyone's phones and keys out of their pockets and wheel the bikes into the van too. They're nice bikes and we may be able to strip them for parts or sell them. Dozer will know what to do with them.

I remove my shirt and force a lump of it into the wound in my stomach. Fuck, it hurts like a motherfucker. I think it's only adrenaline keeping me going. It's more my side than my stomach, looking at the damage. I tie a piece of my top around my waist, holding it in place, and I tie a piece around my bicep where I've been clipped. Fuck, I hate getting injured. It's a massive inconvenience.

As I try to drag Dumb and Dumber closer together, I realise I'm exhausted. I've barely eaten all week, so I give them both a kick in the fucking face, and grab the jerry cans. There's some fuel in them, so I douse Dumb and Dumber, and splash some around Jose and Franco, throwing some over Hugo still dangling outside. I take all their jewellery, watches, wallets and anything else that will be useful.

I strip anything valuable out of Miguel's car and drive it into the barn, undoing the petrol cap and leaving a length of fuel soaked T-shirt hanging out of it, then I set fire to the fuckers using the rest of my T-shirt and a bit of left over fuel and the cigarette lighter from the van. All the dry hay really helps, and within minutes, the barn's engulfed.

As I take off, the fuel tank in the car explodes and it makes me smile. I screech off with Miguel hog-tied and my bounty of two bikes, five phones, four watches, three rings, a fucking gordy bracelet, two necklaces, a Swiss Army knife, AR15, a smug arse fucking grin and a partridge in a pear tree!

Everything hurts as I barrel down the road towards the MC. I hold on to my side as the blood oozes through the T-shirt and I put my foot down. I just need to make it back before I pass out. I can see the garage up ahead. As I drive through the gates to the garage I'm greeted by about twenty of the guys all pointing their guns at me, screeching to a halt as I cut the engine.

Steel

The guys on lookout have sounded the warning siren. There's a van driving erratically heading this way. We all pile out of the door, some guys staying around the clubhouse and some of us heading over to the garage. I stay beside my brother, and the Fucked Up Five are beside us too. We all raise our guns, except for Ares.

It's a show of strength and confidence in us. The van screeches to a halt, the driver's door swings open, and the figure rounds the front of the van. My breath is taken from me, and my hand slowly lowers my gun. It's like everything's happening in slow motion.

She's the most beautiful woman I've ever seen. Her hair's dishevelled in a high ponytail, the blonde shimmering in the sun, giving her this almost angelic halo-like glow. Her face is mottled with bruising in various colours, blood splatters over her cheeks, and her body's glistening with sweat and blood splashes. She has a rag tied around her arm, one at her waist and one on her thigh.

She's only wearing a bra and jeans. As she rounds the front of the van, her muscles flex. I can see a sleeve of tattoos. She makes eye contact with me for a split second, and I think I notice a slight twitch to the side of her mouth as she glances across to find Ares.

"Yo, Boyband!" she bellows. "Do you have somewhere for… overnight guests?" He's beside me, arms crossed. He nods once, as she turns to head to the back of the van, giving us all a view of her full back tattoo. A female, pin-up style Grim Reaper, leg resting on one of three gravestones and a raven sat on one of the others, a finger raised to her lips and holding a scythe over her shoulder. It's stunning, she's stunning, and the most piercing blue-grey eyes stand out in the all-black and grey design.

She has a gun stuck into the back of her jeans, and she's breathtaking. She swings the back doors open and jumps up into the back of the van. It starts shaking as a hog-tied body flies out onto the ground, rolling to the side, followed by the boot she has clearly kicked him out using. He looks unconscious or dead. Jumping down from the van, she yells again.

"Viking, Tank, put my guest somewhere safe till I get cleaned up!" They both move at her command, no question about it.

"Dozer, get your arse over here!" Dozer's stood in the garage. Without hesitation, he walks over to her. She claps him on the shoulder, and gestures inside the van. Fuck knows what's in there.

His eyes light up like fucking Christmas, and he turns and shouts, "Casper, Roach with me!" They jog across in front of me towards him.

"Dice!" Just that one word has my brother running towards her. "Front seat!" She points and he nods, pausing for a second in front of her before he goes. They clearly share a look. Viking and Tank are already dragging her guest away. Casper and Roach emerge from the back of the van, each with a bike, rolling it towards the garage as Dozer barks orders at them.

"Priest." Nodding, he walks towards her. As he reaches her, she leans in to talk into his ear. Whatever she says, he nods. As she goes to move away, he grabs her hand and squeezes it. Her eyes soften as she gives him a single nod and he releases her.

She walks over towards us. "Miss me, Boyband?" He steps forward and drags her into a hug. She whispers something into his ear and he nods, stepping back she glances at me, then back to him. "I need a phone, a drink, a burger and a suture kit!"

Ares reaches into his pocket and unlocks his phone, handing it to her, but before he can say anything, I step forward. "Follow me."

She glances at Ares and he gives her a nod. She nods as she steps in behind me. She has the phone already to her ear. "Bitch face… I'm good… No… I'll let you know when… Stay safe, K.F.D, motherfucker!" She tosses the phone back to Ares.

I turn to her, cocking a brow in question at her. She shrugs at me as she strides past. She grabs the door to the clubhouse and storms into it.

She goes straight to the bar, leaning over it and reaching behind. "Motherfucker!" She winces as she grabs her side. I have my phone out and send texts to

Barbie and Doc, stuffing my phone back in my pocket. She's stood at the side of the bar gripping her side, chest heaving as she gulps down tequila straight from the bottle, letting it fall from her mouth. Her eyes meet mine as she licks her lips, dropping the bottle to her side.

Fuck, I want so badly to be that tequila on her lips. I turn and head down the corridor towards my room, which is next to the med room at the end of the hall opposite Ares's. I step inside.

She follows me in while looking around. "Why am I in here?"

I point to the bathroom. "Med room's next door. I'll grab what you need, towels on the rack." I step out and shut the door behind me. I stop dead in my tracks and take a breath, adjusting my cock in my jeans. It's totally inappropriate to have a boner when she's covered in blood and injured, isn't it? "Fuck!" I'm just about to head into the med room when someone clears their throat next to me. Looking over, Ares's there with a smug grin on his face.

"You good, Brother?"

I nod.

"Sure you are." He laughs.

Taking a deep breath, I step into the med room. When I come back out, he's gone. I head back into my room. I hear the shower going, so I grab a T-shirt from my drawer for her to put on. Then, because I'm an asshole, I put it back and grab a Harley tank with a skull on it. My cock twitches at the thought of her wearing it.

A crash breaks my deviant thoughts, and before I know it, I'm in the bathroom. She's knocked everything off the bathroom shelf onto the floor, and she's hanging onto the wall with her eyes closed, panting. She's under the spray of water in her underwear and the scraps of fabric over her wounds. Her jeans and boots are discarded on the floor. I tear my own boots off, strip out of my jeans and T-shirt and step into the shower with her.

"The fuck you doing?" She flinches and snarls at me.

"Helping!" is all I say as I grab the shampoo and start rubbing it into her hair. She flinches at the contact.

"I can do it my fucking self, you need to get out!"

I think it's supposed to be threatening, but it comes out breathy and sultry as she wobbles and flattens her hand on the tiles. Dropping her head down, she gasps for breath.

"Look, woman, I'm trying to help! You've lost some blood, you're about to pass the fuck out, just steady yourself on the wall and let me fucking help, okay?"

Glancing over her shoulder and looking me dead in the eye, she says, "I don't like... being... touched. Especially by people I don't know!"

"Okay, bare minimum contact. Just support yourself on the wall, okay?" Looking back at the wall, she nods and takes a deep breath as I scrub and rinse her hair.

She sags against the wall. I grab her around her waist to hold her up, and she hisses out in pain.

"Sorry! You good?" Taking another deep breath, she shudders at my touch. Nodding, I grab a washcloth and scrub quickly at her skin to get most of the blood off. She still has the fabric tied around her waist and bicep, but the one on her leg she took off with her jeans. That one's running with blood. I rinse her off.

"Let's get you out so I can look at the wounds." She steps out of the shower and she drops onto the toilet.

"I can do it myself." She gasps as she bends forward, resting her head between her knees. I step out of the bathroom and sling on some clean boxers. I take the med kit back into the bathroom, putting it onto the counter beside her. She sits up and reaches over, flipping the lid and grabbing out the suture kit. Grabbing the tequila from the counter, she pours it straight onto her leg.

She hisses out, "Shit, fuck!"

"That's the first time I've been called a shit-fuck before I've even got my cock in."

Glaring at me, she spits, "Real funny, big man!"

She rips at the suture kit with her teeth while wiping the wound with some gauze. She threads the needle and starts to stitch herself up, pinching the wound together on her thigh.

"Not the first time you've done this, huh?"

"Nope," is all she says as she continues stitching, eighteen in total, neat as fuck. Then she rips the fabric off her left bicep and pours more tequila on it.

"Bullet?" I question.

"Just a graze," she replies but continues to stitch it with approximately ten more stitches. It's not just a graze, but I keep my mouth shut. Then there's a knock at the door, and it swings open.

"Steel?"

"In here, Barbie!" My voice echoes around the bathroom, and I think I see her shudder and her skin pebble. I look down at her as Barbie comes into the bathroom.

"Fuck, Ray!"

She looks up at him, softening. "I'm good, Barbie, thanks, don't worry, okay?" She smiles at him, a kind smile, but it doesn't reach her eyes. Barbie slides the tray onto the counter and I frown at it.

"What the fuck is all this?"

He shrugs at me. "It's what she likes." She smiles at him again, reaching out for his hand, a genuine eye-creasing sunshine smile as he grips her hand for a second, nods and backs out of the room. I'd just asked him for a burger, like she said, but he's brought in a chocolate shake, burger with cheese, lettuce and tomato, fries and onion rings.

What the fuck? He never cooks like this for us. He's more a basic kind of guy. If you ask for a burger, you get a thin frozen burger and a bun, that's it! This fucker looks homemade, juicy.

She clearly has the guys wrapped around her finger. I think back to how not one of them had looked to Ares for instruction. Thinking about it, I hadn't either!

There's a moan that breaks me from my thoughts, and my eyes shoot to meet hers as she moans around that fucking burger. Jesus, I'm screwed! After a few more bites, she swallows it down with the shake.

Then, taking a deep breath, she asks, "Are there some tweezers in there?" She points at the med kit.

Cocking my head at her, I ask, "What the fuck you need tweezers for?"

Pointing at her side which still has the fabric wrapped around it, "Bullet," is all she says.

I shake my head. "We need Doc for that." I grab my phone out of my pocket to see how long he will be, but she grabs onto my wrist. The contact burns, staring at where she holds me. It feels like the whole world just stops, stops spinning, stops everything. I look into her eyes, and they're swirling grey, almost like a tornado. She gives me a pleading look, telling me that she doesn't want anyone else to see her like this.

"It's just Doc! You know him, right?" She nods, taking a deep breath. She releases my wrist, and the whole world shifts and starts spinning again. I almost feel like I'm about to lose my balance. What the fuck is happening? I call Doc. "Bullet removal, my room, now!"

A few minutes later, he walks in. Leaving her in the bathroom, I go to meet him at the door. I explain that she doesn't want to be touched, so he has to make it quick. I lay a towel on the bed and fetch her over, supporting her as I lay her down.

"You good, Ray?" Doc asks. Taking a nervous breath, she nods. He sits on the bed at the side of her, and I walk around to the other side, standing next to it.

"I'm gonna cut this off, okay?" He points to the fabric. She nods and takes a deep breath, looking over towards where I stand, but not at me. She closes her eyes as soon as she feels him touch her. She grits her teeth and flinches. He looks at me, then goes back to what he's doing.

I sit down on the bed and take her hand. She gasps at the contact and shoots her eyes open, glaring at me, trying to tug her hand back. I tighten my grip. I rub the back of her hand. "How's that?" I ask.

"Tolerable!" she whispers.

"Good, concentrate on that, nothing else." She nods, staring at our hands. She grips me tighter. Jesus, this girl. She grits her teeth, but not a single tear comes out, and she doesn't make a single noise. No more than a few gasps and clenches, as Doc's rooting around in the wound, trying to find the bullet. A few minutes later, he claims he has it, and cleans the wound, stitching her up. She never takes her eyes off my hands encasing hers.

Doc hooks her up to an IV and gives her some antibiotics to help with infection, then he tells her to eat and rest. I grab the rest of her food and sit facing her on the bed. She sits up slowly and finishes it all.

"What's your name?" she asks in the softest of voices. After hearing her bark orders at the others, it catches me by surprise.

"Steel," I reply, and her skin pebbles at the sound of my voice. She flicks her gaze to meet mine. I twitch the side of my mouth, but give no other indication that I know it's my voice alone that has done that to her. I grab a blanket off the chair and lay it over her.

"Steel?"

Fuck, that sounds good, her saying my name like that, all breathy and shit.

"Thank you."

"Get some rest, Sunshine. You're gonna need it!" She freezes as I say that. Her gaze is unreadable, but there's something in her eyes I can't make out. They glaze over for a split second before she nods and slides to lay down.

Once she's asleep, I head out to the bar to catch up with Ares and figure out what's happening. Ares's sitting at the bar, rather than his normal seat in the booths. I slide in at the side of him, signalling to Roach to grab me a tequila.

"How's she doing?" He sighs.

"She's a tough motherfucker, she's out now for a bit! She stitched her own arm. Ten stitches in that, and eighteen in her thigh, cleaning it with fucking tequila. Then I fetched Doc to remove a bullet from her side that she was gonna try and sort herself. He stitched her up and put her on an IV and gave her antibiotics." I shake my head and smile at what I thought was myself.

"What the fuck's wrong with your face?"

"What?"

Pointing, Ares huffs, "Your face?"

I rub at it. Maybe I have some blood or something on it.

"You're fucking smiling?"

"Am not!" I spit.

"Are too."

"What are you, five?"

Ares punches me in the arm, laughing. "She's something, ain't she?"

"She sure fucking is!"

Meeting Doc at my room to remove the IV, we both step through the door, but she doesn't stir. She doesn't even move.

"Just take it out. Yeah, I'll keep an eye on her."

Nodding, he moves around the bed, removing the IV and heading for the door. "She may be out for a while. I slipped her a little something into the IV. Don't tell her, though. She'll have my balls for a necklace."

Laughing, I let him out as the Fucked Up Five came barrelling down the corridor. "We wanna see her!" Viking says, ever the front man.

"She's sleeping!" I bark at them, crossing my arms over my chest filling the doorway.

"So?" Tank barks back at me.

"Chill, Brother! Keep it down, yeah!" Nodding to my room, I step back, letting them in. They stand frozen for a second, taking in her passed-out body, assessing her before all moving as a unit. Viking and Tank move around to her left, Tank reaching down and running his fingers across her stitches and dried blood on her bicep, while Dice and Blade go to the right side, gently pulling back the covers to see the bullet wound then covering her back up. Dice drops gently on to the bed, grabbing her hand in his. Bringing it to his face, he rubs the back of her hand over his cheek and closes his eyes for a second. He kisses the back of her hand and lowers it to his lap. I mean, that kind of winds me up, but not one of them bats an eyelash that she's only in her underwear. There's something going on between them all.

Priest's at the bottom of the bed next to me. It feels like he's holding his breath. Touching him on the shoulder, I ask, "Priest? You okay?" Taking in a deep breath, he looks at me with a flash of fear then relief filling his eyes.

He nods. "We thought we lost her." Taking in all their stricken faces, I feel envy. They know her and I don't, yet I feel protective of her, yet mostly jealous that they are here, and they are clearly something to each other, but I can't work out what.

We all just stand there and watch her sleep. After around forty minutes of silence, Tank asks, "Did she say what happened?" I shake my head, sighing as he strokes a stray hair behind her ear. I mean, Tank, the motherfucker who could crush a skull in his bare hands. He's literally as wide as he is tall, yet seeing him so gentle with Ray, I can't help but wonder what they are to each other. We start chatting quietly amongst ourselves, all asking different questions but then the subject's her, always her.

"Is she gonna be okay?" Dice asks. I nod, hoping I'm right. She seems okay.

"Do you need us to grab anything for her?" Viking asks.

I shake my head. "She just needs rest!"

"How long do you think she'll sleep for?" Priest turns to meet my gaze.

"A lot longer if you all shut the fuck up!" she barks in a sleepy grumpy voice.

We all shoot to face her as she slowly opens her eyes. "It's like a motherfucking mothers meeting in here. Can you fuck off and converse elsewhere? I need my beauty sleep!"

Letting out a shaky breath, Tank grabs her hand. "We thought we lost you!"

"Seriously?" She laughs. "What part of me looks like a fucking damsel in distress needing to be rescued? At what point did you forget who the fuck I am?"

Breathing out a solid breath, Tank looks at her face with her light smirk on it. "Sorry, Reaper." He breathes, smiling back at her.

She winks at him, and all the tension leaves him. He kneels beside the bed and kisses her hand. She reaches for his face and cups his cheek, bringing both hands to hold her hand in place. He lets out a breath and closes his eyes and just stays there for a minute while she strokes his cheek!

"We should let you rest," I say. They all take turns to lean in and kiss her cheek, whispering things in her ear before leaving.

"Do you need anything before I leave?" I ask her.

"You stay. I should head back to the van so you can have your bed back." She goes to sit up, but then grabs at her head as if she feels dizzy. I grab her, laying her back down.

"You should stay here. I can sleep on the chair." I point over to the corner.

She shakes her head. "No, I don't wanna put you out. I need a shower and clean clothes before I can sleep again, so I can head back there and get settled."

"Let me help you, okay? You can wear something of mine. You will be more comfortable here!" She gives me a questioning look, but she nods.

I help her back into the shower to remove what's left of the grime, blood and tequila. I turn my back while she slips out of her underwear and then wrap her in a towel. I lead her back to the bedroom. Giving her my tank, she slides it on. She's naked underneath, and fuck, she looks good. I can see some side boob and my cock twitches and shit. I really shouldn't be perving on her, but fuck!

Rubbing a hand down my face, I lead her to the bed. She climbs under the covers and I grab the blanket off the top and start walking over to the chair.

"Steel." Fuck, my name on her lips does something to me, and I think in that moment I will give her whatever she asks for.

"We can share the bed. I'm sure I can keep my hands to myself." She grins at me, barking out a laugh.

"Sure? I'm sure you can, Sunshine." There's that look again, the pebbling of the skin, a slight flush of her cheeks. But that look. What is that? Is it when I call her Sunshine, or is it just the sound of my voice? Walking around to the bed, I strip down to my boxer shorts and climb in carefully to stay away from the stitches on her arm. We both stare at the ceiling for a while before I hear her breathing steady, and that's it, she's asleep.

I listen for a while to the sound of her breathing. She seems so peaceful. After about an hour or so, I start drifting in and out, not quite asleep but not quite awake. She twitches, and my eyes fly open to check on her, but she's just fidgeting in her sleep. She moves again, sliding closer to me. It feels like she's chasing my warmth. There's a slight chill to her skin as she brushes against me.

I reach out to touch her forehead, and she feels cool there too, but as she feels my body heat next to hers, she shifts, turning her back into me. and my arm, that has touched her head, she grabs, pulling it around her. I slide my other arm under her neck and pull her into me. Fuck, she feels good against me like this, spooning her. Her fingers intertwine with mine, and she rests our hands under the tank on her stomach. I try to pull away, but she has me in some sort of death grip. I give up and bury my face in her hair. She smells like me… like… *mine!*

Ray

I don't think I'm still asleep, but I don't think I'm awake either, I feel so warm and fuzzy. My head spins a little. I shuffle to get comfy, but there's something hard in my back. I push back into it, still in the haze of sleep. I gasp as I feel a rough thumb graze my nipple.

I freeze, then the body behind me shifts, and the smell of him engulfs me, immediately making me relax. He smells like fresh, sea air and forests with a hint of something spicy. I inadvertently grind myself into him, which makes his hand on my breast squeeze and flick my nipple again. Pulling me tight and taking in a deep breath, he stills, freezing in place.

My butt grinds into his boner, his arm under my neck, pulling me in. His other hand is under the tank he has lent me, cupping my breast and brushing over my nipple. It's then I'm aware that the tank is up around my ribs, and I'm naked. He backs up and moves his hand from my boob in one quick motion. Shit. I shudder at the loss of contact, immediately feeling cold.

"Morning, Sunshine. Shit, sorry." He slides his hand out from under my top and rolls onto his back, blowing out a breath and rubbing his hand down his face before adjusting his dick in his boxers.

I roll slowly onto my back, wincing as I twist. "Looks like it wasn't me that couldn't keep my hands to myself." I laugh out, forcing out another breath.

"Fuck, I'm sorry, I didn't realise I was… " he trails off.

"Copping a feel," I finish for him. He laughs the most amazing sound which goes straight to my pussy, and I have to clench my thighs together. He grins at me, and fuck, it's the most gorgeous thing I've ever seen. He has dimples for days, and his eyes look like liquid metal swirling with lust. I bite down on my lip.

He climbs out of the bed, muttering to himself, "Fuck, I need a cold fucking shower!" He shuts the door behind him. I actually laugh, and I feel comfortable in the situation. What was that all about? Beside the fucking hot, sexy-as-fuck body and those beautiful eyes, and those fucking dimples. And that scar. I kinda want to lick. Fuck, I need to get out of here!

Taking a breath, I inch out of bed when, behind me, there's a knock at the door. I walk towards it. I become fully aware that I'm in a tank that belongs to a guy whose bed I have been in, and although nothing has happened, I'm naked underneath. Swinging the door open and leaning on the frame, I grin at Ares.

"Boyband!" I wink at him. "What do you need?"

He shoves a phone at me. "It's Scar!"

Pulling it to my ear, I say, "Hey, bitch tits!" Boyband rolls his eyes and goes and sits down on the bed. "Yeah I'm good… I'm gonna go deal with our guest, call ya when it's done and you can come back, okay?... K.F.D... Miss your face, motherfucker... Call you later."

Tossing the phone back to Boyband, the door creaks as Steel comes out of the bathroom, towel around his waist, slung low so I can see the water droplets sliding down over his rock hard abs and Adonis belt. Fuck me. I subconsciously tug on my lip ring. He has a gorgeous tattoo over his pecs and chest, and up onto his shoulders, a raven in flight swooping in with two skulls one on each pec, front and centre grasping for prey. Fuck. I notice another droplet of water snake it's way over his toned chest before descending and bumping over every single ab before getting sucked up by the towel. I really, really wish I was that water droplet. He scrubs another towel into his hair. I lean against the door, taking in the view.

"Ahem." Boyband clears his throat. I shoot a glare at him and he rubs the side of his mouth. "You have a little something right there." Before I can stop myself, I reach for the corner of my mouth and they both laugh. "Drool, Ray... It's drool."

Boyband rolls back onto the bed, laughing, and Steel leans on the bathroom door, smirking as he rubs his jet black hair.

"Fuck you, arsehole!"

Sitting back up he points at us both. "Meeting, my office, thirty minutes!" Pushing past me, he looks at me again and wipes his mouth, laughing before walking out and heading towards his office.

"Argh, I'm gonna kick his arse!" Suddenly, all the breath goes out of me, and I can feel his warmth at my back. My breathing stutters. I close my eyes, feeling like I can't breathe. I'm encapsulated by his smell, that spicy undertone with the smell of the sea air and forest. I'm aware of every single inch of my skin, feeling like electric pulses are shooting across it. His hand falls to my waist, and I lean back into him, feeling like I can't support myself.

"Ray?"

My breaths are coming in heavy, my chest rising and falling rapidly, my pulse thrumming in my veins.

"Ray? You okay?"

Shaking myself, I step forward into the hall away from him. Turning around to face him and my breath falters again. Fuck, he's beautiful! I reach up and cup his cheek. He closes his eyes, and I run my thumb down his scar. He nestles into my palm as his hand slides up to the back of my neck. My breathing hitches, and he opens his eyes, staring into my soul. I don't know what comes over me. I mean, I don't kiss guys, like ever, I can't stop myself though. It's like I've been possessed, and at this moment, all I want to do is devour his lips.

I lean up onto my tiptoes and crash my lips into his. He freezes for a second before reaching his other hand down and gripping my arse cheek. He pulls me into him as I devour him, drinking him in like my favourite liquor, like my life depends on it. I run my tongue along his lips, and he opens up and lets my tongue in. I flick it against his, and he groans at the feeling of my tongue ring running along his tongue. He pulls me closer and slides his tongue against mine even more.

After what feels like forever, we break apart, breathing ragged, short breaths, panting, and flushed. We just stare at each other.

"Ahem!" I spin around to fucking five grinning faces.

"Fuck my life!" Steel barks out the biggest laugh that shoots straight to my clit. Rubbing a hand down my face, I stomp back into his room, muttering under my breath, "I need a fucking cold shower!"

Walking into Boyband's office I'm greeted by Dozer, Tank, Dice, Blade, Viking, Steel, Priest and Boyband, all falling silent as I push through the door.

"What up, guys! Miss me?" They all smile, coming in for a hug.

"Don't fucking do that to us again, you little shit!" Tank laughs, squeezing far too tight. I wince, but I can't find any fucks to give in that moment. I hug him back.

"Hey, beautiful!" Dice grins at me, and pulls me in for a hug and a kiss. I can see Steel in my peripheral vision, and he doesn't look happy.

Dozer grabs me next. "Fuck, Ray, I'm so sorry." Then he steps back and rubs the back of his neck while looking at his boots. "I've been at the lodge!" He grins at me and I return his smile, before getting grabbed by Priest, then Blade.

Viking steps up and touches my cheek. "You gave us a scare, little 'un!"

"Sorry, guys!"

All the guys hug me except Steel, but he gives me a smile that makes my fresh underwear damp.

"What's wrong with your face?" Turning, Dozer's pointing at Steel.

"Nothing!" he barks out looking away.

"Is that a… a fucking smile on your face?" Tank smirks.

"Nah, can't be!" says Viking, huffing a little.

"I can't remember the last time that happened." Priest laughs.

"Fuck you all." Steel grabs my wrist, spinning me towards him and pulling me in for the most exquisite kiss. There are cat calls and wolf whistles going on around us, but he just kisses me harder, and I fucking melt into him like some silly little girl with a crush. I cant find a fuck to give at this exact second.

"Alright, alright, enough of that. We have shit to do then I need to get my girl back."

Breaking away, out of breath but still held in Steel's embrace, I look over my shoulder cocking a brow at Boyband. "Your girl?"

"Yeah, my fucking girl, so let's get on with it!"

Ray

After a couple of hours of going through everything that's happened, Dice shares all the information he retrieved from the phones.

"So, do you guys think we could use this information about Miguel to come to some kind of arrangement with the Castillos? You said they were the most powerful family in the state, and you have tried to get a partnership with them before, so you think we could use this to our advantage?"

"We?" Boyband smirks. "You one of us now, Ray?"

Smiling, Tank asks "Yeah, Reaper, you one of us?"

"You think you're tough enough to be one of us, little 'un?" Viking grins.

"Definitely gonna need that name change." I laugh out.

"What ya thinking, babe?" Priest waggles his eyebrows at me.

"Well Fucked Up Five is a little redundant now there's six of us." I grin back.

"Ah, the little sister we never knew we needed till she wrecking balled into our lives!" Blade grins at me.

"Psycho Six?" I shrug.

"Psycho Six?" Dozer smirks. "How very fitting!"

"Psycho Six," Tank repeats. "I fucking love it!" He swings me around and kisses my cheek. "Perfect!"

"That settles it. You're the Psycho Six! And Reaper? One shitshow at a time. Now what the fuck are we gonna do about the Castillos?" Boyband bites out.

"Leave that to me." I grab Miguel's phone, scroll through the contacts and hit the call button, putting it on speaker phone.

"Miguel?"

Her voice comes through like butter, her subtle accent sexy but you can hear the power in her voice.

"Carmen? Carmen Castillo?"

"Who is this?"

"Me? I'm your new best friend. You can call me Reaper."

"Reaper? And why would I want you as a new best friend?" she purrs.

"Because I've just saved your daughter Catalina's life without you even knowing it was in danger. You're welcome, by the way!"

"Is this some kind of joke?"

"On the contrary, I'm serious! Deadly!"

"I'm listening."

"You might wanna take a seat, Carmen, while I fill you in … "

We fill Carmen in on the whole situation. She's coming to have a meeting with us, but in the mean time, I'm gonna fuck with Miguel a little. It's only fair!

I walk up to the barn where I've been told they are keeping Miguel. As I come to a stand still outside the doors, I can hear a rumble of hushed voices. Pushing through the doors, the whole place falls silent; you could hear a pin drop!

Fucking hell, the whole club's here. What the actual fuck? Here's me thinking I'm gonna have a quiet word. It looks like the Reapers have other thoughts. I hold my head high and stride into the barn. I'm still wearing Steel's Harley tank with the skull on, which I've tied to the side forgoing the bra. If I'd have known the whole club was gonna be here, I would have at least put one on. I'm now flashing major side boob. I have on a pair of ripped black jeans and my tools are stuffed in my new rock trail boots as I walk in. The club parts like the red fucking sea, and I nod.

"Gentlemen, what a surprise!" I strut through the centre of them all. I get to the back of the room, where Miguel's tied by his wrists and ankles to a chair. There is an empty barrel upturned in front of him like a table, and a chair for me to sit in front of. Walking up to the chair, I sit down, smiling at Miguel.

"Hola pendejo… extrañame?"
"Hello asshole… miss me?"
"Scar?" he says with a shaky voice.
"Puedes llamarme Segador."
"You can call me Reaper."

I laugh at the look on his face. "Firstly, when you kidnap someone, you should make sure you have the right person!"

Leaning back in the chair, I lift my leg up, placing my foot on the top of the barrel and leaning forward to remove my hunting knife from my boot. I move back again but leave my leg up. I start picking my nails with the knife without even looking in Miguel's direction.

"Secondly, when you kidnap someone, you should make sure they don't speak Spanish. Estúpido."

"Idiot."

Looking up at him, I cock my head to the side. I point the knife at him. "Those ropes look a little tight! Are they too tight, Miguel?"

Looking at either wrist, he nods, gulping down as his gaze rests back on my face. I lean forward. It hurts like fucking hell, but I grin, not showing an ounce of pain. I see his gaze shift so he's looking down my top, and he swallows, making his Adam's apple bob in his throat. I grin at him.

"Let me help you, Miguel!" Leaning over the barrel, I cut his right wrist free, but keep ahold of his hand and stroke the back of it to pull it to rest on the barrel. He's still looking down my top! Making my voice all breathy, I ask, "Is that better, Miguel?"

Swallowing again, he nods. I can see the bulge in his trousers and I smirk.

"You like that, Miguel?... The view, that is?" Still circling my left thumb in circles on the back of his hand, I hold it across the barrel. His gaze never lifts from my tits as he nods. Wiping my hand across the back of his, he never flinches until I slam the hunting knife straight through his hand, right up to the hilt, pinning his hand to the barrel. He lets out a piercing scream and starts trying to tug his hand free, but he can't do anything. Dropping back in my seat, I reach into my pocket and fish out the matches. Reaching into my other pocket, I pull out the Swiss Army knife. He gasps as he sees the knife.

"Mine now! Franco won't be needing it where he's gone!" I take a match from the packet and with the blunt end, I sharpen then place it on the barrel. Miguel's panting now, sweating and wincing, tears streaming down his face. I take out another match and do the same. I can hear people moving, shifting from one foot to the other, but not one of them says a word. Taking out another match and repeating the ritual, sharpening the end to a point, I put it down on the barrel, get another, and repeat!

Once I have five matches, I put the knife down on the barrel, picking up a match and studying the end. Miguel's breathing heavy. I have been silent while I have painstakingly sharpened every match, flipping the match so the sharp end points to Miguel. I grab his middle finger from his hand that's pinned to the barrel. He's eyeing me with confusion, his breaths ragged sweat beading on his forehead. All will become clear shortly.

Holding his finger in place, I put the point of the match under his finger nail and stare him straight in the eyes. I start to push so slowly. The screaming starts almost immediately.

"Stop please, Sc… Reaper! …Please… I will tell you what you want to know."

I cock a brow at him. "There's nothing I want to know, Miguel. There's no information you can give me that I need!"

Leaning forward, I flick the end of the match, and he screams again as it vibrates under his nail. It's pushed all the way into his nail bed.

Taking the second match, I push it under his thumb nail.

"Fuck!" he bellows out, snivelling. I just smile at him, picking up the third match. I take his little finger, resting the match against the underneath of his nail.

It comes out as almost a whisper. "I have information! If you promise… to let me live… I can tell you everything… everything about the Castillos… The Hellhounds… Shay, everything!"

Pushing the third match under his little finger, he sobs out.

"P-p-lease!"

I push so slowly he starts gasping. I think he's gonna have a panic attack.

"It was Shay, it was all her!" he screams as I push in a fourth match. "She wanted you… Scar, dead. It was… her… All her!"

"Tut-tut, Miguel. I thought you would be made of stronger stuff than this. And you thought you would overthrow the leader of the Castillo Cartel when you're a snivelling douche bag.

"You think I don't know that? You do realise that you, Jose, Hugo, and Franco did nothing but speak in Spanish about your whole plan. You think I wasn't listening? You, my friend, underestimated me, and that was your biggest mistake. But by all means, continue to underestimate me further. That's always fun… for me!"

I slide in the fifth match to another scream. "I know all about your plan to overthrow Carmen." He gasps as if I'd been making up the whole 'I know Spanish' shit and wasn't really listening.

"I know all about your plan to pin it on the Reapers. I know all about the plan with the Hellhounds and how you were gonna sell me. I know all about the human trafficking, I know you were planning on double crossing the Hellhounds." I stand. I walk around the back of him so I can see all the guys there. I have my suspicions on who the rat is, but this next piece of the puzzle will tell me for sure.

"You think I don't know you were fucking Shay?" There it is my proof. The slightest twitch, the widening of the eyes, the slightest inhale. Got you, motherfucker!

"You think I don't know that she was in love with you, but you were gonna betray her and have her sold right along with me?" Reaching down to my boot I slide two of my throwing blades into my hand as I stare right in the guilty party's eyes.

"Did you know she was fucking another of the guys here, Miguel?" His shocked gasp tells me all I need to know as I stand up and launch the first blade, hitting him straight between the eyes. He gasps. I throw the other one, which embeds straight in his neck. His eyes go wide as he grasps for the blade and for breath before collapsing into a heap on the floor. "Consider the rat exterminated."

Everyone in there stares down at Casper's lifeless body, everyone except Roach. It's because of him I suspected Casper in the first place. I wink at him, and the biggest smile comes across his face.

"Nice work, kid!" I grin. "Your intel was priceless. Roach, you did good!"

Everyone around the barn is sharing looks with each other and glancing backwards and forwards towards Roach. He beams with pride. I'm pretty sure he will get patched in now!

Walking back around to sit in front of Miguel again, I take out another match. He's sweating profusely and panting, but not as much as before, so I light the match and hold it to his middle finger, and just watch it slowly burn down the match till it reaches his finger, the smell of burning flesh hits the air. Screams and pure panic spread over him as I just sit there, watching his skin redden and crisp and his nail shrivel. It's the paraffin the match's soaked in that keeps it lit.

As he screams and screams, the match goes out and he calms down. I light the second, rinse, repeat and onto the third. At that moment, my phone rings. I answer it

"Dónde estás ahora?… enviaré a alguien."

"Where are you now?… I will send someone."

Hanging up, I stand and walk over to Viking, whispering in his ear, he nods then leaves. Leaning back in my chair, I light the final two matches and watch as they destroy the ends of his fingers.

Next thing, the door's open again, and in walks Viking followed by two guys in black suits. The MC guys part again for them to enter as I rise from my chair and stand to face them.

Miguel's still whimpering as the three men come to a stop in front of me. Viking turns and steps to my side as the two guys in suits step outward, leaving Carmen in the gap.

Miguel gasps and starts crying. "Carmen, thank god. You're here to save me from these savages. They've kidnapped and tortured me..."

Miguel lets out a sigh of relief, and as I give him the stink eye. He smirks. Ha! Motherfucker thinks she's here to save him. Carmen's dressed in a white blouse unbuttoned to her cleavage, showing the black lace along the cup of her bra, a black pencil skirt, stockings and a pair of black Louboutins. She has thick long dark hair to her waist in luscious waves, and caramel coloured skin. Pulling down the bug eye sunglasses she's wearing, I can see her dark chocolate eyes. She raises her arms to me.

"Mi nueva mejor amiga."

"My new best friend."

Stepping into her, we hug each other like old friends.

"So good to see you, Carmen!" She's absolutely gorgeous.

"I'm here to take my trash back with me." Miguel gasps as she speaks in her subtle accent.

"Of course, Carmen. Would you like it alive and kicking or would you prefer me to slit its throat so it's less... whiny?"

Laughing, she says. "I will take him alive and kicking. We have some issues we have to... discuss."

I nod in acknowledgement to her. "Tank, Viking, would you mind wrapping Carmen's... trash to go? And see it's delivered to the boot of her vehicle."

They both nod and advance on Miguel, who starts screaming. Viking punches him in the head and knocks him out.

"Ah, so much better. Thank you!" Carmen purrs and bats her lashes at Viking as he goes all Mark Darcy and pretends to bow and remove a hat he isn't wearing.

He waves his imaginary hat and bows. "Milady," he purrs right back.

Cocking a brow at him, I mouth, "What the fuck?" at him as he shrugs.

Ares steps forward and saves us. "Carmen, it's lovely to meet you. I'm Ares. Would you care for a drink while we talk?"

"I would, Ares, thank you. Maybe... " As she nods toward Viking, pausing.

"Viking?" I question.

"Hmm, Viking! Yes, maybe he would like to join us."

He gives her the biggest smile and nods, dragging the unconscious Miguel out of the barn.

Carmen turns to the suit guys.

"Ve con ellos, asegura a Miguel y espera con el vehículo... I'm quite safe here!"

"Go with them, secure Miguel, and wait with the vehicle... "

With that, they nod, following after Viking and Tank. Ares and Carmen head to the bar.

Wafting my arm around my head. "Someone clean this shit up!" As I stride to leave the barn.

"Ray… Reaper?" Turning, Roach stands looking slightly embarrassed as all the guys watch him. His eyes flick around, taking them all in, staring at the floor and kicking the dirt with his boot.

"Thank you… for, erm… believing in me!" Turning around and striding towards him, I grasp his chin, tilting his face to look at mine, and he blushes.

"You did good, kid! I'm proud of you, without you saying anything, I wouldn't have suspected Casper! It took a lot of guts to speak out against a brother!" Winking at him, I give him a kiss on the cheek, then pat where I just kissed.

As I turn and walk away, rounding the door, I hear, "Ahem!" in that low, gravelly, sexy voice that can only be Steel. I pause just outside the doors to listen.

"Do you have a little crush on my woman?"

"Erm… I mean… your woman? …Well… erm." But then I see Roach straighten up, stand tall through the crack in the wood of the walls on the barn, and take a deep breath, looking straight in Steel's eyes even though he's the same height as me, and Steel must be six foot four.

"Yes!"

"You gonna try and steal her from me, are you, kid?"

Using the name I called him, I can hear the smirk in Steel's voice.

"If she gave me even the slightest inkling that I stood a chance, yes!" he says with total conviction.

"Even if I would kill you?" He's totally playing with him. I can hear the playfulness in the way he says the words.

Roach takes a deep, shaky breath. "Totally worth it!" I can hear the grin in his tone, and I smile to myself. He's such a sweet kid! And the way Steel called me his woman, I don't want to admit it yet, but fuck, I like the sound of that. My thoughts are broken by a chorus of laughter as I hear what must have been the guys clapping Roach on the back. Time to make my exit. I jog down the clubhouse, grasping my side, knowing I should not be doing this!

I walk inside to speak to Carmen. This seems more like a social drink than a meeting, so I give Carmen my number to arrange a meet and make my apologies. Now this is over, my priority is fetching Scar back.

"Ares, I'll be back later. I'm heading to grab Scar!" His eyes twinkle as he goes to get up to come with me before realising he really should stay with Carmen, nodding to me as he sits back down as Viking waltzes In.

Carmen's gaze falls to his, and they could have been the only ones in the room. Fuck, this could end very badly, but not my problem as I walk through the front doors and towards the van.

Before reaching the van, I hear someone calling my name. "Ray!" Turning, Steel's coming from the back of the clubhouse. "Fancy going for food?" He has on a black T-shirt stretched tight across his muscles, dark jeans tight on his thighs and looser from the knee down, tucked into a pair of biker boots with his waistcoat thingy, which I'd been told is called a cut, over the top, which has his name on one side and "Enforcer" on the other.

"Sorry, I'm just heading over to grab Scar."

"You really shouldn't be driving, you'll pull your stitches, and you really should eat. So why don't I take you for food then we can head to grab Scar? Sound like a plan?"

Shit, he's gorgeous, and I'm pretty sure he could get me to agree to anything while he's standing there with his jeans hung low on his hips and his hands stuffed in his pockets.

"Sure!" And with that, he stalks towards me, slides his arm around my waist, and leads me towards a truck at the end of the parking lot. Opening the door for me and helping me in, he removes his cut as he gets in the truck.

Driving down the road, I glance over to look at Steel smirking. "So, your woman, huh?"

He cocks a brow in my direction. "Eavesdropping, eh?" I shrug

"Tab hanging, we call it, but whatever."

"Tab hanging, haven't heard it called that before!"

I shrug again. "So... what makes you think I'm your woman?"

"It's inevitable."

"'Scuse me? Inevitable?"

"Yup!"

Barking out a single laugh, I glare at him. "Oh... you're serious?"

"Yup!" He grins, fucking dimples and all.

"Is that all you're gonna say?"

"Yup!"

The absolute wanker just stares at me, grinning.

A little later, we're pulling into the diner where Demi works, and I grin, hoping she's on shift. Stepping out of the truck, I shut the door. I hear someone shouting from behind me and turn around to see Dwayne jogging across the truck stop. I come around the back of the truck to meet him.

"Hey, Ray… You okay? I've not seen you for a while." He throws his arms around me and pulls me into a hug. I'm totally taken back, and not quick enough to lift my arms to stop him, he crushes me to him, so it's more like I'm groping his pecs. I shove slightly so he gets the hint.

"Sorry, fuck… Sorry. I've just… missed you, is all."

"It's okay, Dwayne." I mean… missed me?

Steel steps to my side, sliding his hand around my waist again and I roll my eyes. "Dwayne," he spits with contempt.

"Steel… I, erm… Didn't realise you two know each other!"

"We do," he says.

At the same time, I say, "We don't." We both turn to glare at each other.

"Anyway, I'm glad you're here, Ray. Maybe we could go for a drink sometime?"

I inhale, just about to answer, when Steel shoots out, "No!" He turns me towards the diner.

"Steel!"

He kisses the top of my head. "They do amazing milkshakes here!" He winks at me, and I'm so fucking dumbfounded that I trip along the truck stop next to him with his arm around my waist, pulling me along.

"I need to go to the bathroom, grab a booth." I just need to breathe, so I slip into the bathroom while Demi's serving a customer with her back to me. I just need to take a breath before I see her, as fuck knows what's going on with Steel!

As I come out the bathroom Steel's back is to me, and I can see a pair of feminine arms wrapped around him as he bends down and kisses whoever the fuck he's holding on the head. What the actual fuck? I'm seething. I can feel myself vibrating, and I want to stab someone to death with a blunt spoon.

"Ahem!" I cough out, crossing my arms and popping my hip out. And fuck me, as he turns it's Demi in his arms. My mouth drops as Demi's gaze swings to mine, grasping her mouth with both hands.

She chokes out. "Ray?" Next thing, she's sobbing and runs straight at me, throwing her arms around my neck and crying all over my shoulder.

I rub her back and whisper into her hair. "I'm okay!"

She looks up into my eyes. "Fuck, Ray, I was so scared."

Looking over at Steel, he mouths, "What the fuck?" Squeezing Demi, I release her. She keeps her arm around my waist and stares across at Steel. Looking down at Demi, then across to Steel.

"You two know each other?" I raise a brow at Steel which I hope says, w*hat the fuck, you wanker! Saying I'm your woman, and yet you're groping my friend, motherfucker? I will so cut your dick off and beat* *you with it. You'll beg me to murder you, which I will gladly do with that blunt spoon I referenced earlier, you absolute bellend, arsehole, cunty bollock, fuck-facing dickwad!* But I think it was more a, "Explain twatty?"

Demi looks confused. "Wait, you two know each other?"

Steel nods at her. "How do you know each other?" he asks.

Demi shrugs. "Long story!"

"More importantly," I interject, "how the fuck do you two know each other?"

Steel's literally beaming at me pointing with the smuggest of grins plastered across his face. "Are you jealous, Sunshine!"

Huffing and crossing my arms. "No!"

"Baby, you know I only have eyes for you," he says, stalking across the diner, lifting me gently off my feet and pulling me in for the most exquisite of kisses, where I literally forget my own name. As soon as his scent engulfs me, I'm whisked away to a forest by the ocean and that spicy undertone makes my thighs clench. Breaking apart, he rests me gently on my feet, cupping my face and staring deep into my soul. "Fuck, woman, I'm going to marry you one day soon!"

My breath hitches as there's a high-pitched squeal, followed by Demi jumping all over us in excitement.

"Ow! What the fuck, Demi?"

"Oh my god, I can't believe it. We're gonna be proper sisters, like real sisters. I can't believe it. I'm so excited I could scream!" Then she does. "George... my brother and sister are getting married to each other! Isn't that amazing?"

"Oh my god! Don't ever, ever say that sentence again!" I curse.

Then she spins to the whole diner, saying, "She's not my real, real sister, and he's my half-brother, so not wrong! But when she marries him, she's gonna be my real, real sister and that will be so amazing!"

"Fucking hell, Demi, sit the hell down. We are not getting married!"

She pouts at me. "What? Wait, why not?"

Scrubbing a hand down my face, I glare at Steel, who looks so happy I can't do anything else but smile at him, pointing a thumb at Demi. "She's your sister?"

Nodding, he pushes her into the booth and slides in beside her. I sit down across from him. He slides his hands across the table and grips mine. I just shake my head. What the fuck else am I gonna do?

"Facepalm emoji!"

Steel cocks a brow, and Demi literally starts to hyperventilate.

Ray

Pulling up at Pa Bernie's after explaining everything to Demi, I take a deep breath.

"You okay?"

I nod. "That was just a lot. I wasn't expecting that… well, shitshow at the diner, and it caught me all on edge."

"You know I mean it, don't you?"

"Steel, you've known me twenty-four hours at most, and I probably slept for fourteen of them!"

"I knew you were special when you got out of that van, dripping in blood and barking orders at the guys, orders that not one of them questioned, by the way! And when you turned and I saw your tattoo, I knew you were meant to be here, and when I woke up wrapped around you, I knew I never wanted to let you go, so like I say, inevitable!"

I blow out a deep breath. "Let's just stop the crazy talk for now and go grab Scar. We can talk about this later."

As he climbs out of the cab of the truck, just before he closes the door, I hear, "Inevitable!" Closing my eyes and taking another deep breath, I turn to get out of the truck as Steel opens my door for me, puts his hands on my waist, lifts me down, tucks a stray strand of hair behind my ear and leans down to kiss my neck. "Inevitable!" Stepping back, grabbing my hand, he leads me to the door, knocking on it.

The door swings open, and Pa Bernie's there, mouth open, before he grabs me and pulls me in for a hug. There's a hitch in his voice and tears in his eyes. "Fuck, Squirt!"

I just squeeze him as my eyes water too. Fuck it, I'm glad to be alive! Stepping into the house, Ma sees me first and she drops to her knees and sobs into her hands.

I run to her and kneel beside her. "I'm okay, Ma, I'm fine."

She nods as she hugs me. "Fucking hell, Ray!" Pulling back like I've been shot, the sheer shock of those words on her lips. I have known her all my life, and I've never heard her swear, I mean ever!

"Ma?"

She just hugs me. "Shh, my child, that's how worried I am!" I just hug her back. After a while, we both climb to our feet, looking over at Steel, he just smiles.

Bernie has his hand on his shoulder, shaking his hand. "Come in, son! Let's have a drink. I think we need one. Don't you?" We all nod.

Before I can say anything... "Bran, Dane, Scar, your sister's home!" The next seconds are a blur, almost like a stampede. There's a thunder of footsteps along the corridor upstairs that continues down the stairs as all three of them barrel into me, sweeping me in their arms.

"OW! Motherfuckers, I've been shot, and stabbed, and shot, ya know?"

"Fuck, sorry." Bran lets go.

"Soz!" Dane breathes as he also lets go.

Scar just squeezes me harder. "I don't give a fuck. I'm never letting go again ever, ever, ever and then even longer, so there!"

Hugging her back, I turn to Steel and whisper, "She's the drama queen of the family!... Ouch, fucking shot, ya know!" from the dig she gives me in the ribs.

"You deserve that, dickwad!"

"Missed you, fuck face."

"Fucking love you twat waffle!"

I squeeze her back. "K.F.D."

Looking at my face, searching for something, I've no idea what, she breathes, "K.F.D."

Dane wraps his arms around us both. "K.F.D."

Followed by Bran encasing us all and repeating, "K.F.D."

Steel takes us all in and looks at Bernie, who looks at us, and then back to Steel, and shrugs. "It's a them thing, they've done it since they were kids, then when they met Scar she joined in. Who the fuck knows."

Clapping him on the shoulder and tilting his head to the kitchen, he says, "Drink."

Steel nods and follows him in.

"Fuck, Ray, I'm so sorry... I... "

"Shut the fuck up, bitch tits!" Scar just nods. Looking at her beautiful face, still bruised and battered,

I know as long as she's alive I will die for this bitch. After explaining everything to everyone all over again, I then drop the bombshell that Bran is dating Demi and Steel's her big brother. Well, I might have actually not used the words dating. It may have been boning or shagging or both, either way, the attention was taken away from me for a short while.

As we're leaving, Ma gives me a gift bag. As I open it, it's a brand-new phone. "The boys told Bernie yours took a swim, and you not being able to let me know you were back safe really bothered me, so here, I hope you like it!"

"Thanks, Ma. You didn't have to, but I love it. Thank you!"

I give her the biggest hug and whisper in her ear, "I'm sorry, Ma. I love you!" Pulling back, she wipes a tear from her cheek, nods and steps into Pa Bernie's arms.

Gathering Scar, we head to the truck to drive back. Arriving at the clubhouse, Scar gets out the truck, and Boyband's there, waiting.

"Fuck, princess, don't leave me alone again, okay?"

Throwing her arms around him, he lifts her up, and she wraps her legs around his waist as she yells, "See you sometime tomorrow, fuckwit!"

"Knob off, dick face!"

"K.F.D."

"K.F.D." Sighing, I climb down from the truck heading around the back of it. Steel heads towards me. "Thanks for taking me to get Scar."

"Anytime."

"Maybe I'll see you around?" I kick at the floor, becoming very interested in the concrete all of a sudden.

"Yeah, you'll definitely see me around." He smiles as I turn to walk away to the van. I'm bollocksed. I just need a good day or so of sleep. I reach the van. I look towards the truck, but he's gone. I let out a frustrated breath. I'm kind of glad he hasn't followed me, but also disappointed that he hasn't.

Maybe being on my own is for the best. I need to process what's happening. Getting myself ready for bed, I plug my new phone in. Dane's already set it up, so I'm good to go.

I take a massive swig of tequila, then head into the bedroom at the back, sliding my naked body in between the cold sheets. Bliss and sleep!

There's a loud knock at the door of the van. I roll over and pull the covers over my head. "Fuck off, I'm not in!" I whisper. Loud knocking again shakes the van. "Get fucked! Leave me alone," Still whispering but hoping they will get the message, I check the clock. It's 1 a.m. There's another knock, and it all goes quiet, so I turn over and go back to sleep.

It's dark and peaceful when a dream stirs, foggy at first, but then all my senses come alight. The bed dips at the side of me. I smile. I feel the warmth. First, it engulfs me, then his scent. He smells like freedom and the open roads, the outdoors and motorbikes, leather and dirty promises, but then feels so warm, safe. Moaning, I shuffle back and relax. Huge arms encompass me into a tight embrace, and I can't help but feel at home.

It's dark again. There's a hard body pressed behind me, a warm breath making the little strands of hair near my shoulder flutter. He has one arm under my neck and the other wrapped around me. Am I still dreaming? I grind my arse back, and I'm tugged firmer so I wriggle more.

Placing a kiss on my shoulder, he breathes, "Shh, baby, go back to sleep." I shuffle against him, then drift off again. When I wake up the next time, it looks like morning. The van is bright, but the warm body is still hanging on to me for dear life. Then there's a moment of realisation I'm not actually alone.

"What are you doing here? …How'd you get in?"

Placing a kiss to my shoulder, he mumbles, "Couldn't sleep… Scar's keys… Shh, it's early!" Kissing me again, he squeezes me against him.

Shifting in his arms so that I'm facing him, looking at his beautiful face, I trail my finger down his scar. "How?"

"Long story."

"I've got time."

"Some other time."

"Okay." I go to get up, but he grabs me in a bear hug. "Why are you trying to ruin it? Stay!"

Huffing, I ask, "What time is it?"

"Four," he says, never opening his eyes, never even looking.

"Hey, you didn't even look."

He shows me his watch. It's 4 a.m. holy shit. I'd slept the whole day and most of the night away. I can't get back to sleep, so I just stare at his beautiful face, trailing my fingers down his cheek, along his stubbled jaw and across his full lips and down his neck, along his collar bone over his tattoo, down to his holy hot as hell nipple piercings.

I feel the rumble before I hear him. The vibration starts in the middle of his chest, vibrating till the word comes out, breathy but gravelly, "Creeper." There's a slight kick to the corner of his mouth, but his eyes stay closed. He shifts, pulling me in closer, his dick hard and pulsing, digging into my thigh. I gasp. It's at that moment I realise we're both naked.

As I move my thighs, I feel my arousal coating them. "Fuck!"

"I was hoping to wait till we're married."

"'Scuse me?"

His eyes opened slowly, swirling like a storm. "You said you wanted to fuck, I was just stating I'm not that kind of guy. You're gonna have to put a ring on it first, Sunshine!"

I push back from him. Well, I try, but I only get so far. "Who climbs into bed with a complete stranger? Naked, might I add?"

"Who lets a naked stranger into their bed? I mean, some people, huh?"

"Argh, Steel, what are you doing here? You can't just creep around naked sliding into people's beds!"

"Not people's, just yours!" Closing his eyes again, he pulls me into his chest, but his warmth and scent overtake me, and my thighs slide against each other. I know I want him. Before I can think, I push him back as I straddle him across his hips, just below his rigid length.

Gasping, he asks. "Ray, what are you doing?"

"Just getting comfy. Thought we could chat and see what... comes up?" I roll my hips, rubbing my clit over his dick, groaning. I don't know what's gotten into me with him, but it's like everything I've ever thought has been thrown out the window. I want him to kiss me, I want him to touch me and I certainly want him to fuck me. It's playing tricks on my mind. He takes a deep breath, then moves his hands to my hips, as I try to roll my hips again, he holds me still. "Do you want me?"

"Yeah!"

"Does she want me?"

"What?"

"You act like you and Reaper are two different people, so which one of you wants me?"

"Her! Me! Both."

"I'm not here to play games, Ray, I want you, but I want forever with you. I don't want a quick fuck and onto the next, I want you. All of you, and I want you to want all of me, too. Are you fucking Dice?"

I take a shaky breath, and he sits up and kisses me like he's trying to take my last breath, cupping my cheek. "I want you and I want you to want me. I will wait for you to figure it all out, but I won't wait forever, and I don't share. Either you'll marry me or you won't, but until you decide what you want, I'm not playing games, Ray! I will love you, I will burn the world down with you, I will stand by your side, and I will always have your back. Until you can say the same, I should go!"

"Steel, wait." But he's already lifting me off him, placing a kiss on my head and stepping towards the door. "Steel, how can I decide all that when I don't know you? I know nothing about you."

"That's the kind of stuff we'll find out together as we go, but if you can't commit then say. I'll leave you with your thoughts… See you around, Ray. You know where I'll be when you decide what you want."

The bedroom door clicks, and he's gone. "WTAF?" It seems like a lifetime ago, not just Friday that I was shot, but it still hurts like a motherfucker, so I'm gonna do what I do best. I'm gonna shower, relieve my blue lady balls while I'm in there, and then I'm going to work, cos that's just how I roll and fuck Steel, I know fuck all about him, and yet marriage? That escalated so fucking fast, and not in the way I was hoping. How can you decide to be with someone and know nothing about them, jackass?

Ray

"Holy fuck! What the hell are you doing here?" Dozer yells across the garage at me.

"Well, I owe you a week's work. I said I would work last week and we would leave at the weekend. I may have had a minor setback, but I'm here to make my week up. I will be heading out Friday lunch, though, so you've got me till then! What do you want me on?"

"Your back, in your bed, in your van, that's what I want you on, Ray!"

"Come on, Dozer. Beauty won't like that and you know it!"

"Fuck you, Ray. Go. Now!"

"Either put me to work, or I'm heading elsewhere now. Up to you!"

"Fuck you, stubborn-ass bitch! Fine, take the Harley. Full service, noise under braking. I'm going to get a coffee!"

"Fine, but while you're dobbing me into Scar, don't forget I take mine black like my soul with three sugars!"

He flips his middle finger as he walks away.

I shout, "Tell Boyband I said hey while you're ratting me out to him too!" I spin around and get to work. Needless to say no one comes to bother me. Scar knows I will kick off if she does, so she also won't let the others come at me either. It's nearly lunch before I get my coffee. Obviously, Dozer's avoiding me. It's like I've never been away.

I take my coffee and finish up what I'm doing, do another few bits and say I'm done for the day. "Catch ya tomorrow!" Dozer scowls and mumbles, but I head out and back to the van. Fuck, I need to get away from all these fucking dudes!

Ray: I need to get away. Girls weekend?
Demi: I'm in!
Ray: Scar, how about you?
Demi: Where are we going?
Ray: Leave it with me, be ready about lunchtime Fri!

I weigh my options, but have no idea what we can do. I sit in the van all alone, and can't think of a single thing, so I start scrolling through my contacts.

Ares... nope.
Blade... nope.
Bran... nope.
Carmen...

Hmm, maybe, just maybe. I hit dial anyway. What do I have to lose?

"Reaper? Everything okay?"
"Hey Carmen. Call me Ray, everyone else does!"
"Okay, Ray, how can I help you?"

"Well actually, me, Scar, and Demi thought we might head somewhere for a girls weekend from Friday lunch. Then I thought, why not invite you? Maybe we could get to know each other without the lying, kidnapping scumbags and… Have some fun!" I'm not sure why I shrug, because she definitely can't see it!

"Unfortunately, Reaper… Sorry, Ray, I'm with my daughter, so I can't go away … "

"No worries, it's just a thought, take care and I —"

"Wait, Ray… "

"Yeah?"

"I can't go anywhere, but why don't you and the girls come here? I mean, I could use some girl time. We can have drinks and… hang out by the pool, or have a BBQ. What do you say?"

"Really? I say yes, that's a massive yes. What shall we bring?"

"Just yourselves and swimsuits. See you Friday. I will send you the address!"

Ray: Okay, sorted. Bring your swimmers. Scar, you in?
Demi: Ooh, where are we going?
Ray: Surprise!
Demi: Boo!
Ray: 'Laughing emoji'
Scar: I'm in.
Demi: Finally.
Ray: Thought you'd been fucked into a coma, bitch tits!

Scar: Well, if you weren't a little bitch, you could be in your own fuck-coma.
Demi: Ew, with my brother? 'barf emoji'
Ray: I'm not with your brother.
Demi: Then who? Don't you go cheating on my brother. I will cut you!
Ray: Fuck you, Scar!
Scar: 'Middle finger emoji'
Ray: I'm not with your brother or anyone else. Can we just not talk about boys, please? They give me a headache.
Scar: Fine.
Demi: Fine.
Ray: See you both Friday lunch.
Demi: 'Thumbs up emoji'
Scar: Bitch tits out!

Right, I need to get out of the van and go somewhere I won't see Scar and Boyband, or Steel! Fuck my life!

Ray: Gym in twenty.
Roach: You just got shot!
Ray: No shit, Sherlock! Gym in eighteen.
Roach: Okay.

Well, that was easier than I thought. Best get ready for the gym

After a great session with Roach and pointing him in the right direction, even injured, I still put him through hell. I open the door to the van.

"Are you fucking serious?" The booming, gravelly voice sounds across the parking lot. I wince as my fingers still on the door handle, turning to face him. I cross my arms over my chest.

"You bellowed?"

"Too fucking right, I bellowed. Are you fucking kidding me right now? Roach has just come in the clubhouse saying you were at the gym, and when I said what the fuck, you should be resting, Dozer piped up that you've been to work today! So, like I said, are you fucking serious?"

I sigh. "Steel, it's nice that you care, really! But I know my own body, and I'm fine, so if that's all?" I turn to grab the door, but it's ripped out of my hand. "What the fuck, Steel?" Mother fucker is taking liberties now.

"What the fuck, Ray!" he yells. "You've been shot!"

"I know! I was fucking there! I was the fucker who got shot! Now kindly fuck right off and get out my face before I fucking nut you!"

"Woah, woah, woah, easy there." Two hands push in between us, pushing us apart. "Time out, guys!" Turning and glaring at Tank, he raises his hands up in submission. "Steel, why don't you go get a drink, and Ray, why don't you… show me around your van!"

Glaring at Steel, I step into the van. I can hear them whispering as I step in, but I don't give a flying fuck, so I grab the tequila. Tank walks in and shuts the door behind him.

"Bedroom at the end, shower room to the left, closet to the right. Dining room, kitchen, living room. Are we done here?"

"What's going on?" he questions, cocking a brow at me and tilting his head.

"I got shot!" I blow out a breath, releasing my anger. I'm not angry with Tank, and I'm not going to take it out on him.

"I know, but what's going on?"

"I got shot, and now people expect shit from me and just… wanna tell me what the fuck to do, and boss me the fuck around, and make me feel shit. I don't know what to do. I just… " I sigh out a breath.

"You just what?"

"I'm just done, Tank. I'm done! I'm going to bed!" I turn and stalk to the bedroom and shut the door. I still have hold of the tequila, so it's lights out for me!

Ray

Walking around the corner to the garage, I can hear low chattering, so I flatten to the side of the building, coming right to the side of the garage doors. I lean back against the wall and kick up my foot, leaning it on the wall, bending my knee. I take out my Swiss Army knife and pick at my nails while I'm tab hanging.

"She's gonna hurt herself," Steel says.

"You tell her, then!" Priest huffs.

"I tried. She wouldn't even talk to me," Steel argues.

"Or me!" Tank mumbles.

"What were you even arguing about?" Priest asks.

"She went to the gym with Roach," Steel tells them, the fucking snitch!

"The fucking gym. Is she serious?" Viking barks out.

"That's what I said, but she got in my face and started shouting back at me… " Steel whines.

"Yeah, she's got a bit of a temper," Priest adds.

"A fucking *bit* of a temper? That's an understatement," Blade replies.

"So, what are we gonna do?" Tank questions. "We can't just let her hurt herself!"

"Scar says they're going away somewhere at the weekend," Ares tells them.

"Where? She never said," Steel sounds pissed.

"Maybe that's because you were shouting at each other!" Tank's clearly pissed too.

"Fuck you!" Steel sounds like a five-year-old.

"Fuck you more." As Tank joins him in foundation, or what is it they call it? Ah, yeah, kindergarten!

"Guys, this isn't helping. We need to come up with a plan together." Dice tries to rein them in.

"What can we do?" Priest asks.

"She won't listen," Blade hisses.

"She's so fucking stubborn," Steel huffs.

"Well, maybe if you didn't stake a claim within five fucking seconds of meeting her and telling her you're gonna marry her. I mean, fuck, Steel, what were you even thinking?" Dice spits at him.

"What, can't handle the competition? I was thinking she's perfect and everything I've ever wanted and… Fuck, are you two fucking?" Steel sounds so defeated.

"What? No, we're not fucking." Dice is clearly pissed now too.

"Fuck," Steel spits.

"Fucking hell!" Viking spits too.

"I am gonna marry her!" Steel sounds so confident in that statement.

"Not fucking helping, Steel!" Dice spits again.

"I'm gonna take her out for breakfast; then we can talk," Steel informs them.

"Do you honestly think taking her somewhere that openly gives you knives is a great place for you to talk?" Dice asks.

"They're pretty blunt, as far as knives go." Steel smirks. I can hear it in his voice.

"I bet she could kill you with a fucking spoon if she really wanted to." Dice laughs at him.

"Yeah, I reckon she could chop his dick off with a spoon," Tank informs him.

"Yeah, I reckon she could skin you in under five minutes with a spoon." Priest almost sounds proud.

"I reckon she could remove his eyeballs and his testicles in less than three." Blade grins.

"Why am I the one you're all aiming her anger at? Maybe, just maybe, it was one of you that upset her." Steel tries to convince them.

"Nope, it was you!" Priest sounds smug.

"Yep, you!" Tank adds.

"Definitely you!" Ares laughs.

Then there's a big sigh. "Fine, I got a little overexcited and maybe scared her away a little, but I will figure it out. We just need to talk, okay?" Steel's clearly trying to reason with everyone.

"Fine," Priest answers.

"Okay," Tank says.

"Agreed," Viking replies.

"Sure." Blade's clearly done with this whole conversation.

"She won't do it," Dice grinds out.

"Give him a chance," Ares pleads.

"He can't fuck it up any more than he has already," Dice says again.

"Fuck you all," Steel spits!

There's the sound of footsteps.

"Oh, shit!" Steel barks out.

"Yeah, oh fucking shit," I retort, still holding my position against the wall as Steel comes barrelling out through the doors.

The others arrive after the "Oh shit" from Steel and fall silent. "So, gentlemen." I stop picking my nails and eye Ares, Blade, Tank, Viking, Dozer, Priest and Dice before swinging my gaze back to Steel, then closing the knife and stepping up to his chest.

"Do we have a problem here?"

He looks at them all, clearly looking for backup, and they just stand there. They know me better than he does, and none of them make a move. He looks back at me. "No!"

Holding his gaze till he looks away, I turn, walking through the middle of them into the garage. I can hear the sighs, and when I turn back around, they are all gone. Even fucking Dozer. Brilliant. How long will he avoid me today?

Just when I think I'm being avoided and doing a great job of avoiding everyone, I get a message from Ares.

Boyband: Need a favour.

Bane of my existence!: What up, Boyband?

Boyband: I'm calling you.

Bane of my existence!: Why didn't you just call me to start with?

Bane of my existence!: What a totally pointless text thread.

Bane of my existence!: You really are a dick.

Bane of my existence!: Do you know that I can totally text for ages, so if you're calling, you need to hurry up?

Bane of my existence!: I might get bored and turn my phone off. Just because I can. To wind you up.

Bane of my existence!: Because I'm fucking hilarious.

Boyband: Fuck, you're annoying.

Bane of my existence!: 'Laughing emoji' 'middle finger emoji'

After speaking to Ares on the phone, it doesn't look like I'm avoiding anyone. He has a job for me tomorrow night, so I might as well get on with it.

I need to get away, so I head over to Dwayne's bar. It isn't ideal, but I can park up outside, and at least I have a bed for the night if I get totally trashed. I take a shower and go to grab my phone, then remember I don't wanna talk to anyone, so I leave it on the table and head across the truck stop, walking into Dwayne's like I don't have a care in the world. Striding over to the bar, Dwayne eyes me, then smiles.

"Hi, Ray. On your own?"

"Yeah. Tequila, please, Dwayne." He pours the drink and shifts uneasily. *Please don't bring it up, please, please, please*, I recite through my mind.

"Soo, how ya been?"

Fuck, fuck, fuck. This is so awkward. "Yeah, good buddy, you?" That's right, I hit him with the buddy line, to which he grimaces and nods as if to say, "Okay, I get it."

"So, you and Steel, huh?" Fuck's sake, why can't I get away from Steel? He's everywhere, all-consuming, all fucking gorgeous and ripped and hot, and… fucking hell, what am I doing? I just smile and shake my glass once. He fills it up. I ask him to start a tab, and I'll settle up later. He nods, and I go to sit in the corner by myself. I need to figure shit out. My head is all over the place.

So normally, I fuck guys like I did Dwayne, with minimum contact, no kissing, hugging, or anything of that nature, but why? Tapping my glass, I contemplate the reasoning behind it. Hmm… why? I don't hate guys. I feel uncomfortable when I get attention I don't want, but the guys at the MC, I don't seem to mind. In fact, I instigate it a lot of the time, especially with Dice. I climb into his lap a lot, I mean, a fucking lot! And Tank, I didn't think twice about being so close with him on his bed with his arm around me, and I laid out on his chest. I even hug Boyband. They feel like family, which leaves me confused.

Is it the guys or the situation? Is it the fact that back home, Reaper's locked away for extremely long periods of time? When I let her out, that's usually when I fuck someone or worse. Well, Jer, so is it her needing that control? When I met up with Jer, she didn't object, when normally, I would get an uneasy feeling beforehand with other guys. Steel… I mean, I woke up in his arms—twice, for fuck's sake!

Why doesn't she object to these guys? All of a sudden, my hackles are up. Just before I see a hand reach for mine.

"Well, look at you. Aren't you a sight for sore eyes!" The guy purrs, looking at his hand, then his face, and then his hand again right where it meets mine.

"Move it or lose it!"

He laughs, but the next thing, Dwayne's in between us, whispering in the guy's ear, "Look man, I say this with the utmost respect, but seriously, you really don't wanna go there with this one." He looks over Dwayne's shoulder at me, and I gave him my very best psychopathic glare with added sociopath thrown in for good measure.

"I think I can handle this little thing," he spouts.

Dwayne shrugs, but before stepping away, adds, "Any damage she does to you and this place is on you. Cash upfront before you try your luck!" I bark out a laugh, and the guy hands Dwayne a hundred dollars. Then it's Dwayne's turn to laugh. "Yeah that's not gonna cut it! I need at least five hundred dollars." Then turning and looking at me, I nudge my thumb up. "Six hundred." I nudge again. "Eight hundred. I'm gonna need eight hundred dollars."

"That should just about cover how fucked up I'm feeling tonight, Dwayne." I stand up to look at the guy. I crack my fingers and my neck, never taking my eyes off him, and taking a look at my eyes, he takes a step back. I step around Dwayne, and then the guy is gone.

"Fifty each?" Dwayne shrugs.

I laugh, clapping him on the shoulder. "Nah, keep it for last time. I'm, erm, sorry about that!"

"Yeah, don't worry, they deserved it. I'll send another drink over. You look like you could use one."

"Thanks, Dwayne, I appreciate it."

So I clearly objected to that guy. Well, Reaper did. She felt him before I did. Hmm, interesting. I need to test a theory. I just need to figure out how.

After squaring my tab with Dwayne, I'm about to leave, but I'm the only person left, so I sit at the bar. "Dwayne, can I ask you a question before I go?"

He looks at me dubiously. "Erm... sure."

"Okay, so let's say I'm asking for a friend."

"Is that friend you?"

"Maybe!"

"Okay, shoot."

"Okay, so my friend fucked this guy, kind of. But didn't... wasn't... couldn't... " I huff a sigh.

"Look, Ray, just say what you need to say. I know I'm not in the running, so hit me with it. Maybe we can be friends?"

"Really?"

"Really. Now shoot!"

"Okay, so when we fucked..."

"Oh... okay, we're just gonna go straight to it... Yep, okay... Right, I'm listening... "

"Okay, so when we fucked, I didn't finish, and I didn't let you touch me. What colour were my eyes?"

"What?"

"My eyes, what colour were they?"

"How the fuck am I supposed to know that, Ray?" Blowing out a breath, he looks at them now. "Now they're really blue, like the colour of cornflowers or sky. I don't think they were blue. That feels like the wrong answer. Now they look bright and almost happy."

"But not before?"

"Not sure, but something's different."

"Okay, I want you to lean right in my face and stare into my eyes."

"Okay!"

"Okay, is this what my eyes looked like?"

"No, I don't think so. I mean, does it matter what your eyes look like? It seems like an odd question to me."

"Okay, give me a second." I close my eyes and think, *okay, bitch, show me what I'm missing here, come out, come out, wherever you are*. At that, I can feel my skin buzzing with excitement clenching my fists, my hand shoots up, and I grab Dwayne's throat, throwing my eyes open.

He gasps, then winces out, "That's it, like that, they looked like that, stormy that's what they were like, swirling and stormy, almost grey, fuck… Ray, can you let go of my throat now… Please… I might come in my pants if you don't!"

Shaking myself, I take a step back and take in a deep breath, leaning forward. I hug Dwayne. "Thanks, you don't know how much that helped." After, he hugs me back. I don't even flinch or get disgusted like I thought I would. Hmm, maybe I've changed. I need to get some kind of contact with Steel, but I think I might wait till after the weekend. Call me chickenshit if you like, but I'm just gonna leave that scab alone a little longer. That's if I can keep on his good side tomorrow, as there's no getting away from tomorrow night. Fuck, fuck, fuckety, fuck!

Ray

Ray: Gym, fifteen minutes
Roach: You sure? We worked hard the other day. Don't you need to rest, you know, with the injury and all?
Ray: Gym, twelve minutes.
Roach: On my way! Chill.
Ray: Dick!

So after keeping Roach busy for an hour, we shower at the gym. I tell him I want to have a drink with him to talk through some new training bits. The kid has been working hard. If it wasn't for him, I wouldn't have known about Casper. He deserves this. So as we walk down to the clubhouse, we chat about nothing in particular.

Swinging the door open and heading in, everyone's standing there, waiting. Ares, Steel and Dozer front and centre. The look on Roach's face is priceless.

"Erm, everything okay, guys? Are you waiting for drinks? If you give me a second, I will be right with you!"

Ares takes a step forward. "Hang on, Roach. Before you go anywhere, we need to talk."

"Shit, that doesn't sound good. I can sort it whatever it is, I can fix it, Ares, I'm sure… "

"Fuck's sake, Roach, shut the fuck up and listen, knobhead!" I bark out at him, scrubbing my hand down my face and throwing my gym bag in the corner.

"Sorry… Yeah, sorry. Erm, what was it?"

"We're patching you in, kid!" Ares claps him on the shoulder.

"What the fuck?" He gasps.

"That's right!" Ares chuckles. "You proved yourself loyal by your actions which helped us get out of a tricky situation. Now, you ready to get tatted up?"

"Fuck yeah!" he sings out, and we all clap him on the back. The group parts to find the guy who works at the local tattoo shop, ironically called Tatts, sitting there with a chair and a tattoo machine ready.

Just before Roach makes his way over to the chair, he turns and hugs me, tears in his eyes. "Thanks for believing in me, Reaper, I won't let you down!"

"I know you won't, kid. Now, go get that tat before the arsehole changes his mind!" I laugh out, and Roach just smiles at me and heads to the chair.

One and a half hours later, he's finished. He's been handed a bottle of whisky. Apparently, his drink of choice when he started, and now he's finished, he has to sit on the bar and drink until the bottle's empty, or he falls off the bar.

Who makes this shit up? Seriously! I stay till he passes out and is carried to his room, then I slip out the back and head to the van. Operation Avoid Everyone Till After The Trip commences again.

Friday lunch, I'm packed and out the door. Grabbing Scar and heading to Demi's, we're on the road.

"Where are we going?" Scar asks for the millionth time. We've only just picked Demi up, so we still have a way to go, but, "It's a surprise" doesn't seem to be cutting it anymore.

Ah, well, tough shit. They will have to wait. They then decided it would be fun to ask me questions about Steel. You know, just to make me squirm, but fuck them. I will drop them in the middle of nowhere and pick them up on the way back if they keep being arseholes.

Finally, as we pull up to the gate, two security guards in suits with guns come to the window to speak to me, smiling. As they get to the window, one speaks in a heavily accented voice, "Reaper! Nice to see you again. If you drive up to the main doors, someone will be with you to collect your bags and park your… vehicle for you!"

"Thanks." I smile back as we drive through the gates. The fence goes all the way around the villa, and it looks massive pulling up. We get out of the van with the bags.

Three young Mexican guys come to grab them for us. "We will take these to your rooms. If you would like to follow us, Senorita Castillo will meet you by the pool for drinks in around thirty minutes!"

Dropping into step behind the guys, we can see the villa is actually a square shape with the pool centrally outside, eating area, sun loungers and outside cooking area and what looks like a dance floor all in the centre.

"Ah, very security conscious, nice design!" I mumble to no one in particular. We walk into our rooms. Three separate double rooms, all with their own bathrooms, two on the left of the corridor and one on the right.

I take the one on the right, and as I do, there are big double sliding doors at the back leading out to the pool area. Once we've dropped our bags and changed into something more appropriate, we head outside.

There's a bar tucked away in the corner, which I hadn't seen before, and the bartender's making cocktails, so we go over to him. We're two cocktails in when Carmen and her daughter Catalina show up. Catalina's a carbon copy of Carmen. She just looks slightly younger, more from the shape of her body than anything else, but at nearly fifteen, she is absolutely stunning.

I give Carmen a grin and walk over to her to give her a hug. Look at me, getting out my own head and then hugging Catalina too.

"Reaper, it's fabulous to see you. So glad you could make it. I hope your rooms are satisfactory?" she asks in her subtle accent. However, her English is exceptional.

Carmen, Demi, and Scar go over to the table and sit with their cocktails. Catalina's eyeing me curiously.

"What do you wanna know, kiddo?" I ask, grinning.

She takes in a shocked breath. "Know?"

"Yeah, I can totally see the questions flying around in your head, so come on, sit down with me and ask away!"

"Really?"

"Yeah, sure!"

"Did you really save me? How did you know? Why do they call you Reaper? Is Ray your real name? How many men have you killed? Did your tattoos…"

"Easy, tiger!" I cut in, laughing. "One question at a time."

Blowing out a breath, she fixes her gaze on me again. "What's your real name?"

Before I give her the answers, I cut in with, "Right, ground rules!"

"Ground rules?"

"Yep, you wanna know my secrets, right? Then we have to build trust. You'll have to give me some of yours, too. A secret for a secret!"

"Is your name a secret?"

"There are not many people who know my real name, my family, then some of the people I went to school with if the teacher slipped up and used it, but not many!

"If you want to know my secrets, we will have to make a pact. Our secrets are ours to share with each other, only you can't share mine with anyone else, and I won't share yours. Deal?"

She thinks for a moment. "So, if I tell you something, you won't tell my mum…?"

"Can't and won't unless it's a matter of life or death!"

Letting out a shaky breath, she says, "Do we need a blood pact?"

I raise a brow at her. Well, that escalated fucking fast, but I have a feeling whatever it is, this girl is gonna need my help with it sooner rather than later, and I'm gonna have to be ready.

"Would you like to make it a blood pact?"

Thinking again, she chews on her lip. "Yes!"

"Well, okay, then!" Rising, I lead her to my room, where I get out the Swiss Army knife and give it to her. She looks at me, then down at her hand, then back at me. "You don't have to do this. I'm not asking this of you."

"I know, but I want the vow to mean something. I want to trust you, and I want you to trust me. There aren't many people here I can talk to, and you seem… well, from what my mother says, you seem like a handy person to know!"

I smile at her, really smile. "I will make you a promise right here, right now. You pick a code word, and if you need me, you just say or text that word, and I will drop everything and be right there, no questions."

"You would do that?"

"I take my vows very seriously, so yes, I will" Taking the knife, she looks at me, then pauses, pushing the knife into the fleshy part of her palm above her left wrist. On it, she carves a small heart the size of a thumbnail. Showing me, I take the knife from her and mark my hand the same, then push it against hers.

Blinking, eyes filled with tears, she says, "I don't have anyone I can trust other than my mother, and some things I can't talk to her about!" Sniffling, she tries to blink back the tears.

"Hey, it's okay. I'm here. You can tell me anything. Has something happened?" Glancing over to the door and back to me, she nods.

"Catalina, has someone hurt you?"

"Please don't say anything, don't call me Catalina. He says it, and I don't like the way he says it."

"Okay, what about Cat, Lina, or Tali?"

"Tali? Tali, I like that."

"Okay, kiddo. Tali it is. So who hurt you?"

When she doesn't reply, I tug her arm and sit on the bed next to her.

"My real name is… Sunshine!" A tiny, shocked gasp leaves her lips as she raises her eyes.

She looks at me and smiles. "Sunshine?"

"Yeah, my mum chose it. She died when I was four. After that, my dad couldn't bring himself to call me it, so he called me Ray instead, he said I was his ray of sunshine, so I've gone by Ray ever since."

"He works here!" Tali hangs her head. "Kind of, anyway. He's not hurt me… yet. But he touches me when no one's looking. He's high up in the organisation, and I don't know if my mother will believe me or do anything."

"What's he done?"

"If he's near me, he will slide his hand up my legs to my underwear, and he will pinch my ass and my breasts if he can get away with it!"

"Is he here this weekend?" Looking at the floor again, I grab her chin.

"Your mother will believe you, and I'm sure she will kill him for even thinking he can lay a hand on you."

"You can't tell her. Please don't tell her!"

"I won't, I promise, but if he's here this weekend, I will kill him if you want me to."

"You will?"

"Yes!"

"I can't let you. My mother... she would kill you!"

"Let me deal with your mother. I won't hurt her, and I won't tell her, but I will kill the son of a bitch, deal?" Shaking her head, she looks at the floor again.

"Are you telling me the truth, Tali?" Looking at me with unshed tears and a look that crushes me, she nods.

"Then tell me who he is." I lean down to my bag and draw out my hunting knife. I wrap it in a towel, picking up the Swiss Army knife. I give it to her. "When I was kidnapped by your mother's ex-men, this belonged to one of them.

"I took it when I murdered him. It's yours. Keep it close in case you need it. Stab him with the pointy end!" A small laugh falls from her lips.

"Now, let's head back to the pool, and if you see him, you say the code word. What's it gonna be?"

She thinks for a moment while biting her lip. "Santa Muerte!"

"Ah, Mexican Grim Reaper!" I smile at her.

She gives me a genuine smile. "It seems fitting. Reaper!"

I laugh as I rise to my feet. I pull her into a hug, and she takes a breath and then sobs. I hold her for what feels like a lifetime. Hearing the faintest noise, I look towards the door and see Carmen. I raise my finger to my lips, and she nods and backs away. I can see the hurt in her eyes, but she doesn't say anything. A few minutes later, Tali pulls away from me and wipes her eyes.

"Go wash your face. We will head to the pool before someone comes looking for us. Remember the word and use it when you need to, okay? I will not let him touch you again!"

She nods and scurries into the bathroom. Fuck, that got real heavy, real fast, and this is gonna be one of those make-or-break moments, as I'm gonna kill that motherfucker, and it's gonna be brutal. I just hope that Carmen won't take it as an act against her, but if she does, I'm gonna have to be ready.

I need her to trust me blindly. And for that, I need to talk to her without giving any of what I know away. Just another day in the life of Reaper. It's getting far too easy to blur the lines I have kept in place for so long. Maybe my dad and Steel were right!

Tali exits the bathroom.

"You good?"

She nods.

"Okay, I need you to trust that I won't tell your mum what's happening, but I do need to ask her to trust me. If I kill someone here, she needs to have the heads up, okay?"

She chews at her lip and nods. "You won't tell her, though, will you? I don't want her to look at me like I'm... damaged or fragile."

"Can you defend yourself?"

She shakes her head.

"Okay, while I'm here, I will show you some things, just in case we don't get the outcome we want, okay?"

She nods and smiles. "You'll really teach me?"

"Yeah, kiddo, I will." Slinging my arm over her shoulder, we walk out of the room and back towards the pool. Carmen eyes me curiously and cautiously. I need to speak to her, but I won't betray Tali. She needs me, and I won't let her down. I shake my head slightly at Carmen, and she looks away. I can see a sadness in her eyes, but she stiff upper lips it, and I know I will have to explain myself later, well, as much as I can, but I won't betray Tali. She needs to know that my word means something!

After having a few more drinks around the pool, Carmen orders us all food, and we sit and eat it outside. It's so warm, and by the time it gets dark, there are heaters which she has flicked on to take the edge off. We drink until the early hours, talking and laughing and then head to bed.

When I wake the next morning, I have an uneasy feeling, so I shower quickly and head to grab the others, sliding my knife in my boot, so I'm prepared if needed. We are spotted loitering in the hall, and one of the staff members takes us to the dining room.

Carmen is already eating breakfast. "Morning, ladies. I must say, what a fantastic evening I had. I really enjoyed your company."

Smug grinning at her, I say, "Carmen, you almost seem surprised by your own admission!" I waggle my eyebrows at her as she breaks out in laughter.

"Reaper, I must say you're not what I expected. I do find you and your friends extremely entertaining, and it's a pleasant surprise to feel so at ease. I hope we can build a true friendship, as I think that could be beneficial to us both."

"Strong women need to support each other and straighten each other's crowns. I'm always down with adding another queen to our group, and I look forward to growing this friendship. That said, Carmen, would you mind a word in private?"

Frowning at me, she nods. "Of course. Why don't I show you around the grounds?"

Grabbing a couple of the Pan Dulce as we head out, I follow her to the main doors and out into the gardens after we are far enough away from the house.

Carmen clears her throat. "I'm assuming this is something to do with what I saw in your room yesterday."

Chewing my breakfast, I nod. These are amazing, but I'm not gonna let some sweet bread distract me from what I need from Carmen. "It does, Carmen. What I'm about to say isn't going to instil your trust in me. However, I need you to know that no matter what goes down, it needs to happen, and I need you to trust that!"

"That sounds very cryptic, Reaper, and we barely know each other. While I do have an element of trust in you, you've already saved my daughter a fate which would have been worse than death for her, you were in reality saving yourself, and that information was a bonus."

"You are correct, Carmen. I did save Catalina by saving my own skin, and after meeting her, I'm glad I did. We had a talk… this is what I need you to trust me on."

She pauses and turns to look at me.

"Before you say anything, Carmen, please understand I mean no offence by this, but I cannot tell you what we talked about."

I show her my palm and explain the secret for a secret pact we made, and that I won't break that.

"My word is what I live by, and I've given my word to your daughter. We've agreed that I will do a favour for her, and when she calls upon me, nothing will stop me from carrying it out. I hope you understand that I can't tell you what or why, and I'm asking you to trust me blindly and allow me to do this. I don't want to make an enemy of you, Carmen, but if that is the cost of fulfilling my promise, then so be it."

"Reaper, I really don't like the sound of this. Can you tell me what's happening? Why does my daughter need a favour? I need to know what's going on. Is she in danger?"

"I'm sorry, Carmen. I can't tell you any more, but I will insist that Catalina considers discussing it with you. All I can say is I've promised her I will do whatever it takes to fulfil my promise to her, and I promise you won't be hurt or injured in any way while I carry it out. That's all I'm willing to say!"

"Is whatever you're going to do… will it keep my daughter safe?"

"Most definitely, Carmen. I would not put her in danger. We made a blood pact. She needs to trust me, and that's what she wants in return."

Blowing out a breath, she says, "Reaper, you must understand, I am the head of the Castillo Cartel. You understand that if you do anything to cross me, I will bring the full force of the cartel down on you? I really don't want to lay a threat at your feet, but this is my home. I brought you into it, into my daughter's home, and I have gone against my advisers and given you free rein. Have I not been a gracious host? This is more than I've allowed in a long time, but I see something in you. I just hope it won't blow up in our faces!"

"Carmen, I can assure you that if this blows up, it will be in my face, not yours, and I will trust that you will do what is necessary, but I made a vow to your daughter, and above all else, that is my priority. All I ask is that whatever happens, Scar and Demi are not held responsible. They know nothing at all!"

"Reaper, you're making this extremely difficult for me to understand."

"I know, Carmen, I do understand, and don't think I'm taking this lightly, but in reality, I need you to trust that whatever Catalina has asked me to do, she has her reasons, and for now, those reasons mean you will have to wait for her to feel like she's ready to tell you.

But I promise I will keep her safe. You have my word on that."

"Do we need a blood pact too?"

Laughing, I smile at her. "Will it make you feel better?"

"Can I get back to you on that?"

"Sure!" I laugh. "Now come on, let's head back. I need some more Pan Dulce, and then I need to check if I'm gonna sink or float!"

We walk back in comfortable silence, but I keep the lookout for anything untoward. By the time this weekend is over, I know I will have blood on my hands, and I may be fighting for my own life, depending on how Carmen views my actions.

The day comes and goes, and the evening crawls in. As we are having dinner, Carmen informs us that some of the family are coming to visit and that she has arranged a cocktail party for us all. As we head back to our rooms, we all find a garment bag and a shoe box on our beds. Demi's is a beautiful emerald green cocktail dress with a puffy tulle skirt and matching Mary Janes.

Scar's is a beautiful, full-length red silk gown that clings to her curves with a slit right up the thigh and dips right to the base of her spine with a cowl neck front with black high-heeled pumps. Mine's a stunning black satin floor-length gown. It's simple and elegant, with no bells and whistles, no slit. It's backless, showing off all my tattoos with cross-over shoestring straps, and when I open the shoe box, there's a note.

Reaper,

To keep Catalina safe, you might want to wear your boots. You can "accessorise" them with the outfit.

C x

I take that to mean that although she doesn't know what's going on, she wants me to be ready. She has seen me keep my weapons in my boots and no doubt knows I will be packing, so to speak. Although the dress is tight, as it skims my hips, it flares out slightly, so I strap on my thigh holster and load two of my throwing knives into it and then add my New Rock Trails.

I slide my hunting knife down the side, dropping my dress. It coils around me without drawing attention to my weapons. I also get Scar and Demi to do me a fancy updo, and I add a throwing knife to that, too, so it looks like a hair clip. When I'm all suited and booted, I head off to the party.

I'm introduced to the main players of the cartel. Most of them pas, uncles and cousins, and then I'm introduced to Carmen's brother, who I immediately dislike after talking to him for less than ten minutes. I have figured he's a pig and doesn't care for Carmen in the slightest. I will be keeping an eye on this slimy bastard.

Catching the sight of Tali out of the corner of my eye, I make a beeline for her.

"You look stunning," I whisper in her ear. She blushes. Her dress is similar to Demi's but in silver. She seems distracted.

"Santa Muerte?" I breathe into her ear, but she shakes her head, so that means the brother's out. "Is he family?"

She shakes her head again. Well, at least that's good news. "He's my uncle's Lieutenant." I nod and glance around.

"Stay close, okay? Don't go anywhere on your own, even the bathroom. Come get me first, okay? Do you have your knife on you?"

Nodding, she taps her breast. "It's in my bra!"

"Good. If for any reason anything happens, I want you to scream 'Santa Muerte' as loud as you can over and over, and remember what I said about the knife?"

"Stick 'em with the pointy end."

"Yep, stab first!" I tap the side of my neck, then tap my groin.

"Ask questions later if they're still breathing, okay?" While messing around in the pool today, I taught her where to stab that little knife and hope if she needs to, she will.

We head to the bar and get a drink. We both get fancy non-alcoholic cocktails. I need to have my wits about me tonight. If her uncle's here, then his Lieutenant will be too. A few family members ask Tali to dance, and she does. Carmen's making the rounds but keeps checking I'm close to Tali. Every time I catch her eye, I just nod, watching as Tali dances around the dance floor. Demi and Scar are sat chatting with the barman.

I give them the nod towards Tali, and they nod silently, telling them I need to keep an eye on her and them letting me know they are good. After looking around again, I see Tali at the edge of the dance floor, wide-eyed and with a look of sheer panic on her face. Making eye contact with me, she mouths, "Santa Muerte."

I nod, looking behind her to the guy who has her arm in a vice grip and is slowly stepping back to avoid attention. I catch a glimpse of what looks like a blade pushed into her ribs, but I can't be sure, so I make my way quickly towards them, grabbing a cocktail from a table.

When I get close to them, I stumble. I walk past, tipping the drink down myself and his sleeve. He lets Tali go for a brief second, and she makes a dash for it. I stumble into him again and slur my words slightly. "So sorry."

"Maldita perra estúpida!"

"Fucking stupid bitch!" he mutters as he brushes off his sleeve.

I bat my eyelashes at him. "That's the nicest thing anyone has ever said to me."

Keeping up the drunk pretence, rubbing my hand up his arm, I say, "So strong!" and then, flicking to his eyes. "So handsome!" I bat my eyelashes and try to suppress the gag and eye roll. "So, handsome, what's a girl like me gotta do to get a guy like you to escort her back to her room?"

"Dios, eres estúpido."

"God, you are stupid."

Clearly, I know what this twat's saying, but I really need to rein it in and get him away from here and in my room, where I can kill him and hide the body, all in a night's work. Smiling again and rubbing against him, I slide my hand up his body and over his shoulder.

"It's so hot here. You want to help me out of my dress?" Leaning up, I lick along his neck, and he grabs me around the waist. He drags me against his body, pushing his dick against me and rubbing it into me. Fucking gross. I'm gonna enjoy this. I stumble again, and he grasps hold of me tighter.

"You're a filthy little whore, aren't you? I'm gonna make you sorry you bumped into me." He grabs my arm tightly and starts to drag me inside. "I'm gonna fuck that stupid mouth of yours so hard, you won't be able to talk for a week. Then I'm gonna fuck that tight little ass of yours till I make you bleed. That's only for starters."

I smile at him as he turns to glare at me. I stumble along beside him.

"You really are simple, aren't you?" I cock my head to the side and bat my eyelashes again.

"I don't understand Mexican. It's a beautiful language, though!"

He runs his hand down his face. "You think I'm speaking 'Mexican?' You really are a dumb whore!"

I smile at him again. "What did you say? I don't understand."

He says more slowly, "I said you have beautiful eyes!"

I flash them at him and take over, leading him down the corridor. "My room is this way." Leaning into him, I rub my hand across the front of his dick. "I want you to fuck me till I scream."

I stumble again, and he catches me by the arm. I fumble with the door and push it open, letting him inside. I push him back so his back is pressing against the bathroom door.

"I want to fuck you in the shower." I open the door and push him in. I start pretending to undo my dress. "Take your clothes off." I grab him by the tie and pull him into me, licking his lips. "Hurry, I need you," I slur out.

He drags his tie off and kicks his shoes off as he undoes his trousers. "I'm gonna fuck you raw, you stupid bitch!" he spits out, and I grin at him.

I reach up to my hair and pretend to fumble with the clip, pulling and huffing in frustration. He undoes a couple of buttons on his shirt and pulls it over his head. He's standing in boxers and socks. I can feel the grimace from my boots.

I'm disgusted, and so's Reaper. He grabs the back of my neck and pulls me towards him, smashing his mouth into mine. I give him a bit of tongue before pulling back and smiling. "You're so fucking sexy." He grins at me and pulls me into another kiss.

I moan and try not to puke and reach up again and grab my throwing knife, sliding my other hand around the back of his neck while we kiss. He's rough and gropey, and a total cunt, so I smile as I kiss him back, then plunge the blade straight into the side of his neck, right into the carotid. Removing the knife immediately, I then stab it in again into the front of his neck, pushing him backwards and crowding him into the shower cubicle. He gasps and goes to cry out, but I push the blade deeper, then release it again. He's drowning in his own blood, gurgling and choking it down and as he slumps onto the floor of the shower, eyes wide as I smile down at him.

"You underestimated me, motherfucker! That was fun! Catalina sends her regards!"

Trying to stand up, he gurgles, and that's it, game over. Lights out, and I smile as he slides down the tiles. I take a look at myself in the mirror, grimacing at the blood down my chest and across my face. Stepping over him in the shower, I turn it on and wash myself off, dress and all, till the water runs clear. I spray the floor where the blood has sprayed and send all the stray blood down the drain.

Taking a look at myself in the mirror and touching up my make-up, and rinsing off my knife, I tie my hair back up. Not as fancy as it was before, but I doubt anyone will notice. I towel off my dress. It's still warm out, so if I can get outside and maybe near a heater, my dress will dry pretty soon, and hopefully, no one will notice.

Walking through the house the opposite way, I come out near the other side of the bar and slide in beside a couple who are deep in conversation. Well, he has his tongue down her throat.

I order two cocktails and neck one. The next thing I know, Carmen's shouting to me. I turn round, and she calls me over, wandering over to her. She's standing with her brother and Catalina. "I hope you're having a good night."

"I am, Carmen. What a lovely gathering."

"Thank you. My brother has taken quite a shine to you and wondered if you would like to dance!"

"I would love to, Carmen." I take her brother's hand and pull him over to the dance floor. Carmen grins the biggest shit-eating grin at me and as we swing around. I flip her off, and she barks a laugh at me.

I think he's called Carlos. Who gives a fuck, anyway? He pulls me in close. "You are an exquisite woman. I would like to have a night with you."

"Why, Carlos, I am flattered, but unfortunately, I'm recently engaged, and that would be terribly unfair to my fiancé."

"Hmm." He pulls me closer, grabbing my arse and grinding his dick into me.

I smile up at him. "I'm so terribly sorry, Carlos. I must take my leave. Thank you for the dance. It was a pleasure meeting you." As I move to walk away, he grabs me hard around my upper arm. "I don't like being told no."

Leaning into him and whispering into his ear, I slide my hand up his chest. "I'm sure you don't, Carlos, and while I'm in your sister's home, I'm trying to be respectful, so I'm going to give you this piece of advice."

I step even closer and push into him. "I know exactly who you are, but you... you have no idea who I am and what I'm capable of. While you still have your dignity, I suggest you remove your hands from my body. I implore you to realise I'm not the woman for you and allow me to leave civilly, or I will remove them."

He smiles a vile, vicious smile at me.

Leaning in, I grab his balls and twist, and he squeaks. When people look around, he pretends he doesn't know where the noise has come from. "Go on, Carlos. Underestimate me. That'll be fun!"

As I twist again, he holds his breath, and I give him the biggest grin.

"I'm going to release you now. I think you should walk out of this house immediately and go home before I make a show of you." I lean up and kiss him on the cheek, giving just a little tug before releasing him. "Thank you for the dance, Carlos. It was a pleasure." Stepping back, he grimaces at me and leaves the party. Catalina comes straight over to me, throws herself in my arms, and sniffles.

"Hold it together for me, okay?" I whisper into her hair. "It's done. You don't have to worry anymore. I do think you should tell your mum, though."

She nods. "Will you tell her with me?"

"Of course." We head over to Carmen and sit down with her. She's at a table away from the party. Most people have left now, so Tali looks at me, and I nod, taking her hand in mine. Once she has told Carmen the full story, Carmen's vibrating. I put my hand on her arm. "Calm down. It's dealt with! People don't need to suspect anything, so just smile and nod." She does, then looks between us.

"Where is he? Did he leave with my brother?"

"No, your brother left after I threatened him when he tried to force himself upon me, but his Lieutenant is in my bathroom."

She cocks a brow at me. "What's he doing in your bathroom?"

"Not a lot, not really… the fucker's dead!"

Then she looks at me, and then at Tali, and bursts out laughing.

"Jesus, Reaper, you're something else!" I smile at Tali and then at Carmen.

"I know, right? I'm the goddamn gift that keeps on giving!" This time we all start laughing, and Demi and Scar join us as we head to the bar and get more drinks, then head to the dance floor. We dance until the early hours and then head back to our rooms.

I shower properly in Scar's room before heading back to my room to sleep. When I get there, the bathroom door is open. As I look inside, the guy's gone, and the room's spotless. Smiling, I shut the door and step back into the room, climbing into bed. I pick up my phone, the alcohol giving me some courage. I check my phone for Steel's number, but it isn't there. I check under Colby, but still nothing, so I go through the whole phonebook till I find him. When the hell did he change his name to that?

Wife: Steel?
Husband: Ray, where are you?
Wife: Awayswith the girls.
Husband: I know that. Where?
Wife: Carmen's.
Husband: WTAF you doing there?

Wife: A psarty
Husband: Are you drunk?
Wife: Yehs.
Husband: Is that yes?
Wife: 'thumbs-up emoji'
Husband: ···
Husband: ···

He's typing, and those three fucking dots show up, then disappear, then show up again. I wait, and I wait, and then I fall asleep.

Ring, ring, ring.

"Yeah?"

"Ray?"

"Yeah?"

"What are you doing?"

"Sleeping."

"Are you okay? Do you need me to come to fetch you?"

"Nah, I'm good."

"Are you?"

"Yeah, call you tomorrow."

"Yeah, sure. You sure you're okay?"

"I'm good… Steel… Thanks, night."

"Night."

Fuck, just hearing his voice makes me miss him. What the fuck am I doing? This guy… I don't even know where to begin. He's everything I didn't even know I wanted, and he seems to feel the same for me too. I've decided there's no me and her anymore. I am her, and she is me. I am Reaper!

Waking the next morning, fuck, my head's spinning after everything. I shower again and return to bed when there's a knock at my door.

I whisper-shout, "Come in!"

The door swings slowly open, and standing there is Steel! Sitting up, I gasp. "What are you doing here?"

"After speaking to you last night, something felt off, so I woke Ares. He called Scar, and she told him some story about you killing a guy, and then I had to see you were okay."

I tap the bed at the side of me. "Come here."

Shutting the door, he stalks into the room, sliding onto the bed.

"Get in. We need to talk."

Huffing out a breath, he turns and faces me, looking into my eyes. It's like he can see into my soul. Like he knows what I need before I do.

He reaches up and tucks a strand of hair behind my ear. "So… you killed a guy, huh?"

"I did."

"You okay?"

"Not my first, and I'm certain it won't be my last. I'm good. Get in. I'll tell you what went down, well, as much as I can. Some bits I promised to keep private."

He nods and strips down to his boxers.

"What are you doing?"

"Getting in."

"Why did you get undressed?"

"Who gets in bed fully clothed, Ray?"

"Fair point." Taking a breath, I explain everything except Tali's secrets, and then, gazing at me like I'm the sun and he's the moon, he leans in and kisses me.

"I can't promise you forever, Steel."

"What?"

"I don't know how to do that. I'm just coming to terms with Reaper and me being one." I point between us. "I don't know how to do this. I don't know how to do *us*. All I know is that at the moment, I don't wanna be without you. I want to see what it looks like to be with you. I want to see where this goes, but I can't promise you forever. That I can't do.

"I know you want me to choose you forever, but I can't decide that after a few weeks. It's too much. I've never done relationships properly. It's all too much."

"Okay."

"Okay?" I breathe out.

"Yeah, okay."

"Steel, what does that mean?"

"It means as long as you're willing to commit to me and only me, and try, I'm willing to try too."

"Really?"

"Yeah, really, Ray. Let's just take it steady, okay, and see what happens."

Nodding and snuggling into him, I feel the tightness in my chest ease. I feel the warmth from him seep in, and I feel like this can really be something. I feel the part of me that's Reaper that I normally keep separate almost purr. He quietens that side of me, too.

I fall asleep again. When I wake, it's to knocking on the balcony door. Stalking over to it, I see Tali outside, shuffling her feet.

"Hey, kiddo, what's up?"

"Erm, I can't find my mother. She's not in her room. I looked where she would normally be, but she's not there."

"Hey, don't panic. I'll grab some clothes and come with you to find her, okay?"

Then the gorgeous rumble of Steel's voice comes from behind me. "She's fine."

Spinning round and stepping back, Tali steps into the room. "Who are you? Do you know where she is?"

"Tali, this is Steel, he's my—"

Steel cuts in with. "Fiancé."

"Fiancé?" Tali repeats at the same time I do. She raises an eyebrow at me, then smiles.

"Nice to meet you. So where's my mother?"

"She's in a… business meeting."

"Meeting?"

"Yeah, don't worry. She's fine, okay?"

Tali nods but looks at me again, and I nod. "Can't hurt to go look for her anyway, can it?"

"Nope, she's fine. She will come to find you when she's done."

"Steel, what are you talking about? Who's the meeting with?"

Blowing out a breath, he asks, "If I tell you, will you stay here and not go looking for her?"

"Fine," I huff out.

Glancing over at Tali and back to me, he says, "I didn't come alone, okay? Once I said where I was going, Viking came with me. He called Carmen before we set off, and she met him at the gates. She's with him somewhere."

"Viking?"

"Yep, Viking!"

"Oh, Viking," Tali says.

Glancing over at her, I ask, "What do you know, kid?"

"Erm, just that she has a thing for him... Ew, maybe I don't wanna find her right now. Do you guys wanna hang out by the pool?"

"Yeah, sure, kiddo. We'll be there in a sec, okay?"

Nodding, she backs out the door. "Nice to meet you, Steel."

"You too, kid!"

It's lunch before we see Carmen and Viking. They both arrive by the pool. Carmen looks extremely relaxed.

Viking's wearing shorts. He throws a pair at Steel. "Thought you could use these."

Tali's staring open-mouthed at Viking, blatantly eye fucking him as much as a fifteen-year-old can. It's slightly uncomfortable.

Steel's sat there in his jeans and T-shirt barefoot and looking incredibly hot in more ways than one. He goes back to the room and comes out in his shorts. Fuck, he's sexy, and I'm not the only one to notice.

"Tali, you have a little something at the corner of your mouth." Reaching up, she rubs at the side of her mouth as I laugh. "Drool, Tali... It's drool!"

She flushes red. "You're horrible." She grins back at me.

"I know, right? That's why you love me!"

Coming up to me, she hugs me. "I do love you. You're right!"

I kiss her on the head. "Last one in the pool's a dickhead!" And I run off and dive bomb into the pool, followed by squeals from Demi, then Tali, Scar, then next, Viking and Steel are whooping as they jump in. We all look back at Carmen.

"Nope! I am the leader of one of the biggest cartels in the States. I am not doing that!" Pointing at us all in disgust, the next thing we know, she's squealing as Viking has climbed out of the pool and is sweeping her out of her chair into his arms.

"Have a little fun, babe," he purrs at her, and she leans in and kisses him. Then he walks to the pool, and she squeals again as he jumps in with her in his arms. She comes up spluttering and punches him in the arm, to which he replies with a massive belly laugh.

Turning to Steel, I mouth, "Babe?" He just shrugs, so we spend the next hour hanging off the boys trying to dunk them and splashing. We only come out when food starts arriving.

After packing our bags, we stand at the door, waiting to leave. Carmen has asked Viking to stay for the week. She said they had some business to discuss. No one argues, and we leave him behind as I go to climb into the van.

Tali comes running out to me, throwing her arms around me. "Will I see you again?"

"Hey, of course. Why don't you get your mum to bring you to the club for a visit sometime?"

"I can come to the club?"

"Of course, you can!" I raise my hand, pointing to the scar that's healing on my hand. "Forever and always, kiddo!"

Smiling up at me, she taps her own. "Forever and always."

I give her a kiss and a hug, and we jump in the van and head back home. Jesus, home…? That says a lot! Pulling out of the gate, I ask, "Scar, Demi. Come up here. We need to talk."

"What's up?"

"What's happening with you and Boyband, and you and Bran?"

They both exchanged glances. "What's happening between you and my brother?"

"I asked about my brother first."

"Oh my god." Scar barks out a laugh. "You're both brotherfuckers!"

And we all burst out laughing. "Seriously, guys, what the fuck are we doing here with these guys? What about our tour of the States? What about going back to the UK?"

Scar shakes her head. "Do you even have to ask? You said let's go home, and then you're talking about going back to the UK. You didn't say back home. You see the club as home now, don't you?"

"I think so. Fuck!"

"Me too. I wanna be with Ares!"

"I wanna be with Bran, but I wanna move closer to you all. Maybe Ravenswood? Maybe Bran would want to live with me."

"Holy shit, you guys wanna move in together? I can't believe it, one of my best friends and my brother. Jesus, we're really building a family. What about you and Ares? What's gonna happen when our visas run out?"

"I've been speaking to Dad, and while you've been at work, I've been looking for premises to branch out here. There are a couple of places in Ravenswood that are suitable, and Ares would have us on retainer, so we already have one client.

"Dad seems to think it's a good move as he's thinking he might move here too, so he can be close to us."

"Wow, shit. You really are serious about this guy."

"What, and you're not serious about Steel?"

"I don't know what me and Steel are. I have no fucking idea."

"My brother is crazy about you, even I can see that, and now I know he's part of the MC, and that's why he always stayed away. I'm hoping I can get to spend more time with him, and all that's because of you. If he hadn't met you, I still wouldn't have much of a relationship with him!"

"You think he's changed since meeting me?"

"Totally, Ray. It's like you bring some of your light to all his dark. He's not so standoffish and moody anymore. Apparently, he closed down after his mum and our dad died. Mum was still pregnant with me when everything went down, so they never told me what happened. He was sixish. My mum said he was there when it happened, but she wouldn't give me the details!

"He was always getting in trouble after that and ended up in juvie for a while when he was sixteen. He was nearly eighteen when he came out, and then he moved out and stopped showing up. When Mum fell ill, he helped me out and came to see me a little more, but still not very often. Now, I feel like we could actually have a relationship. I want what you, Bran and Dane have!"

"Well, fuck!" I breathe.

"Just please give him a shot. You could be great for each other!"

"But how would that even work? It's not like I have a law degree and can move here to work. I'm gonna have to go back to the UK soon, and then what?"

"We'll figure it out. Dad's been looking at ways to sort it. He just needs more time!"

"So, we're staying?"

"Yeah, we're staying."

"Yay, you're both staying!"

As we pull up at Demi's to drop her back, we promise to go have a look at some properties at the weekend in Ravenswood. She will make some appointments for the morning, and Scar will book some for the premises in the afternoon. I need to talk to Dozer and see if there's a job for me. I need to know if I can stay here for myself, not just for Steel.

I need my own thing. I just hope that the MC can be it for me, too, even if things go south with Steel. Pulling back up at the MC, Steel's already back and in the bar. We head in, and Scar runs straight up to Ares, wrapping her legs around him and kissing him like she hasn't seen him in far too long.

"Fuck, princess, I missed you!" He kisses her back, then he walks through to his room, kissing her while she hangs off him like a fucking spider monkey. Shaking my head, I walk over to Steel at the bar.

"Hey, you!"

"Hey yourself." I lean in and kiss him just because I feel like it, and he turns on his stool and pulls me in between his legs and wraps his arms around me and kisses me back.

"I could get used to this," he murmurs against my lips.

"Wanna try?" I smirk at him and kiss him again.

"Fuck yeah!" He grins, there's an almighty roar and I spin around in time to see Tank flying at me. He grabs me out of Steel's arms and spins me around.

"This place ain't the same without you!" Looking over his shoulder, the rest of the gang's there. "Come to play, Ray?" Priest asks. I look around at Steel. He smiles and nods.

"I've got some stuff to sort out. You should go hang out, and I will see you later, okay?"

"Okay."

"Dice? Can you help me with some shit?"

"Yeah, sure, Steel. What ya need?" Steel nods in the direction of the corridor, and they both head off, so I stay with Priest, Blade and Tank and play doubles at pool. By the time I'm ready to go, Steel still hasn't come back, so I head to the van. I need to be up for work at stupid o'clock.

Ray

After speaking to Dozer and making up as we left things pretty shitty between us, he says he would be happy to offer me a permanent position. It's what he has wanted all along. Apparently, it's me that needs to get my head out of my arse and stop being a little bitch and realise this is where I belong. I mean, rude, but totally fair!

He wants me to commit right now as he has work coming out of his ears, and Beauty loves me being around as she actually gets to spend time with Dozer. She must have a screw loose if she wants to spend more time with his miserable arse, but each to their own and all that shit. The lodge is coming together since I'd finished most of it before I was rudely interrupted. They are gonna move in soon, so if I stay, that will be sooner.

I just need to figure out how to do it all legally. I don't need the money as I have an income from the Adventure Centre and the family businesses. Shit, the Adventure Centre. How can I walk away from my family? My pas, Cade, Steven and John. I need to speak to them too.

Finishing up for the day, I head back to the van. Texting Roach, I tell him to meet me at the gym in an hour and a half. I sit down to FaceTime with my pas. It's morning there. As their faces appear on the screen, my eyes well up, and the first thing I say is, "Fuck, I miss you guys!"

"Miss you too, Squirt." They all sing out together, grinning at me.

"It's too fucking quiet around here without you! Hey, you have a tan!" Cade laughs out.

"How are you and Scar doing after everything? You both all healed up?" John asks.

"Yeah, we're good, all healed now. I'm back in the gym and training one of the guys here, so it's been great."

"Have you figured anything out?" Cade asks.

"I think so. I'm gonna see if I can stay. That's what I want to speak to you guys about. I'm unsure, as I don't want it to be like when Bernie left, and we didn't see him for ages. Sorry, but FaceTime isn't enough for me. I need to know I'm gonna see you guys!"

Steven sighs and smiles. "How about we make a deal? You come to see us every year, and we will come to see you every year, so at least we can see each other every six months. What do you say, Squirt? You wanna commit to that?"

"Six months? Fuck no! I can't live with that, twice a year. Three months, at least. I suppose I can live with that." I sound almost dejected.

"You suppose?" JJ asks.

"Yeah, I just miss you. I've not been away from any of you this much, ever. I'm fucking twenty-three, for fuck's sake. I may have a little separation anxiety!"

"Fuck off!" Cade barks out. "I don't doubt you miss us, Squirt, but anxiety of any sort, you're talking out your ass!"

"Hey, it was worth a try to get you to feel sorry for me!" Although I really do mean it. I feel like I have just learned to be one, but I'm splitting with Reaper all over again.

"Twat!" Steven laughs.

"Rude!" I laugh back. "Right, I'm gonna head to the gym. Call you in a couple of days, okay?"

"Love ya, Squirt!"

"Love you all, ya knobheads!" Blowing them kisses, I end the call. I know they think I'm hard as fucking nails but with my dad gone, I'm actually struggling a bit without them, especially Cade. He's always been my go-to. And without him, without them, I'm a little lost, if I'm honest.

Walking into the gym, Roach is already there. "Hey, kid, how's it going?" He's in shorts and a vest top and looks like he's raring to go.

"Are those some muscles I can see coming? You're looking good!" I punch him in the arm as I walk past. "Ready to ramp it up now I'm healed?"

"Fuck yeah, Ray, bring it on!"

"Oh, you're gonna be so sorry and sore tomorrow!" I make my way over to the ring. "Come on, kid, let's go!" Taking the pads into the ring, an hour and a half later, he collapses onto his back.

"Fuck, Ray, I'm done… I think I've died!"

As I laugh, that booming voice comes from the door. "Fuck Ray, you sadist! You okay, kid?"

He lifts his head off the canvas. "No, Steel, I'm not!" Then he drops it back down again and is panting for breath. He's a sweaty, panting mess, which I take as a win for me.

"Same time tomorrow?"

"Hell yeah!" He wheezes. "Can you just leave so I don't have to try and get up while you're here? I don't know if my legs will work. You've totally kicked my ass!"

"Okay, Kid. You gonna be okay?"

"Maybe?" He laughs, and I grab my shit and leave with Steel, walking back towards the van.

Steel grabs my arm. "Where are you going?"

"I need a shower."

"Grab your stuff and come back to mine. My shower is better, and my bed is comfier!"

"Oh, I'm staying, am I?"

"Do you not want to?" He cocks a brow at me as if he hasn't considered that an option.

"Yeah, I want to!" So I grab a bag of stuff from the van and follow Steel inside the clubhouse. Dice shouts at me as I walk inside. Steel takes my bag and tells me to come through when I'm done.

"What do you need, Dice?"

"I wanna ask you about your plans." He nods toward the direction Steel left in. "Ya know, are you seriously wanting to stay?"

"Fuck, Dice, shit. I'm sorry, I just got swept up in the whole kidnapping, Steel saga. I never thought!" I drop into the chair beside him. "I'm sorry, Dice. I never thought how it would all look!" I scrub a hand down my face. "Not a problem. I can fix this, don't panic!"

"What the fuck are you talking about?"

"You know, me and you, and now whatever this fucking thing is with Steel. I'll tell him I changed my mind. I'm with you, and we'll carry on as we were, yeah?"

"What the fuck, Ray?...You'd do that? Give up Steel, I mean?"

"Dice, you know I love you, yeah! I'd do anything for you!"

"Including giving up what makes you happy? I would never want that, Ray. Can we carry on as we were, though? I kinda need my ride or die!"

"Seriously?" My face lights up, and I jump into his lap, hugging and kissing him. "I fucking missed you!"

"I missed you too!" He grabs me, and we just hold each other for the longest time.

"Who's been flapping their lips, anyway?" I ask as we finally pull apart. "I want to, but not sure how to achieve it with being here on a tourist visa."

"Well, I've been trying to look into it, but I can't find your visa information, so I need a little more from you. Do you have your driving licence on you?"

"No, it's in the van with the visa."

"Give me the keys. I'll go and get it."

"Before you do, the issue might be my name." I glance around to make sure no one's looking. "You know Ray is not my real name," I whisper.

"Fuck, of course, with everything that's gone on, I never even thought! Jesus, rookie mistake! Well, that'll be why. Give me the keys. I will go and see what I can sort out!"

"Can you keep that between me and you? My name, I mean?"

He nods, and I tell him where everything he needs is, and off he goes, letting out a shaky breath. I head to Steel's room, knocking. I stand and wait for the door to open.

"Hey, why are you knocking?" He looks puzzled as he opens the door.

"What else should I do?" Shrugging, I just look at him, confused. He grabs the front of my top and drags me to him, pulling me in for a steamy kiss.

"Next time, just come in, okay?"

"Okay."

"You wanna shower first?"

"Sure." Walking into the bathroom, I turn around to close the door.

But Steel's right behind me. "Wanna hand?" he says, smiling, stepping in closer and causing me to back up a step. My breath hitches as he smiles at me with those fucking dimples, and I lose my goddamned mind. He kicks the door shut behind him and takes another step, grabbing me around the waist and pulling me into him. Gazing up at him, I'm flustered and can't think straight.

I don't think I have ever had someone cause me to react this way. Normally, I'm so calm and controlled when it comes to stuff like this. It's an action more than a reaction, but now I can hear my heart pounding in my ears. My skin's tingling. I'm physically vibrating, still fully clothed, and he's only touching my waist on top of my clothes, I take a deep breath.

"Fuck!"

He cocks a brow and smirks at me.

"Did I just say that out loud?"

He nods, grinning back at me. "You okay? You look a little… flustered there."

I mutter under my breath. "Fuck you, Steel. It's not my fault, okay? My body seems to have a mind of its own around you!"

"Really?"

"Shut the fuck up, will you?"

He takes a step, pushing me back a bit further, then kissing the crap out of me. As I come up for breath, he smiles down at me. The next thing I know, his hands are going from my waist to my leggings and pushing them down. I gasp as my pants go down with them. Bending down, he takes off my trainers and socks and whips my leggings and pants off swiftly. His hand is on my stomach, and he pushes me back against the wall, dropping to his knees. His other hand grabs my leg and lifts it over his shoulder as he thrusts his face between my legs and licks straight up through my lips.

"Fuck, Steel, I've just been at the gym!" I gasp out as I grab onto his hair. I fully intend to hold him back. I'm sweating my tits off from my workout. I'm totally gross, and it's all a bit much, a bit quick, but he licks me again, releasing my leg to rest over his shoulder, plunging a finger inside me.

My head falls back, my grasp tightening on his hair, and I shamelessly ride his face while he laps and nips at my clit, pumping his finger inside me, then swapping to two. I can't think straight. It's too much and too little all at the same time. I grind onto his face I can feel him grin against me.

I gasp his name, and he grins again, then my leg shakes, my chest rises and falls rapidly, and my heart is pounding in my chest and my ears. I can feel it pounding through every inch of skin, and as the heat and the electricity rise up and start to tingle through my body.

"Steel!" I gasp again as he flicks my clit with his thumb. I start to clench around his fingers and his tongue.

"Fucking Hell, Ray!" He breathes against my clit as he bites down. My vision blurs, my breath hitches, my core spasms, and my orgasm rips through me.

"Fuck!" he whispers as I come against his face, lapping at me and pumping and stroking and biting, and I can't hold myself. My leg collapses from under me, but he has me pinned against the wall. I see stars and hear the ocean crashing. I'm vibrating and out of breath, and I can still feel him smiling against the inside of my thigh as he bites down on it. "Perfect, absolutely fucking perfect."

I can't speak. He nips the inside of my thigh again, and I shudder against him, letting my leg drop to the floor. He slides up my body pinning me to the wall. I have my head cocked back against it, eyes closed and panting. He kisses up my neck along my jaw, and then he kisses me. I can taste myself on him, but for some reason, it's so sexy, and I'm so turned on and flushed. I can't think straight. All I can concentrate on is the feeling of him against me.

"You good?" I open my eyes. His intoxicating, swirling grey eyes are sparkling. His smile is the most beautiful thing I have ever seen, and those dimples wreck me every time. Staring in his eyes, I try to catch my breath.

"I'm fucked, aren't I?"

He just grins at me. "Not yet!" He smiles as he devours my mouth again. I melt against him, reaching one hand to the back of his neck and the other grabbing his arse to drag him in closer to me. I kiss him back, for all it's worth. As the kiss becomes less frenzied, I break away.

Grabbing the back of my top and pulling it over my head, leaving me just in my sports bra, I grab at his jeans and undo them, pushing them and his boxers down his legs. He kicks off his boots and then his jeans and, grabbing the back of his top in one swift motion, he pulls it over his head.

I rip my sports bra over my head and stand panting, naked, just taking him all in. His body is to die for, like Michelangelo has carved it. That raven across his chest with its wings spread over his shoulders on each pec, its wings surround those skulls, and its claws are front and centre as if it's coming to grab its prey. He has the Reaper tattoo on his right bicep and a 'D' on his left wrist. He has both his nipples pierced. My breath catches in my mouth, and I tug on my lip ring. I think I might pass out when I stare into his eyes.

His eyes are running all over me. "Fuck, you're so beautiful."

Smiling at him and panting, he's clearly still having an effect on my body. I lean forward, rubbing one hand up over his pec, flicking his nipple ring, causing him to bite his lip as I slide my other hand down, encasing his dick with my hand, running my hand up the length of him and flicking my thumb over the tip, sucking in a deep breath he rests his head on mine.

"We should stop before we can't," he whispers, closing his eyes.

"What?"

"We should stop."

"You're fucking kidding me, right?"

"No… I need to stop!"

Moving my hand up and down his shaft, I lean up and bite his bottom lip. "Really?" I lick across his lips with my tongue ring and plunge my tongue into his mouth, twisting my hand and running my thumb across the head and squeezing, dropping my other hand to his balls, cupping and tugging gently.

"Jesus, fuck, Ray!"

Running my hand up and down his shaft, I quicken my movements, causing him to gasp as he looks directly into my eyes. His pupils are blown, his breaths hitching every time my thumb passes over his head.

"Please, Ray!"

"Please stop, or please carry on?"

"I don't fucking know, Jesus, Ray. Fuck!" So I quicken my hand, twisting up and down his shaft, tugging on his balls and licking across his jaw. He's now leaning over me, hands on the wall behind me, head lolled, eyes closed.

I kiss and bite down on his neck, and he starts to thrust into my hand, quickening his breaths, and when I hit the spot just below his ear, I sink my teeth into his neck. His breath stutters, and with a feral growl, his dick swells. He erupts, pulsing streams of hot come across my stomach. I keep pumping until he stills, and then I brush my thumb over his tip, causing him to shudder and gasp while his eyes fling open and he comes down from his high.

I reach up my thumb, sliding it over my tongue and my piercing, and suck his come off it.

He stares into my soul. "I'm so fucked!" he breathes as he reaches a shaking hand to cup my face and pull me in for a devastating kiss.

When we break apart, I shake my head. "That's something we both agree on! So, what do we do now we've both agreed we're fucked?"

He gives me a god-honest, panty-dropping if-I-was-wearing-them smile, and I know I'm a goner.

"Marry me?"

"What the fuck?"

"Marry me!"

"Steel, that's insane."

"And?"

My breath comes out all shaky. "I don't know what to say. Steel, I barely know you."

"Fuck, Ray, say yes!" Staring into his eyes and him back into mine, he leans into me and kisses me, slowly running his tongue against mine. All my fight is gone, he's almost giving in to me, almost gentle, but it's so intense and leaves me panting for breath.

He whispers against my lips. "Marry me?"

Then he kisses me again, the passion rising. I can feel my thighs slicking, he slides his hand over my stomach, sliding between my legs and running his leg between and kicking my foot out, running his hand between my thighs, between my lips, and I gasp. He kisses me again, taking my breath away, whispering against my lips again.

"Marry me, Ray?" He thrusts his fingers inside me, rubbing his thumb across my clit and his tongue into my mouth in a punishing rhythm, my breath hitches again as my orgasm starts to build, and I gasp into his mouth.

He whispers again, "Marry me?"

I'm trembling. "You're playing dirty, Steel!" I moan into his mouth.

He kisses me again and carries on, thrusting his fingers in and out, in and out, and rubbing at my clit, quickening but then slowing his movements, making me pant and my breath hitch. My thighs shake, and my chest pounds. I'm so close, but he's playing dirty, dicking around, edging me. I'm starting to get frustrated.

"Marry me?" He keeps bringing me to almost orgasming, then backing off. I start to gasp. Anticipation is driving me insane again, bringing my orgasm to the point of destruction, only to slip away slightly. I swear I'm gonna kill him.

"Marry me?" He breathes into me, pinching at my clit. I start seeing stars. He smiles against my lips, then licks down across my jaw to my neck. Finding the same spot I bit on him. He licks across it, quickening his thrusts with his fingers and thumb, then biting down and sucking as I tighten around his hand, causing me to shout out his name while I come undone.

I'm thrashing against him and the wall. It's so intense from being on the edge for so long. While I hit the peak of my orgasm, he sucks my neck into his mouth so hard I know he's leaving a mark. He bites down while I clench around his fingers, and while I come over his hand, he whispers, "Marry me?" against my neck.

I cry out, "Steel… Fuck… Yes! …Yes! Fuck yes!" I'm panting, a total mess. My pupils are blown, and I'm gasping for breath. I'm flushed and totally destroyed.

I come down, my legs shaking, my skin burning where he touched me, come running down my thighs, and he lifts his hand to his mouth, licking his hand and each finger into his mouth. "Fuck, you taste amazing. I can't wait to call you my wife."

I'm still panting and gasping for breath, and my vision still contains black spots, but I'm slowly coming back to normal. "You're kidding, right? Are we really doing this?" I pant out. "This is fucking insane!"

He's grinning at me. "You said Yes!"

"Yeah, I did." Fuck, how the hell did he get me to say yes? Well, I know how… but fuck."

"You can't take it back!"

I stare into his eyes, searching his face. I'm not sure for what, but whatever it is, all I can see is his desire. He wants this, me to be his wife, and the more I look into his eyes, I find I want it too. Fuck, I want that so much. I hope it isn't the orgasm talking, as that has blown my fucking mind, but god, I want him!

"No, marry me?" I smile at him.

"Fuck yeah, I'll marry you." He picks me up, swinging me around and kissing me like I've just given him the moon on a stick. Then, as he places my feet back on the floor, he kisses me again.

"Fuck, I'm so happy right now. I will spend the rest of my life trying to make you feel as happy as you've made me. Come on, let's go tell everyone!"

As he grabs my hand and tries to drag me out of the bathroom, when I pull back, he frowns. "You don't wanna tell everyone?"

"Erm, no. Not right this minute…"

The look on his face is hurt, maybe sad. I laugh, cupping his face with my hands. "Baby, I'm naked and covered in your come!"

He stares down, and a smile spreads across his face. His smile gets wider as he looks back up at me. "Fuck, it looks good on you!"

Then we both bark out a laugh. He pushes me back into the shower and turns it on. "Let's get you cleaned up. Then we can figure out who to tell first!"

Steel

She's pacing back and forth in our room. Fuck, *our* room. That sounds so good. She's chewing the side of her thumb. She's still in her towel from the shower, and I'm getting dressed. "Hey, you okay?"

"Steel, what if I can't stay? What if I have to go back to the UK? What happens then?"

"You won't. We'll find a way, okay? I promise!"

She nods but continues to pace.

"Ray!"

"Yeah?" she breathes out as she shoots around to look at me.

"Beautiful, I love you! We'll be fine. Now, can you please put some fucking clothes on? I'm trying not to fuck you till after we're married, and after everything we've just done before and during the shower, I feel I need to warn you that I'm hanging on by a very fucking thin thread as it is."

She lets out a shaky breath. It looks like she's been holding it forever. "You love me?"

"Fuck yeah, I love you. Of course I do. I'm not playing, Ray. This is real for me!"

"Shit, Steel… "

I step in and kiss her. "Hey, I know it's early days, and you're probably freaking out. I love you, Ray, but I know you're not ready to admit that yet, and that's fine. I understand, okay? But seriously, you need to put some fucking clothes on because I'm about to lose my goddamned mind!"

She lets out another breath. "Okay."

I turn to finish getting dressed. I'm wearing my boxers and jeans. I make it two steps. "Steel?" As I turn to face her, she bites down on her lip ring, which drives me crazy, and as she looks at me, my jeans become very tight in the front, and I'm sure my cheeks flush. It feels like the temperature rises about twenty degrees. I step towards her. "I love you!"

My mouth opens and closes, then opens again, and I just stand staring. She takes a step, closing the distance between us. She gently kisses my mouth and breathes into it. "I love you, Steel!"

I grab the back of her neck, pulling her in for a bruising kiss just before her body slams into mine. I rip her towel off, spin us around, and throw her down on the bed. My body covers hers, my thigh rubbing between her legs. She gasps into my mouth as she instinctively wraps her legs around my waist, and I grind into her. I know she's the one writing the rules here. I'm totally okay with that. There's no fight for dominance between us. She will win every time.

She grabs onto my hair in one hand, smashing her lips against mine and forcing her tongue into my mouth, pulling me into her with her legs. She grinds into me, and her breaths start coming in shallow pants.

I grind myself into her, and the friction through my jeans is delicious. It's rough and dirty, and fuck, she lights me up like a fucking Christmas tree.

Gasping, she grinds into me again. I rise up on my arms, looking at her face as I grind myself into her again and then again. The friction from my jeans is driving me crazy, my already sensitive dick's throbbing with need, and she clings to me and shamelessly grinds herself against me. I thrust harder, causing her back to arch off the bed.

I lean down and lick around her nipple. Then as she starts to buck, gasp, flinch and thrust against me, her breath stutters as another orgasm rips through her. I bite down hard on it and fuck, every cell of my skin burns and tingles as she thrashes and bucks and cries out underneath me. I bite down again, then lean over to the other, looking up at her as she gasps again, and just as she takes a breath, I bite down on her other nipple and grind into her, dragging her orgasm out. Then she can't breathe, she stills, her eyes close, and I'm pretty sure she blacks out for a split second. My hand cups her cheek, and I kiss her mouth so slowly, but I grind into her again, slower this time, almost like I'm making love to her slow and sensual.

"Steel, you need to fuck me now! I can't take it anymore. It's too much. It's not enough. I need to feel you inside me!"

"Sunshine, I want that so, so much." I grind into her sensitive pussy, and she gasps as I grin against her.

"Fuck I want you so bad, Ray!"

"Steel, now! I'm not gonna beg, but for the love of Hades, just fuck me." She's gasping and writhing under me as I slowly dry hump her, almost like I'm trying to slowly force her through the bed. "Steel!" she snaps as I thrust painfully slow against her clit, then I pull away, kneeling up, there's a massive wet patch where she's come on my jeans, and as I stare at her, I can't help but smile. She drives me crazy. Even from underneath me, I'm under no illusion this woman will make me give her what she wants. I tried. I've given it my best shot to hold out till I'd put a ring on it, but I concede. She's a force. She's an all-consuming, bow down to god. I will worship at her altar till the end of time.

"I can't wait any longer. Fuck, Ray… what are you doing to me?" I reach down and undo my jeans, sliding them and my boxers that have a wet patch at the front down to my knees. I grip my dick at the base and squeeze hard. "Fuck, give me a sec, or I'm gonna blow my load as soon as I'm inside you."

I let out a breath. I lean down, still gripping my dick, lining the tip up with her wet, slick, pulsing pussy. She feels so soft, so wet, so much like home. As both of us just stare for a second...

Bang. Bang. Bang.

"Steel, you in there? Steel, open up!"
"Fuck, it's Ares!" I whisper. "Brother, I'm busy. What do you want?"
"Dice just spotted Shay's car in Ravenswood. We're going after her now!"
"Fuck, I'm coming!" I sigh.

Breathing out a shaky breath, Ray laughs. "At least one of us is!"

I grin at her and kiss her again. "I won't be long!"

"I'm coming too!"

Of course, she is! I laugh as she pushes me off her, grabs her clothes, throws them on, stuffs her knife in her boot, and runs out the door to the bar.

She's in her ripped jeans and hoodie, and she goes to throw herself on the back of my bike when Ares shouts, "Ray? No, I need you to stay here!"

"Fuck that. I'm gonna kill that bitch!" she barks at him.

"She's heading this way, Ray. I don't have time. I need you to protect Scar. No one else will do it like you, Ray. If we find her, I will bring her back, but please, I need you to keep her safe for me!"

Ray yells, "Fuck!" at no one in particular, and she nods. "Go quick, find that bitch, and drag her back here!"

With that, we shoot out with a rumble of bikes.

Ray

I run back to the clubhouse. I need to get to Scar. Trying the handle on Ares's door, it's locked, so I bang on it.

"Scar, it's me. Let me in!"

Bang, bang.

"Scar, come on! Fuck!"

Backing up a step, I kick the door in, and it swings back, dinting the plaster. I take in the room. There's no one here. I rush to the bathroom. Nothing.

"Fuck, Scar!" I bellow out, and I storm back out into the hallway. "Think!"

Pausing, I quiet myself, taking steady breaths, closing my eyes and listening. That's when I hear it, the slight creak of a door blowing in the wind. Someone hasn't closed the back door properly. I slide out of it, unable to see anything as it's dark, darker than dark. I step around the building. Everything's silent. There, I hear a raven, its short, repeated, shrill calls echoing through the woods. I head in that direction.

I grew up around ravens and know this sound is made when trespassers are near, so they've been disturbed. Sticking to the trees, I run fast and as silently as possible. I get past the barn before hearing a twig break and a scuffle. We're heading towards the lodges now, so I power on. I need to get around them and surprise whoever has Scar. I grab a handful of pebbles, stuffing them in my hoodie pocket, before diving back into the trees. I'm getting closer. Scar's putting up a fight, trying to stop herself from being dragged.

I speed past them in the trees while they're on the path. As I come around, I throw a stone in the direction I have just come from, and the man who's dragging her stops. I throw one to the side of him, and he spins again, grasping Scar in front of him and holding her against his body. I throw two, this time in opposite directions, and as he glances around, I step out behind him and put my back to the tree, bending my leg and placing my foot on it behind me.

I have my knife. I mean, fuck, I can remember my knife but never think to pick up my bloody phone. Pulling my knife out and picking at my nails, I say, "They won't come out until I say!"

"Fuck!" He spins round and faces me, holding Scar against himself between us.

"You're surrounded, so it's gonna go like this: you're gonna let my sister go, and I won't kill you!"

"Fuck you!"

"Chill, there's no need to be aggressive. Shay's not coming for you!"

"What? Shay? I don't know who that is!"

I laugh at him. "Ah, come on, pull the other one. It's got fucking bells on it. Are you fucking her? She did tell you *why* she's having you do this, didn't she?"

"What you talking about?"

"What reason did Shay say she wanted you to take her?" Pointing at Scar with my knife but keeping my back against the tree, then going back to picking my nails.

"She ruined her life. This bitch here ruined Shay's life!"

I laugh at him again. "She's fucking Shay's ex. That's why she wants her gone, so she can get back with him!"

"That's a lie. She loves me. We're gonna be together once we've killed her!"

"What's your name?"

"My name? What the fuck has that got to do with anything?"

"I like to know who I'm killing."

"Thomas! You won't kill me, though, not while I have her!"

"Did you ever watch the *Twilight* films, Thomas?"

"What? You wanna talk about fucking vampire movies!"

"Yeah, Thomas, you're actually Riley Biers!"

"What the fuck you talking about?"

"Shay is Victoria, and Scar here has nicked James. She's just trying to get him back. You do know that when I kill you, she's not gonna give a shit?"

"You don't know anything!" he snarls at me.

I laugh again. "Ah, she really does have a magical pussy!"

"The fuck?"

I point the knife at him again. "Do you realise she's already sent two other guys after her?" I point the knife at Scar again. "Poor Casper. Took my knife between the eyes for her, and poor Miguel." I shake my head. "The Castillo Cartel collected him after I had a little fun. Word is he's been skinned and then filleted, and then... anyway, you get the picture of what's gonna happen to you."

He starts looking around, so I throw a couple more rocks. "Hold your positions!"

He spins back to me.

"So if you let her go, I won't kill you, but if you spill one drop of her blood, I will give you a Columbian necktie! Choose!" I shout at him, making him flinch.

"Shay's not gonna come for you. She wants Ares, not you! So what's it gonna be, boy?"

I can see the panic in his eyes as he darts them back and forward.

"If... if I let her go, you won't kill me?"

"Correct!"

"Shit, shit. Fuck."

Hearing a car in the distance, I keep talking. "So, what's it gonna be? There's an expiry to everything, boy, and yours will be up in five... four... three... two..."

"Okay, okay, fuck!" He pushes Scar forward.

"Smart choice, kid." I get near to him. I lunge, grab his wrist with the knife, and he drops it. I spin around him so I'm now behind him, holding his arm across his body and my knife to his throat.

"Scar, I need you to run like fuck back to the club, grab your phone. Call Ares, and lock yourself in Steel's room... Now!" She doesn't need telling again. She just runs. I see the headlights coming in the distance around the pond.

"Now listen to me good. She's gonna tell me to kill you. I can either do it or act it. Either way, she needs to believe I've slit your throat. If you wanna live, when I run the knife over your throat, drop your head, and start making choking noises, convulse in my arms for about one minute, then I will drop you to the ground. Stay there! You hear me?"

Wide-eyed, he nods. "Please, just don't kill me."

"Don't make me kill you!" He nods as the car slows about twenty feet in front of us, headlights blinding us, but Shay opens the door and steps out behind it.

"Hey, honey, you okay?"

"Shay, she's gonna slit my throat. Help me!"

"Tell him, Shay, that you don't give a shit about him. You just want Ares back. Well, you ain't gonna get him, girl!"

"Honey, you know I love you. We're gonna be together!"

I make a load of retching noises. "Oh, please!" I move the knife to the far side of his throat. "You know you're living on borrowed time, Shay. I'm fucking coming for you, bitch!"

"You're a fucking psycho!"

I bark out a laugh at her. "Oh, sweetheart, you have no fucking idea! I'm not just a psycho. I'm one of *the* psychos, part of the Psycho Six. You may have known them as the Fucked up Five, but they've had a little… upgrade!"

Although I can't see her because of the headlights aimed right at me, I know she has just shat herself. *Yeah, you fucking should*! "I'll be coming for you, Shay. If I have to, I will burn the world down, but I am coming!"

"You can go to hell!"

Well, I almost piss myself laughing a psychotic laugh at her. "Oh, sweetheart, didn't you hear? Hades himself rescinded my invitation, even they don't want me down there. Who the fuck do you think sent me here?" I smile a manic grin. "I am the motherfucking Reaper!" Everything falls silent. "I'm gonna give you to the count of I'll slit your boyfriend's throat, and he's done gasping and twitching for breath till I come for you, so I suggest you run, and run fast, and run far, and when he's dead, bitch, there's nothing on this earth stopping me till I rip your soul out!"

I swipe my knife across his throat. He gasps and gargles as he drowns in his own blood, and I smile as he thrashes while Shay stands frozen. He's trying to grip his throat to hold it together, but it's no good. He's dead already. "Run, Forrest, run!" I bellow as she jumps in the car and speeds away.

He sags and gasps before I drop him to his knees then he falls on his face. I grimace. "Shit! Sorry, I forgot not to kill you, oops!" I bend down and wipe my knife on his clothes as I hear footsteps pounding from the clubhouse. "Everyone alright, boys?" They stand looking at me, then the body on the floor, then me again. "Fuck, Ray!" Dice gasps out.

"Jesus!" Tank breathes out.

"Bloody hell, quite literally!" Priest breathes out a solid breath.

Steel's silent, staring at the body and then at me. He walks over to the body and knocks him onto his back to see the full extent of my handiwork.

"Shay got away!"

Steel glances back at the body and back to me. He sweeps me up into his arms. "Fuck me. You're fucking perfect!" Sweeping me into his arms, he kisses me like he's missed me and can't live without me, and I wrap my legs around him and return it right back.

"Erm, guys… " Tank trails off.

"Ahem!" Priest coughs out.

"You are two sick motherfuckers. You know that?" I pull back from Steel, smiling at Dice.

"Thanks for noticing, Brother!" I wink at him.

He barks out laughing, shaking his head. "I need a fucking drink!"

"Me too," Tank chimes in.

"Me blooming three!" Priest turns and struts towards the clubhouse.

"Wanna fuck me against the tree?" I smile against Steel's mouth, kissing and nipping at his lower lip.

"Fuck, woman, you're driving me insane!" He flips me up over his shoulder and smacks my arse as he walks down towards the clubhouse. I let out a throaty moan as he runs his hand down his face. "Fuck, you're gonna drive me to an early grave, and I'm gonna die with a boner I can't get rid of!"

Laughing, I slap his arse, then squeeze it. "Mmm, I hope not. I'm not nearly done with you yet!"

Stomping into the bar with me still over his shoulder, he drops me straight in front of Ares and Scar's table. Scar's sat in Ares's lap, and he's hugging her close. Steel slaps my arse, knocking me a step forward towards their table.

"Well?" Steel nudges me.

"Well, what?"

"You gonna tell 'em?"

I grin at him. "Now?"

"Yeah, now!"

Roach is at the bar. I walk over and climb up on top of it. "Listen up, dickheads!" I wait for the hushed whispers and chattering to die down. "Just want to let you all know that Steel and I are getting married!"

Then I jump down from the bar, grab the tequila bottle and strut across to Steel. He sweeps me up in a ferocious kiss, and before he can drop me, there's an almighty scream and then a flying Scar diving off Boyband's lap and straight at us.

Steel manages to catch her, but she doesn't give a shit; she's still squealing.

"Fuck, knobhead!" I laugh at her.

"*Married*? You're a total twatty douche-canoeing, dickwadding cockwomble!"

Barking out a laugh at her, I sweep her into my arms and crush her to my chest.

"Thanks for coming for me!"

"Always. K.F.D, remember!"

"K.F.D!" She hugs me back like she never wants to let me go.

Back in Steel's room after a few celebratory drinks, I pick up my phone and add a group FaceTime, calling all my pas at the same time!

"Squirt, you good?" Bernie comes through first.

Cade says, "Yo, Squirt. 'Sup?"

Then JJ and Steven ask, "Hey Squirt, how's it going?"

"Squirt?" I hear Steel chucking behind me.

I turn and glare at him. "Don't you fucking dare!" I point with my best stern face. He sucks his lips in, biting down on them and huffing through his nose. "I'm warning you!" Then looking back at the screen, I say, "Hey, guys!"

"Who are you talking to?" Cade asks.

"No one!" I reply before I think it through.

"Ouch, wounded." Steel drops onto the bed clutching his chest.

"God, you're a fucking dickhead!"

"Steel, is that you?" Bernie asks.

"Hey Bernie, you good?"

"Yeah, I'm good, son. You?"

"Yeah, I'm good, thanks, Bernie." He grabs the phone off me and, standing up, walks over to the other side of the room. "Guys, while we've got you all together, firstly, it's a pleasure to meet you all, I hope we can all meet in person soon, and secondly, I want to ask your permission to marry your daughter?"

"Fuck, Steel!" I breathe out from the bed.

"Marry?" Cade barks out, "Ray?" He laughs. "Yeah, sure, kid, if you can get her to say yes, that I would like to fucking see it. Maybe you can get her in a fucking dress while you're at it!" he barks out another laugh. "Married? As fucking if!"

Then Bernie chimes in, "Married, you two? Seriously!" He huffs out a laugh too.

Steven turns to JJ. "Is this one of those meme things or something? I don't get it."

"No, a meme is a picture with a phrase or writing or something, fuck, I don't know what it is," JJ spits out.

"Is it a TikTok or something?" Steven asks, and then everyone's staring at Steel.

"No, gentlemen, I'm deadly serious. I want to ask for Ray's hand in marriage, and I hope to see you all at the wedding if you agree, if possible… Ray?"

Sighing, I step up, and Steel pulls me in front of him and holds the phone at arm's length so they can all see us both. Then there's a squeal from the background.

Bernie whips around. "Fuck, Marie, you scared the shit out of me!"

She rushes in and grabs the phone. "Hi Ray, baby. It's a yes from us. We love you together. I can't wait. Let me know what you need, a dress, flowers, anything. I can't wait. I'm so excited. I need a dress, something fancy!"

"Something… mother of the bride-y!" I smile at her, and then she screams and bursts into tears.

"Really? Do you really want that? Me, mother of the bride, oh my god. I would be honoured! Oh my god, Bernie, did you hear that? I'm the mother of the bride.

Ray, call me, and I will do whatever you need. Let me know your desired colour scheme, and I will match my outfit. Bernie, I'm going to have a look for a new outfit!" And then she's gone. I'm grinning at her reaction.

"Cheap shot, Squirt!" Bernie says, shaking his head.

"Hey, she's been the only mum I've ever known, so no, not a cheap shot. She deserves to be there as my mother."

"Yeah, but now you know we can't say no, as Marie will throw a fit. Well played, Sunshine!" Cade barks out.

"Hey, watch it!" I grimace at him! Then he just laughs. Fucker.

"Right, I'm going now. You lot can talk amongst yourselves, I will speak to you tomorrow, and you can let me know what you think!"

"When's the wedding?" John asks before I can hang up.

"Erm… we haven't set a date yet. I just wanted to run it by you guys—"

"Four weeks on Saturday," Steel interrupts. "Let us know. Thanks, guys. See you soon!" Steel says, then hangs up.

"Four weeks?" I gasp.

"On Saturday," he retorts.

"What the fuck, Steel? We can't sort it that fast!"

"I just wanna marry you, baby. The sooner, the better!"

"Fuck."

"Yeah, I wanna do that too, and I can't wait much longer, so four weeks on Saturday, okay?"

My skin tingles, my breaths come in short, and my eyes well with emotion as I try to contemplate what the actual fuck is happening.

"Four weeks?" I sigh.

"On Saturday!" He smiles back.

"You're fucking mental!"

"You fucking love it!" As he sweeps me up into his arms and spins me around. "Right, let's get back to the bar; you need to spend some time with Scar!"

There's a round of applause and a few cheers as we head back into the bar, and we are greeted by everyone wanting to get us drinks. I head over to Scar. "You good?" I ask.

"Yeah, knobhead. I'm good!" she says. Standing up, I hug her.

"Ray, fancy staying in the van tonight? I could do with a girly night."

"Always, Mrs! Are you sure you're good?"

She whispers in my ear, "Yeah, just need a break."

So after devouring my husband-to-be, we set off back to the van.

Scar

"I will come to get you at seven and take you for breakfast at the diner so we can talk to Demi," Steel tells Ray, as we leave the clubhouse. I can't help but feel a bit down.

"Hey, you okay?" Ray nudges me as we walk to the van.

I shake my head. I open the door, stepping in. Once Ray has closed the door, I break down and just cry.

"Hades, fuck, Scar. You're okay. I've got you!"

I sag into her, she drags me to the bedroom and gets me into bed, snuggling into me and hugging me tighter, pulling the covers up around us. She just holds me until I stop sobbing.

"You done?"

I nod. "Sorry, just a lot to take in. First, I was beaten up by Shay, then you were kidnapped and shot and stabbed, and then I'm kidnapped, and now you're getting married, and it's a lot, emotionally. It's making me question everything!"

"Firstly, I'm gonna kill that bitch. Don't you worry about that. Secondly, I'm back, I'm fine, and I killed them! Thirdly, I got you back and killed him! Fourthly, holy fucking shit, I'm getting married. What the actual fuck?"

Huffing out a breath, I hug her tighter. "You are ridiculous!"

"I know, right?"

"How did you know Steel was the guy you wanted to marry?"

"Fucking hell, Scar. Can we start with an easy one!"

"I'm gonna go get the tequila for these questions! Pjs on!"

As she heads to the kitchen, I change, climbing back into bed.

"I have tequila and the last bag of Haribo!"

Sliding out of her jeans and her boots and putting her knife on the bedside table, she climbs in at the side of me!

"Should I start carrying a knife?"

Ray just rolls her eyes at me like I'm fucking stupid.

"Is that a yay or a nay?"

"Scar, I love you dearly, you are my world, but if you start carrying a knife, I will never hug you again!"

I bark out a laugh at her ridiculousness yet again. "I can't believe you're getting married!"

"Fuck, Scar, I know! What the fuck?"

"How did you know he was the one? Because I've met the guy, and honestly, he terrifies me!"

"Honestly, that first day back, he took me to his room. I was in his shower when I nearly passed out. I clung to the fucking wall trying to stop myself from falling and knocked everything off the shelf. He came in, didn't say anything, stripped down to his boxers, climbed in the shower, and held me up while he washed my hair. He looked after me and then held me all night. And I've never felt like that. I dunno how to describe it. It just felt right.

"I woke up in his arms, and I freaked out a little, but not enough to move or do anything about it, and then I kissed him, and it's almost like I've never had issues letting people touch me. He's always touching me, kissing me, and it feels perfect! Fuck, I sound like a right girl now!"

"How did he propose?" She flushes a little, and I laugh. "I don't think I've ever seen you embarrassed!"

"Fucking hell, Scar, he edged me till I screamed yes."

"Edged you? As in 'edged' you?" I burst out laughing. "Fucking hell, Ray!"

She shakes her head at me. "Tell anyone, and I will stab you!"

"But you do wanna marry him, don't you?"

"Yeah, Scar, I really do. It feels like I know nothing about him while also feeling like I've been with him forever! I just feel like he was made for me. What about you and Ares? How's that going?"

"Can we talk about you some more?"

"Come on, Scar, spill. What's going on? You haven't wanted to leave his side, and yet after what went on, you bail?"

"He saw me as weak after Shay, and I didn't want him to see me weak again. I wish I was more like you. When she was kicking me while I was down, I just kept thinking you would have killed her by now, and when that guy grabbed me and dragged me up the path, all I could think was Ray would have killed him by now, and you did! I think Ares deserves someone more like you! I think I need to take a step back and regroup, ya know!"

"You know Shay's like me, and he didn't want her. He wants you because you're not like that, Scar. Your strengths lie elsewhere! You're a fucking goddamn queen. You're intelligent, funny, and fucking sexy as fuck! Don't overthink anything. He wants you!"

"What if he changes his mind, Ray? What if he decides he doesn't want me?"

"Easy!" She waggles her eyebrows at me, grinning. "We kill the motherfucking dickhead, steal his bike and ride off into the sunset. Thelma and Louise style!"

"Didn't they both die?"

"Semantics!" She laughs out loud.

"Thing is, I can take him, so it's not a worry."

I just laugh at her. I mean, what else can I do? "I don't want to have kids."

"Where the fuck did that come from?"

"I was just thinking, with you getting married and everything… Are kids on the cards? And while I think, fuck yeah, I would make an awesome aunt, I really don't want kids of my own… Not now… Or even ever!"

"Fuck, I want kids!" She shakes her head. "I never thought I did till I said yes, then now I have all these possibilities, and I do want kids!"

She opens the Haribo bag, and we both grab a handful and slouch back into the pillows.

"Fuck!" She breathes around a mouthful of jelly sweets.

"Fuck!" I breathe out in reply.

Washing them down with fucking the rest of the tequila. I don't remember much after that.

Steel

"I will come to get you at seven and take you for breakfast at the diner so we can talk to Demi."

As the girls leave the clubhouse, I turn to Ares. "That thing I talked about doing? Is it still good?" He nods.

"You got Bernie's number?"

He raises an eyebrow at me. "Yeah, Brother, what you up to? Not getting cold feet already, are you?"

"Fuck no! I just wanna do some stuff, and best you don't know what, plausible deniability and all that!"

Laughing and rolling his eyes, he throws a set of keys at me. "They're the only ones, so don't lose 'em!"

Nodding, I grab Bernie's number and head to my room. "Hey Bernie, it's Steel."

"Steel? Everything okay, son? You're not having second thoughts already, are you? I know she's a lot!"

I bark out a laugh. "No, Bernie, no second thoughts; why do people keep saying that? And she's just the right amount! Anyway, I wanted to ask you a favour."

"Ah, not even officially part of the family yet, and you wanna favour, hey? What toys do you need?"

"Toys?"

"Yeah, that's why you called, isn't it? Because of my… contacts?"

"Bernie, I think you've got the wrong end of the stick. I wanna do a surprise for Ray, but I need a bit of help. She's gone to the van for the night with Scar, so can you come here? If you park in front of the garage, I will meet you there!"

"Ooh, how cryptic. I love surprises. I'm on my way. See you soon!"

I open up the group chat and message Dice, Viking, Tank, Priest, Dozer and Blade as I head to the bar to grab a quick drink.

Steel: Guys, we're on! Meet me there in thirty minutes, stealth mode, though. Don't let anyone, and I mean *anyone,* see you!

Tank: 'Thumbs-up emoji'

Dice: 'Thumbs-up emoji'

Viking: On my way back now, so I will be a little late. See you there.

Blade: 'Middle finger emoji' sorry 'Thumbs-up emoji'.

Priest: K.

Dozer: I'm literally sitting beside you at the bar, you twat!

Steel: 'Middle finger emoji'

We all agree after an hour of going backwards and forwards on what I want. "So we all know what we have to do. Bernie, will Marie give me a call, please? And Dozer, can you get Beauty to call me too? Is there anything I've forgotten?" I look at everyone. They're all shrugging and shaking their heads. "Bernie, you know what to do with the pas, yeah?"

"Yeah, got it sorted, don't worry. You sure this is gonna happen in four weeks?"

"It had better! Right, let's call it a night. Just be quiet as we leave!"

Steel: Hey, Brother, all sorted. Can you send me "on a job" for three weeks in a few days? I need an alibi.

Ares: Yeah, is this gonna bite me in the ass, though? I do not want to be on your wife's bad side. She's scary!

Steel: Wife! I love the sound of that! Ah, you scared of little ole Ray?

Ares: No! I'm scared of the motherfucking Reaper. That bitch is insane, and you would be wise to be wary, too. Don't make me regret this, Brother!

Steel: We're good, Brother. She's gonna be fine, don't worry. I got you.

Ares: Fine!

Operation Surprise Ray is underway. Fuck, I hope she likes surprises. As I head to my room, I can't stop thinking about her. I want to crawl into bed at the side of her. I want to smell her, that citrusy tang with that woodsy undertone and when she's been at work, the smell of bikes on her makes my dick throb. Or maybe it's just her, just the thought of her has my jeans tight and uncomfortable. Why the fuck I am abstaining till after marriage is beyond me.

I have no fucking idea. I just want it to be pure and special, but in the same breath, when I kiss her, and she slides her tongue over mine, and I feel her piercing, it makes my dick twitch, and all I can think of is her slowly sliding it up and over my dick while licking around my head.

I can't wait to tell her to get on her knees and take my dick like a good girl. Still, I also want her to tell me to hold the headboard like a good boy while she rubs me through the bed, preferably on my face. I have so many, many dirty thoughts running through my head that the only way I'm not gonna do everything I want to her now is if I'm "away," but at the same time, I don't know if I can actually leave her. I mean, I feel like I can't breathe when she's not around. I barely know her, but I feel like she's my whole world at the same time.

This is all-consuming, and I'm not sure it's healthy. Still, if she wants to burn the world down, I will hand her the torch, step back and film it for her. Still, I also can't wait to bury my dick in her, no matter how intense my thoughts get or how skewed things become. It all boils down to that. It all comes back to her, the feeling of her body wrapped around mine. She's all I can think about, all I can feel.

I want so badly to be buried inside her to the point that I don't know where she begins and I end. I want to see if she fits like a glove. I want to be her everything. I want to be her be-all and end-all, and mostly, I don't want to breathe without her. I wonder if I'll finally give in and take what's mine, or if I'll let her consume me, which is more than likely what will happen. I've never bowed down to anyone, but for her, I will worship at her feet and give myself to her willingly for her to do as she pleases with me, and when that happens, will it feel like home? Or will she destroy me? Only time will tell, but either way, I'm so fucking far gone; it doesn't matter at this point.

Ray

After talking to my pas last night, it turns out they can't make the wedding, but they're gonna fly out a few weeks later to see us. I can't even believe how gutted I am, but apparently, Pa Bernie is gonna make sure it's live-streamed for my pas, but disappointment doesn't even begin to cover it.

My palms are sweaty walking into the diner; I've no idea why. Maybe it's because my pas aren't coming, maybe I'm having second thoughts, maybe I can't do this without them, maybe I think Demi's gonna be the same. I mean, they said they're happy for me, just can't make it blah, blah, fucking blah or whatever! After last night and talking about it with Scar, it now seems so fucking real.

Steel grabs my hand. "Don't back out on me now, Sunshine!" I grimace, and he stops dead in his tracks. "What is it? Why do you grimace when I call you Sunshine?"

I sigh. "Do we need to do this now?"
"Yup!"
"Great… It's my name, okay?"

"What?"

"Sunshine! It's my birth name. I'm literally Sunshine Reins. Fucking facepalm emoji!"

"Firstly, facepalm emoji? You're gonna need to explain that one, and secondly, Sunshine? …Wow, that's cute. I like it!"

"Now, will you not say anything and keep this to yourself? I'm suddenly not gonna be as scary with a name like fucking Sunshine!"

"I won't tell anyone, but I'm still gonna call you it. I like it! My little Ray of Sunshine!"

"That's where Ray came from. My dad… he didn't wanna call me Sunshine after mum died, so Ray kinda stuck."

"I'm not gonna stop calling you it unless you really want me to." He gazes at me with those liquid metal swirling grey orbs that melt my soul and those fucking dimples that I'm sure will make me murder anyone he asks me to. Every time I look at him, I just keep thinking, damn, I'm fucked, and I truly am!

"Okay, enough stalling. Let's do this!" I laugh as he drags me into the diner. Demi throws her arms around us and hugs us before heading off to order our food. When she brings it back, she sits and has a coffee with us. We then proceed to tell her the news, which ends up with her coffee all over the table when she jumps up screaming. Fuck's sake, everyone is far too excited by this wedding.

Heading into work, I know we have a busy week ahead, so fuck knows when I'm gonna sort out a wedding in four weeks. Well, shit. As I walk into the garage, Beauty's there.

"Hey, girl!"

"Hey, Mrs! What you doing here?" I almost sing at her as I cross the garage to hug her. Who would have thought it? I've become one of those people that hugs everyone I know. Fucking weird, right?

"I'm your fairy godmother."

"Who the fuck? What now?"

"I'm a party planner, so Steel's asked me to help out!"

"Well, fuck me. Thank Hades himself for you. I love you. You're my new favourite person!" I sigh out a massive breath. I have no idea what I've got myself into.

"All I need is a colour theme from you. I can sort as much or as little as you like."

"I don't know what to say."

"Come on, let's hash some ideas out in the bar." She grabs my arm and starts to drag me out.

"Beauty, I can't. I have to work. Can you meet me later?"

Dozer lets out the biggest laugh. "Ray, this is the wedding of the century. Work can wait, and you're marrying Steel, which means you're here to stay, so it's a win-win for me. Go, take the morning off, and come back when you know what you're doing. Trust me, my old lady will sort you the best of everything!"

I grab him and give him a kiss on the cheek. "Thanks, old timer!"

"No worries, kid. Just remember my favourite cake is red velvet, no, lemon, wait… no, death by chocolate."

"Yeah, yeah!" Beauty jibes. "We get it. You love cake." She grabs him for a filthy snog, making me blush and slightly damp as it makes me think of Steel.

"Not as much as I love you!" He smacks her arse as she walks away from him.

Sitting at the bar, Beauty grabs a binder from her bag to give me a tonne of options. "Shouldn't Steel be here for all this too?"

"Nah, he said to give you whatever you want." She digs in her pocket, shaking a credit card at me, then slipping it back inside for safekeeping.

"Seriously? …I don't know, I never envisioned myself with a boyfriend, let alone a fiancé. I mean, what the fuck happened, Beauty? I've been here all of two minutes, and now I'm moving to a totally different country, packing up my whole life for a guy I haven't even fucked yet."

"What?"

"Yep, he wants to wait till the wedding. I mean, is it the 1900s?" I bury my head in my hands and scrub the palms of my hands into my eyes. I mutter, "What the actual fuck am I doing?"

"Hey, are you having second thoughts?"

"Honestly? No, I'm not, which is what I think is scaring me the fucking most. Beauty, have I lost my goddamn mind? I mean, it's like I've had a personality transplant since being here. The trouble is, I can't say I don't know who I am anymore, as I don't think I've ever been any more me than I am right now. What if I have a brain tumour? That could be a possibility, right?"

Beauty barks a laugh, making my head fly up to see if she's still in her chair. With the energy behind that laugh, she should possibly have ended up thrown on the floor.

"Oh, Ray! You are so perfect for each other! Right, let's pick some shit and spend some money!"

Sticking my hand in my pocket, I grab my card out, too, throwing it on the table in front of her. "Here, put it all on there, but I need mine back later to sort something to wear."

"I've already booked you an appointment to look at bridesmaids' dresses next week and wedding dresses a couple of days later."

"Wedding dresses? Shit, seriously? A dress? Like an actual fucking dress? Scar put you up to this, didn't she?"

"Speak of the devil." Beauty laughs, nodding behind me. I'd messaged Scar and told her to come help as I'm hopeless and not interested in all this shit. Fuck's sake. I don't care about some fancy arse wedding. I just want to marry Steel, and that's enough for me.

"Fuck, I need a drink!"

Four hours later, I'm starving, so Barbie makes us some food, and Dozer joins us. I ban any talk of the wedding before I end up with a headache. Beauty's amazing, I give her a few ideas, and she's running with it. I mean, fuck, she's a demon at planning shit. I ask if we need a priest or whatever. She says that's already sorted, so that's the main thing. Dice has said that as soon as we get a marriage certificate, he can get me a green card. It will cost but can be rushed through, so I give him the details off my card and tell him to use whatever he needs. There's more than enough in there with everything my dad left me and the monthly income from the Adventure Centre as well as our "other businesses." I'm not worried. How do I explain to Steel my income, though?

After eating, I need to get to work. I have had a girly enough morning. I need to get some grease under my fingernails and on my face to feel like me again. Bernie and Marie have invited us all over for dinner, so I know it's gonna be more wedding talk, so I head back to the garage, leaving them all talking amongst themselves.

"Hey, kid, you good?"

"Yeah, old timer, I'm good! It's just a lot, ya know!"

"Just let Beauty do her thing honestly, she's the best there is, and there will be minimal shit for you to sort out if you want it that way. If you need any time off, let me know. I can work around stuff! Word has gotten round that you're staying, and we've got work coming out of our asses, but they're also willing to wait as they only want us to do it, so we have time, okay? But also, I'm sorry for all that shit that went down before you… ya know, went away. The fucking lodge looks amazing. I don't know how to thank you!"

"Thanks, Dozer. I appreciate it, I really do, and how about we call it even? Just get the fucking bathroom finished so you can move in soon, okay? You're coming tonight, aren't you?"

"Deal. Yeah, we'll be there, kid!"

And then I throw myself back into my work, get filthy, and have the best afternoon. I have grease in my hair, under my fingernails and in places it shouldn't be as I'm not careful, but hey, that's what showers are for, right?

Heading over to Bernie's, we're in a convoy. Ares and Scar in front, me and Steel behind but next to Viking, Beauty and Dozer, then the rest of the Psycho Six behind them. Bran's going to fetch Demi and meet us there.

When we get there, Marie has laid the table full of salad, coleslaw, cheese, and everything else you can think of, and Pa Bernie is at the grill with steaks, chicken, and all sorts of crap. I mean, I don't know how many they're feeding, but fuck me, we could eat for days and still be shit left over. The guys all grab beers and group around the grill. So cute, really.

The girls and I sit at the table. Beauty runs through a few things quickly but then says we're done, really. She knows what to do, and I'm gonna leave it with her. I'm gonna have to pick bridesmaid dresses if I'm having them and my own, of course, but other than that, she's gonna sort it all, which is a total relief. Scar asked if she could help, and Beauty jumped at the chance.

"So, while I have you all here, I've decided I want you all to be my bridesmaids, so will you come with me in a couple of weeks to pick the dresses…?" The squeals. Fuck, my ears!

"Marie, will you come too? This is probably the only time I'm ever gonna do something this girly. I mean, what the fuck am I playing at here? I feel like I've been tricked into my worst nightmare, and it's like a car crash, and I just can't look away!"

"Jesus, Ray!" Scar barks. "Bit specific and totally morbid, but whatever, anyway, what colour scheme are we going for?"

"I don't fucking know. We'll pick when we see the dresses. Now I'm gonna go get drunk with the boys because all this girly crap is making my balls shrivel up and die. I need tequila!" Getting up from my chair, shaking my head, and rubbing my temples, the girls all start laughing. I let out a groan and walk over to the boys.

"Pa, the girls are being wankers. Please shoot me now. Put me out of my misery, I beg of you!"

Bernie laughs too. "Fucking hell, Ray, you're such a drama queen!" Steel just cocks a brow and frowns at me, then grins.

"What, you're not even gonna save me either?" I give him a pout, and the bastard just full-on belly laughs at me. Next thing I know, I'm being swept up into Viking's arms, and Tank is crushing around us both.

"Ah, poor baby," Viking purrs. "Did those mean girls not play nice?"

"Nope!" I do sound like a baby, and they all start laughing, even Tank, so I elbow him in the ribs. "You're a dickhead, you're a twat waffle, you're a cunty bollock, and you are an asswipe, and you are a butt-squatch. You're a knobhead. You're a cockwomble, and you, my friend…" I say, pointing at Steel. "Are fucking lucky that I love you because I am never ever, ever doing anything like this again, ever!" Steel just stops, mouth open, staring at me while everyone else goes quiet and starts looking around for anything to focus on but us.

"You love me?" he asks, more of a whisper than anything else, but I look at him, confused. "You do remember I've told you before? Do you honestly think I'd say yes and not be in love with you? Seriously?"

"But you've not said it in front of actual people before."

"What, you want me to change my mind? Only love you in… private?"

"No… but?"

"Yeah, you said that already!"

Next, he lunges at me in a frenzy, smashing our mouths together and pulling my lip in between his teeth, nipping and sucking, then plunging his tongue in, and I'm gone, lost and breathless. Once we pull apart, everyone has left us and gone over to the table. Most of them have their backs to us as if they're trying to block out that image, and I can't find any fucks to give, so I kiss my fucking husband-to-be again like I goddamn mean it, and then he whispers into my mouth.

"I fucking love you too!"

We all crashed at Pa Bernie's because we all had far too much to drink by the end; let's just say it got a little messy. After managing to get back to the club this morning, everyone heads off their separate ways Dozer, and I head to the garage to work, both with a bitch of a hangover and a busy day to boot. Fuck, last night was a bad decision. Well, the drinking part, anyway!

Steel rescues us at lunch with burgers and milkshakes, and I swear, I love him more in that second than ever until he says those four stupid words, the fucking stupidest fucking words ever invented, which immediately cause me to want to punch someone in their junk, throat or both! Maybe that's just the hangover talking, but fuck.

"We need to talk!"

I'm not in the mood for 'we need to fucking talk' talks. "I'll meet you in your room when I've finished, okay?"

So we finish early, as we're both still hanging, and I call in at the bar for a tequila or four which, to be honest, is the best decision I've made all day, so fuck yeah. I go knock on Steel's door.

"What the fuck are you knocking for?" He screws up the front of my shirt and pulls me to him. "You smell so good!"

"What the fuck? I'm hungover, and I've been at work all day. I stink like a polecat!" I sniff my armpits and screw my face up.

He smells my hair and my neck. "You smell like gasoline, and have you been welding? Fuck yeah, that's it, that's so sexy." Then he sniffs my hair again. "And something… fruity."

"Nice! Petrol, welding and fruit, bork!"

He just laughs and pulls me in through the door, kissing me like he's not seen me for a week.

"Right, I need to talk to you."

"Argh, do you have to?"

He just laughs at me again, dickwad, and smiles. He's so devastatingly handsome. I can't get enough of those eyes, and those dimples are going to be my downfall.

"Sit down, and I'll grab you a drink. You're not gonna like this."

I groan and move away to sit in the chair at the far side of the room. I'm being dumped. I know I am. He's made his mind up. This is a total mistake, he got it wrong, and now he's cutting his ties, game over, end of story. Hasta la vista, baby! I run my hand down my face and groan again.

"Hit me with it. Pull the plaster off. Just yank. One swift go, go on now before I change my mind!"

"So, you know when you went and got kidnapped, and Ares called everyone back to fake find you, well, I kind of was in the middle of a job, and I need to finish it before the wedding."

"Oh."

"Oh?"

"Yeah, I thought it was gonna be done. Sorry, Ray, it's been real, like, and I'm like so over it, so let's like call it quits while we still can and just be friends, okay?"

"That's what you were expecting?"

"Yep."

"Why the fuck would you expect that? Jesus Christ, Ray, that's what you've been thinking all afternoon?"

"Yep."

"Fuck!"

"I didn't say it made sense. It was just what I was thinking. I'm not used to all this!" I gesture wildly between us.

"All what?"

"All this. Me, you, feelings and shit!"

"Ray, you're such a fucking guy!"

"You saying you're the girl in this relationship, baby?"

He shakes his head. "Yeah, I think I am, but fuck, I wouldn't change it. I have to be so in control 24/7. I'm the Enforcer, but then you come in and steal my thunder, but bring the sunshine with it and cause everyone to fall in love with you, but also to be a badass motherfucking bitch that I can be a bit more… I don't fucking know, sensitive. I can actually let my guard down instead of having to be so fucking manly all the time!"

"Ah, baby," I say, pushing him back onto the bed and climbing up his firm sexy ripped body and staring into the swirly grey vortexes of his soul, the pink fullness of his lips, the dimples that will be the death of me, and I push myself up with my hand on his throat, and squeeze slightly. He gasps, and his face falls serious as he takes me in, straddling him, my hand wrapped around his throat, and he reaches his hand to my wrist and holds it there. I rock my hips over his straining jeans and smile down at him.

"I have a little secret hobby that I think you're going to love, but I'm gonna save it till after the wedding, but for now… " I trail off, rocking my hips again and squeezing just a tad harder. His pupils dilate, and his tongue flicks out and licks his lips. He's staring into my face like he's here to serve me and me alone.

"Do you want me to fuck you, Steel?" He looks away, trying to calm himself, so I rock my hips again, this time grinding into him a few more times and keeping my grip firm. He gasps as I lick up the side of his face, and his eyes flutter closed. He takes a few steadying breaths, which don't seem to help. "Steel? Do you want me to fuck you?" I rock again, but he keeps his blown gaze on me, taking another gasp. He nods his head, so I rock a few more times. "If I fuck you now, will you regret it?" He shakes his head but can't look me in the eyes. I grab a nipple through his shirt and twist. "Don't lie! Will you regret it?" And he nods.

"I'm sorry!" he whispers. I smile down at him and start grinding myself on him. Well, we don't need to have sex to both come—time to make a mess in his jeans. I start riding him fully clothed, and his cheeks flush, and I lean in and kiss him a little. Then I rock again and flex my fingers, eliciting another gasp, "Ray!"

"Fuck!" I kiss him, then pull back and flex my fingers again, cutting off a little more airflow. He should be starting to buzz and feel a little lightheaded, so I grind and flip my hips. As I feel his thighs tense below me, I grin. "Come for me!" I demand, and I keep on grinding against him as his breaths become shorter, and he's panting for breath and staring into my soul like it owns his, and he stutters and stills. I feel him pulse through his jeans.

Letting go of his throat, he stays still for a while before glaring at me. "Fuck, Ray, what the hell am I supposed to do now with boxers full of come and a dick that's throbbing to be inside you… but also wants more of that?" He gestures to all of me, smiling down at him.

"When do you need to leave?"

"In the morning." He sounds a little sheepish at that.

"Fine. And how long will you be gone for?"

"I'll be back for the wedding, promise!"

"Fucking hell! Best make it count, then! So you're still holding out on me and waiting till after the wedding?"

He takes a shaky breath. "Yeah, I wanna wait."

"Go and clean up then, and we can move my shit in here, then talk!"

"You coming?" He nods towards the bathroom.

"If I do, we both will be, and I won't stop, so just go. It's better to remove the temptation and close the door… and maybe lock it so I can't get in. I'm really trying, but my inner Reaper wants to shout 'fuck it' from the rooftops while I tie you to the bed and ride your face!"

Stuttering out a laugh, he heads off but doesn't look convinced he's making the right decision. After his shower and emptying the van, it turns out Scar's stuff has been gone for a while. Who knew? Steel tells me he wants me to give up the van and stay in his room while he's gone, and then we can live here for a bit until we get sorted. He has also booked the van to be taken back tomorrow, so I will need to take it, and Beauty has offered to follow me. Steel tells me that we have to drop the van off at a specific rental place which is a two-and-a-half-hour drive, so that's most of the day gone. So we decide to make a day of it after and go visiting.

Saying my goodbyes to Steel and sending him on his way, telling him to stay safe, I have an uneasy feeling. Something's not quite right. Scar and Beauty are waiting for me at the garage, and seeing as Steel is gonna be away and I don't have to be back at work till tomorrow, I make a call.

Scar heads off with Beauty. They'll meet me at the diner so we can pick Demi up and then head over to drop the van off. After dropping the van off, we head to Carmen's to stay overnight, and I give her the details for the wedding and tell her I have a surprise for Tali on the day. Tali's at a friend's house, so we sit around the pool and have a few drinks.

"So Carmen, what's the deal?"

"What deal?" she asks.

"You know the business deal that kept Viking away for nearly a week?" Then we all burst out laughing.

"I've never had girlfriends before… I don't think I like it!"

"Ah, come on, Carmen," Scar asks.

"It's not like we didn't see you guys together before we left. There was no business. That was all pleasure!"

"Ooh, if looks could kill, Carmen, we would be toast! Come on, spill."

"Guys, this isn't fair. I don't know… I don't do feelings. I normally order a guy for my needs. You know… a professional! But Viking is just so… "

"Dreamy," is Scar's input.

While Demi adds, "Sexy."

Unlike Beauty's reply, "God-like."

On the other hand, I have seen him in his shorts and go with the obvious, "Hung like a donkey?"

"Ray!" She blushes. "That is not the only reason." This causes us all to laugh, and when Carmen realises her words, she punches me in the arm.

"I actually think I hate you, and you are... how do you say it… a knober head?"

"Knobhead!" I reply smiling.

"Yes, definitely one of those." We spend the rest of the night laughing and talking and having some chill time, which is what we all need.

I'm not even hungover at work as we had taken it steady-ish for us lot, anyway. Me and Dozer have worked hard trying to get ahead as we know I need some time off for dress shopping. Urgh, not my idea of bliss! The week goes by in a blur. Beauty's keeping me vaguely informed on what she's doing. We still need a colour scheme, but fuck, I like grey and black, so maybe that, with a bit of white thrown in, seems good to me. The guys will probably wear their jeans and cuts as we are getting married on the grounds behind the clubhouse.

I blink, and a few more days have passed, and I decide to go shopping on my own. I have no idea what to wear, but Marie has told me about a boutique that does evening wear, tuxedos and stuff if I want something like that. I head off there, then to the dress shop, then a department store and then I make my mind up. I'm only doing this once, so I'm going big or going home.

After picking an outfit, I stash it in the cupboard in Roach's room. I think he will be the least likely to tell anyone it's there, as he knows I will kick his arse. He has really come on leaps and bounds in his training, and it's really starting to pay off.

Beauty's an absolute godsend. I'm still pissed that my pas aren't gonna make it to the wedding. I mean, I get it. I know they just can't all leave the centre, but I was kinda hoping at least one of them would make an effort. Out of all of them, I thought Pa Cade would be here.

I have decided on the colour scheme. Steel's still away, but the guys are sorted. I'm assuming that's jeans and cuts, and hopefully clean boots would be nice. Beauty has sorted the food, I have asked for a hog roast, she's done decorations, organised the officiant, absolutely everything. We just have to sort the bridesmaids dresses. We've put it off till now as we've just been so busy at the garage with people hearing

I'm getting married. They want things sorted before I have some time off.

The next few days pass pretty much like the last few weeks, in a blur of work and wedding shit. Steel's still away, which sucks, and the wedding is just over a week away. I'm starting to panic slightly. However, I've had some news this morning that is helping me, and that's that Pops is on his way. His flight will be here in a few days time, and I can't wait to see him.

I've got the afternoon off, and me, Marie, Scar, Beauty, and Demi are heading over to the shop, and after speaking to Carmen, I've got everything I need. There's a little dress shop in Ravenswood, but they have a bigger store in Gosport Harbour, so if we need anything, we can get it shipped. The store is on Main Street, and there's a dead-end alleyway to the side of the building between that and the florist. I park there as I can't be arsed to walk. While Beauty heads to the florist to check on something, we stand on the street discussing the wedding, and Marie shows us a picture of her outfit.

"Ma, it's stunning. You're gonna look amazing." I grin at her.

"Ray, I'm so excited to be a part of the wedding. I don't have a daughter, but I've always felt like you were mine, really. You know we love you. I just can't wait to see you and Scar all dressed up. It's gonna be a beautiful wedding!"

Beauty joins us, and we all walk into the boutique. The girls try on every fucking thing imaginable. I'm having nightmares of drowning in tulle and lace, and there are bows and everything. I'm totally overwhelmed. They have tried cocktail dresses, evening gowns, ball gowns, mermaid dresses, skater dresses, sun dresses, even maxi dresses and anything else they could find, and just when I'm losing the will to live and considering stabbing myself in the eye with a stiletto, I get up to have a wander, basically to de-stress, but as I'm rummaging, I find these amazing dresses. They are perfect.

"Excuse me?" I call over to the saleswoman. "What are these on this rail?"

"Ah, these are orders ready for customers to collect or that have been cancelled."

"Which ones are these?" I quiz, pointing at a set of dresses wrapped up.

"Bare with me. I need to grab my order form." Coming back ten minutes later, she tells me this is a cancelled order if I want them for a discounted price, as there has already been a significant deposit left for them, I have to take the whole order, though. There are six dresses altogether, but I only need four. The girls try on the dresses, and there are enough different sizes that they fit nicely, and it's by far cheaper to have the six. I take them as is!

As we're heading out of the store to Steel's truck which we'd borrowed, we're all laughing and joking, finally feeling like this is the last hurdle as we round the corner to the truck. I walk between the wall and the truck. The girls start to climb inside and load in the dresses and shoes.

I have my back to the alley, and I'm talking to Scar as Beauty, Demi and Marie are climbing in, hearing a noise behind me. I spin around, shoving Scar to the floor. The gunshot rings out, and I grab my side. Motherfucker! I bend down and grab Scar, pulling her up and shoving her behind me, moving toward the truck's open door, using my body to shield her. I can hear her screaming as blood runs down my side but looking around the alley. I see the fucking bitch responsible.

"Oh, you made a big mistake, motherfucker. Don't think you're leaving this alley alive!"

The most sarcastic laugh bubbles out of her throat. "You've taken everything from me. I'm gonna end you, psycho!"

Reaching into my back pocket, I shove the keys to Scar, who's sat in the back. "Climb over and get everyone the fuck out of here, now!" Scar jumps to action, shooting into the driver's seat and slamming it forward, screeching out of the alleyway and down the road!

"So, bitch tits, what's it gonna be, fast or slow?"

"What the fuck you talking about?"

"How you die." I shrug. "Either way, one of us isn't leaving this alley alive, and my money is on you."

"I'm gonna end you. You took them all, Miguel, Casper and Thomas!"

"Who the fuck's Thomas?"

"The guy whose throat you cut in the woods! I'm gonna make you pay!"

I need to keep her talking and make her mad so she gets sloppy. Time to throw a little extra pizazz in my piss-off-o-meter, especially for her. Fire away, and let's hope I don't get shot again. Here goes nothing.

"Ah, I thought he was called Riley, Riley Biers. You know who I mean, Victoria, don't you?"

"His name was Thomas, you know that you fucking psycho. I'm gonna fucking kill you." She points the gun at me, and I run full pelt at the wall. She fires, but I've already moved as I hit the wall about fifteen bricks up with my foot, and I propel myself off the wall, flying towards her. She has fired where I was, not where I'm gonna end up. The flicker of recognition in her eyes makes me realise that she knows she's made a grave error in judgement. She gasps as my fist connects with her temple, and she winces and crumbles to the floor on her knees. Landing at the side of her, I jump around her back, getting her in a headlock and shaking her.

Once my grip's seated with her head at an awkward angle, I whisper in her ear. "Any last words, motherfucker?"

"Go to hell!"

"I've already told you, been there, done that, invitation revoked!" Laughing, I drop sharply with a satisfactory crack, and then she's limp, one snapped neck. Ain't no motherfucker coming back from that. I drop her body to the floor. "You shouldn't have underestimated me, motherfucker! That was your first mistake!" I grab my phone. "Scar, you safe?"

"Yeah, we're around the corner, didn't wanna leave, so I'm about three minutes away!"

"Brill. I need to disappear a body and fix this hole in my side. Can you give me a hand?"

"Already on my way!" Scar's called ahead, and as we pull into the car park, Ares's there, waiting.

"You!" He jabs his finger towards me. "Are gonna send me to an early grave? Can you please stop getting stabbed and shot? Steel is gonna have a fit, especially this close to the fucking wedding, Ray!"

"Hey, fuck you. It's your psycho fucking ex who got all shooty and leary! Totally not my fault."

"So what happened? Where is she now? I'm gonna send the guys out to retrieve her and end this!"

I lose my shit and bark out a laugh. "I'm insulted, fuck face, that you think she's not in the back of the truck with a broken neck."

"You fucking serious?"

"Deadly, motherfucker!"

"Shit, Ray, get your ass inside. Doc is in the med room waiting!" I turn and look at the ashen faces of the women who are my closest family.

"Girls, can you take the dresses to Steel's room for now, and Demi, can you take Ma home while I get patched up? You all good?" I look over them all. I can see Marie has been crying, and Demi looks like she's about to throw up. Beauty and Scar seem to take it in their stride, although I think Scar's a little shaken. I give them all a smile and head inside, knocking on the door and shoving inside.

"Fucking hell, Ray, you're definitely single-handedly keeping me in a job."

"Then you're welcome, I guess!" He gives me a genuine smile and cleans and stitches the wound before dressing it. It's only a flesh wound and is about an inch higher than the last one. Good job Steel doesn't give a fuck about scars, as I'm getting quite the collection. However, he's gonna lose his shit when he finds out I was shot. Best ring him while I get patched up.

"Baby?" He sounds sleepy.

"You sound tired. Are you sleeping okay?"

"Not without you, Sunshine. I miss you!"

"I miss you too, handsome. I need to talk to you, though. You okay for a minute?"

"Yeah, sure, baby. What's up?"

"So I had a little mishap… "

Doc spits out a laugh. "Little mishap!" he mutters under his breath.

"Who the fuck's that, Ray?" He sounds agitated.

"It's okay. It's just Doc!"

"Doc! What the fuck, Ray?"

"I'm okay. It's only a scratch! A little flesh wound, nothing life-threatening. I'm good, ok!"

"Fuck, I'm coming, okay? I'm coming. I'll be there soon!"

"Steel, I'm okay, aren't I, Doc?"

"Yeah, she's good, Steel! More of a bullet graze than a gunshot wound. Few stitches and a little scar, but no problem!"

"Who the fuck shot you, Ray?"

"Shay!" Shit, I wasn't gonna say shot. Fucking Doc and his big mouth!

"Fuck, she dead?"

"Yeah, she's dead."

"Good girl! I'm gonna get back as soon as I can, okay? Can you rest up for me, please?"

Good girl. Fuck me, that did all sorts of fuzzy things to my nether regions. Totally inappropriate while Doc's stood so close. "Yeah, I'm gonna head to bed now, okay? Don't rush back for me, but if you're finished early and you're back sooner, that would make my day!"

"Okay, Sunshine!"

I hang up, get cleaned up and crash.

The next morning, I wake up with a warm body spooning me, a dick pressed into my back and that smell, he's all-encompassing and I smile and go back to sleep suddenly content. I feel whole again. Who knew that's what I must have been searching for this whole time? It's him!

Waking up in a blur, I feel at ease, and as I open my eyes, I shift slightly as strong arms squeeze me tighter, pulling me back to his body's warm, firm planes. I rub my arse back into him as he groans into my neck before nipping at it and kissing down it. The groan that comes from my lips is almost pornographic.

I feel him smile against my neck as he whispers into it. "Good morning, beautiful!"

"Hey, gorgeous! When did you get back?" I roll over in his arms, causing a wince as I knock my side. I nuzzle into his neck. "I missed you!"

"You did, huh?"

"Mmm, I did." I lean up and kiss him like I can't breathe without him, and it feels like that lately.

"Did you get everything done that you need to?"

"Nearly. There are some bits I need to sort, but I can do that from here, so I don't need to go back."

"Mmm." I kiss him again, only this time, I add a little nip to his bottom lip, sucking it into my mouth and running my fingers into his hair. I clench my fist and pull his head back so I can bite down on his neck, and then I lick across it as he groans. Pushing my thigh over his hip, I push him back, straddling his body so my arse is pressed into his dick. "Be a good boy and put your hands on the headboard!" I slide my hand from his hair around his throat. I hold him in place, not under any illusions that this monster of a man couldn't move me if he wanted.

But knowing that he allows me to control him is so fucking sexy. Adding slight pressure to his throat, he steadies his hands on the headboard, "Ray? Don't..." Leaning back slightly and lifting my weight off him, I reach into his boxers and release his massive dick. It's solid, and I can feel it pulsing in my hand. His breaths come in shallower, and his pupils dilate at my touch as he inhales a shaky breath and then releases it steadily.

"Trust me?" Without breaking eye contact, he nods. I rub my thumb across his head, a slight bead of pre-cum already waiting for me. I rub my thumb through it and down his shaft, flattening my body to his while still holding the pressure on his neck. I kiss him, then pull his lip into my mouth, biting down and tugging at the same time, slowly pumping and twisting his dick as my hand rises up and down it. I hold it firm, although my fingers don't reach each other.

I kiss him again harder and pump a little faster. His breath hitches, and his chest flushes. His dick pulses, and I get high on the feeling that I'm the one affecting him like this. He's a slave to my touch. He trusts me to hand over complete control to his pleasure, and at that moment, I know I will love him forever as I twist and pump. His breaths stutter.

"You gonna come for me, baby?" Nodding once, his eyes flutter shut for a split second. I know he's gonna blow his load, but I want to taste it so bad. Before he opens his eyes, I let go quickly, sliding down his body and laying between his legs. His eyes fly open as I grab him and force him between my lips. Gazing up at him, I continue pumping him, only this time into my mouth, swirling my tongue around him, grazing my piercing around the head of his shaft as he bucks against me. He convulses beneath me, gasping, and then he freezes, holding his breath, and roars as he comes straight down the back of my throat, pulsing with every shot of come as it slides down, and I swallow like the greedy girl I am. When he relaxes and begins to breathe again, and only when his dick has started to soften and stop releasing into my mouth, I lick around him and pop him out of my mouth, smiling up at him.

"Fuck, Sunshine, I was not expecting that." He's still panting and out of breath. His lips are plump from where I kissed him before, and I'm desperate to kiss him. As if he knows my every thought, he pulls me up his body and devours me like he's starving.

"Fuck, tasting me in your mouth is literally the second best thing ever!"

"Oh yeah, and what's the first?" I question, kissing me again till I'm breathless, then pulling back. His eyes twinkle as he shoves me over with his hand on my chest, holding me down. He slides between my legs.

He grins up at me. "Tasting you on my lips!" And then I think I pass out as he devours my pussy licking and nipping and biting, sliding fingers in and out of me, teasing my nipples with his spare hand, pinching and tugging while I orgasm all over his face. He doesn't ease up. While I'm panting for breath, he slides his other hand down and pumps that in and out of me a few times before sliding down between my cheeks.

I gasp at the intrusion as he slowly pushes inside my arse. Still, as he pumps in and out, then adds another finger while continuing to pump inside my pussy and nip at my clit, I know I definitely black out then. The spots in my vision become bigger and blacker, and the breaths in my throat become almost none existent. As I gasp for breath, my back bucks off the bed. I fist one hand in the covers and the other in his hair. I shamelessly ride his face while he's pumping into my pussy and my arse, and I can't focus on anything, only him and his hands. His mouth, that sinful fucking mouth, and those talented fingers that play me like a harp. I shudder and blink as I gasp and try to gather some resemblance of having not lost my damn mind to this devastatingly all-consuming man feasting between my thighs. As I gasp and come back to reality, he pauses, grinning at me from between my legs, then licks the whole way through my pussy from bottom to top, making sure he has every last drop of me.

As I try to drag him up for a kiss, he shakes his head. "If I slide up you for a kiss, I know my dick will have a mind of its own, and I will lose all control, so I'm just gonna stay here a minute while I gather myself, okay?" He bites down on my inner thigh, and I gasp and stutter out another breath.

"Fuck you and your self-control!" I laugh out at him, and he bites me again and rolls out from between my legs. I lift myself up onto my elbows as he stands at the side of the bed, tucking his dick back into his boxers and untwisting them, wiggling his eyebrows at me.

"Want me to take you out for breakfast?"

"No!" I pout, sticking my bottom lip out for added effect. "I want you to fuck me through the bed till I don't know where I end and you begin, and I don't know my own fucking name!" He barks out another laugh.

"All in good time, Sunshine, nearly there, not long now!" I drop onto my back, throwing my arm over my face and groaning. All I can hear is him laughing as he starts up the shower.

"Motherfucker!" I whisper out after him. While I'm sulking, my phone rings out. There's still a week till the wedding, and Pops should arrive tomorrow night. It's probably Scar letting me know the arrangements. As I grab my phone, I see it's Pa Bernie.

"What up, B-dog?"

"Hey, Squirt, you working today?"

"Yeah." I look at my watch. "In about an hour, whaddya need?"

"Can you come for dinner tomorrow? I need a favour, just you, though. Well, you and Dice, if possible. I need him too!"

"Yeah, sure, Pops is arriving, but I think Scar will want to grab him alone. I will check with Dice, but I can't see it being a problem. Is everything okay?"

"Yeah, I just got a job, and I need your guys' help with it. That's nothing to worry about. It just needs to be a bit hush, that's all!"

"No worries, see you about six, any problems, I will give you a bell! Love ya!"

"Thanks, Squirt. Love ya too!"

Reaper: You got plans tomorrow? Need a favour.

Dice: Nope.

Reaper: Is that nope to the favour or nope to the plans?

Dice: Plans.

Reaper: Cool, Bernie's, dinner at six. Pick me up?

Dice: K.

Reaper: Okay, Chatty Cathy, I thought I'd messaged Tank for a minute there! Gotta get ready for work. I can't have you talking the hind legs off a donkey all day. Some of us have work, ya know, okay? See you later. Wear something pretty, okay? xxx

Dice: Twat!

Reaper: 'Laughing emoji' 'Middle finger emoji'

Ray

As I finish work the next day, I head to the van for a shower, realising I don't have it anymore and head into Steel's room. I knock, but there's no answer, so I shove my way in, and he's laid on the bed, reading, looking sexy as all fucking hell, shirtless, barefoot and with jeans swung low, his massive hands holding that delicate book as he peers over the brim of it at me.

"Whatcha reading?" I purr as I walk in.

"Why the fuck are you still knocking?" he retorts back, and I just shrug.

"I gotta get ready to go to Pa Bernie's. What are you doing tonight?"

"You mean apart from missing you while you're out on your date with Dice?"

I spit out a laugh at him. "Are you jealous of me and Dice going to Pa Bernie's?"

"Nope!"

"You want me to blow you before I go?" I waggle my eyebrows at him.

After relaxing it into his lap, he pulls the book back up to his face. "Now that you mention it, I kinda do… but I should say no as it's getting harder and harder to stop it from going any further! …Fuck, Ray, you make it so goddamn difficult!"

"Soo… is that a yes or a no then?"

He closes his eyes, tips his head against the headboard, and drops the book onto the bed. "Will you keep all your clothes on?"

"I will."

"Argh, why is it so difficult to say no to you?"

I bark out a laugh. "You make it sound like this is going to be such a chore for you, baby, and also, I'm just irresistible!" I crawl up the bed and kiss him, "Hey!" I say as I smile into the kiss.

"Hey." He returns before I slide down and lay between his legs, slowly unbuttoning his jeans and tugging them and his boxers down a little. I free his cock and lick my lips. It stiffens in my hand, and I lick my piercing up the length of his dick and across the head. As the pre-cum starts to seep out, I lick across it again and then plunge my mouth down, engulfing his dick with it. When it hits my gag reflex, I swallow, able to then go a little further before pulling back.

"Fuck Ray!"

I lick all the way to the top again and repeat it again and again.

"Fuck," he whispers, and I hum at him. "Mhm?"

"Shit, Ray." He jolts, and I chuckle. "Fuck!" he spits out again. "Be a good girl and do that again. I liked it!" As I take him in my mouth just before the gag, I hum and swallow, taking him deeper, then humming again before pulling back. He's gasping, and he runs his fingers into my hair, and I wink at him as he forces my head back down. In fairness, it doesn't take much forcing, but looking up at his face... fuck, he's gorgeous. I dip again, and he thrusts up into my mouth. I grin and hum around him as his breaths become more ragged, dipping again and twisting my hand at his base to follow my mouth, I cup his balls with my other hand and gently tug and twist and suck and hum, and he gasps, his pupils blown, his breathing ragged, and his hand curling into my hair, and the other into bed.

"Fuck, baby, I'm so close! Fuck, you're such a good girl, baby, just like that." He gasps out. I nip at the tip, and he thrusts into my mouth again before stilling and holding me there while he comes down the back of my throat, licking and sucking till he releases my hair. I slide up and straddle his waist as he grabs my hips and grinds me down. "Fuck, I want you so bad!" He rocks me back on him again, and I groan.

"I'm going for a shower if you wanna join me!"

"Ray!" His warning tone is meek at best. I chuckle as I head for the bathroom. When I turn over my shoulder, he's scrubbing his hands in his hair and down his face as if he can wipe the desire away. His eyes meet mine as I peel my long sleeve T-shirt over my head, flick off my bra, and palm my tits. He groans as I step into the bathroom, shutting the door behind me.

"Fuck," I mutter as I climb into the shower. I'm gonna have to sort myself out, as I have given myself blue lady balls. I scrub myself clean, and as I rinse off, I take the shower head and point it at my clit, leaning back against the shower wall. I change the setting on the head to the solid jet. I gasp as it changes and hits my clit, "Fuck!" I gasp out as I reach up with one hand and pinch my nipple. I rock my head back so it's resting on the tiles while I angle the shower head so it's destroying my clit, I gasp as it hits the spot, and I rock it left and right, rubbing the jets across my now swollen clit. I hear the door click open.

I turn and give him the filthiest grin. "You joining in or just watching?"

He takes a deep breath. "Watching!"

Turning my head back to lean on the wall, I pinch and pull at my nipple, cupping and squeezing my tit, directing the jet back across my clit and pushing it a little closer. It's barely an inch from me, and I flex and rock my hips as if riding the shower head. Fuck, that feels good. I close the distance as I ride the head, pinch my tit and tug and grope, and rub the shower head again, getting faster with the motions as I pant. I'm literally grinding on the thing now, and there's no stopping my orgasm. It hits me like a freight train. It's a good job I'm leaning against the wall, or I would have collapsed.

I keep the shower head there while I freeze and pant through it before I let myself come down fully. I turn and look at Steel. His breathing's heavy, his pupils blown. The bulge in his jeans doesn't leave much to the imagination. Without breaking eye contact again, I angle the shower head to that sweet spot and bring myself to the peak again, pinching and tugging at my tit and grinding down harder on the shower head. I never break eye contact, and neither does he. He's frozen in the doorway, and I can't take my eyes off him. Fuck, he's sexy, jeans tight on his thighs, barefoot, bare chest, messy black hair from where I've scrunched my hand through it, sparkling grey eyes swirling as he watches me.

I start gasping and writhing against the shower head, my vision blurs, I see stars, and once I start to orgasm, I have to close my eyes to concentrate. At the peak of it all, I feel hands run up my body, my eyes fling open, and he's there, right in front of me. As I continue to come undone, he cups and pinches my tit and slides his other hand behind my neck as he leans in and kisses me, making me gasp and pant all over again as my breaths come in shorter. As I come down from my orgasm, I drop the shower head to the floor, and it's spraying up against us as he presses me against the shower wall, pushing his body against mine, teasing his thigh between my legs. Still holding my neck in one hand and my breast in the other, he kisses me like a drowning man.

He runs his hand from behind my neck down my body and between my legs, running his thick, rough fingers through my lips, pressing them inside me, pumping in a few times before pulling his fingers to his lips and rubbing them across his before sucking them in and licking them with his tongue. He removes his fingers and repeats again, running his hands down my body and pumping in his fingers.

"Fuck, Steel, I need you so bad." He freezes and then takes a step back, looking me up and down before stepping back towards me again, thrusting his hand inside me and pumping while flicking his thumb across my clit. It's all too much after two orgasms already, but also not enough at the same time. I feel so empty. I need to feel him pounding into me, I reach down to undo his jeans, but he grabs my wrists together with one hand and forces them above my head, pinning me to the wall.

"Steel! ...Fuck's sake!" He rubs punishing circles across my clit and pumps inside me. He flicks his fingers, and fuck, he hits my g-spot, and I'm flying. I scream out his name, but he continues. I can't tell if he's punishing me or worshipping me, and my brain doesn't care. It's completely fried. I ride his hand while screaming out around his mouth. I try closing my legs, too many sensations all at once, but he lifts his thigh higher, keeping my legs apart for him as I buck and writhe against him, catching against the wet denim. I see stars and fireworks, and I'm pretty sure I black out at least twice before my legs buckle, dropping me onto his thigh as his body crushes me against the wall of the shower, water still spraying up around us. He cups my face while I pant and try to blink my eyes into focus.

"Fucking beautiful!" he breathes into my lips. "You're fucking perfect!" As I blink at his face in wonder, he picks me up, shuts off the shower, leaves the head swinging, and carries me over to the towels. Grabbing one, sliding it around me and carrying me out to the bedroom, he sits on the bed with me sideways across his lap as he tucks my hair behind my ears, smiling at me with those swirling eyes with promises of forever, those devastating dimples and that filthy mouth. I sigh as his eyes shoot up to meet mine. I cup his face.

"I fucking love you!"

He smiles back. "I know!"

I huff a laugh at him. "Twat!"

He grins and kisses me so that I know without saying a word how much he loves me! We stay like that till there's a bang on the door.

"Stop fucking. You're late. I've been waiting outside for ten minutes, Ray. Hurry the fuck up!"

"Fuck, Dice, I'm coming!" As I jump off Steel and run around, grabbing and throwing clothes on, he lays back on the bed, still in his wet clothes, ankles crossed, back against the headboard, resting his arm behind his head, and I freeze. "Fuck me. You are beautiful."

"Beautiful?" He laughs.

"Yep, absolutely. Fucking devastatingly beautiful!" Leaning down, I give him a kiss. "I've gotta go! Miss you already!" I laugh and head out the door.

"'Bout fucking time!" Dice does not look happy. "I'm fucking starving, so hurry up and get your ass on my bike, ya twat!"

I throw my arm around him and kiss his cheek. "Love you too, Dice!"

"Yeah, yeah, I fucking know!" he barks back out. We head out to the car park.

Climbing off Dice's bike, he looks at me. "So, what's this all about then?"

"Beats me?" As we head inside, Pa Bernie is waiting.

"Everything alright? You guys are late!"

"Someone"—Dice points at me—"wouldn't put another someone down for two minutes!"

"Figures!" Pa huffs as we sit at the table. Pa takes a deep breath.

"Okay, what I say can go no further. You both understand that?" We both look at each other and then back at Pa and nod. "Okay, so you know a bit about Ray's pas and me?"

"A tiny bit, but no specific details."

"Okay, let me start from the beginning then. I was a Navy SEAL, me, my buddies, Cade and Sebastian, we were in our twenties. We did a mission combining our unit with the British SAS, and that's when we met Daniel, Ray's dad, Steven, and John. The six of us hit it off. We became brothers and remained really close. Sebastian and his wife Julie had a kid, a boy named Daniel-Cade Miller. He would have been about six-ish when Ray's mum finally became pregnant with her and her brother Bas.

"Daniel had decided he wanted to retire and start his own business before having kids. We'd been talking about it for years, putting money away, so we had already set retirement in motion. That was when the Adventure Centre started. We all talked about it and decided we would all join forces and create something from all our training. We were getting ready to open, just doing the finishing touches, when Marie and I found out we were pregnant with Bran. It was perfect; the Adventure Centre was ready. Sebastian was supposed to come with us but decided he needed some more money to set him up, so he took another tour before retiring. Anyway, partway through his tour, something happened. We still don't know what. Most of the files are redacted, and we can't get a straight answer.

"So anyway, he got sent home early, medically discharged. He was injured while on tour, but not severely, according to the information we managed to acquire. It didn't make much sense! After he got home, Julie called us and said he was totally different. Something was wrong with Sebastian. She said his behaviour was irrational, erratic and almost like he had PTSD. We told her to take Daniel-Cade to a hotel and stay there till we got there. The Adventure Centre wasn't quite open yet, and Marie and Ray's mum weren't ready to have the kids for months yet, so we headed to the States.

"When we got to the hotel, Julie never checked in. We headed to their house, and it was already a crime scene. According to the police, some other woman had turned up at the house as Julie was ready to leave, saying she was pregnant with Sebastian's baby but didn't know he was married until he came back from tour and was behaving weirdly. After talking it all out, they decided to confront Sebastian together.

"Daniel-Cade was in his room, and when Sebastian came home, it all went to shit. He had some kind of episode and attacked Julie and the other woman. We never did find out her name. The neighbours heard the shouting and called the police. By the time the police got there, all hell had broke loose. Sebastian had Julie by the throat with a gun to her head on the porch, and the other woman was holding Daniel-Cade behind her in the front garden, begging Sebastian to let Julie go, but he wanted to swap Julie for Daniel-Cade. He couldn't bear to be parted from his son.

"They think a policeman got too close, and Sebastian freaked, shot Julie, then shot himself. The woman was taken into protective custody with Daniel-Cade until everything was sorted. When we arrived, they wouldn't tell us anything. We contacted CPS, but they wouldn't give us any information because we weren't technically family.

"After three weeks of contacting every military contact we had, we found out that the woman had taken custody of Daniel-Cade as she was the closest thing to a family the state could find, which is bullshit. We were his family. He knew us. He didn't know her from fucking Adam. Anyway, she was carrying his half-sibling. Because of the nature of the case, a judge signed off on it and also allowed her to change his name and seal his records. We've been unable to find him even with all our contacts we tried for years. After a few years of no new leads, we decided that every year, we would try another PI and pay them for a month to see if they could uncover anything else. It was like he just vanished.

"We still don't have any information. We don't even know if the other woman had a boy, a girl, or even who she is."

"So is this what you need me for, to try and locate this kid who will be what… thirty-ish now?" Dice asks, puzzled.

"Well, not exactly. See, we know who the judge is who sorted this all out, but we've been unable to crack him over the years. Anyway, the other day, he contacted our security firm. He has no idea it's me, but he needs a security detail for a charity event. It's high profile, and he has a lot of enemies. The event is in nearly five weeks."

"Okay, so why do you need me and Dice?"

"I thought if he had a male security guard, he would leave them standing outside doors, keep them away from his laptop, maybe. But as a girl, we could pass you off as an escort. He would be more likely to write you off as less of a threat and let you into his office so you can snoop around."

"So where do I come in? You want me to be the security too?"

"No, I was hoping you would have a device or something that Ray could plug into his laptop or something to take control or download or something, I don't know. I've not really figured it out yet, but if we can find Daniel-Cade, we can bring him home. He was meant to grow up with us, to be with us, and this is the newest way we've had in years!"

After brainstorming for the majority of the night, we come up with a plan. Dice is gonna create a device that will download the contents of the laptop but also plant a virus that will give him access to the servers that hold the information so we can break in that way, too. It should give us access to things that aren't on the laptop. I'm gonna be the pretty little distraction. That way, I can turn up at his office and poke around a little before heading to the event as his chambers will be locked down, and it will be difficult to even get into the building normally, but under the guise of taking him to the event, we can waltz right through the front fucking doors.

As we leave Pa Bernie's, Dice turns to me. "Fuck, that shit's bad! I mean, I hope someone would have fought this hard for me."

"Yeah, we grew up hearing about Pa Sebastian. That's where my brother got his name from, we called him Bas, but his full name was Sebastian, and obviously, his son was Daniel after my dad and Cade after my pa. I wonder if he had a brother or a sister, and I hope he was happy growing up. I know my dad and my pa split the business, so Pa Sebastian's portion has been going into a separate bank account all these years."

"Fuck, that's gotta be worth a fair bit."

I shrug. "I would think so, that place is a gold mine, and we have other businesses, too. I know it gets split six ways. I now get my dad's portion."

"Anyway, before we can figure all this out, we need to get you married. Only a few more days. How're those feet doing?"

"Feet?"

"Yeah, are they getting cold?" He grins.

"Nope, my feet are toasty, Dice. I've never been happier, and it's nearly a week!"

"BLURGH!" He spits out, making puking noises. "You broke Steel, you know that, don't you?"

"What the fuck do you mean, I broke him?"

"He was tough, stabby, and non-smiling, and now look at him. He smiles, laughs, jokes, and is all mushy!"

"Dice, I hate to break it to you, but in that case, I've broken you, Viking, Tank, Blade and Priest too. Tank only spoke in grunts and now makes full conversations. Viking is fucking Carmen, so maybe his behaviour is down to Carmen, but you've all mellowed and are influenced by my magnetic personality!"

He barks out a laugh. "Yeah, right!"

"Ah, Dice, that laugh just proves my point!"

"Dammit!" It's now my turn to laugh at him.

"Shut the fuck up, Ray, and get on the bike!" Slamming my helmet on, I can't help but chuckle as we speed back to the MC.

I text Steel when we get back, but there's no reply. I need a drink, though, so we sit at the bar. There's only the two of us here necking a couple of shots. We don't speak a word when the third has gone down. Dice turns to me.

"This is really fucked up, isn't it? You've all been looking for this kid for years, and nothing?"

"Yep, just vanished. It would be easier if we knew his name, but we have nothing to go on, and I know it bothers all my pas. They miss Sebastian and want to do right by his son. It's just been so long!"

After a few more shots, Dice asks if he can look at all the evidence. "Maybe I can find something you know that someone else has missed."

"It really can't hurt!"

"Right, I'm off to bed, Ray. I'll let you know how I get on with my gizmo!" He laughs and walks away, smiling to himself.

That's what Pa kept saying. "Make me a gizmo."

"Facepalm emoji!" I mutter to myself and head to our room. *Our* room. I like the sound of that. I may even just walk in and not knock. As the door creaks ever so slightly, I peer in, but Steel doesn't stir. He's fast asleep. Walking to the side of the bed, I strip off. Just as I go to sit on the edge of the bed to get in, the covers fling back, and strong arms wrap around me, dragging me in and throwing the covers back over us.

"I missed you!" He kisses my neck and breathes in my hair, then groans. "You're naked!"

"I am!"

He groans again. "What do you have against my nakeds?"

"My body and my dick, and my dick wants to be inside those nakeds. That's the problem."

"That sounds like a you problem, not a me problem!" I laugh.

"Bitch!" He pulls me closer and grinds into my arse.

"That doesn't seem to be a productive way to help your problem!" Groaning again, he reaches up and tweaks my nipple.

"Ouch, motherfucker!" I gasp out before it turns into a throaty moan.

He chuckles into my neck as his hand migrates down over the planes of my stomach and between my legs, pushing his fingers inside me, I groan, and he groans as he removes his fingers to suck them.

"You're so wet!"

"Well, stop grinding into me, and stop sticking your fingers inside me then, maybe, just maybe, I won't be wet all the time. Oh, and stop looking at me, stop being so goddamn bloody gorgeous, and stop giving me butterflies every time you flash those dimples. Then maybe… Nah, I still can't see it happening. I've just been wet ever since I met you. You wanna take advantage and slide right in? We're only a few days away. I won't tell, I promise!"

He bites down and chuckles into my neck again, causing a moan to creep out.

"Sorry, Sunshine, no can do! I have morals, you know!"

"Argh, morals are overrated!" I grind back into him. Then I twist in his arms, reaching between us and sliding my fingertips across his stomach, making him buck against me, sliding my hand down the inside of his boxer shorts, rubbing the palm of my hand into his dick as it flinches and thickens even more than it already is.

"You're playing with fire!" he warns in that sexy, gravelly voice that vibrates into all the special parts of me.

"Oh, and the voice thing… you can't talk to me. If you don't want me to want to jump you!" I kiss him breathlessly, then pull back. "Your voice does all sorts of sexy things to me and my nether regions, and now I don't think I can help myself!" Flexing my fingers, I squeeze and kiss him again. "You're not gonna be the type of husband who denies his wife nice things, are you?"

"Wife! I really like the sound of that." I twist my hand up and down along his length.

He breathes out, "Ray!"

Smiling up at him, I ask, "Yeah, gorgeous? Whaddya need?" I keep twisting and squeezing as I slowly move my hand up and down his shaft. I slowly kiss him, raking my tongue along his lips.

"Ray!"

"Tell me what you need, baby." I kiss him again, slowly, like I'm trying to steal every last breath from him. Sucking his bottom lip into my mouth, I gently bite down, tugging on it as his eyes roll into the back of his head. He's panting and breathless, and his chest is rising and falling. His pupils are blown, and as I reach down and tug on his balls, he shudders, so I speed up ever so slightly, causing another shudder.

"Ray!" He grabs the back of my neck, dragging me in for a devouring kiss, stealing my breath right back. I quicken my pace, and his breath stutters again.

I feel him thicken in my hands. I groan and whisper into his mouth. "Now be a real good boy and come all over me, baby." His balls enlarge in my palm. He gasps more urgently this time. He stiffens as he comes all up my front. Rubbing my thumb over the head, he shudders and hisses at me. Taking in a shaky breath and staring into my face, he says, "You are a fucking goddess!"

Smiling at him, he pulls me flush to his chest, sliding me up his body to kiss me, rubbing his come into both of us. "Baby?"

"Yeah?"

"Are you really gonna make me wait?"

"Good things come to those who wait!"

"Better things come to those who take advantage of the filthy things I have going around in my mind right now!"

He shakes his head and laughs at me. "Ray, it's less than a week, that's it!"

I pout. "Fine!"

He kisses my forehead. "Do you want a shower?"

"Nope, I don't care if I'm covered in come. I wanna sleep if you're not gonna fuck me!"

Twisting me around and pulling my back to his front, he wraps one arm under my neck and the other around my waist. He holds me against him so I can feel his cold come between us. He slides the hand around my waist, down over my stomach.

"Steel!" I warn.

"Yeah, baby?"

"Now who's playing with fire?"

"I just wanna return the favour, that's all, baby!" he purrs into my neck right before he bites down on my shoulder.

"Fuck, Steel!" His hand slides down my stomach and reaches between my legs, but his other hand clenches around my throat, and I gasp, which turns immediately into a moan. Fuck, that feels good. Sliding his fingers through my lips and circling my clit, he bites down on my neck again. "Steel!" I gasp out. I reach up and tug at my nipples.

I can feel him start to grind into my arse as he gently squeezes my neck. I tug and pinch at my nipples and shamelessly ride his hand like it's my full-time job. Fuck, that feels good. This guy really is the man of my dreams. He knows how to let me lead, and he knows how to make me follow, and at this moment, as I think about if I have lost my mind or not, he pinches my clit, reminding me of exactly where I am at this moment. He flicks my clit as he pushes two, then three fingers in while he circles it with his thumb thrusting into me. As I push back into him, he grasps my throat tighter.

I start seeing stars, my vision blurs, and my breath stutters. I succumb to the overwhelming need to explode, so I do, trying to scream out his name, but it comes out as a gasp. As I shudder and buck against his hold on me, he doesn't stop. I come, and I come hard, and I might have passed out, but he doesn't stop.

"Steel!" I force out a gasp. "Steel, I can't."

"Yeah, you can, baby, for me, be a good girl and come for me again, all over my hand, keep going!" Biting down on my lip, I can taste blood. I'm pulsing and vibrating while he continues straight into my second orgasm. I can't function. I'm clawing at my tits, pulling on my nipples while he restricts my breath to the point of almost panic. Well, I would have panicked if it wasn't him, if it wasn't the man I trust with my life, if it wasn't the love of my life, my everything, my reason for being and the reason I'm whole for the first time ever.

In that moment of realisation, I release. I let go and let the feeling overtake me, closing my eyes and shuddering through the sensations he's enticing out of me. I can feel his heartbeat pounding on my back, my clit pulsing against his thumb, my insides clenching down on his fingers, strangling the feeling out of them, and as the last shudders come to life. He clamps down on my neck, cutting off my breath altogether, as the last of my orgasm rips through me.

Once I stop convulsing, he releases my neck, and I gasp out, drawing in lungs full of air, gasping, and the influx of oxygen causes my brain to feel light and floaty.

I remember him kissing my neck and licking it as he whispered, "So fucking beautiful, you're such a fucking good girl. Sleep, baby, sleep." As my blinks become one long one, I drift into the most peaceful sleep, hardly surprising as I'm totally wrung out and exhausted. All I can think about as sleep claims me is, fuck, we haven't even gotten to the good stuff yet. I'm screwed! And then the darkness seeps in and claims me. I welcome it as I'm right where I'm meant to be.

Ray

The next week passes fast. It will soon be the wedding. Steel has been working hard trying to finish the job, and I've been trying to get ahead at the garage so I can take some time off. We've barely seen each other.

Waking up, I call Scar. "Hey girl, I can't get hold of Pops. I haven't seen him since he got here, and I was hoping we could go for lunch. Which hotel is he in? Thought I might just pop by and kidnap him."

"You can't. He's... Not there... He's... Helping me... Erm... we're looking at offices today. Sorry, Ray!"

"Oh, okay, so will I get to see him before the wedding?"

"Probably not, Ray. We're heading to sort some legal stuff out tomorrow before I come for your hen get-together, sleepover thing!"

"Oh, okay. I will just see you in a couple of days then!"

Ray: Demi, are you doing anything today?

Demi: Yeah, sorry, Bran and I are going to some viewings. I will see you in a couple of days for the sleepover, though. x
Ray: K. x

Well, this sucks, it doesn't look like anyone's around today. I might as well head to work. As I walk out the front of the building, there's an almighty screech. "What the hell are you doing wandering around? You're supposed to be out of the way, so you can't see me setting up. Who's in charge of occupying you for the fucking day, as they're sacked!"

"What the fuck are you talking about, Beauty!"

"Shit! Ray, we're setting up out the back for the wedding. You can't be here, so you need to leave!"

"Can't I help?"

"Nope!" Holding her finger up to me, she pulls out her phone and dials.

"Hey, Steel, someone's dropped the ball. We need to get Ray away from here. She's literally stood right next to me, wanting to help. Who is on Ray duty today? …Okay… Hmm… Okay… On it!"

Passing the phone to me, I ask, "What the fuck's going on?"

"Hey baby, so it's like this, you were supposed to be taken out for the day while we get this stuff ready, and it looks like that hasn't happened for whatever reason, so… wait in our room. I'm gonna sort it, okay? Give me thirty minutes, please?"

"How come you get to help, and I don't?"

"Because I want it to be a surprise, and you love me, so you're gonna let me do this. Wait in the room. Thirty minutes, okay?"

"Fine, but you owe me!"

"Love you!"

"Yeah, yeah, I'm going to the room for thirty minutes. If no one comes before then, I'm coming to help, like it or not!"

I hang up, toss the phone back to Beauty and stomp back inside. Twenty-six minutes later, Dane's hammering on the door.

"Ray, it's me. Come on. We're going out for the day!"

I sling the door open and smile at Dane. "How much did you object?"

"A shit tonne!"

"How much are they paying you!" He kicks his boots against the door frame, grinning. He doesn't answer. "How much, Dane?"

"Dad says he'll give me $100 to keep you busy all day, plus expenses!"

"Expenses? Limit?"

"Nope!" he says back with an evil chuckle.

"Ah, so easy! Almost like we've been doing this forever!" I sling my arm around my lil bro.

"So what are we doing?"

"I don't know, what's fun, can keep us busy all day and will cost a bit?"

Scratching his head, he thinks for a minute. "It's about a two-hour drive!"

"And it's...?"

"A theme park!"

"Like rollercoasters and shit!"

"Yeah, like rollercoasters and shit. What do you say, Ray?"

"Let's do it!" As we run to the car, we jump in and high tail it out of there! An hour and forty-five later, we're pulling into the car park of the massive theme park. We buy the queue jump tickets, VIP passes, the works. We play every carnival game that you have to pay for and win a shit tonne of crap which we carry around every ride. We eat candy floss, ice cream, waffles, and more ice cream and sweets, and then Dane's sick after one of the rides, so we go on it again, and we take a shit tonne of photos till we're exhausted.

"Wanna drive back, or shall we get a hotel?" I ask him.

"I think if I try to drive, I will pass out, puke, or both." So we head to the nearest hotel.

Wife: Back tomorrow. xx

I then turn my phone off. One, because I don't have that much charge, and two, because I'm an arsehole, so there. We climb into the twin beds, put shit on the telly, order room service, and pass out!

Waking up, we head downstairs for breakfast. "Hey Dane, thanks for yesterday. I appreciate it!"

"That's what little brothers are for. You know I missed you when we moved back here. I'm glad you're staying! I would like to spend more time with you. If you want to, that is."

I launch myself at him and give him the biggest hug ruffling his hair. "I fucking love you, ya know!"

He grins at me. "I fucking love you too! Now let's get breakfast, then head back. You're getting married tomorrow!"

"Gulp!"

"Did you just say fucking gulp?" He asks, bursting out laughing at me.

"Yep!"

"Fucking facepalm emoji." He grins. And that's it. We both lose it in the corridor of the hotel. By the time we make it for breakfast, our sides hurt, and our cheeks are sore, and I'm so ready to get back home and marry the love of my life.

Turning my phone back on, it blings, and blings, and blings.

Steel: Okay, baby, have fun. Miss you. xx

Pa Bernie: You two fuckwits best hurry up home.
Pa Bernie: Your Ma's going out of her mind with worry.
Pa Bernie: What are you two up to? If you get into trouble, I'm gonna whoop your asses.
Pa Bernie: I'm not bailing you out if you're locked up. You can rot in there, knobheads!
Pa Bernie: That's it. It's official. You're both fucking dead.
Ray: Love you too, on our way back. xx

I show Dane my phone.

"Well, that escalated quickly. Glad to see Dad automatically assumes that we're in jail! Nice!"

Slinging my arm around him, we head home to face the music. As we pull up to the front of the clubhouse, Steel's standing there waiting for us. I jump out and run at him, throwing my arms around him and kissing him senselessly.

"Fuck, I missed you!" He breathes into his kiss.

"Missed you too, big man!" Putting me down, he glances over at Dane.

"Yo, D-man. Thanks, buddy. I owe you one!" Dane gives him a nod and a two-finger salute.

"No probs, anytime!" He walks around to his boot. "What the fuck are we gonna do with all this shit?"

Steel walks around and peers in. "Holy fuck, what did you two do?"

There must be at least thirty random stuffed animals and toys of all colours and varieties. "I'll be fucked if I know. I only want the Reaper!"

"Reaper?" Steel questions. I dig into the back and pull it out. It's a Grim Reaper about a foot tall with a scythe over his shoulder. I waggle it at Steel.

"Holy shit, that's fucking adorable!" He snatches it out of my grasp.

"I know, right?"

"Anyway!" Dane interrupts. "What the fuck am I supposed to do with the rest?"

"Children's home?" I answer.

"Kids' hospital." Steel shrugs.

"You could give them to your girlfriend."

"Argh, we broke up. You know we did."

"Save them for the next relationship!" I grin.

"You're fucking ridiculous. Love you, twat knuckle. See you tomorrow!"

"Later, cunt muffin!" I bark back at him,

Steel just looks baffled, shaking his head. "I have no idea how to respond to that."

Dane just climbs back in the car and speeds off, waving through the back window as he goes. I head off to go inside.

"Where the fuck are you going?"

"Erm, shower? I'm minging!"

"Sorry, baby, no can do. We need to head out for food and then pick Demi up."

"What? I can't even have a shower?"

"Nope, not got time. Come on." Great, I bet I stink like a polecat in yesterday's clothes, same pants and everything. Lovely!

Heading towards Steel's bike, I slowly slide my hand over the seat and along the gas tank. "This really is a stunning fucking bike! How come you all have the same one, just different colours?"

Steel shrugs, looking at me through half-lidded eyes, a smile on his face, dimples out and proud. "Me and Ares got them, and then the other boys loved them, so they copied."

"That's it?"

"Yep, that's it, simple!"

"Well, that's not as interesting a story as I hoped it would be."

"Come on. I wanna take my fiancée out for food one last time!"

"And your fiancée can't be freshly showered to do it?"

He laughs, pulling me away from his bike.

"No bike?" Pouting, I stroke my hand back off the seat.

"Not today, baby. Gotta pick Demi up!"

"I'm so gonna fuck you on that once we're married!"

His eyes glisten at me, and he licks his lips. "I'm gonna fucking hold you to that!"

Smirking, I slap his arse as we head to the truck.

Pulling up at the diner, we head inside. Demi isn't working this afternoon. She's done the morning shift, so she can head back home and grab her stuff, and we're gonna pick her up after we eat. Scar, Demi, Beauty, Marie, Carmen and Tali will stay with me in the clubhouse tonight. All the guys have gone out to the lodges up the top end of the property.

I still haven't seen Pops yet. I hope I get to see him tomorrow! We sit in our usual booth, and Steel messes around, fidgeting with the sugar, resting my hand over his as I sit opposite him. "You okay?"

"Yeah, I just want to talk, you know, before tomorrow. Before it's too late."

"Well, shit, that sounds ominous!"

He gives me a small smile, but not a dimple in sight.

"Shit! Okay, hit me with it."

Looking up at my face, he lets out a breath. "So I want to make sure you're... happy to go ahead tomorrow, that I haven't forced you into this, that you haven't just got swept along. I want to give you an out and also talk about deal breakers?"

"Shit, baby, you having second thoughts?"

"No. No, nothing like that. I just want you to know what you're getting into... I'm not the man you think I am—"

"Huh?" I gasp. "You mean... you're not a virgin?" I ask with a half smile, half smirk.

"Sorry, baby, I'm not a virgin!" He half huffs.

"Well, it was nice while it lasted!" Rising to my feet, I think I see the lump in his throat and his eyes gloss over. Sitting back down, I grab his hand again. "Baby, you're scaring me, okay?"

He looks back up, meeting my gaze. "I did some time in juvie when I was younger. I haven't been the best man I can be. I feel like there are things about me you should know before you commit for real... I want kids! And as much as I love you, I can't bring myself to share!"

"So you did some time in juvie? What for?"

"Stealing cars."

"So you suck at stealing cars. At least say you got better at it, or do you still suck at it?"

He smiles at me. "We got a fuck tonne better. That's how me and Ares got the money together to buy the old farmland for the club!"

"Okay, so you're not a total failure then."

"I suppose not!"

"And you want kids?"

"I do!"

"I'm not saying no, let me just put that out there, but I wanna get settled first. I wanna be us for a bit before we figure that out, but I'm not averse to the idea!" With the hugest grin on his face, he picks up my hand and kisses it. "I'm not sure what you mean by sharing. What are we not sharing?"

"You, I'm not prepared to share you!" He huffs out again, totally losing me along the way.

"Okay, what are your deal breakers?"

"I just want kids and wanted to tell you about juvie and the not sharing. I didn't know if that would put you off."

"Are you fucking serious?" I laugh. "Have you met me? Have you seen the things I've done, and you think wanting kids, sharing whatever you mean by that, and a stint in juvie is a dealbreaker?" I shake my head. "You really wanna go down this route?"

Nodding, he rubs his thumb across the back of my hand.

"Right, hold on to the seat of your pants, as I think mine are way worse, and you might be the one changing your mind!"

He shakes his head at me. "Never!"

Letting out a calming breath, I close my eyes for a second. "I can't tell you the full story of how Scar and I met. It's not my story to tell, but what I can say is I was nearly fifteen. I killed two men, slit one's throat and stabbed the other eighteen times. Scar begged her dad to take my case and save me, and he did. He got me off of the murder charges, and I walked away scot-free, but I did do some time in a detention centre for it while waiting for it to go to trial.

"Scar and I were together for about six months after we first met. You know, like *together*. I killed three men, then killed my own dad to provide me with an alibi for the deaths of the three, not to mention the countless other people I've killed, beaten up, stabbed and shot. I also killed six guys when I was kidnapped, leaving them in a barn and setting a fire. I killed… I kissed a guy to lure him to my room, then killed him at Carmen's. I killed Shay by snapping her neck with my bare hands, and I fucked Dwayne… kind of!"

"Anything else?"

"Erm, off the top of my head, I think that's it, but there's a lot of shit I've done, so if you're looking for an out, I think I've given you more than one to go on. Definitely more than you gave me!"

"What about the Dice thing?"

"Dice?"

"Yeah, when I first met you, I was told you were fucking Dice, and I kind of tried to be okay with sharing. I actually thought if I didn't see it, it wasn't happening, so I tried not to look. I never asked you to end things with him, but he was also with you first, and I kind of got swept up with everything, and I kind of just lied to myself and said I was okay with it. But the closer we get, I can't ignore it anymore. I think that's my deal breaker… I can't share!"

"Steel, baby! I can't believe you think I've been fucking Dice this whole time, and you haven't kicked off. Also, when would I have time to fuck anyone else? I'm not or never have fucked Dice! We're close, yes, and lines were slightly crossed in the beginning, but we've never fucked! Is that why you've hung back?"

"One of the reasons. So you're not fucking him then?"

"No, baby, I'm not!"

He huffs out a breath and scrubs a hand down his face. "You mean all this time I've been trying to turn a blind eye and accept something that wasn't even happening? Fuck's sake!"

"Hey, it's okay. Look, you can ask me anything. I will always be honest. There are things that I can't share as they're not mine to share, I will always tell you that, but everything else is fair game, okay? Just tell me if there's anything you can't deal with. I mean, I hit you with a lot."

He blows out another breath. "I'm not overly thrilled about three of those things. I'm just hoping I can get past them."

"Which bits?"

"The bit where you crossed lines with Dice, kissed a guy at Carmen's and fucked Dwayne. I'm really having a hard time with the Dwayne one, but I think if you told me what happened with them, I could get past it!"

"Deal!"

"Deal? Easy as that?"

"Yep, I'm an open book! I have a deal breaker, though, two, to be exact. I won't tolerate lying. I can't abide by it!"

"Oh shit!"

"Well, that sounds like a confession of guilt before we start!"

"I can't tell you why I lied, but I have been for weeks. Just please know it's for a surprise, and I wanted to throw you off the scent."

"You lied?"

"I did. I'm so sorry I didn't ..."

"Hey, we're only just setting the rules, so anything beforehand is null and void. Next time, I want you to be honest. Just say it's a surprise and leave it at that. No other explanation needed!"

"Really?"

"Really!

"And the second?"

"You cheat, you die!"

"Wow, just straight in there, huh?"

"I won't tolerate a single betrayal. If you even look at another woman slightly inappropriately or get emotionally involved, I will de-dick you and bury you in a ditch!"

"I agree to those terms!" He holds out a hand to shake. I shake it.

I peer down at him. "Promise?"

"I promise to be honest. I promise to be loyal, and I promise to be yours."

"Forever?"

"Forever, Sunshine!"

"Then we have a deal!" With the goofiest grin, I melt. I slide around the booth and straddle his lap. Wrapping his arms around me and grabbing my arse, he drags me into him, chest to chest, both our breathing becoming erratic, eyes unblinking and dilated, a stare of a thousand promises passing between us.

I reach up and cup his face in my hands.

"Why do you have such an effect on me?" I gaze into his eyes, totally gone for this man who rewrote my rule book and burnt the old one to ash!

"When people are made, they're made in pairs, one single heart and mind split into two and sent off into the world. Maybe they'll find each other; maybe they won't. You"—he reaches up and puts the flat of his hand on my pounding heart—"are the other half of me!"

And he shrugs like he hasn't just said the most romantic thing in the world, and the lump that appears in my throat is gonna fucking suffocate me. My eyes glaze, and I take a stuttering breath before taking another steadier deep breath.

CLUNK! "I'll just set these down here!" the waitress says as she places our food on the table behind me. I bow my head forward to his and chuckle.

He smiles up at me and kisses my cheek. "Now shift your ass, woman. I'm hungry!"

"Dick!"

He kisses me again, and I slide off his lap and round to the other side of the booth. We eat in almost silence, but it's a comfortable silence exchanging glances and smiles as we eat. It's the happiest I've ever been.

Steel

I jump out of the truck and grab Demi's bags. I put them down on the floor and scoop up my fiancée for the last time. I spin her around. "I'm gonna miss you, don't do anything crazy without me, okay?"

She chuckles and nuzzles into my neck, wrapping her legs around my waist.

"I'm gonna go wait inside!" Demi blushes at the side of us.

"Demi, wait, can I have a word before you go!" She nods as I turn back to Ray.

I give her a kiss, one, to remember why she has agreed to marry me, and two, so she will miss the hell out of me and three, to make sure she will turn up tomorrow!

"See you tomorrow. I'll be the one at the end of the aisle!" I kiss her one last time and release her. I slap her ass as she bends over to grab Demi's bags. She gives me a wicked grin that promises all sorts of crazy dirty things when we're married. Fuck, I love the hell out of that woman. She heads inside, and I turn to Demi.

"Soooo..." I say as I scratch the back of my neck and kick concrete with the toe of my boots.

"Soooo..." she repeats.

Oh, fuck, why can't I speak to my own sister the way I can to Ray? "I know I've been a shit brother. I honestly thought keeping you away from me was for the best... after seeing Ray with her brothers, the guys, and even you and Scar. I realise that I need to improve. I need to do better!"

Blowing out a breath and looking to meet her gaze, she's stood, hip popped, arms folded. She has a look about her. She's changed since meeting Ray. We all have. She's more confident, and she isn't the mousy little sister I often ignore and boss around when I bother to see her.

I smile, but she doesn't return it. Fuck, she's gonna make me work for this. That's totally Ray's influence right there. Shaking my head, I take another breath.

"Go on!" She nods. "You're not totally fucking this up. Keep going!" My eyes shoot back to her. She never swears, I mean never.

"Ray's rubbing off on you!" I point out.

And she shrugs. "Maybe!" She smiles.

"It suits you! ...Anyway, I want us to be closer. I want to be a proper big brother. I want what they have. I want that with you. Can we start again?"

Her lip quivers, and her eyes glaze over, and I step forward, pick her up, and hold her to my chest.

She sobs out. "I've felt so alone for so long!"

"I know. I'm sorry!"

"I love you, Colby Steel!"

I sigh as she uses my full name. No one calls me that. It's strange but nice strange.

"I love you too, Demi Jones."

She grins up at me, sniffling. "I think you're gonna be a great big brother!"

I wipe the tears from her cheeks with my thumbs. "Well, I can't get any worse!" And we both laugh. "Now go keep my delinquent fiancée out of trouble for one night, and I will see you at the wedding!" She nods as she goes to walk away.

"Demi!" She gazes back over her shoulder. "Save me a dance, yeah!"

And with a grin that I want to see more often, she kisses me. "You can count on it, big bro!" And she skips inside, and my heart skips a little, sad at the sister I have missed out on, but a little happy at this new relationship we're gonna be able to forge. I head to the lodges where the guys will be and text Scar.

Steel: Just dropped them off

Scar: K.

Steel: Keep her out of trouble. It's only for one night!

Scar: If you think I have any more control over her than you do, then you've no idea who the fuck you're marrying.

Steel: Fair point. At least try for me.

Scar: I will do my best, have a good time. Don't get shit-faced.

Steel: You too! Thanks, Scar.

Ray

I grab the handle of our room. It's locked, so I waggle it again. It's never locked. What the fuck? Ares's door bursts open.

"In here, dipshit!" Scar laughs out into the corridor.

"What the fuck are we doing in there?" Demi comes down the corridor, all puffy-eyed but smiling.

"What the fuck happened to you?" I toss her a confused look.

She throws her arms around me. "You broke my brother, and it's the best thing ever!"

"Erm… you're welcome!" Laughing, we both turn to Scar, and she's hugging us both. Jesus, these emotions will be the death of me. Who knew finding the man of your dreams and the place you belong, with most of the people you love, would be so emotional? But then I feel a slight pang of sorrow knowing my pas won't be here tomorrow, which then makes me realise my dad won't be here either tomorrow.

As if sensing my shift, Scar squeezes us both tighter. "You've got us, Ray, Always!"

"I know, it's just—"

"I know," she replies.

"Come on, let's get in there!" We head into Ares's room. It's bigger, way bigger than Steel's. There's a sitting area with a sofa and TV, and there are two beds. As I look closer, one's Steel's.

"Why is Steel's bed in here?"

"Because we're staying in here tonight, the boys have gone to the lodges, so Carmen and Catalina are staying in Viking's room, and Demi, Aunt Marie, and Beauty are gonna crash here with us! Then we can get ready tomorrow together. I've got everything you need right here, snacks, tequila. You name it, I have it."

I smile, but I know they won't have what I truly want at that moment. My dad. "I'm gonna go check on my outfit, won't be long!"

Walking to Roach's room upstairs, I knock on the door, and then my phone blings as I grab it out of my pocket. The door swings open, and Roach's there with his phone in his hand, looking down. I see it's him that's messaged me, and we both laugh.

"Great minds, eh?" He smiles.

"Totally!" I grin back, shoving my phone back into my pocket.

"I was just heading out. Steel has invited me up to the lodges with the guys!"

"That's great, Roach. I want to know if I can leave my outfit here. I don't want anyone to see it yet!"

"Yeah, sure. Here, I got a key for you, so you can use my room if you need to. I'm taking everything with me that I need!"

"You sure?"

"Yeah. Can I talk to you for a sec before I go?"

"Sure."

He steps back, lets me in, and gestures for me to take a seat on the bed. He looks worried. He's chewing his lip and shifting back and forwards.

"Roach, spit it out, will ya?"

"Sorry, Ray… I just want to say thank you for everything… I really appreciate all you've done for me, and… I… Well, just thanks!"

"Roach, why does it sound like you're saying goodbye to me? You going somewhere, kid?"

He looks down at his feet and shuffles again. "No, I just… you know… with the wedding and all… I just thought I might not see you now, that's all."

Jumping up from the bed, I throw my arms around him. "Are you fucking kidding me, dipshit? Firstly, you're not nearly skilled enough for me to walk away from your training. You'll do yourself a fucking injury. Secondly, fucktard, you don't get to think shit like that. You're stuck with me. I told you when you trusted me to come to me about Casper, I would always be there for you, and I meant it, so, twatty, hug me like you mean it and fuck off to play with the boys while I have to do girly shit or something wank like that, okay?"

He pulls me into a hug. "I do fucking love you, Ray, and if things don't work out with Steel, I will try and kick his ass for you!"

"Deal, big lad!" I kiss his cheek. "Now fuck off!" I laugh and head back downstairs, tucking the key in my back pocket.

I decide I'm not ready to go back to the girls. I just need a breather. My dad's kicking my arse today, it's a real struggle, so I head out to where the wedding's gonna be held. As I walk down the aisle between the seating to the archway at the end, there's a raised platform in front of it. I stop in the aisle, looking up at the stars. I'm overwhelmed with emotion. I lay down on the ground, staring straight up towards the twinkling sky.

"You up there, Dad?" I huff out. "Fuck, I miss you... I wish you could be here... I wish you could have met him... And my new brothers... And sister... I think you would have loved them all!"

There's a lump in my throat as I stare at the twinkling stars and wonder if there really is anything up there. If there is, then I definitely won't be going, I've got a one-way ticket downstairs, but I'm sure they will lock the doors as soon as I arrive, motherfuckers.

"I wish the pas would have been able to come... Fuck, I have all these people here, but at this moment, I feel so alone... The one I want is you, and you're gone... You're not gonna see me get married... You're not gonna get to give me away... Steel wants kids, and as much as I think I do too, I can't help but break my heart that they'll never know you... Am I doing the right thing? ...Should I have waited till the pas could be here? ...Should I have let Steel get to know me first? What if he doesn't like the real me? ...I don't even know what the fuck I'm talking about... I've been more me here than ever, so if that doesn't put him off, I suppose he's not going anywhere... I'm so in my own head I just really think I need a hug... A big, fuck off, Dad hug... And a good talking to ...I fucking miss you, Dad. I hope you know I'm sorry for everything. I wish I could have saved you. I love you. I hope you're looking down on me tomorrow, and I can make you proud."

I huff out a sigh, and a few tears stream down my cheek. I can't bring myself to give a shit! Staring at the stars, they blur in and out of focus, and I just concentrate on breathing.

"Mind if I join you, Squirt?"

"Shit, Pa, you scared the crap out of me!"

"Fuck off. You didn't even flinch!"

"The inner me was terrified."

"Bullshit, Squirt, you would have heard me shut the lodge door and every step I made on my way down here, and you know it. Now budge over!" Shuffling nearer to the chairs but staying laid down, Pa Bernie lays down beside me. He leans over, wipes the tears from my face, and lays back down. "Whaddya need?"

"My dad… and my pas!" I whisper out with a stuttering breath. Reaching under my neck, he pulls me to his chest, and I break down and sob, and he just holds me for what feels like forever.

"I'm done!" I say as I shakily pull away from him, sitting up. He slings his arm around me.

"He'd have loved him, you know."

"You think?"

"Yeah, even the little time I've spent with him, he worships the ground you walk on. When Scar called him to say you'd gone, he was out that door like lightning, had to drag the big motherfucker back!"

"Shit, he didn't think I was having second thoughts, did he?"

"Nope! Are you?"

"Nope!"

"Didn't think so!" Grinning down at me, he pulls me in and kisses my forehead. "So Squirt, what's it gonna be? Do you want me to get Steel? I left the dozy twat pacing back and forth, he will probably have worn a hole in the floor by the time I get back, or you gonna play being girly?"

I huff out a breath. "I should do the girly thing, I suppose. Can we go shooting after the wedding, though? And axe throwing, and maybe paintballing? I think I will have had enough of the girly shit to last a lifetime!"

He barks out a laugh at me. "Whatever you want, Squirt!"

"Thanks, Pa. I love you!"

"Love you too, Squirt. Now fuck off before you have me crying!"

Laughing, I jog back to Ares' room. Before bursting through the door, I message Steel.

Wife: Sorry, I'm good!

Husband: Where are you? I'm coming to get you!

Wife: Nah, I'm good honest just needed a moment, rough day!

Husband: Second thoughts?

Wife: Never! xx

Husband: You'd tell me if you did, though?

Wife: You'd be the first to know, but never happening.

Husband: Phew, I was slightly worried.

Wife: Maybe, but not about me having second thoughts. You know I love you too much! Now fuck off

and enjoy yourself. Meet you at the end of the aisle tomorrow?
Husband: It's a date. xx
Wife: xxx

I push through the door. "Holy shit, you scared the crap out of us!" Scar spits at me as I burst in.

"I'm good. Sorry, guys, I just needed a minute!"

"Carmen and Catalina are five minutes away, and then we can get this party started."

I give everyone a hug while I wait and clean my face. "Let's do this!"

I struggle to sleep as I'm so excited. I just want to be married to Steel. We barely drank last night. Instead, we all had our nails done, which I suppose is cute and isn't the worst thing in the world. The girls pampered me. Carmen brought some expensive treatments, chocolates, and champagne, which tastes like cat piss, but is apparently very expensive, so I drank it and kept my thoughts to myself for a change.

It was a lovely gesture, really. We're becoming this close group of ragtag women who really shouldn't have anything in common.

"Can I say something to you all before we start getting ready?" The girls all pause to look at me.

"What's up?" Scar asks, half curious, half panicked. Maybe she thinks I'm having second thoughts.

"Nothing. I just want to say thank you all for last night and today. I might not get a chance later, although some of us haven't known each other long. I really love you all, so thank you! Oh, and Carmen and Tali. I have a question for you both?"

Carmen and Tali look confused, and Carmen replies, "Anything. What do you need?" I nod to Scar, and she walks over to the dresses.

"Will you be my bridesmaids?"

Tali lets out the biggest scream and runs at me, throwing her arms around me. "Oh my god, oh my god, I'm gonna be a bridesmaid!" She's chanting, and as I look at Carmen, her eyes have glossed over.

"Is the big bad cartel queen a little taken aback over there?" I joke.

She just nods and walks over, pulling me into a hug, too, whispering in my ear. "If you tell anyone, I will gut you like a pig, *perra*!"

I bark out a laugh and hug her tighter. "Your secret is safe with me!"

The girls go to town getting me ready. I still haven't shown anyone my outfit. I told them the colour theme was black, white and red. I want my hair half up, half down and over one shoulder. They curl it in long loose waves down my back before pinning it off my face and to the side. Scar has some little white and red flowers that she pins in my hair, and then Scar does everyone's make-up. She does a subtle smoky eye, with slightly winged liner, false lashes but again subtle ones, and Carmen's red lipstick so we all match. The dresses are all-black, strapless, sweetheart neck cocktail dresses with red ribbons at the waist, which we have added ourselves to help with the fit, as Tali's is a little big. It just helps to pull the waist in slightly. Carmen's is a little tight on the bust, but she says it makes the girls look fabulous, so she's not bothered.

I have bought them all Louboutins, the classic black heeled pump with the red sole, so fitting with the rest of the look, and they have all had their hair styled the same as mine since they said it looked so cute. It's time for me to get dressed.

I send Scar to get my outfit. She promises she won't look, and I trust her.

Back at Ares's room, I slip into the bathroom alone. I will need some help to zip it up, but I want to surprise them. I open my bag and take out my fancy bridal pants. I have picked a white lace pair with a tiny blue rose at the front, my something blue on the hipster shorts. Come on. I was never gonna be there in a thong with stockings and suspenders.

I have had a custom-made garter belt, which is a thigh holster for a small blade I slide in. Not that I'm expecting trouble, but I have learned never to go anywhere without at least a blade. I throw on my New Rock Trail boots and slide my blade inside, these are my FMBs, my Fuck Me Boots, as we call them back home, but I thought of them more as my "Don't Fuck With Me Boots" when I slide a blade into them. I think maybe tonight they will actually be my "*Fuck* Me Boots." Fingers crossed. I know I should have gone for maybe a high heel shoe like the girls, but I want to be me, so these are also my something old.

As I stand and look at myself in the mirror, I feel sexy. I hope Steel thinks the same. I worry at my lip ring. We haven't had sex yet. I mean, we've done a lot, and I mean *a lot* of other stuff, but he won't fuck me till we're married, and now I'm worried, what if it isn't good?

What if, after all the hype, he doesn't enjoy it? I shake my head. I know it won't be like that. I'm just having a moment. I'm not a good girl. I'm not even a good person, I've done things, things that would make a grown man cry, and I just hope that he loves me as much as I love him, regardless of how fucked up I am. It's just a little jitter. I will definitely be keeping to myself.

Opening the garment bag, I look at my dress. Yes, I know, dress! A fucking *dress*! It's white satin and lace, has a halter neck and a sweetheart neckline, and is completely backless. It clings to my figure, making me look shapely for a change. It's a mermaid cut with a small train that I can clip up later for dancing. As I slide it on, I feel like a movie star. I look so different. As I hold the front, I step out into the room.

"Can someone help me fasten this up…?" I trail off at the look on their faces.

Every one of them has their mouths open, frozen where they are just staring.

"What is it? Is it too much? Not enough? Do I look stupid? I look fucking stupid, don't I? Trying to be something I'm not… I knew I should have worn my fucking jeans. The guys are gonna be in their jeans and cuts, and here's me in a fucking dress…"

"Shut the fuck up! You're spoiling the moment!" Scar scolds me.

Marie's eyes fill with tears. "Ray, baby girl, you're a vision. I'm so proud to be your mum today. She would have thought it was perfect. You're stunning!"

I give her a kiss on the cheek. "I love you, Ma. You've always been a mum to me, not just today. Please don't make me cry, though. I've done enough of that!"

She chuckles, and she steps forward. "Your pa wants you to borrow this." She pulls out a silver and diamond flower hair clip. It's stunning. She shrugs. "Something borrowed. It was your grandma's. Your pa's mum lent it to me on my wedding day, then when she died, Bernie kept it, hoping you would get to wear it one day."

"Oh fuck, it's gorgeous. This best be waterproof make-up, Scar. I'm really struggling here!"

She steps back, wiping her own tears, and walks around to fasten my dress for me.

"Well…?" I question the rest, still standing there catching fucking flies.

"Ray!" Scar says, but then nothing else either. This is very, very good or very, very bad. That's the only time Scar will ever be lost for words!

"Fuck, Ray, Steel's gonna shit a brick!" Beauty gasps.

"Is that good or bad?" I question.

"Fuck, that's good!" she exclaims.

Tali looks in awe. "When I grow up, I wanna be just like you; you're beautiful and badass!"

I give her a face-splitting smile.

"Hermosa, perra loca. Te amo!" *"Beautiful, crazy bitch. I love you,"* Carmen says.

I smile. "Thank you, but less of the crazy, okay? I love you too!"

I suddenly feel a little shy when I look at Demi. "So what do you think, Sis? Yay, or nay?" I glance down at my dress and smooth out the imaginary creases.

Demi shakes her head. "I can't right now. I'm barely holding it together. If I start saying what I think, I'm gonna cry and ruin my face, then you'll ruin your face, and... not happening!" Grinning, she just gives me a thumbs-up.

I laugh and shake my head at her. "Thanks, Demi. You all look fucking beautiful. Right, let's take some quick photos before we head out!"

We get outside the clubhouse, and Scar stands front and centre, Beauty and Demi behind her, and Carmen and Tali slightly behind and to the side in an arrow formation.

"Ma, will you walk me down to Pa?"

"Really?"

I smile and nod. "I can't think of anything more perfect."

"I would love to!" She gushes. Pa Bernie is giving me away as my other pas can't be here.

Apparently, there's a photographer and a videographer, so they won't miss anything. Taking a breath, we walk around the side of the clubhouse towards the green out the back. The girls are covering me from view, they really do look stunning, and Ma... she looks hot as hell. She has a fitted red and white flowered dress, with the same shoes as the girls, a black bolero jacket with a black and red fascinator and as Scar has done her make-up, she has the same shade of lipstick as the rest of us. As we turn to go around the building, I glance over to my right, and I can see Steel at the end of the aisle.

"Holy fuck!" I gasp as I meet his gaze. His smile widens, and his eyes shine. His dimples melt my fucking heart. My breath stutters and I feel like I'm floating. His raven black faux hawk is styled but still has that look I love, like I've run my fingers through it. His grey eyes twinkle even from this distance.

Fuck, this man is handsome. It's then and only then that I realise he's wearing a suit, a fucking suit. I was expecting jeans and cuts, but he has on a black tailored suit showing his body shape with a black shirt and a red rose for his buttonhole. Ares's standing next to him in the same suit with a white shirt and white rose buttonhole. Pops is behind them with a book in his hands. Wait… is Pops officiating the ceremony? Well, fuck me.

Steel tosses a wink in my direction, and I melt. That's when everyone looks around. There are a few gasps and mumbles, but I can't take my eyes off him. As we step forward, the rest of the guys are waiting to escort the girls down the aisle.

Dane steps forward and takes Scar's hand, and then Beauty steps forward to be greeted by Dozer, who gives her a kiss on the cheek and links arms with her. Bran greets Demi, Carmen's collected by Viking, and he leans in and kisses her telling her she looks beautiful.

Then he glances over her shoulder and winking at me, mouthing, "You look fucking amazing!"

I smile as I feel my heart swell with all the love I feel at this moment. Tali's met by Roach. He looks really handsome and is really growing into his features. Gone is the weird kid with a scrawny gangly body. He's filling out nicely, he's never gonna be massive, but he's gaining an athlete's physique. Tali blushes.

He lifts her hand into the crook of his elbow and leans over. "I'm Roach. You look beautiful!"

She smiles a shy smile and looks away slightly, shy and a little embarrassed. He glances at me, almost as if he's asking if he's doing okay, and I give him a smile and a wink. They do look cute together. As Ma and I get to the front, Dice, Tank, Blade, and Priest step forward.

Blade leans in and pulls Ma's hand to his mouth, giving it a kiss. "We would be honoured to escort you to your seat, Marie!"

Dice takes Marie's other hand and kisses it too. "Marie, you are a vision of beauty!"

She smiles at them both as Priest gives me a wink, and Tank gives me a smile.

"You all look so handsome," I whisper. They're all dressed in matching suits, white shirts, and white buttonholes as they move away. Pa steps forward, but there's movement to either side of him, and my jaw falls. My eyes glaze over, and I blink and blink again as I try to focus.

Standing there are Pa Cade, Pa Bernie, Pa John and Pa Steven. My lip starts to tremble, and my hands start to shake. I'm trying to hold my shit together but losing it by the second.

Pa Cade steps forward as I reach for him, "Hold it together, Squirt, we got you. You look fucking beautiful! I'm so proud of you." He kisses me on my cheek, his eyes glazing slightly too, as he stiff upper lips it, and drops to the side of me. Pa Bernie falls into the other side, squeezing my hand, even though I have hold of my bouquet. It still feels surreal, like they're not actually here.

Pa John comes and gives me a kiss on my forehead. "You didn't actually think we wouldn't come, did you?"

Pa Steven comes up and kisses my other cheek. "We've never missed a doctor's appointment, a school play, or a court hearing. What makes you think we would miss you getting fucking married?"

"God, I've missed you all so much. How long are you staying for?"

Cade laughs. "Trying to get rid of us already, Squirt?"

"Never!"

"We're here for a month. We've missed you too, kiddo!" John says.

The lump hits me hard, then. My dad always called me kiddo.

Cade notices. "Come on, Squirt, let's add another family member to this ragtag band of fuck ups we love so dearly!"

I grin at them all. "He did this, didn't he!" It isn't a question. It's a statement. I know Steel has arranged all this. I'll never know what I have done to deserve this wonder of a man.

I just hope I don't fuck it up. He's too good to lose! They surround me and turn me towards the aisle. Just as I'm about to step on the aisle, the '*Wedding March*' plays out across the field. At the end of each row of seats, there's a bouquet slightly smaller than the girls' in red and white roses. My bouquet is slightly larger and hangs longer at the front. It's made up of mostly white and red roses, but there are two black roses in the centre.

I look back to Steel, the archway is now covered in red, white and black roses, and a black carpet is running between the white chairs. Each chair has a red, white, or black ribbon tied in a bow around it.

Fuck, Steel and Beauty really have made this beautiful. A massive marquee is behind the raised area where Pops, Steel, and Ares are standing. The girls are all side by side to the left of the raised platform, and all the boys have separated to the right behind Steel.

Looking across at all the club members and their families, all the men are dressed in black suits with red shirts, and the women and children are a mix of black white and red. When I said the theme was black, white, and red, I thought of a few flowers and the bridesmaids, but everyone in the club has stuck to it like glue. They all look beautiful as I try to smile at everyone.

While I'm walking, I'm gripping my pas tight, as if I think they might not be real and disappear at any given moment. I can't help but keep looking at Steel. He takes my breath away as we step toward the raised platform. Pops steps down, leans over and gives me a kiss on the cheek, speaking so only I can hear.

"You look beautiful, Sunshine." Before stepping back, he then asks, "Who gives this woman to be married today?"

Cade, Bernie, John, and Steven reply, "We do!"

They all kiss my hand, and Cade holds it while I step up towards Steel, he winks at me, and they sit down on the front row next to Ma.

As I reach up and take Steel's hand, he pulls me towards him and lifts me off the ground, kissing me like we are already married.

After a little while, Pops coughs. "Ahem, we haven't got to that bit yet!"

There's a chuckle throughout the seats, and I blush slightly. Fuck, I'm never gonna live that down. We step back a little and grin at each other like idiots. Thank heavens for the expensive lipstick. It's still where it's supposed to be and not all over Steel's face.

Giving us a moment to take a breath, Pops asks, "Ready?" We both look at each other and nod.

"Do you, Ray, Sunshine Reins, take Colby Steel to be your wedded husband, to cherish in love and in friendship, in strength and in weakness, in success and in failure, to love him faithfully, today, tomorrow, and for as long as the two of you shall live?"

Never faltering, never taking my eyes from his, I reply, "I do!"

"Do you, Colby Steel, take Ray, Sunshine Reins to be your wedded wife, to cherish in love and in friendship, in strength and in weakness, in success and in failure, to love her faithfully, today, tomorrow, and for as long as the two of you shall live?"

Holding my gaze and smiling wider than ever, he nods. "Fuck yes!" he breathes out.

Everyone cheers as he sweeps me up in his arms, swinging me around and kissing the life out of me.

"Ah, fuck it, I now pronounce you husband and wife, as you were!"

But we're still kissing, and I don't give a shit that all these people are staring, cheering, and whooping. These people are now my family. Next thing I know, we're being hugged and kissed by the bridal party. When Beauty hugs me, I grin. "Fuck, girl, this is amazing. You're so talented. I can't thank you enough!"

"You're welcome, but the majority of it, Steel did. He told me what he wanted, and I made it happen. You're beautiful together!"

Steel grabs my hand, and we head over to the field at the side of the tent. Everyone's gathering there for photos, the whole club and their families. As I walk to the photographer, I ask her for a few specific photos for myself, and she nods. After taking a few with everyone who attended, the families are sent to the tent to find their tables. We take more photos, and then the club members go to find their families. We then do all manner of family-based photos. The guys all look so handsome, with their top two buttons open on their shirts, all suited and booted.

After all the photos, we head inside, where people are sitting around. There's a dance floor in the middle, a massive long table at the top. To the right, there's a bar and on the left is the food, a hog roast. Fuck yeah, I'm starving. A pudding table and sweet counter for the kids, well, me, mainly me. All the tables surround the dance floor, and all the chairs have white covers and either red or black ribbons around them. On the tables, there are centrepieces of roses floating in bowls with gems at the bottom and tea lights floating inside. There's a table in the corner with children's games, toys and colouring books with pens. All the toys Dane and me won are set as favours in place of the children who are invited. They all have a cuddly toy, and the ones that are left over are on the children's table. It's adorable, and there are so many happy kids with their new toys as we head to the top table and find our seats.

Everyone starts clapping and cheering again. Fuck, this is surreal. It feels like I'm a celebrity.

One little girl is swinging around her toy on the floor, and she catches sight of us. She comes over to the table. "Are you… are… you Reaper?"

I smile and nod. "I am, and what's your name?"

"I'm… I'm… Matilda."

"I'm glad you could make it today, Matilda. Your dress is so pretty."

Next thing, her mum is grabbing her up. "I'm so, so sorry; she didn't mean to intrude. She didn't realise. I'm sorry."

I raise my hand to her. "Hey, she's fine. It's okay!"

Then a guy I've seen a couple of times comes over. "Sorry, Reaper!"

"Hey, it's fine. Matilda and me are having a conversation, isn't that right, princess?"

She nods. "Mum, Dad, stop embarrassing me. I'm talking to Reaper. When I grow up, I'm gonna be just like her. I'm gonna be beautiful, and I'm gonna kill bad guys and..." She looks up at Steel and blushes. "I'm gonna marry the most beautiful man in the world, and he's gonna kiss me like Steel does Reaper, and I'm gonna live happily ever after. The end!"

I can't help but smile. Leaning over the table, I say, "Well, Matilda, you realise you're a very strong and intelligent young lady, and you can be whatever you want to be, so I hope that one day you'll invite me to your wedding when you marry that most beautiful man in the world."

"Really, you'd come to my wedding?"

"If you invite me, I will come. I would love to!"

Her mum nervously reaches for her. "Come on, Matilda. You've taken up enough of Reaper's time!"

I smile at her mum and hold out my hand. She shakes it, "Please call me Ray, and I've always got time for anyone in this club. You're always welcome if you wanna chat, or the kids do."

She actually smiles a genuine smile. "Thank you, Reaper... erm, I mean Ray, I appreciate that."

I grin, and as they walk back across the dance floor, I shout, "Matilda!"

She spins around. "Yes, Reaper?"

"Don't forget my invite, remember okay?"

"I won't!" She grins back at me like I'm a god, a princess, or both. A lot of the club members know me by reputation, and with Steel being their Enforcer, they are right to be wary, but I don't want them to feel they can't talk to me if they want to. I sit back next to my husband.

"Hey, wife!" He grins at me.

"Hey, my gorgeous husband!" Leaning in, I give him a mother of all kisses, and then there's a bang on a microphone. As I glance behind me, there's a stage with a band on, and Ares is asking for everyone's attention!

"Hello, everyone. You all know who I am, and if you don't, what the fuck are you doing here?" He barks out a laugh. "I'm not gonna ramble on. I just want to say, Ray, you and the girls look beautifully stunning today, and I can honestly say there hasn't been a dull moment in our lives since you arrived. You've made my best friend one of the happiest men alive, and by making your sister Scar tag along, you've made me the other happiest man alive. I just want to say welcome to the family!

"As an honoured tradition, when an old lady marries into the club, we have a cut made with 'property of' and her husband's name on the back. However, due to unforeseen circumstances, this hasn't managed to happen this time, so instead, we got you this. This is from everyone here. Ray, can you come up here, please?"

Looking at Steel, he smiles and shrugs. Rising from my seat and heading to the stage, I climb the few steps and stand beside Ares. I mutter under my breath as I walk over to him. "Boyband, what the fuck are you doing?"

Grinning, he puts his hand over the mic. "Just shut the fuck up and get over here!"

Turning around, I look out at everyone's smiling faces. Ares hands me a box. Undoing the red ribbon and white wrapping paper, there's a black box inside. Opening the box is a leather cut. Looking over at Ares, I'm confused. He has just said it isn't a 'property of' cut, so pulling it out of the box, I hold it up, looking at the back of it first. It's the Reapers logo that's on everyone else's cut. As I hold it up, everyone cheers and whoops as I turn it to face me. Looking at the front, it has 'Reaper' on one side and 'Enforcer' on the other, with the one percenter patch on the shoulder.

Turning back to Ares. "I don't understand?"

"Welcome to the club, Reaper. Consider yourself patched in!"

"What the fuck?" My mouth hangs open, and then I close it, then open it again and look at all the smiling faces at me. "Wait, I haven't even prospected. How is this… huh?"

Ares's laugh booms out through the mic. "Holy shit! I've left Reaper lost for words!"

Everyone in the tent bursts out laughing as I flip them all off. "Motherfuckers!" I mutter under my breath.

"As it's your wedding day, we will wait a few days before we make it official and get you tattooed in, so after that, everyone, grab some food, dance, drink, enjoy yourselves and welcome Reaper to the family!"

Everyone stands up and cheers again, clapping, as I sling the cut over my dress and head over to Steel, spinning around. "What do you think?"

"Fucking perfect!" He drags me into his lap.

"I don't understand. Why does it say 'Enforcer?' That's you. I … I …"

Steel puts his fingers to my lips. "When Ares asked me to vote on if we should patch you in or not, I told him I didn't want you away from me, not because I think you can't take care of yourself or anything like that, but since I met you I can't bear to be apart from you, and after seeing you in the barn with Miguel, fuck, I wanted to join in so badly, so what better way to be together than to actually work together, too? So I'm going to be the Lieutenant, and you'll work alongside me as the Enforcer!"

"You sure you're not gonna get fed up with me!"

"Never!"

I kiss him again, and we get lost for the longest time, lost in each other's eyes, in each other's minds, and especially in each other's lips. When we finally break away, it's because I can smell Scar stuffing her face beside me, and my stomach rumbles.

Steel drags me over to grab food, and when we get back to the table, we have drinks, and the band begins to play a few steady tunes for some background noise. Once we've finished eating, the guys slide the long tables together to make it a big square table and shove it to the side nearer the bar. We all sit down again and start chatting. There's me, Steel, Scar, Ares, Viking, and Carmen. Apparently, Tali has gone to sit with Roach at one of the other tables. Carmen thinks she has a little crush.

Demi, Bran and Dane are with us all, my pas, Marie and Tank, Priest, Blade and Dice. We laugh and drink.

The girls are in the guy's laps, so we can huddle closer together.

Dice whispers over, "Bernie, I've got the gizmo working!"

"Fuck yes!" is Bernie's reply!

Steel turns to Cade. "So what was it like bringing these guys up?"

Cade laughs. "Hades! It was a fucking nightmare. How much have they told any of you about their childhood?"

They all look at each other and shrug. Only my pas, Marie, Bran, Dane, Pops and Scar know how we were brought up. The others know bits but not specific details.

Bernie laughs. "So Ray had a twin brother, Bas. He was… a dick even from being young. No matter what we did, he thought he was better than us all, and he made Dane, Bran, and Ray's lives miserable. When Ray's mum died, he got worse, but in fairness, he was always an arsehole. Bas just beat them all up and bullied them!"

JJ continues, "So we decided to give them a little hand. Did they tell you about our jobs?"

"Yeah, you run an Adventure Centre in the UK!" Steel answers.

"Yeah, well, we do now, but we were all military SAS and Navy SEALs. We were well trained, so we started the kids on a little self-defence… but it escalated."

"You can say that again!" I bark out, "I could shoot a gun by the time I was seven, my axe throwing and knife skills are second nature, I can hot wire a bike or car or any vehicle, I'm a shit hot mechanic in case any of you didn't realise. Really, we were trained in mixed martial arts. It just depended on who we were spending time with that day. I can build a bomb, I'm proficient in parkour, we can dive, me and Bernie have our own code we can speak in and decipher, and Bran and Dane have pretty much the same skills. We were trained basically as child assassins!" I shrug, and Bran and Dane laugh!

"Anyway," Bernie interjects, tossing me a scowl. He hates when I use the child assassin description. "They had… opportunities other kids didn't."

I roll my eyes.

"Bas didn't want anything to do with them, and although we had brought them up together, he wasn't interested, so he stayed away. Even from being little, Ray and Bran and eventually, Dane were inseparable but fought like cat and dog," Steven continues.

"We did not!" Dane shoots out. "We never fought. We always had each other's backs… OW!" I kick him under the table, and he turns to me. "Bitch," he mouths.

"See!" JJ cuts in. "They never stopped!"

Everything goes quiet as Dane, Bran, and I are in a stare-off.

"Nope!" I say.

"You sure?" Bran asks.

"Theme park!" I reply.

"Fuck!" Dane spits.

"We should," Dane says.

"Maybe it's time." Bran shrugs.

"Fine!" I cross my arms over my shiny new leather cut, and we all just sit there staring at each other. Everyone around the table is casting glances at each other, not having a clue what we are arguing about.

"You're the oldest!" Bran points out!

"By two fucking months, arsehole!"

"Still, you know the rules!"

"Dickhead!" I huff at him.

"Okay, so it's like this, we never fell out, we always had each other's back, and we never fought between ourselves properly. We might have enjoyed a bit of rough and tumble, but never an actual proper fight!"

"I beg to fucking differ!" Cade says. "I've lost count of how many teeth you've knocked out of each other's faces and skinned knees. There's even been a broken bone or two, and don't get me started on black eyes!" Shaking his head, he looks at our faces.

"Come on then, spill. You fuckers are up to something!"

Dane sighs. "So remember when Bas hit me and blacked my eye? I must have been four or so. These guys would have been what, five or six?"

Marie speaks up. "That was the first time one of you had really got injured from the other!"

Dane asks. "Do you remember what happened?"

"Erm, we sent Bas to bed with no supper and took you out for ice cream, and you got a new toy, an Action Man if I remember rightly?"

"Correct," Bran says, smiling at his mum.

"The next week, I fell over and skinned my knee and was just told, jump up, Squirt, you're okay."

Steven looks thoughtful for a minute. "Yeah, because that was an accident. That was different!"

"Exactly!" Dane laughs.

"I don't get it," says Bernie

"Okay, listen closely, as I'm not gonna repeat it, and maybe tomorrow, I will deny ever saying anything. We figured that if one of us was injured by another, we got ice cream and a toy. The one who did it got no supper; however, if it was an accident, we got fuck all!"

I can see all my pas frowning, and the boys are now leaning in, listening closely. Scar smirks. We told her about it years ago when she became one of us.

"So, when we injured ourselves, which was a regular occurrence, another one of us would take the blame. They would get to pick the toy when they got sent to bed. The one who wasn't involved would sneak them a snack while the injured one got ice cream. It was a win-win situation!"

"What about the black eyes? Lost teeth? All that stuff?" JJ questions.

"We were kids that climbed trees and rode dirt bikes. We fell over, tripped on stuff, played and got caught by a stray accidental elbow." I shrug.

Cade cut in. "So what about all the teeth?"

Dane replies. "Mainly, they just fell out when they were ready."

Marie looks shocked. "What about Dane's fractured arm?"

"Fell out of a tree!" Bran grimaces.

Bernie laughs. "You little fuckers. So you never fought!"

"Not once!" I shrug.

"When we made you apologise after, you always hugged all three of you, even when one of you wasn't involved, and did that K.F.D. thing. What's that all about? You never told any of us!"

"I would kill for them!" I say.

"I would fight for them!" Dane replies.

Bran finishes with, "I would die for them!"

"Kill for you, fight for you, die for you!" Scar chirps in, and we all smile at her.

"Wait…" Bernie pauses. "When was the last time any of you fleeced us?"

Grimacing, Dane pulls a face. "The other day!"

Steel barks out a laugh. "Holy shit, you guys are devious as fuck. I wish I'd grown up with you all!"

Frowning at Steel, Cade grumbles, "Yeah, that's just what we needed, another of you fuckers pulling the wool over our eyes. How did we never know this? I mean, six of us brought you up, and we didn't figure it out. We had training in hand-to-hand combat, hostage negotiations, and information extraction, amongst other things, and three pissant kids conned us for years, and you did last week? When? Who? What?"

"Erm… sooo, you know how no one came to take me out for the day the other day? Bran had agreed, knowing he wasn't gonna make it, so when you rushed around at the last minute, you asked Dane to hang out with me! We saw an opportunity, and we took it!"

"Yeah, I did, and he said why should he? He would rather stick a hot poker in his eye!" Bernie scratches his head, looking confused.

I bark out another laugh. "Yeah, and then what did you do?"

"You fucking little wankers!" Bernie lunges over the table at us, but we lean back and laugh. "You fuckers! Dane protested… really fucking hard about having nothing in common any more. You were just his annoying sister, blah, blah, blah! So I offered him one hundred dollars!"

The whole table erupts.

Dice grins. "Fuck, Bernie, he fleeced you!"

"You reckon? Add expenses on top of that too!"

Steel high-fives me. "My wife is a criminal mastermind!"

Bernie sinks his head into his hands. "Nearly eight hundred dollars you guys fucking spent. I should have known you were up to no good when you didn't come back!"

Turning to Steel, Bernie laughs. "You know what? She's your fucking problem now, son. See how you like that!"

Crossing his arms over his chest, Bernie huffs. The pas look confused, and I think there's a little pride in there too.

Steel pulls me into his chest, resting his chin on my shoulder. "Bring it on," he speaks in my ear, then kisses my cheek. I grin like a motherfucker.

Bernie shakes his head. "Bastards!" he mumbles.

"Let's make a toast." Pa Cade rises from the table. "To Ray and Steel and to all those who can't be here today, to those we've lost along the way!"

"To my mum and dad, I love you guys!" I raise my glass.

"To Bas… " Pa Bernie raises his glass. "He was a dick, but he was still family!"

Pa JJ follows, "To Sebastian and Julie."

Pa Cade raises his Glass. "To Daniel-Cade Miller. We're still looking for you, son!"

We all raise our glasses, but Steel remains seated and frozen, looking around. He has a frown on his face.

"What's up, baby?" I wonder if he wants to toast his family.

"Why did you say that name?"

"Which one?" Pa Cade cocks a brow.

"My name? That's me!"

I turn in my chair. "What's you?"

"That was my name!"

"Steel, what are you talking about?" Pa Cade asks.

"My real name. It was Daniel-Cade Miller. How do you know that name?"

My glass clatters to the table. My pas, Bran and Dane and Ma sit there open-mouthed.

"What do you mean that's your name?"

"I was born Daniel-Cade Miller. My mum was Julie and my dad was Sebastian. That was my name before it got changed, it's all I remember from before!"

"You're serious, Steel? You're not fucking with us? You're really him?" It's almost a whisper, and if I weren't listening to it, I would have totally missed it.

"Yeah!"

"And Demi's your real sister?"

"Half-sister, same dad," he replies.

"Holy shit!" Pa Cade shoots up from his chair, pulls Demi closer to him, and he grabs her from Bran's knee and swings her around. "Holy fuck, I can't believe it… after all these years, she's a girl!"

Pa Bernie rises slowly to his feet. I climb off Steel's lap, and he takes hold of his face. "You're really him, son?"

Steel nods. "Ray, what's going on?"

"Jesus fucking Christ!" Pa JJ says, looking at Steven, who replies. "After all these years, they found each other. If that's not fate, I don't know what is!"

"Ray?" Steel speaks again as Pa Bernie pulls him to his chest. Ma's crying and the rest of us are in total shock. Everyone goes quiet, exchanging glances as to where the fuck do we start explaining this shit fight?

"What are the fucking chances of that!" Dice says more of an exclamation than quizzing anyone, but still, holy fucking shit.

I grab Steel's hand and pull him away from Pa Bernie. "Come with me!" He's so shocked, but so am I. What the fuck just happened? He's frozen, so I tug a little, and we head outside, pulling him towards the aisle where we had the wedding. I sit him down on the raised platform.

"You good?"

He shakes his head, resting my hands on his shoulders, his face in turmoil. I release him and lift my dress. His hands automatically slide up my thigh till he reaches my knife holster.

He smirks, cocking his eyebrows. "You came geared up to our wedding?"

"Always, tell me you're not packing?"

He laughs. "You really are perfect, aren't you?"

"Me? Nah, you're just blinded by my dazzling personality. Don't worry. It soon starts to grate!"

He frowns. "That'll never happen!" He pulls me down so I'm straddling him.

"Do you wanna talk about it?"

He nods. "Where the fuck do we start?"

"So if I tell you what I know, you can fill in what you know, and if we don't have the full picture, my pas will. Well, I suppose *our* pas will."

I shrug, and he laughs. It's a start. "Okay, so my dad, Steven and JJ were in the SAS in their twenties. They were sent on a joint Ops mission with a team of American Navy SEALs. Sebastian, your dad, Cade, and Bernie were among them. They became best friends, thick as thieves, you might say. Anyway, you came along, and then a few years later, my mum got pregnant with Bas and me. Well, his name was actually Sebastian, after your dad!"

"Your brother was named after my dad? Why?"

"When my mum and dad decided they wanted a family, he wanted to leave the SAS, so he talked the others into retiring and setting up the business together, hoping to build the Adventure Centre the guys had been talking about for years. Apparently, they had all been putting money away for it, including your dad.

"They were all going to move to the UK. You were supposed to come live with us all. The other guys left the Navy SEALs, but your dad wanted to do one last mission to gather some more money, so the guys headed to the UK to get everything ready until your dad brought you and your mum with him when he returned.

"The guys were ready to open the centre, and my mum was only just pregnant with me, and Ma had just found out she was pregnant with Bran. Your mum phoned in a panic, saying your dad had come home early, medically discharged, but it didn't make sense, and he wasn't himself. He was erratic and confused. They told her to take you to a hotel, and they were coming to get you. Bernie, Cade, Steven, John, and my dad, Daniel.

"Wait, Daniel…? You never said your dad's name was Daniel!"

"Yep, you were named after him and Cade."

"This is a total mindfuck!"

"I know. Bear with me, though, okay?"

He nods, but his eyes are glazing over, and he looks pale, hardly surprising.

"They all jumped on a flight, but it was nearly twenty-four hours later when they arrived. When they got to the hotel, your mum never checked in, so they went to your house. It was already a crime scene. They tried to speak to the police, but they wouldn't tell them anything. They said they were family, and they were here to get you. They were taken down to the station where they were held for questioning, and by the time they got out, you were gone.

"They were told your stepmother had claimed you. They didn't know anything about another woman or even that she was pregnant until they started digging later. They stayed there for ages looking for you. They found a judge who had signed off on changing your name and signing you over to… I'm assuming… Demi's mum?

"She must have been pregnant with Demi at the time. Apparently, when Sebastian came back to the house, he found her talking to your mum, and he lost it, had some psychotic break, and it all turned to shit. I'm so sorry, baby!"

"So... My dad wasn't a bad guy. He was ill or something?"

"Yeah, they think it was PTSD, but the guys couldn't find out totally as his medical discharge was for an injury to his back, but they think he possibly had a severe head injury too, maybe? By the time they tracked the judge down, he had said you were better off away from their sort, and they had put you all into a type of witness protection thing.

"They changed all your names and set you up elsewhere so you could have a fresh start. They've been looking for you for years. Every year, one of them comes back here with everything they have found, and they go to different private investigation agencies and military friends and normally spend a couple of months trying to find a new lead on anything.

"That job Pa Bernie wants Dice and me for, the judge who signed off on changing your name, has contacted Pas security firm asking for security for an event. Pa wants me to go so I can gain access to his laptop, and Dice is creating this gizmo that will allow us to copy it and then let us connect to his servers, hoping we can download the name you had been given to try and track you. All this time, you were right under my nose!"

He takes a few deep breaths. "Well, shit. I don't know where to begin to process that mindfuck. Guess we've been meant to be our whole lives, huh?"

I smile down at him. "I'm so glad I found you, Daniel-Cade Miller, Colby Steel, whatever your name is… you're mine now! Always and forever!"

He kisses me like a drowning man, and we stay like that for the longest time, basking in the moonlight, held in each other's arms, till someone clears their throat behind us. We turn to face Pa Bernie and Pa Cade.

"You good, son?" Bernie asks. Steel squeezes me a little tighter.

"I think I will be."

"You wanna talk about it?" Pa Cade asks.

"Nah, I'm gonna need some time to process, then I think we should all talk together, but not today, not now, it's too… much, ya know?"

"I know, son. We're sorry we couldn't find you sooner. We tried; we really have all these years."

I climb off Steel, and he stands facing the guys. "Come on. I need a fucking drink!"

Pa Bernie claps him on the shoulder. "Whatever you need, son!"

"We're here now!" Pa Cade adds, and we head inside. The party has picked up. There are drunk people dancing and singing to the band on the stage, the food is going down too, and the kids are running around, hyped up on excitement and sugar. It's amazing to see what this man has done for me.

Walking back over to my other pas, they all give Steel a hug. Demi's sitting on Bran's lap, still in shock.

She jumps up and flings herself at Steel. "Are you okay?"

He hugs her tight. "I'm okay. We'll be okay." He turns her around to see everyone's smiling faces, happy to have found them both.

She smiles up at him. "We are, aren't we? We're gonna be okay!"

He nods.

We have a few more drinks, and Steel's phone rings. He waves it at me and goes outside. "Who the fucks phoning him? Everyone's here!" I look around, and everyone important is at our table.

They all shrug.

Steel comes back into the tent. "It's here!" Grabbing my hand, he looks over my shoulder. "Come on, you lot!" As he drags me outside and towards the clubhouse, followed by the rest of us, there's a white van parked outside the front of the clubhouse. It's rocking as we come around the corner. We all gather there.

"What's going on?" I don't trust rocking vans, especially after the kidnapping incident.

"Wedding present!"

"You got me a van?"

"No, twat, I got you what's in the van."

"Oooh, what's in the van?" Scar questions from behind me.

"Surprise!" is all Steel says, standing behind me, chin on my head and arms wrapped around me, holding me against his warm body. The guys from the van slam the back doors and come to me.

"Sign here, please, Mrs Steel."

I look at Steel, and he smiles and nods. Mrs Steel, fuck, I like the sound of that! I have no idea what I'm signing, but I trust this man with everything that I am, so I do. The guys get in the van and drive away, leaving what can only be described as an orgasm on wheels.

A Harley Davidson Night Rod Custom in the same matte black as Steel's, but his has silver rims and accessories, while mine has rose gold. Fuck, this is sexy. He releases me as I walk over to the bike and slide my hand down the tank and across the seat.

"This is mine?" I ask, really unsure what's happening right about now. Steel only nods., "You bought this for me?" He nods again. "Steel, this must have cost a fortune. I can't take it. It's too much."

Laughing, he grins. "Too late now, beautiful, you signed for it. It's yours, all bought and paid for. Hop on. Let me see how sexy you look on it!"

Hitching up my dress, I cock my leg over the bike.

"Only you would wear sexy ass biker boots and a blade to your own wedding!" Ares barks out a laugh.

"Two!" I lean down and tap my boot! Grinning like a motherfucker, I start the bike up, and the rumble through my thighs causes an involuntary moan.

Steel chuckles. "You like?"

"I fucking love it!" I start tucking my dress around my thighs and under my butt.

"Whoa, whoa, where the fuck do you think you're going?" Steel grabs the keys and turns the bike off.

"Hey, no fair! You can't give me a bike and not let me ride it!" Folding my arms over my chest. "That's almost like telling me I can have the same dick forever but not letting me use it! ...Oh wait, you already did that!" I know I'm being a brat but no fair! "I can't have two sexy things in my life and not be able to ride either of them. That's just cruel!"

Looking over Steel's shoulder, I can hear tittering and scuffling as the others back away. I also hear Pa Bernie mumble.

"Come on. This may not end well for Steel!"

"You, husband!" I poke him in the chest. "Are a fucking fun sponge!"

"A fucking what now?"

"Fun sponge!" I mutter, huffing out a breath.

"We can go out tomorrow, just the two of us, up to the campsite and take a picnic. How about that?"

"Fine, but if I don't get to ride my bike tonight, then... " I grab him by the front of his trousers and pull him forward. I lean up and kiss him, wiggling my eyebrows at him. He picks me up off the bike, pinning me to his body.

"You can have anything you want tonight once we get back to our place!"

"Our place... I like the sound of that!"

"And I don't want you to think I forgot, so in a couple of days, we need to go and collect our rings, okay?"

"Rings?"

"Wedding Rings! You didn't think we were gonna get married and not have rings, did you?"

"I never actually thought about it."

He laughs at me and shakes his head.

"Come on then, let's get back to the party. I'm hungry!" sliding my hand over the bike again.

He laughs. "You're always hungry!"

"Let's not let it turn into hangry then, as you'll be wanting a divorce, okay?" I pull him along behind me as I rush back for more hog roast.

As I've finished stuffing my face, I walk along the edge of the dance floor towards the sweet table when there's a squeal.

"Reaper!" I spin around as six little kids barrel towards me. And fuck, that's more terrifying than being kidnapped!

"Matilda! What's up, kiddo?"

"Reaper, I told my friends that I knew you and you were coming to my wedding, and they said I was lying!"

I bend down to their level. "Huh, they did, did they! It's not nice to tell lies, but it's also not nice to not believe your friends. Do you normally tell lies, Matilda?"

She looks at her shoes, and the others all nod.

"Okay, well, Matilda is gonna stop telling lies, or I'm not coming to her wedding, but if she promises to always tell the truth, then I'm going to go. Deal!"

Matilda nods. "I promise, Reaper!"

"Good, so you guys go have fun, and I will see you at your wedding, okay?"

As they turn and walk away, one little girl says. "Oh my gosh, I can't believe we just talked to Reaper, and she's going to your wedding. Do you think if I stop telling lies, she will come to mine?"

"She's my bestest friend. I can ask her and put a good word in for you, so maybe she will!"

"Would you do that?" the other little girl asks.

"Sure!" Matilda shrugs. I have to laugh; they are so cute. As I stand, strong arms tighten around me. He's taken his jacket off, his sleeves are rolled up, and his tanned arms hang around me as he leans in, engulfing me with his heat and smell. It makes my head spin and my toes curl in my boots. It feels like the earth tilts every time he's near me, pulling me into his own gravity.

"Quite the following you have there, Reaper." He nips at my shoulder.

"Mhm," I mumble as I melt into his strong arms and tight grip.

"Dance with me?"

"Of course, you dance too! How are you this perfect?"

"You're just lucky, I guess!"

"Yeah, I'll agree with that." We melt into each other, dancing to the band, playing some ballad love song I don't notice. Gazing into Steel's eyes, I reach up to cup his face. "You've made me the happiest woman alive!"

Leaning down and kissing me. "I promise to try and make you feel like that every day!" We dance for a couple of songs, and then they bring a chair to the middle of the room.

Ares takes the mic again. "It's time for the garter and bouquet toss!"

"What?" I ask.

"I have to remove the garter with my teeth, then toss it to all the men. The one who catches it will get married next, and then you toss the bouquet, and same for the women."

"Oh, okay, this isn't awkward at all in a room with kids in it!"

Steel laughs and drags me over to the chair. Everyone gathers around the edge of the dance floor, women on one side, men on the other. The women are behind me, and the men behind Steel. He gets down on his knees and shoves my dress back, eyes lighting up when he catches sight of my garter holster and knife combo again.

He grins at me. "Fuck, that's so sexy!" I tip my head back and laugh. Leaning down, he licks up the inside of my thigh so painfully slowly. All the air and sound get sucked out of the room, and then it's just us. As he looks up at me with those swirling eyes promising me the world, I can't take my eyes off him. This gorgeous creature is mine.

I can't believe how lucky I am to have found him. As he gets to the garter, his teeth nip the inside of my thigh, making me wetter by the second. He takes a deep breath. "I can fucking smell you from here. It's driving me mad. I want to plunge my tongue inside you so badly. I don't think I can stand up. I've got the biggest boner!" he whispers against the inside of my thigh before biting down on it, then grabbing the garter by his teeth, slowly straightening my leg out, and sliding it all the way down my leg and over my boot. He screws it into a ball as he stands, and all the guys step forward as he tosses it over his shoulder. Roach catches it, and immediately after going bright red, he looks over to Tali, who blushes a little.

I'm taking note of where she is. Ares hands me my bouquet. "Now, it's your turn!"

I grab the bouquet and toss it over my shoulder straight at Tali, and she jumps up and squeals as she catches it. The music starts up again, and everyone joins us on the dance floor.

After a while, a lot of the families start to leave, and everything is winding down. We head around, thanking everyone for coming and saying our goodbyes. Heading back to the clubhouse, it feels like we've been gone for days, not just since this morning, as we walk between the clubhouse and the garage.

Steel grabs my hand. "You got time for one more surprise?"

"Steel, fuck, this whole day must have cost you a fortune, and I checked my card, and Beauty hasn't spent anything on it, so what gives? You can't pay for everything. I really appreciated today. It has been wonderful, but it's too much, Steel. You do realise I'm loaded, right? Well, I suppose now we're loaded!"

"Well, one small surprise then, please I've already done it, so you can't take it back now!"

"Fine, but then we will sort this all out tomorrow, okay?"

"Yeah, okay."

"I mean it, Steel!"

"Okay, I said okay. Alright, now come on, this is great. You're gonna love it! Close your eyes."

So I close my eyes, and the next thing I'm being flung over his shoulder, fireman's lift type, and we're heading up some metallic stairs from the sounds I can hear. "Where the fuck are we going?"

A door opens as there's a clunk, and I'm dropped to my feet. "Open!"

Opening my eyes slowly, I see we are in an apartment, newly renovated, open-plan, with a large kitchen to the left and a living area to the right. There's a table and chairs to the back of the kitchen and sliding doors out to what looks like a balcony.

"Are we above the garage? Fucking hell, Steel, is this where you went?"

"Yep."

"You did all this?"

"I had help!"

"And you were here this whole time!"

"Yep."

"Fuck, Steel… this is beautiful."

"You wanna live here together then?"

"Hell yeah. How am I ever gonna repay you for everything?"

"Maybe you could start by showing me the bedroom?"

I bark out a laugh. "Finally!" Grabbing his hand, I walk towards a door.

"Bathroom," he whispers.

I turn to the other door looking at him. He shakes his head, there's only one other door, so I head towards it. As I step through the door, it's into a large room with a door on the back wall and one to the right. There is a large bed with sliding doors to a balcony on the left. Everything is in greys, blacks, and whites. It's beautiful.

"Steel… I don't know what to say. This is beautiful."

He pulls me to him. "Wanna finally show me how appreciative you are?"

"Hell yeah!" I swing around, pointing at the zip. He slowly, painstakingly pulls the zip down, inching the dress over my hips and pooling it on the floor, leaving me in my white pants, knife holster and New Rock Trail boots.

"Fucking hell! I thought you looked mind-blowing in that dress, but you're definitely load-blowing out of it. You look so damn sexy!" I kick the dress away from me.

"So, husband, whaddya wanna take off, and whaddya wanna leave on?" Reaching down and hooking my fingers into the waistband of his trousers and pulling him with me as I back towards the bed, once the backs of my legs hit the bed, I reach up and unbutton his shirt, sliding it off his strong shoulders, when it pools on the floor, he kicks his shoes off, while I undo his trousers and slide them down his legs.

Putting his hand on my chest, he pushes me back so I fall on the bed. Taking the rest of his clothes off, he stands there, completely naked, and fuck me. It's a fucking beautiful sight. I lift up onto my elbows to drink him in. If I had ordered him out of a catalogue, I couldn't have picked a more perfect partner. Licking his lips and smiling down at me, he crawls up my body, kissing, nipping and licking his way up to my mouth before devouring me while grinding his body into mine.

I'm overwhelmed with anticipation, and sensations take over me. I have waited what feels like so long for this release. I don't know If I can contain myself. I reach down to undo my boots.

"Leave them on. Leave it all on. Knives and all."

"Kinky fucker!" I kiss him and roll him onto his back, straddling his waist. His palms caress my breasts, sliding down to my waist. He pulls me down onto him, grinding into me. I gasp.

"Fuck me, beautiful!" He reaches over to the bedside table, sliding the drawer open. There's a stack of condoms.

I shake my head, leaning over and closing it. "We're married now. I want you, bare. I want to feel you come inside me. I'm clean. I got tested a few weeks ago."

"You did?"

"Yeah, just to be on the safe side. I wanted this to be… a first for me!"

"And me!"

"You've never?"

"No."

"We can use a condom if you prefer, I—"

"No." He shakes his head. "I don't want that!"

"I just want you to fuck me, beautiful. I wanna feel all of you," I say to him, reaching between my legs.

I lift off him, palming his dick in my hand. He's already solid. Hard, proud, and pulsing, I bring him to my opening, pushing my pants aside. He holds my hips as our eyes meet, and I slowly lower myself onto him, stretching me in so many delicious ways. His breaths come in heavy as mine stutters. As I get to the bottom, I gasp and let out my breath, I'm so full, and Steel clamps down on my waist, holding me in place. I cock my head back and close my eyes. I try to rock forward but only manage a fraction of what I'm trying to do.

Steel interrupts my train of thought. "Wait!"

"Wait? You ok?"

"Yeah, just don't wanna blow my load like a thirteen-year-old. Just gimme a second. Fuck, you feel so amazing!"

After a few seconds, he twitches inside me, and I start sliding backwards and forward, grinding into his pelvis. He grips my hips hard enough to bruise as I ride him like it's my motherfucking job. His pupils are blown, his breaths are stuttering, and his fingers are in a bruising death grip on my hips. I grind into him harder, and my clit starts to swell and pulse.

I can feel the electricity rising through me. I push my hands up along his chest and wrap my fingers around his throat. I lean in slightly. His eyes grow wide, and his breath stutters more violently. I throw my head back as everything starts tingling. I can feel the heat rising up from my core, and I erupt, my orgasm taking over. As I do, I throw my head back again, and I clench my hand as my pussy clenches and convulses around his throbbing dick.

He roars, "Fuck!" as he approaches the edge with me. I can feel him pulsing inside me and filling me with his come. I can feel my whole body. It feels like it's on fire, being burnt from the inside out, as he gasps for air, still gripping my hips and grinding me into him. I can feel him soften inside me, but he grips my hips tighter, firmer, and starts to grind into me again. Fuck, that feels so good. I can feel his dick softening and the come sliding around between us, coating my thighs, soaking my clit, making my clit swell more, feeling the intense pressure and the burn from the friction. But I can't bring myself to get off, I don't know how long we stay like that. It feels too intense, too sensitive, and I can't find a fuck to give to make me wanna stop, so I grind again, harder but slower. Sliding against his body, every nerve ending tingling with a cold burning sensation, lazily enjoying the feel of him beneath me, he gasps as he starts thickening again, his eyes wide, his smile spreading.

I'm totally in awe of this man as he quickens our pace, grinding me into him as he pulls down on me. Fuck, I bite my lip. I'm gonna come again. I can feel the build-up, running a finger down my face. I lean forward to kiss him just as my clit hits another angle, the hard planes of his body rubbing deliciously against my pebbled throbbing clit. Theres come everywhere now, it feels so good, coming again like a Mac truck, and I scream out his name.

"Steel!" I pant into his neck, and as I pant into him again, erupting, adding more come to the mess, I collapse on his chest, both of us panting. "Holy shit!" I pant out. "That was fucking amazing!" I feel myself twitching from him still being inside me, but as I go to ease off, he grabs me.

He holds me to him. "I'm not ready to stop yet. I don't want to not be inside you." He pulls me in tight.

I pulse my pussy, and he moans out, so I carry on, "Be a good boy, and hold on, baby!" Within ten minutes, I'm coming on him again. By now, he's fully hard, so he rolls us over so I'm underneath. He lifts my leg and rests it on his shoulder, and leaning into me, he lifts his upper body off mine and thrusts into me like he's trying to drive me through the bed.

"Fuck, Steel!"

He pounds again and again, making my insides feel amazing and my outsides even more so. He keeps pumping. "Fuck, wife, you're beautiful."

"Say it again!" I whisper out.

"You're beautiful!"

"No, the other thing!" I moan.

"Wife? Fuck, wife, you're so perfect." As he says 'wife,' my breath hitches, and I fall over the edge after him again.

"Fuck, husband, you're so goddamned gorgeous!" He pounds into me again and again. I come again and think I actually black out as he fires his load into me, still pounding into me, trying to push me through the bed. Fuck me, was I here for it. Best sex ever. He collapses on top of me, sweaty bodies sliding together. He reaches up and tucks some hair behind my ear, and goes to get off, but I hold him tight.

"Stay!" His dick's softening inside me, and something about that feeling's turning me on. I can feel come seeping out of me onto my thighs, and I grind into him.

"You like that, huh?"

"I don't know why, but it feels amazing." Steel slowly and carefully starts to move inside me again, and I gasp.

"Fuck Steel, I'm losing my goddamn mind."

The feel of all that come and his soft dick sliding inside me is so hot. I roll him gently onto his back again and sit on him, slowly grinding myself into him.

"You're gonna make me hard again!"

"Is that such a bad thing?"

"No, it's sexy as fuck. Now be my good girl, and don't fucking stop."

So I don't, because I want to be his good girl at that moment. I carry on the cycle for the next few hours till, at some point, we fall asleep or pass the fuck out. When I wake up, I ache, and as I go to move, there's a weird sensation. His dick's still inside me, and my pussy convulses like the filthy whore she is. I'm laid on top of him, rolling my hips slightly. He moans. I'm still in my underwear, boots, and knives. I roll my hips again, and I can feel him hardening again.

I kiss up his neck, along his collarbone, and then to his mouth as I slide my tongue in. He moans and starts to kiss me lazily. I'm unsure if he's still asleep, so I kiss him again and grind myself into him. "Morning, husband!"

"Fuck, morning, wife. I wanna be woken up like this every morning." Grinding down again, he flips me over. He holds my gaze as he slowly and torturously pumps his hips. Lifting my arms above my head, he pushes down into me.

I moan, pinning my grip above my head. He slides up and down me, grinding into my clit and pushing me over the edge. It isn't long before he follows me over. We are a sticky mess, and holy shit, it feels good. Sliding off me, he holds my hand and pulls me up. "Let me show you the bathroom," he says as he pulls me into him for a knee-trembling kiss.

He picks me up and throws me over his shoulder, smacking my arse. "I think I need you to fuck me in every room, on every surface, before we leave here."

I reach down and slap his arse. "Deal!"

He slides his hand up the inside of my thigh and straight into my still-slick pussy, and I groan and clench around his fingers. "Fuck, all I can smell is us. That's so fucking sexy!" he murmurs, pumping his fingers in and out of me while I gasp as he carries me into the bathroom. He takes me straight into a massive walk-in shower with a bench all the way along one side. He turns the water on and stands me up.

I lean up and kiss him. "How do you want me?"

"Fuck, I don't think there's enough blood left in any other part of my body to decide that!"

I turn away from him and bend over. "Show me what you got!"

He moans and wipes his hand down his face. "Fuck, Ray, you're gonna fuck me to death!"

Looking over my shoulder and winking at him. "I'm happy to die trying!"

Grabbing my hips, he slams into me, driving straight in without a second thought. "Fuck, you were made for me!"

"Oh shit, Steel!" He pounds into me. I slide my hand between my legs and start rubbing my clit.

"Holy fuck!" he spits out as I catch his balls and rub at the base of his shaft as he impales me. I can feel my legs start to shake and the heat rise. Black spots flick over my vision. Closing my eyes, I place my free hand against the wall and rub faster. His arm comes around me to hold me against him, and his other hand slides up my body, sliding around my throat and pulling me off the wall holding me flush against his body. Squeezing my throat a little more, not enough to cut the circulation or stop my breath, just enough so I know it's there till I gasp and I lose it. I'm falling over the edge. It's more like plummeting over, my body flush with his, my head back on his shoulder, his large rough hand banded around my waist, and his thick fingers gripping around my throat. I can't tell where he finishes, and I begin. Closing my eyes, I continue to frantically rub while I power through my orgasm, and he follows me over, spilling inside me till we both collapse against the wall. Panting, Steel turns and sits on the bench, pulling me into his lap.

"Fuck you're insane!" Turning to straddle him, I grab his face in my hands and start slowly kissing him. His hands grope my arse. As we sit there, then I feel his dick twitch against my leg. "Again?" I ask,

He laughs. "I think my dick is always gonna be ready for you. Maybe we should get washed and dressed and go get some food!"

"Sounds good!" I say as I rock my hips against him before sliding back to get off his lap, but his hands clamp down on me.

"Well, it's rude not to use it now. It's hard!"

I laugh. "You're insatiable." I slide my hand between us, positioning him against me and sliding him right in. He shudders against me, and I slowly ride him, nice and steady kissing him up and down his neck while he clamps down on my nipples with his teeth until we both come again and then we really do clean up and head out, as we walk down the steps. "Steel!"

"Yeah, baby, what's up?"

"Can you show me the rest of the place later? I've barely seen it, and the bits I did see, I didn't really see as I was focused on someone else!"

We head into the bar. I'm itching to get out on my bike, but Steel says we have spent all day in bed, so we need to be sociable, and the picnic will have to wait till we get our sex drive under control. Everyone's in the bar, so we all sit together and have a few drinks.

Steel and I keep yawning, and everyone's taking the piss. After a few games of pool with the guys, Steel and Demi speak to our pas.

Pops comes over and gives me a hug. "How are you doing, Sunshine?"

"I'm good, Pops. It made it so special yesterday that you were the officiant. I can't thank you enough!"

"Good, anything for you, you know that, right? I want to talk to you, anyway. I know you and Scar will stay here now, but I think that without you guys, there's nothing at home for me. I know Scar's looking at premises for a law firm. What would you think if I semi-retired out here?"

I throw my arms around his neck. "You would really do that for us? Seriously?"

"I'm really thinking about it, and being a criminal lawyer and the new... family business we've acquired. I think it could be good for all of us!"

"Pops, that would be great. I would seriously love that."

"I wasn't sure how serious Scar and Ares were and also if she would want me so close, cramping her style. I know we've spoken about it, but I'm not sure how serious she really is or if she just agreed to make me happy. I thought you were the safer option."

We both laugh at that. "Me, the safer option? That's a sentence, not many people will ever say… It's a yes from me as long as it's not just for us!"

"I actually kinda like it here, and I've never seen you or Scar as happy. It's definitely something to really discuss!"

"Why don't we go for lunch tomorrow, you, me and Scar? We can talk it out and look around Ravenswood or further afield if you like. Scar said you'd been looking at premises already, but I'm assuming now that was just a ploy so you didn't see me before the wedding and let anything slip."

"It was. What about Steel?"

"I'm sure he can manage without me for a few hours."

Suddenly, I'm grabbed from behind, and my neck is nipped. "Nope, can't manage without you, not even for a second!"

I burst out laughing. "You're ridiculous!" I tell him as he nuzzles into my neck.

"Ready to go?"

"Sure, I'm going to lunch with Pops tomorrow. Will you be okay without me?"

"Yeah, actually, me and Demi are going out with the pas."

"Perfect. Pops, will you sort it with Scar and let me know what time we're leaving?"

"I will do, Sunshine. Night, you two!" Leaning in to hug me and shaking hands with Steel, we head out.

"I can't wait to get you home!"

"Can I actually look around the place? It would be nice to see it, as you've put so much work into it?"

"Sure, baby, whatever you want!" Throwing me over his shoulder and smacking my arse, we walk out of the clubhouse and across the steps up to the apartment.

"I can walk by myself, you know."

"Where's the fun in that?" He leans over and bites my arse cheek.

"Ow, motherfucker!" And the booming laugh vibrates up through me and seems to resonate between my legs, causing an involuntary groan to slip from my lips.

This causes him to laugh again. "I can smell you now, wife!"

"Then stop laughing, talking, or making any sound while I'm this close. It does all sorts of delicious things to my nether regions!"

He barks out a laugh again. "Steel, fuck!" As we reach the top steps, he puts me down and raises his hands in mock surrender.

Opening the door and stepping in, he says, "Let me show you around while you get your… nether regions under control!"

"Fuck you, arsehole!"

"I love how you say 'arsehole' instead of 'asshole.' How very British of you."

I roll my eyes as I walk through the door. "Fucking ridiculous!" I shake my head at him. As we walk through the door, there's a large kitchen to the left with a generous-sized island in the centre. The cupboards are dark grey, with a lighter grey concrete worktop and grey tiled splash back, the sink is a slate grey, and there's one of those large flexi mixer taps in black. There are four pendant lamps in black over the island and LED downlights under the cupboards and around the baseboards.

I run my hand along the countertops. "These are beautiful!" I open the tall cupboard, where there's a fridge and freezer built in and a dishwasher. Further along, the floor is wooden floorboards with a pale ash grey finish. To the right, there's a media centre built into the wall, finished in grey with games consoles and a sixty-five-inch TV fixed to the wall above it. The wall is papered in a matte black/grey wallpaper with velvet skulls. It's fucking gorgeous. There's a large black leather sofa in a U-shape facing the TV with a stylish black and grey coffee table in the centre. There are different shades of grey cushions all over the sofa, some have skulls on and a grey fleece thrown over the back of it. "This paper is perfect, Steel. This place is amazing!"

He smiles at me. "I'm glad you like it!"

"I fucking love it, and all the skulls… they're so… us!" There are two big windows to the front with heavy black floor-length curtains, and there are silver skulls on the ends of the silver curtain poles, with the TV in the centre of the windows. It's so cosy.

At the side of the kitchen is a double sliding door with a round glass table and six chairs around it. In front of them, one of the wedding centrepieces is in the middle of it. There's a built-in washer and dryer on the other side of the kitchen units. Sliding the door back, there's a balcony that runs the full length of the building that must go over the garage office and store room. Stepping out onto the balcony, there's a built-in grill to the left and a heavy black metal balustrade with lights built into the floor. Just behind it are two large Victorian-looking lanterns, one side of the doors and another set of doors leading into the master bedroom with the same light fittings on either side.

Steel turns the lights on, and I can see the marquee and seating still erected out to where the wedding was. "It seems like a lifetime ago that we got married, not just yesterday!"

Steel comes up behind me, sliding his arms around me and leaning us both onto the balustrade. "It was the second best day of my life!"

"Ah, yeah, and what was the first?" I smile smugly.

"The first day I met you, when you came barrelling out of that van all bloody and badass, barking orders at everyone, and them all doing everything you said without a second thought. I knew right then and there I would follow you to the ends of the earth."

Spinning in his arms and reaching up, sliding my hands up the hard planes of his chest over his shoulders and to his face, I lean up and kiss him. "You are my forever, everything I didn't know I wanted or needed. I don't know what I did to deserve you, but I promise to be by your side no matter what!"

As we lose ourselves in more kisses, they start to heat, and when I grab for Steel's waistband, he grabs my wrists.

"Beautiful, at this rate, you're never gonna see the rest of this place."

I suggestively grin at him as I flick the button of his jeans open. "I've seen much more than I did yesterday. There's always tomorrow!"

"Argh!" he groans as he pulls me back inside. "Why am I the sensible one? Come on. It will take ten minutes. Then you can do whatever you like!"

"Whatever I like… to you?"

He grins at me and shakes his head. "Fine, whatever you want to me!"

"After you've shown me around, I need to head back to your room. There's a box in the wardrobe I need!"

"Really? …Everything from the room is in the walk-in. I'll show you that last!" Grabbing my hand, he leads me back into the living space. There are three doors. The first one leads to the master, the second to the bathroom.

"There's another bedroom?" As I head to the last door and push my way into a corridor, turning back, I look at Steel, confused. There are two doors to the right and one straight in front. There are three smaller bedrooms. "We have four bedrooms?"

"Yeah, I have a feeling that we might end up with a lot of visitors. It's gone from being me and Demi, who weren't that close before you came along, to suddenly this massive group of close family who seems to spend a lot of time together."

"Sorry!" I grimace at him. "I know we can be a lot, especially when we're all together, and now I'm part of the Six, too. I appreciate we are a lot, and if we're too much, you need to say, especially now we know who you are. My pas... they're actually all my dads. They brought me up and treated us all the same.

"I got no favouritism from my dad over Bran and Dane, just like they didn't from Pa Bernie, but as old as you are now, they know who you and Demi are. They're gonna want to be a part of that, and eventually, they will slide into that dad role. It's just who they are! So, again, it may be too much; you just have to say!"

"I'm actually looking forward to it. I've not been that close with a lot of people before. I mean, I have my inner circle of brothers here, and Ares and I are really close, but since you came along and got kidnapped, we've all just been a whole lot closer, and when they helped me with this place, they hinted at moving in, although I said no, they laughed it off as if they're gonna at least be hanging out here a lot."

"It's just that whole magnetic personality thing again. Hades, you're fucking lucky to have me!" I bark out, laughing as he slaps my arse and grabs me, pulling me into him. We're still in the corridor, but he pushes me against the wall and kisses the breath out of me. I start to tangle my legs around him and climb him like a fucking tree, till my legs are around his waist, and his dick is grinding into me through our jeans. I rest my head against the wall and pant as we grind against each other, biting down on my neck. I arch my back off the wall. "Fuck, Steel, I'm not gonna last the rest of the tour!"

All of a sudden, he stops grinding and drops me to my feet. I gasp out a moan of disappointment, and he chuckles, that vibrating, clit teasing laugh against my neck. I clench my thighs together to get some friction against my jeans, causing a gasp to seep from my lips.

Grabbing my hand, he drags me back out along the corridor. "Come on, dirty wife. You need to see the rest of it before I let you do dirty things to me!"

Walking into the bathroom, on the right, there's a white rolled top, claw foot bath with pale grey sides. There's a twin set of sinks along the back wall with a large mirror above them. To the left is the large walk-in shower with a bench along one side and the toilet to the left at the side of the door. The room is modern, with grey tiles with little white, black, and grey mosaic inserts all around the room and LED lights overhead. The shower is one of those massive shower heads with the rainfall effect. Still, there's also another shower head on the side wall which makes me remember pleasuring myself in Steel's shower while he watched. As I wonder if that's why he went for the double head, his arms slide around me as he nips at my neck. "Yep, that's why there's two."

"I didn't say anything!"

"Nope, but you got that look on your face, the same one you had that day!"

Smiling at him while he nuzzles into my neck, I think this is one of my favourite things he does. Grabbing my hand and dragging me out of the room again and through the bedroom, he says, "I have a surprise for you!"

"I bet you do!" I wink.

"Not that! Not yet anyway, come on!" As he pulls me into the walk-in, all my stuff is on the left, and his is on the right. There's a bench in the middle and a mirror on each side, opposite each other. I skim my hands along the clothes. There's a garment bag which isn't mine, and as I get to the shoe racks, there are three extra boxes.

"What are these?" I question, frowning at them.

"Open them!"

Reaching out, taking the garment bag, and opening the zip, I see it's a black leather biker jacket with a full skull on the back. The leather is so soft. "It's so fucking gorgeous."

"Open the boxes!" Steel claps excitedly. I open the box, and there's a brown box inside. I recognise the box, the logo.

"You didn't."

"You haven't even opened them!"

"Fuck, Steel, this is too much. You've done too much!" I sit down on the bench, staring at myself in the mirror, shaking, and overwhelmed with everything this man is doing for me.

"Hey, you okay?"

I take a shaky breath. "Yeah, it's just a lot, you know? I'm just overwhelmed. You don't need to buy me all this stuff. You don't need to buy me anything!"

"Baby, I need you to listen to me, okay? Really listen!"

Nodding, I wipe my hands down my face and through my hair, turning on the bench to look at him. He takes a seat beside me and grips my hands in his.

"I helped start this MC nearly ten years ago. I work hard. I've never had anything or anyone to spend anything on. Everything I've earned apart from my bike and necessities has just stayed there, being saved, going nowhere. I spent what I had because I wanted to.

"I don't need it, and I want to buy these things for you. Really, they're also for me. I love you, and I want to spoil you, and you can't stop me. In sickness and in health, remember? Let's call this my sickness, so you have to deal!"

"Ridiculous, you are totally ridiculous. You do realise I have more money than I know what to do with, right, and now, that's yours too?"

"So we can buy more of these... what do you call them... FMBs, because fuck, I got hard while I was looking through them, imagining you in them and the things you were gonna do to me while wearing them. Fuck, I want to buy so, so many more pairs!" He waggles his eyebrows at me and, licking his lips, he laughs. "Open them!"

Opening the first box, they say on them: New Rock SHOE PUNK M-MAG018-C5. Opening the box, they are a stiletto pump shoe with black snakeskin leather with small silver metal skulls around them. They have a silver block carved sole and heel, and fuck. They are sexy. I slide them on, and they fit perfectly.

I walk up and down the walk-in. As I walk back towards Steel, he adjusts his jeans and takes a deep breath.

"Next!" he says excitedly. The next box I open says: New Rock BOOT PUNK M-MAG006-S1. These are shiny black leather ankle boots with a black stiletto heel, a big metal skull on the side, and a leather panel across the front, at the top, and across the toe with studs on. Sliding them on, I walk backwards and forwards, doing a little spin.

"Fuck they're nice! ...Next!"

Laughing at his ridiculousness, I slide them off my feet and open the third box. This box is larger. These say: New Rock PUNK M-MAG025-C1, and holy fuck, I think I about come in my pants. Looking at these, I know right away I'm wearing these tonight.

They're calf-high boots with buckles all the way down. The buckles are a skull head on one side with flames on the other, leading down to a studded band across the toe with a studded panel on the ankle and around the heel. There are studs up the front of the whole boot. They have a carved, shaped silver stiletto heel and a carved silver platform. Standing and turning to face Steel, I slide my jeans off and kick them aside. I slide the boots on, slide my top off, grab the jacket and slip that on. I stand in the boots, my black underwear, a black bra and shorts set, and the black leather jacket.

"Holy fucking shit! Babe, that's hotter than hot!"

"I'm so gonna ride your face wearing this!" I gesture to my whole self.

"Yes fucking please!"

I turned to grab the box I have been looking for, shaking it at Steel. "Come on, baby, I've got a lot of things to thank you for!" I wink at him and drag him up.

"Wait, one more thing. Quickly press this top right silver circle on the mirror on my side!"

"What?"

"Last thing, I promise, quick, as I really wanna see those in action!" He points at my boots and grins like a fucking idiot. I place my box on the bench, walk over to the mirror, and put my finger on the circle. There's a click, the mirror slides back, and lights flicker on inside a secret room. Turning and looking at Steel, he nods, and I walk in.

I step in there. To the left, on the wall, is racking with guns. Some of them mine. All mine are on the left, and all Steel's are on the right, my M4A1 assault rifle, my two Glock 19s, and my Beretta M9 and SIG P226. I got them all from Pa Bernie, and underneath them, all in baskets hanging in place, is enough ammo to start a war. "You been getting acquainted with Pa Bernie?"

"Bernie?"

"Yeah, Bernie runs a security firm and does gun shows. We get all our guns and toys from Bernie."

"Toys? Ahh, that's what he was on about!" He points out the ones that are his, like I don't know, a HECKLER & KOCH P30L and HI-POINT 916 9mm LUGER, a Glock 19 and SIG P226. It seems we have similar tastes in guns as well as boots. Stroking my hand over all the guns, the feel of the steel against my fingertips. To me, guns aren't about protection or firepower. To me, guns are sexy.

I buy guns and knives like Scar buys shoes and purses. I choose them for how they look, how they feel in my hand, how they make me feel, and having them touch my skin. I like sleek, I like black, I like simple and understated, but I also like to feel sexy holding that weapon, feeling the power I have while wielding that particular item.

I don't have a favourite gun, per se. It's all about mood for me. I'm a very sensual person when it comes to choosing my weapons. "Oh shit, Pa Bernie's gonna be pissed at you!" I laugh. "Might wanna rethink your gun supplier!"

"I thought Bernie's legit!"

I laugh again. "He is… most of the time. Well, about sixty-five per cent!" I wink at him. To the right are our knives, the ones I got from Bernie at the gun show. Turning to face that wall, to my left are all my knives and Steel's. To the right, my Ontario 6143 M9 Bayonet, Ontario MK III, Gerber Mark II, Sheffield Fairbairn-Sykes dagger, SOG Seal Team Elite, Emerson Combat Karambit, CRKT Tecpatl and also in pride of place in the centre mounted to the wall is my Sniper Elite 385 Crossbow and arrows.

There are drawers beneath. Sliding the top drawer open, inside are my knuckle dusters. Sliding open the next drawer and my Ninja Hunting Rainbow Kunai throwing knives are in there too. "Steel, this is amazing!" I turn back around and slide my arse onto the drawers, leaning back. I kick my legs, snag him around his waist, and yank him towards me. "Do you know how hot weapons make me?"

"You're here in a leather jacket, underwear and FMBs to die for. Do you know how hot you make me?" he growls, reaching between us and cupping his junk through his jeans and squeezing. I grin at him. "I think you've been harder!"

"I thought you promised never to lie!" He grabs my arse and drags me in closer, slamming his hot mouth into mine, forcing his tongue against mine, both battling for dominance. Grabbing the back of his hair and yanking, a growl comes from his depths, making me grin and grind into him, biting down on his lip.

"You like that?" Breathing heavily, he nods, unbuttoning his jeans and sliding them down. I climb down from the drawers, turning and pushing him back against them, sliding back onto the top of the drawers with his jeans around his ankles.

I climb back up, straddling him, forcing him back against the wall, knocking the knives, placing his hands on the drawers and putting my knees on them. "Be a good boy, and don't touch!" Leaning in and kissing him and biting down on his bottom lip, keeping it between my teeth. "Understand?"

He just nods, lowering myself over his dick, just sliding the tip in still with his lip between my teeth. I suck it into my mouth. His eyes roll into the back of his head. His pupils have already blown and match his raven black hair. The lighting here makes it shimmer like a raven's wing, looking almost purple at some angles and emerald at others.

Sliding my hands up his chest, still hovering over him with just the tip in, I pinch his nipples and twist, flicking his piercings. He groans into my mouth as I kiss him again slowly, sliding myself down the length of him. Once I'm fully seated, I rotate my hips a few times. His head lolls back against the wall as I grind myself into him.

I lift almost totally off of him before slamming myself back down. He makes a sharp intake of breath as I twist a nipple again, leaning up and biting down on his neck just below his ear.

"Fuck, Ray!" he gasps out as I lick over the bite mark. Licking along his collarbone, I slam myself back onto him. He tries to pull his hands free, but I have all my weight on my knees, pinning them to the top of the drawers and slamming down onto him again. I slide my hand up around his throat and turn his head away so I can bite down on his neck again, then lick it. Before biting down on his collarbone, he gasps out a shaky moan as I squeeze my hand on his throat, not to cut his circulation off or try and make him pass out, just to hold him where I want him, just enough to say I'm in charge and you will do what I want. Slamming onto him again, my thrust slams him into the wall, and a couple of the knives clatter to the drawers. Grinding into him, his breaths are laboured, and his eyes are rolling, struggling to focus. Slamming myself around him again, his breath hitches.

He's close, I can tell, so I grind myself into him, rubbing my clit against him as I slam down over and over, one hand still on his throat, the other on his nipple, twisting till he gasps out and closes his eyes gritting his teeth.

"Ray!" he roars and gasps as he comes so hard inside me, I feel it in my chest. I carry on grinding into him as he gasps and twitches at the sensation, filling me up, and only once he has finished and sagged in my hold do I plummet over the edge myself. His gaze meets mine as I scream his name while hammering myself home over the edge, but I don't stop gasping and screaming. I carry on till I come again.

As I sag onto him, his hands release from under my knees, and he grabs me around the waist, holding me to him, maintaining eye contact. "Holy shit …where have you been all my life?"

I smile at him while panting. "Trying to find you! Now I have, I'm never letting you go!" an involuntary spasm causes my hips to rotate against him of their own free will, causing us both to groan. Rocking again, I can feel his come starting to run out of me, coating my thighs and his, and I can't help myself rocking again, causing another groan to escape from those gorgeous plump lips of his. Those groans and growls just vibrate straight through me to my pussy, and when I rock one more time, he reaches over, grabbing the heels of my boots in both hands and slamming me into him.

"Fuck!" I moan out. I'm so sensitive, but with the feel of our come sliding around my clit and my pussy, it turns me on so hard, even more now he's starting to harden again, so he slams me into him again and again.

I grab onto his shoulders to steady myself as he drags me forward by my heels again, slamming me into him and making me gasp as my clit slides over him, pulsing and throbbing from the orgasms I've already had. His eyes twinkle as my pussy clenches around him. I can feel him thickening back up inside me as he drags me onto him again, and again, and again, not giving me a second to recover. He's panting, a layer of slick sweat coating us both, biting down on my neck. I slam my head back as he drags me into him again. My breaths are coming in short and stuttered. It's so intense, my clit's so swollen and tender that every slam, every thrust, every slight slide of our skin together is sending electricity through it into my stomach, up to my throat as I gasp for air. I try to hold onto my sanity, slamming me into him by the heels of my FMBs. They really are turning out to be Fuck Me Boots, quite literally.

I start to see black spots, fireworks, stars, the whole shebang as he slams into me again and again. My breath hitches, and my brain short circuits as I grab down to one of my nipples and tweak so hard I know it will bruise, but it's too much and just enough. I can't help the sensations flinging around my body, every nerve ending alight with what can only be described as cold fire burning me from the inside out. Slamming into me again, I'm gone. I blackout and collapse into Steel's arms. As I crash through the other side of my orgasm, holding me tight around my waist, he reaches up and slides a lock of my hair behind my ears.

"Fucking beautiful!" he whispers against my mouth. "How the fuck did I get so lucky?" He kisses me like he's trying to steal my last breath. We rest our foreheads together, panting into each other's breaths.

"So …you like the secret weapons room, then?"

"Erm, it's not bad, I suppose!"

Digging me in the ribs and causing another spasm to radiate through me and me to grind against him, I buck and moan.

"Nope, can't do anymore. Need a minute. Shit, that tickles like fuck, can't cope!" I gasp out as he chuckles against me and kisses me so slowly, like he's telling me the promises he's making for the rest of our lives, reaching up and cupping his cheeks with my palms. "I fucking love you, husband!"

"Fuck, I love you, wife!"

Only Hades himself knows how long we sit there staring into each other gazes and sharing languid and unhurried kisses, tongues tasting and flicking across lips, hands gently roaming skin, totally losing ourselves to the feel of each other. Finally pulling away and sliding me to the ground, my legs are still wobbly.

"Easy there, Bambi!" He laughs as I try to stand in the six-inch heels while waiting for the blood to rush back to my legs so I can feel them.

"Dick!" I laugh as he slides off the drawers, his legs wobbling too, sliding his jeans back up but leaving them hanging on his hips. That delicious Adonis belt directing me down behind his boxers. I lick my lips as he reaches over and kisses the breath out of me, sliding his hands over my shoulder, dropping my jacket to the floor, throwing me over his shoulder, and smacking my arse.

"Fuck, I love fucking you. I can smell us so bad!"

He slides his fingers between my legs, walking me back through the walk-in and throwing me down on the bed. "Wonder if we taste as good as we smell!" He slides his thumbs under my shorts and yanks them down and over my boots, running his thumbs through my lips. I can feel him seeping out of me. "Fuck, that's hot!" Next thing, his head's between my legs, and he's pushing his fingers inside of me, pushing his come back in, as he licks up across my clit. I buck my back off the bed. He licks again. "Fuck, we taste good together!"

Licking and thrusting his tongue into me and plunging his fingers inside at the same time. I gasp out, and as I do, he slides up me, slamming his mouth against mine. I can taste us both on his lips, and I groan. His tongue slides into my mouth and his fingers slide into my pussy, and his thumb rides across my sensitive bean.

"Hades!" I breathe into his mouth. "You're actually trying to kill me!" Grinning against my mouth as he kisses me, our taste filling my mouth with the taste of lust and longing, he removes his hands from me and slowly slides his dick back inside me, slamming my head back against the pillows and my hips up to meet his.

I grab the back of his head and slam his mouth into mine again, breaths panting and becoming more erratic. We are both so sensitive, but neither of us can stop sliding up and down my body, flesh on flesh. There's so much come sliding around that he slides against my clit in the most erotic of ways. My nipples tighten as the heat rises again. "Fuck!"

"Hang on, baby!" Slamming into me again, our breaths hitch and gasp, so sensitive, so delicious, so addictive. I fall over the edge, and he follows me into the darkness. I think we both pass out from orgasm overdose. I'm pretty sure that's a thing!

My mind wakes before I do. There's a pressure on my chest, almost a feeling of restraint. I calm my breath, slowly opening my eyes, only to see the most beautiful, soft, relaxed face across my shoulder and a tight, muscular body pinning me to the bed. Clenching and pulsing my pussy, I groan. He's still inside me. I smile to myself. We must have fucked to the point of exhaustion… Again. Something about the feel of him, semi-hard, semi-soft, makes my hips squirm underneath him, not enough to wake him, just enough to 'wake him' he's so responsive to me.

I pulse again and feel him thicken. Fuck, I feel so horny like this. It's like all those years I denied myself proper touch. Now I can't get enough of it, enough of him. Still with the come from last night covering my thighs and coating my clit, flexing my hips, the tingle shoots through me. Fuck, he really is gonna be the death of me. I've gone from having sex a few times over the years after deciding men just aren't on my agenda to some dirty little cock whore who needs to ride his beautiful, amazingly talented dick constantly.

Sliding my arms around his arse, kneading his cheeks, I roll my hips, closing my eyes as the sensation grows. Fuck, I'm close. I can feel him stir, but I hope he won't mind. I tilt again, gasping as my clit rubs against him, rocking my hips. His eyes slowly open, and a fucking panty-dropping smile creeps across his face reaching down and grabbing my wrists.

He slides my arms above my head. "Morning, wife! What do we have here, then?" Sliding his body up mine and back down again, I gasp again. Fuck, he knows what I'm doing now. He's gonna slowly torture me. "Were you being a dirty little wife and fucking me while I was sleeping?" I nod as I bite my lip, and he slides up and down me again. My eyes roll back in my head. My nipples pebble as his chest rubs against them, causing them to pulse with sensitivity.

Swapping my wrists into one hand, he slides the other down and flicks and pinches my nipple while licking along my jaw, down my neck, across my collarbone, to my other nipple and pulling it between his teeth. Sliding himself back up and down my body creating delicious friction, his muscular arms slide along my toned ones. His nipples pebble as he drags himself back up and down my body, causing another gasp to seep through my lips, initiating a groan that comes from his core vibrating against me.

"Were you trying to come on me without waking me, Sunshine?" I shrug my shoulders. I wasn't intentionally trying to come without him. He is just too delicious not to grind myself into whenever I get the chance. Biting down hard on my nipple and pinching the other, he slides up me, less gentle this time, slamming into me, causing me to see stars. Fuck, I love it when he's rough.

"Be a good girl and hold on to the headboard. Do not move those hands!" I nod, looking up at my wrists. The bed's massive with solid, rustic-looking wood, thick and sturdy. I push my palms against it pushing myself back towards Steel.

I don't want to answer him. I think my voice will betray me and show him exactly how down for this I am. I've been a walking contradiction since I met Steel. I have always been dominant in the bedroom since having a few lousy relationships growing up. I felt I needed to control my own pleasure, and that's what I did. Usually a fast fuck and fuck off was my go-to. I'm always in control, but with Steel, there's a lot of push and pull. He likes to be dominant but also likes me to be, and he will let me. I love the feeling of giving up control for a while, but I find I'm the same. If I feel he wants to be dominant, I step back and allow it, revelling in the total lack of control. It's refreshing and freeing at the same time.

He gently slides his hands down the outside of my outstretched arms down the sides of my rib cage, causing little twitches and flinches. I love it when his whole weight is pinning me down. It feels amazing to know this solid, sturdy Adonis is mine to control when I want, as he runs his fingers back up, taking one nipple between his thumb and finger and squeezing.

I feel my core clench as he groans, causing the vibrations to trickle out all over my body. Sliding his other arm up towards my neck, he clenches tight around my throat, causing a gasp, and my eyes widen, not in fear, but in excitement. He rises up over me and bites down on his lip, pausing for a second before pulling back and slamming into me. I groan out a moan as he bottoms out inside me. Shit, that feels so good. My eyes roll back, and I can't focus, so I just relax into it as his fingers clench around my throat again. He slams back into me, and my eyes fly open to find his gaze. He has the most feral grin stretching across his face as he thrusts back, slamming into me again, trying to drive me through to the garage.

I'm pretty sure he's gonna manage it, too. I gasp as he bottoms out again. The pleasurable, painful feeling of his thick hard dick pounding into me relentlessly makes me spiral. The way he fucks me is addictive. I can't explain it, but I love a lot of pain mixed in with my pleasure, and god, does this demon of a husband of mine know how to deliver. With one hand still on my throat, tensing and relaxing, he thrusts in and out. The other slides down to my hip, pinning me to the bed hard enough to leave bruises.

I'm totally aware of the burning sensation his skin creates on mine. I can feel each fingertip as if it's trying to fuse itself to my skin. Pinning me to the bed, he slams into me again and again, and I become weightless. I feel lightheaded, like I'm floating. My eyes roll in my head, heat spreads all around me, and it feels like the apartment is on fire.

"Look at me!" he growls. That noise causes me to tremble. This vibration in his tone slides around my insides like a pinball machine lighting every nerve, every cell, lighting everything up like he's thrown a Molotov cocktail. My eyes fling open, and I slowly focus on his stunningly beautiful face. I'm in awe of him as he squeezes tighter around my throat and slams into me again.

I gasp. "Fuck! Fuck! Fuck!" I bellow. Shit, this's gonna cripple me. I can feel my insides on fire, my cells melting, my core burning in a raging fire, my heart and lungs white with heat as it erupts throughout my body, urging me to arch into him while he holds me down. My breath stops altogether, not because of his hold on my throat, but just from the overwhelming sensations he's sending through my body.

I roar as I come, never taking my eyes from his, the grey swirling vortexes that threaten to steal my soul, but in all honesty, I think I'd hand it over willingly. My orgasm builds and builds, and I can't hold back. The roar just keeps coming, being dragged out of me from the depths of my core, pulsing through me like an atomic weapon.

I clench, squeeze, and pulse around his punishing dick as he keeps thrusting throughout my orgasm. As I finally come down, my breath shakes out as I feel like I've held it in for an eternity. My body relaxes, physically spent. He thrusts again, tightening my throat and slamming into me one last time.

He thunders through me with a sick intensity. I can feel his streams of come slamming into me, hot and burning my core. I gasp as it all becomes too much, too sensitive, too intense, too emotional. I feel like our souls have just been slammed together with such an intensity that we have finally achieved it and fused them together for the rest of eternity. Relaxing his fingers around my throat, he collapses against me, both of us gasping for breath, the feel of each other's hearts pounding.

Moving my hand from above my head, I slide some of that obsidian hair from his forehead, lean down, and kiss the spot. Unable to say anything, we cling to each other like we need each other to survive. My eyes start to close, my breaths even out, and my whole body starts to ebb gently into sleep.

There's an almighty banging on the door. "You fuckers dead in there, or what?" Snapping our heads up with a groan, Steel kisses my lips as he slides off me, grabs his jeans, and heads out to the door. When he comes back, I'm starfished on my back on the bed, unable to move, totally spent still in my bra and boots.

"Baby, you need to get up and ready. Everyone's here!"

"Everyone...?" I murmur.

"Yep!" He laughs. "Your pas, Demi, Scar and Pops, apparently, are all in the apartment. We're late!"

"Fuck!"

"Nope, no more fucking. We need to get up!"

"Cock blocking bastards!" I mumble out. "Shit, I'm gonna have to walk out there to get to the shower, aren't I? Fuckers!"

Steel laughs, pointing to the side of me. "Ensuite!" This is the only room I still haven't looked around. I hadn't paid much attention to the surroundings when we ended up in this room.

"Fuck, I love you!" As I slide off the bed, there's a small ensuite with a shower still big enough for two with a toilet and sink. Throwing my boots and bra off, I dive in, scrubbing myself clean, and trust me. It took a lot of scrubbing, I ache and I'm tender in all the best places.

Steel leans on the door frame, watching me, then frowning and moving back into the bedroom. "I'll grab us some clothes, I can't stand there and watch that any longer, or I'm gonna end up in there with you, and we will never leave this place, and everyone is still out there waiting!"

Laughing as he walks off, I hurry up. As I get out of the shower, Steel gets in, and then I'm fully aware of his predicament. "Shit!"

"Exactly!" He laughs. "Now fuck off and get dressed. You're distracting me in that towel!"

Grinning, I leave, grabbing the clothes Steel has laid out for me. Red bra and shorts, black ripped jeans, my New Rock Trail boots, and a Harley Davidson vest top which I know is his as it's massive on me, and you can see the red bra through the arm holes. Scraping my hair into a pony and throwing on some red lipstick and mascara, I swan out to the living room.

"'Bout fucking time!" Pa Cade points at me. "What time do you call this?"

I shrug. "I don't know, and I give no fucks!" Everyone laughs as I walk over to the coffee maker and make two more cups of coffee. Steel walks out of the bedroom, still rubbing the towel through his hair, wearing a tight black T-shirt stretched over his muscles and faded blue jeans tight on his arse and thighs and stuffed into his biker boots. Walking over to me, he tosses the towel on the counter, grabbing my hips and spinning me while lifting me to sit on the counter. I run my fingers through his hair, taming it slightly, pulling on the back as I lean in and kiss him.

"Blech!" Pa JJ grimaces. "You two are disgusting!"

I smile at Steel, and he knows exactly what I'm thinking. If they think this is disgusting, they don't want to know what happened most of the night.

Grabbing his coffee, he takes a big gulp. "Okay, so what's the plan?"

"You and Demi are coming with us. We have business to sort out. Scar and Pops get the pleasure of Squirt's company!" Pa Bernie laughs.

"Hey, I'm a delight!"

"Yeah, sure!" Pa Steven laughs.

"Wankers!"

Steel just shakes his head at us all, pulling me off the counter and slapping my arse. "Come on then, the quicker we get sorted, the quicker we get back!" Giving me a panty-wetting kiss, he grabs his jacket, and they head out the door.

Turning to Scar and Pops, I ask, "Wanna have a look around before we go anywhere?"

"Sure!" Pops grins as Scar laughs. "I thought you'd never ask!"

We wander back into the living area. "Fucking hell, Ray, this place is amazing. You really had no idea?"

"Nope, none! I can't believe he got it so right when technically we don't really know each other that well!"

"Yeah, that's not true. You're like the same person. He's just better looking!"

"Bitch!"

"Come on, you two, or we're gonna be late!" Pops throws the keys to a rental at me, some type of minivan. "You drive. You know the area better than me!"

"Why can't I drive?" Scar asks, genuinely frowning.

"Scar, I want to talk to you on the way and don't want you distracted."

"Shit, that doesn't sound good!" Reaching the minivan, I climb in the front, and they both climb in the back.

By the time we arrive in Ravenswood, Scar's crying, and they're both hugging. Pops will keep the firm in the UK, semi-retire out here, but help Scar set up her law firm and work for her part-time. Once they get up and running, it will be a big help as Scar is still considered new and will need to pass the state bar exam, but together, it will set her up.

Pulling into the car park in the centre of Ravenswood, we head over to the estate agents next to the hardware store I'd used for Demi's place. There are three properties we are going to check out. One is an office downstairs with a flat above that already comes with a tenant. It's on the end of the row with Beauty's Party Planning place on it. The other is a big glass double-fronted store, almost twice the size of the last place, with a large apartment above. This is actually next door to Beauty's place. Hers is a double-fronted place too, and the third is a tiny little office above a bakery.

Heading back to check out the second place again, the downstairs is a large open-plan area with enough room for at least four large desks as well as the other things an office would need, with a kitchen and bathroom and two store rooms out the back. It seems like a no-brainer. Going back upstairs, the apartment leads off the office, so it isn't really suitable to rent out, although it does have a separate back entrance from a small courtyard.

Pops thinks it's perfect for him to move in as Scar's going to move into one of the lodges with Ares. They're gonna start doing it up soon. Upstairs there's a large open-plan living kitchen, diner, a bathroom, and two bedrooms, all off the main living area. A door out of the kitchen leads down to the enclosed courtyard, which has two parking spaces and enough room for a table and chairs or something like that.

"It's perfect!" Pops exclaims. "What do you think, Scar?" It looks right out over the big car park that sits in the centre of Ravenswood. There's a little grass area with some trees to one side of the car park, and there's a tattooist run by a couple of the guys from the club. It sits between the gym and the estate agents, looking out across the centre, the estate agents, gym and hardware stores, a couple of clothing stores, a thrift store, a coffee shop, a clothing store, a bank, a book shop, a dress shop and Beauty's place. That's just around the central area. There are more side streets littered with smaller shops.

Scar nods. "It really is." She smiles. "Are we really doing this?"

He grabs us both for a hug. "I have a really good feeling about this!" Pops smiles at us both. We head over to the estate agents and sort out the paperwork.

"We just need to wait for the credit checks to come through, the funds, and then the place is yours. It's empty, so as soon as everything is cleared, it's yours!" the estate agent says, shaking all our hands.

"So today we bought a building!" Scar laughs, skipping out of the estate agents.

"Dinners on me!" I sing to them both.

"Fuck yes!" Scar exclaims, throwing her arms around my shoulders.

Walking over to the car park, we see the pas, Demi, and Steel coming out of the bank. Demi and Steel both look a little pale.

"Hey!" I shout over the car park as their heads shoot up. Steel strides over to me, throwing his arms around me.

"Fuck I need this!" He grabs me into a bear hug.

"Everything okay?" Shaking his head, he just holds me looking over his shoulder. Demi just looks lost. I wave her to come over, and as she reaches me, I drag her in between Steel and me and pull them both closer.

"What the fuck's happened?"

They both just squeeze a little tighter. The pas head over to Scar and Pops. As Pa Cade walks past, he grips Steel's shoulder. "Just a little too much information, I think."

"You said you were gonna go easy! You said you'd fucking look after them and just give them the basics to get their head around it all first! …What the fuck did you say!"

"Easy, tiger!" Pa Cade raises his hands in defence. "We did the basics, bare minimum!" He glares at me. "It was just a little too much, so we're taking everything a little steadier than we planned, okay? Now back her the fuck up!" He nods at me, clearly meaning my inner Reaper is showing, but fuck, I'm so protective of these two.

I nod, knowing exactly what he means. Since my dad died, I have stepped fully into his role, his share in the business. I know how lucrative it is, and that's just the Adventure Centre. I think Pa Cade is saying they don't know about the other businesses yet! We also share the security business with Pa Bernie, among other not-so-legitimate dealings. Everything's split equally, so even though Demi and Steel will have to share their cut, it has been sitting there for twenty-three years untouched.

Dad and my pas take a percentage of the profits and put it back into the business accounts, and then a percentage towards our "other ventures," and then what's left is split six ways. They don't take a wage; they just split the profits at the end of the year as they all live on the property. There isn't really anything they need to spend, so I know what Dad had with interest, they would probably both be getting around six hundred to eight hundred thousand from the Adventure Centre alone.

Demi pulls away first, looking into my eyes with hers glazed over. "Just over a million dollars." She gasps. "Each!"

Steel looks up at me. "What the fuck, Ray?"

I shrug. "What can I say? I told you I was loaded. The pas are extremely competent businessmen.

"I don't know what to do with all this information! Or money, or information!" Steel stares through me, barely registering everything.

"Come on, you. I'm taking us all out to dinner, Mr and Miss Moneybags!" Sliding an arm around each of their waists, they just nod and let me lead them over to the restaurant. It's a smaller Italian place but looks nice from the street. Clapping them both on the back and shoving them through the door, I say, "Welcome to the family!" I laugh out loud.

After eating, I grab a quick word with Pa Bernie. I have a proposition, well, maybe more of an idea I want to run by him. I send Demi back with Steel. I get Scar and Pops to wait for me. After getting back from Ravenswood, I think Demi and Steel could use some time alone together, so I make myself scarce and head to the gym with Roach. After kicking his arse around the gym for two hours, we head inside for a drink. Wearing my cut around this place feels weird. It doesn't feel real.

Ares has said I need to get my ink soon and also attend church to be a fully-fledged member, but with the wedding and everything, it has been a little chaotic. Scar's in the bar with Beauty. After chatting to the girls, I head up to Ares's office. It's about time we had a chat about what's expected of me without the prospecting. I don't feel I have really paid my dues. I knock on the door.

"Yeah?"

Slinging the door open, I say, "Hey, Boyband!"

I slam the door behind me, heading to the couch and lounging on it.

"Hey Ray, come in. Why don't you make yourself goddamn comfy!"

"Thanks!"

"Sarcasm, Ray. Ever hear of it?"

"Erm, I'm not sure, don't think so! You?"

"Fuck, you're irritating!"

I mock a gasp. "Ouch, wounded!"

"If you weren't Scar's sister and Steel's wife, I would totally kick you out of my club!"

"Ha!" I bark out. "Liar! You only just made me a member. You want me for something! What is it you're after, Boyband?"

"I'm not after anything from you, Ray!"

"Ah, this is about Scar, then! Spill, Boyband. I can't help if I don't know what you want! Honesty is always the best way!"

Kicking my feet up on the arm of the sofa and leaning back, I drag a pillow behind my head. "Come on, spill!"

"Fine, but is this a Boyband-Ray or Ares-Reaper conversation?"

Sitting up, placing my elbows on my knees and tapping my hand on the sofa at the side of me, he glances over and comes over to sit next to me. I turn my body to face him and pull my knees onto the sofa.

"Whatever you need it to be… Brother!"

He blows out a breath. "I asked Scar to marry me, and she said no!"

"Do you want to marry her?"

"Well, I… I just thought… "

"That's a no, then!"

"It's not like that. I just never wanted to get married, ever. I can see myself with Scar forever. I can't imagine anything else, and I don't think I ever want to get married …ever."

"So what's the issue then? If you don't want to, and she said no."

"I just don't know if I can lose her. She's my forever, Ray, just marriage isn't a part of that, and I'm worried now she's said no, she's gonna go back to the UK!"

"I think you need to speak to her. Have you seen her today?"

"No, well, not since this morning!"

"Talk to her, honestly. I think you'll be surprised!"

"Hang on, that's not what you came here for, is it? You came to see me."

I smile at him. "I'm not sure what you want from me, Boyband, what the club wants from me. I'm the first woman. I'm the first not to prospect. How do the guys feel about all that? Do they think I'm getting preferential treatment? I wanna make my own way. I don't want it handed to me on a plate, and I still don't know what you do here!"

I scrub my hand down my face. "Now the reality is sinking in. I'm not sure what my role is."

"Okay, so we trade guns and weapons, offer security, safe passage, run the garage as you know, and a bike chop shop. We occasionally steal cars, but that's more of a nostalgia thing, and we own the tattooist in Ravenswood as well as a nightclub at Castle Cove. The guys take turns to run security there, and we launder money through our legit businesses."

"Still not seeing what I can bring to the table unless you want to get a new weapons supplier."

"Firstly, you can't think of anything you can bring to the table? Do you have no ideas about anything? And secondly, a new supplier? Who do you know? You run an Adventure Centre in the UK. Scar's told me all about it! But you do have talents. We can use you, Ray, and what is it they say? Keep your friends close and your enemies closer?" He wiggles his eyebrows at me.

"So you see me as the enemy, nice! Is that all?"

"Look, Ray, you're not the enemy, but you're definitely a wild card, and honestly, I would sooner have you on my side than on someone else's. Steel's obviously told me about the whole 'his dad being another pa' and all that, but I don't get what that has to do with anything."

"So my pas are all ex-military. We run an Adventure Centre in the UK and a security firm here, amongst other ventures. Also, Pa Bernie and Bran run a gun shop and tour gun shows buying and selling guns."

"Huh!"

"Huh, that's all you've got to say?"

"Shit, Ray, I had no idea. I knew you had a lot of hardware, but I didn't know where it came from. It's good stuff, though. I just don't think Bernie could handle the numbers we shift, but I will bear it in mind, we've been trying to make a partnership with The Armoury, but we can't seem to get a leg in at the minute, so we're working with the Cruzes!"

I huff a laugh at that. "No worries, Boyband, but what I came for is that I need an office!"

"I'm sorry, I thought for a minute as the Enforcer, you said you need an office!"

"You're not as old as I thought then, and there's clearly nothing wrong with your hearing either!"

"You know I can go off you quite quickly!"

The laugh that ricochets out of me is legendary. "You, my friend, are a dick! But yes, I want an office. Got anything hidden away or a bunker somewhere?"

"You serious?"

"Yup!"

"Will you help me with Scar? ...And leave *my* office?"

"Yup!"

"Great! The barn's yours. There's a grain storage room under it, have at it!"

"Oooh, thanks, Boyband, that was easy. Oh, and I'm taking down the Hellhounds!" I stand to head out.

"Hold up, motherfucker. Taking the Hellhounds down?"

"Yep, I can either do it, then properly patch in, or I can patch in, and you can come along for the ride. Either way, I'm ending them."

"So, rules for the club, Ray. You can't just go off half-cocked doing your own thing. You're part of this now, so if you have information or a plan, you bring it to me, we hold church, vote, and decide what happens as a club. If it's sensitive, we have the inner circle go through things first, okay?"

"Okay, fine. I've noticed the guys always wear their cuts around here but not when they go out, well, mostly when they go out. Why's that?"

"We like to keep our identities secret, or at least quiet. We only wear cuts when we're riding as a club recreationally. That way, we can pass ourselves off as a motorcycle club that just rides, and not as a one-percenter club. That way, we keep our business to a minimum. A lot of our guys are part-timers, too, meaning they have jobs elsewhere, like you and Dozer with the garage."

Going through the rules with me and chatting about expectations, we decide I'm going to look into the Hellhounds and dig around, as apparently, I'm a unicorn. That's what he called me, something that doesn't exist in the actual club world.

I should be able to go to other clubs without drawing as much suspicion, so that's my plan to gather some information before bringing my idea to the club. Heading into the bar, I clap Boyband on the shoulder. "Just be honest, yeah?"

He nods and heads over to Scar, joining the boys for pool and darts. "Come on, guys, let's see how messy we can make this!"

I laugh as I strut over. "Damn, girl, that cut looks fine on you!"

I twirl around with my best model pose. "I know, right?"

Tank laughs. "You're an idiot!"

"Rude!" I sling my arm around Viking. "So when are you and Carmen getting married?"

"Fuck you, Ray. Don't say shit like that out loud!"

I bark a laugh at him. "Fine, rack 'em up! Dice, can I grab a quick word?" While the guys rack them up and get the cues sorted, I tell Dice what I need, and he says it won't be a problem and to give him a few weeks. Heading back to the table, I snatch the bottle of tequila up and neck, at least five shots worth.

Priest snatches it from my lips. "Hey, I'm playing catch up, no fair!"

"Yeah, well, you're on my team, and I wanna win, so I need you to be able to see straight!"

After playing pool and darts for the rest of the night, I'm absolutely shit-faced. The guys put me in Steel's old room as there's no way we will make it up the stairs to the apartment.

"Isn't it normally the husband that stays out till all hours getting drunk with his friends?" I roll over, squinting at the large imposing figure in the doorway and roll back, groaning. I'm fully clothed, face down, starfished sideways across the bed. My mouth feels like Gandhi's flip-flop, it's too bright, and my husband is giving me the fanny flutters. My head is trying to pound out a resounding no at me, but my nether regions are making me hot and squirmy.

"What time is it?"

"Six."

"Argh, too early!" I grab the pillow and place it over my head as he just laughs at me, walking over and flipping me onto my back. I make a hissing noise at him as my arm flings over my face!

"Ray!"

"Uh-huh!"

"Let's get you home!"

"Urgh, can't I stay here? It's so still and quiet and not outsidey at all!"

"You're ridiculous!" He pulls me to my feet. "Over the shoulder, or can you walk?"

"I can, but I don't want to!"

"Over the shoulder, it is, then." He throws me onto his shoulder and smacks my arse as he walks down the corridor. Tank is yawning in his doorway.

"Next time, text your stupid husband where you are so he doesn't wake me up at stupid o'clock to find your stupid ass!" I don't reply. I just lift my hands, flipping him the bird as we walk past, as Steel carries me draped over his shoulder, head hanging down and arms dangling. I close my eyes and huff out a breath as we head through the bar.

There's a bark of laughter as Ares, Scar and a couple of the guys are in there. "Did you all shit the bed? What's wrong with you people? It's the middle of the fucking night!" I toss out as we head through the bar. I'm normally a morning person, but I'm pretty sure I was drinking till after four, so six is still the middle of the night. Ares laughs again, and I flip him off too.

Steel just keeps walking and smacks my arse again as we head out the door. This time, an erotic moan falls from my lips as I squeeze my thighs together, but that just makes him chuckle, and that just makes it worse as my pants flood and my heat rises.

"Fuck you and your stupid sexiness!" I fire at him as he laughs again, and I groan. "Argh!" I rub my face before letting my arms dangle again as Steel pushes through the door of the apartment.

Demi is just coming out of the kitchen with a coffee. "Morning, Ray!" She chuckles as we pass by. I reach out and snag her coffee right before it reaches her lips. "Hey!"

Lifting up and taking a swig, I say, "Argh, that's good shit!" Steel places me on my feet, careful not to spill my stolen coffee. I slide onto the counter and chug some more. "So, what are we doing today?"

"I need to take Demi back. She's got work today, although I don't know why she's bothering!"

"In that case, then I'm going to bed!" Grabbing him by the neck of his shirt, I drag him to me, kissing him. As I push him back, I slide off the counter. "Come wake me up nice when you get back!" Winking at him, I toss Demi a smile over my shoulder. "Later, gator!"

She just stares at me, shaking her head as I stride into our room. I throw my clothes in a heap and slide into bed, and sleep.

Ray

I wake with Steel's head between my thighs and a smile on my face, "Afternoon, husband." I gasp out.

He grins at me but carries on licking, biting, sucking, and nipping. I grab his hair and shamelessly grind myself against his face. He moans and pulls me deeper, sliding his tongue inside me and sliding it around to my clit, tugging slightly and sucking.

I gasp as he slides a finger in, stroking my insides and making me quiver. As I grind down, he slides in another finger as he starts to pump faster, sliding in another finger from his other hand for a second before sliding down and sliding it into my arse. I groan out and grind into him again.

"Fuck, Steel!" He slides his fingers in and out of me and tongues my clit. The next nip, I gasp and then go rigid. Fuck, my orgasm slides over me, pulsing through me as I try to focus, but I see stars and taste colours. All I can do is tag along for the ride. As the heat rises, my skin pebbles. My nipples harden like bullets, and my eyes roll to the back of my head. Gasping as I come down, Steel grabs my hips and throws me over, yanking me onto all fours. He slams straight into me, bottoming out before retreating and slamming back again. I've barely taken a breath after the orgasm. Everything's tingling, pulsing and I feel like my skin is vibrating with need as he pounds into me making me feel like there's a tsunami raging under my skin.

As he continues slamming into me, he slaps my arse. "That's for staying out most of the night!" I moan and grind back into him. *Slap.* "That's for making me worry and sleep on my own!" Groaning again, I gasp as my orgasm rocks through me, still slamming into me, rhythmically driving me insane. He follows me over the edge pumping into me till he's empty.

Collapsing on my back, he pins me to the bed nipping my neck. "Sleep well?"

"Mmm, woke up better, though. What else do I need to do to get you to spank me?" As he laughs, kissing my neck and snuggling in for a few minutes, we just stay there, his warm breath skating over my skin, making it pebble, but I can't find the will to move. As Steel shifts, I stifle a groan as I feel his come seep out down my thighs. He slaps my arse and slides off me.

"Sorry, babe, but we've got places to go, people to see. Go get cleaned up. We need to leave in"—he looks down at his watch and grimaces—"ten minutes, babe!"

"Shit, seriously?" I dive off the bed and into the shower. Steel must go in the main bathroom as he's walking back into our room with a towel wrapped around him. "Hey, no fair!"

He laughs. "Beautiful, you know damn well that if we don't shower separately, we won't be out of here on time!"

"Fine!" I throw on some jeans, a long-sleeved T-shirt, my biker boots, and a leather jacket. We head out climbing on our bikes.

Steel shouts over. "Keep up, Sunshine!" We peel out of the clubhouse parking lot.

Pulling up outside a nondescript building, bars over the windows, razor wire around the fence and a security guard with a gun at the gate, we're let through. Getting off the bikes, Steel reaches for my hand, and we walk up the few steps to the door. Pressing the button and stepping back to look at the camera, the door buzzes, and we walk in. Inside is a wall with a hatch that has bars across it. There's an older lady behind it. She must be in her sixties.

"Steel, Leonard is waiting for you. I will buzz you through!"

"Thanks, Sandy."

I smile at her as he pulls me through the door.

An older, bald man rises from his chair behind the desk. "Steel, so good to see you again, and this must be the beautiful wife." He takes my hand and kisses the back of it, but it feels sweet rather than creepy, almost chivalrous and gentlemanly. I give him a gentle smile, and as Steel shakes his hand, he walks back around the desk. He reaches into the drawer and pulls out two ring boxes. I look between them and Steel as he snatches them up and stuffs them in his pocket. "Don't you want to check them?"

"Do I need to?"

"I would prefer it that way. If we have a problem, it can be rectified."

Steel steps to the side and quickly glances into the boxes smiling at Leonard, then back at me. "You've outdone yourself, Leonard! I appreciate the rush order." Winking at me, he grabs my hand, and we leave.

As we pull back up to the clubhouse, we climb the stairs to our apartment, walking in through the door. Steel's behind me as he shuts the door. I turn to face him as he slides to his knee, holding out the ring boxes. "Ray, Baby, will you stay married to me?"

I laugh. "Forever, I will stay married to you forever." As he opens the box, my jaw drops. As he takes the rings out and places them on my finger, there's a wedding ring and an engagement ring. They're both maybe silver or platinum. There's what looks like a black diamond in the centre with a black onyx skull on either side and a black onyx rose on the top, and on the bottom, there are some small gems, maybe diamonds edging it. It's fucking stunning, and the wedding band is thin and slides against the other ring. It's black and silver encrusted with diamonds. It's the most stunning thing I've ever seen.

I'm fully aware that I'm standing next to the kitchen with my mouth open, literally shaking. Steel slides the rings on my finger and stands up, cupping my face and kissing me. "I had them made special." Then hands me the other box opening it. A thicker ring with the same skulls and a rose is in the centre. They match perfectly as I slide it out of the box, taking Steel's hand.

"So you wanna stay married to me?"

"Fuck yes!" he barks out as I slide the ring on, and he picks me up and spins me around.

"Fuck, I love you!"

Ray

The next week I spend working at the garage, catching up with my pas, and spying on the Hellhounds. Wearing Steel's joggers, hoodie, and a baseball cap, I've been sliding in with a few of the lower scummy guys. I've been tracking these slimy bastards and even slid into their clubhouse as a hang-around a couple of times. They're fucking gross animals!

I'm going to kill every last one of them and wipe them from existence. From what I can figure out, they're trying to get in with a lesser group, someone who's trying to make waves, Dillon or Dalton or something like that, according to the lower guys. I'm wondering if it's Dante. They're still working toward human trafficking, but the Castillo Cartel and the Reapers have been putting the word out that they won't tolerate human trafficking, so most are running scared, but the Hellhounds are gearing up.

Pa Bernie's been keeping his ear to the ground, and they're looking for gun suppliers. We have contacts with all the local suppliers, so we've put the word out to steer clear. We decide to go ahead with the job for the judge. I've talked Bernie into letting me still do it. I'm hoping we can get information from him that may be of use as at least something we can sell.

Heading into the clubhouse with Steel, the guys are playing pool. Ares and Scar are in the booth with Dozer and Beauty, and Roach is behind the bar. My phone rings. It's Carmen. "Hey, girl, you good?"

"Yes, Ray, thank you, how are you?"

"I'm good. What's up?"

"Nothing. I just had a call from Catalina. She's staying with a friend and asked me to message you!"

"Really? What's she need?"

"Nothing, just asked me to tell you she got top marks on a paper she did for school yesterday."

"Yesterday? I spoke to her last night, and she didn't mention anything about a paper! Carmen, what exactly did she say? Word for word?"

"She said she was staying with her friend for a few days as they were finishing a project and that I need to tell you about getting top marks on her paper!"

"Carmen, what was the paper about?"

She didn't say, just said she was working on a project about Santa Muerte!"

"Santa Muerte? Carmen, are you sure?"

"Yeah, definitely!" As I look around, the boys are all watching me. My body language is tense, to say the least. I must have paled, and I'm pacing while I talk.

"Carmen, you need to listen to me, okay? Lock down the villa, get to your safe room and stay there till I get there. Call Tali's friend and check if she is there, but she won't be. Carmen, she's in trouble, that's why she needed you to give me this message. Do what I say quickly. I'm on my way, okay?"

I don't give her a chance to say anything. I hang up.

"Ares, there's an issue. I'm heading out. I gotta go tool up. Something's happened to Tali. Dice, see if you can track her movements after school today and call me?"

As I head for the door, Steel steps in front of me. "Baby, what's up? Talk to me."

"Tali's gone. I need to get to Carmen!"

"Okay, let's tool up. Leave in five, okay?"

Viking spins around. "I'm coming!"

"We're all coming!" Tank nods.

"Give me five. I can set a search going and then set off; you'll need me there too!" So Dice runs to his room. Tank, Viking, Priest and Blade go to tool up. Ares gives me a nod. He knew things would be serious if I called him by his name and not Boyband.

"Ray, do you need anything?" Dozer shouts as I'm about to head out of the clubhouse.

"I'm good, Dozer. Sorry to leave you hanging again!"

He shakes his head. "Don't worry, just find her!"

Nodding. I run out the door and up to the apartment.

Grabbing my phone out of my pocket, I put in my 'alternative' PIN number, turning my phone into the secure direct line. Ringing twice, the automated voice chimes through as I race through the apartment to the weapons room.

"VERIFICATION."

"Sierra 8674463," I recite.

"VERIFIED! ... IDENTIFICATION?"

"Black Queen, Delta 1."

"CONFIRMED! ... REQUEST?"

"Patch to White King, Alpha 1!"

"White King!" the disguised male voice comes across.

"Request backup on standby, availability?"

"White King and Black Rook available!"

"Await further instructions, full tact ready!"

"Affirmative!"

Hanging up, I grab my backpack and load it up with guns, ammo, knives, grenades, smoke bombs, and knuckle dusters. I grab my jacket and helmet and run for my bike. Steel is hot on my heels, and the boys barrel out of the clubhouse door, packed and ready. We load up and get out of there!

Storming into the villa, I call Carmen. "I'm here. What do you know?"

"I'm coming. Meet me by the pool." She throws her arms around me.

"Ray, what's happening?"

"I don't know yet, Carmen, but we're on it, okay? Bear with me, okay? I got you."

She nods and grabs my hand. On the outside, she appears calm, every bit the cartel queen she is, but when she takes my hand, I can feel the tremble in it. I squeeze ever so slightly, and as our eyes meet, there's a silent plea. *Save her*. I nod once, and then I slide my own mask into place. Tali doesn't need Ray. Tali needs Reaper, and that's what she's gonna get, and whoever hurts her is gonna wish they'd stayed in bed this morning!

Dice grabs his laptop and starts checking footage. About thirty minutes after school ended, Tali walked out of the gates and headed to the coffee cart. She was surrounded and dragged into a van. After showing us a few stills, there were four guys. Three who grabbed her, and one who remained in the driver's seat. I recognise three of them as Hellhounds.

"This has to be something to do with the deal with Miguel! There, those three, they're Hellhounds, and I bet my life on it the other one is too!" Pacing backwards and forwards, I grab my phone.

"Dice, can you track her phone if I call it?"

"If she answers and she stays on long enough, yes!"

"Fuck, what are the chances of her still having her phone on her? Shit, here goes nothing!"

Catalina

I stay behind after school to finish a paper in the library. I've requested the driver pick me up an hour later than normal, but I'm finished earlier than expected, so I head out of the gates and down the street. There's a coffee cart there that does amazing hot chocolate, so I grab one while I wait. Hearing a screech of tyres, I spin on my heels as a van skids to a halt. One man slides the door open in the back and steps out. Another gets out of the door nearest to me, and one comes from the other side of the van. I can still see one of them in the driver's seat. I step back.

"Can I help you?"

Two of them surround me as the other steps closer, grabbing my arm. As I struggle, the others come closer and snatch me up into their grasp and bundle me into the back of the van. I'm pinned face down on the van floor with one of the guys straddling my back while he ties my wrists together behind my back. I'm still wearing my backpack as he slides down my body. He ties my ankles together, sitting back on the bench, the other two are in the front, and there's one guy on the floor at the side of me.

I'm frozen in place, terrified. The guy at the side of me slowly and gently slides his finger up my thigh and starts lifting my school skirt. I start thrashing, and the guy on the bench states, "Do not fucking touch her. Cerberus will string you up!"

"Only wanted a look. Chill, man!"

"Don't be stupid, man. You know what she's for. Keep your hands to yourself!"

I roll onto my back and scoot away from them, sitting against the back doors of the van so I can see them all, we travel for about an hour, and the road seems pretty straightforward. It doesn't feel like they are detouring to throw me off. When the van stops, I'm dragged out of the back doors, my eyes darting around to see where I am. There's what looks like a truck stop as they drag me over to an SUV. A larger man gets out.

"Are you fucking serious? You haven't even blindfolded her. What the fuck are you idiots playing at?"

They hang their heads and shove me towards the guy with the SUV. He grabs me by the hair and shoves me towards the boot of the vehicle. Opening it up, he shoves me in and tugs a bag over my head. After setting off, it's just me and him. We drive for another ten, maybe fifteen minutes.

I'm dragged out of the back of the vehicle, held by the scruff of the neck, and pushed forward. I'm pushed up a few steps. The only thing stopping me from falling on my face is the guys' bruising grip, a door opens, and it's the smell that hits me first, stale beer, stale cigarette smoke and another smell that's sweaty and like sex but also not.

I know what sex smells like as I've walked in on my mum with her... I don't know what to call him... Viking. Anyway, he's kind to me and seems to like my mum, and when he's at the villa, she laughs a lot. She seems to relax around him. I wonder if I will ever see them again.

After the overwhelming smell, the noise is next: clinking glasses and chatter, mainly rowdy men, possibly a bar. As I'm pushed through, there are a few hands running over my body as I wriggle and thrash in the guys' hold. I hear another door open, and I'm pushed through it. Then the noise and smell fade slightly, there's a knocking noise, then a creak, and then I'm lifted off my feet and carried down some stairs. I think I'm in a basement. A musty, damp smell wafts around me, then a sweaty sickly smell. There's a dripping noise, clinking noises almost like chains, and a cold bite around my ankle.

I'm pushed down on a camp bed-type cot, and then nothing but the sound of boots walking away from me. I shuffle up the bed and feel the cold, damp walls till I find the corner and sit with my back against it. Still, hands bound behind my back and bag over my head. I rub my head against the wall, sliding the bag off so I can see my surroundings. There are some crates of bottles in one corner, and there are five more cots with chains. There are three other bodies down here chained to the walls like me.

"Hello?" My voice cracks and shakes. I'm terrified.

"Shh!" a voice sounds from one of the beds.

Taking a deep breath. "Where are we? What's happening?"

"Will you keep it down, or we will all be beaten!"

With a gasp, I settle back against my backpack. It's so uncomfortable. I try to wriggle it so I can get into the zip compartment. My phone is in there. If I can call my mum or Ray or Viking, they will know I'm in trouble. They can help. I start to thrash, trying to bend my wrists towards the bag. Four guys appear as the hatch flings open and heavy boots sound down the wooden stairs. The one at the back is bigger. As the two at the front grab me and untie me, they remove my backpack and toss it over to him.

He rummages through it to find my phone and walks over to me, he slaps me so hard my head hits the wall, and I see stars. "You're gonna phone your mum, you little bitch, and tell her you're staying at a friend's place for a few days. Do not test me, motherfucker. If you tell her we have you, we will kill you!"

I nod, my head still swirling, and I can taste blood. How the hell am I supposed to let her know I'm in trouble? I can't, but then I nod again at him, knowing full well I can get her to give Ray a message. Then these guys will be toast. After passing the message to Mum, I hope she will get in touch with Ray. They throw my phone on the stack of crates near the door and leave again.

"Can anyone reach the crates? Can you get my phone so I can get us help?"

"What makes you so special, princess? We've been here for weeks. No one's coming for us." My phone starts ringing till the answer phone cuts in, then it stops and then rings again. Then when it starts ringing for the third time, the hatch flies open, and the big guy comes down, picking up my phone.

"Who the fuck's, Ray?"

"She's a friend of my mum's, she's… persistent, she freaks out when people don't answer, that's why I always do. She will think there's something wrong if I don't talk to her. She's a nightmare."

"Fine, speak to her, get her off the phone quickly. You say anything, and you're dead, you hear me? Don't screw with me bitch, okay?"

I nod, and he puts the phone on speaker and calls Ray. "What the fuck, Catalina? You know I hate it when I don't get an answer."

"I know, Ray. I'm sorry!"

"Okay, it's fine. Your mum gave me the message about your project, well done, kiddo!"

"Thanks, Ray!"

"So, how long did it take you?"

"Maybe an hour, an hour and a half at most!"

"Ah, good, so your mum asked me to pick you up, okay?"

"Thanks, Ray, I appreciate that!"

"Okay, kiddo, stay sharp. I'll see you soon!"

"Okay, Ray, I love you!"

"Love you too, kiddo. Always and Forever!"

"Right, you little bitch I'm turning your phone off. Fuck it if she gets pissy. You're not gonna be around much longer. We're moving you in a couple of days!"

Ray

"Steel, can I have a word in private?"
"Yeah, sure, baby. You have a plan, don't you?"
"I do!"
"I'm not gonna like it, am I?"
"Not so much, no!"

Taking a heavy breath, he stands from his seat and follows me into the villa, making sure we aren't followed and we aren't spied upon by any of Carmen's guys. At the moment, I don't trust any of them. Someone knew Tali's driver wasn't picking her up till later. Someone here is working with the Hellhounds, and until I find out who, and they have been eradicated, I trust no one.

I don't trust anyone but my brothers and my husband, period. "I need to go in alone. If I go in as a club whore, I can walk straight in the door, no questions asked!"

"Are you fucking kidding me? They will recognise you!"

"They won't, trust me. They're shallow and useless. They won't even put two and two together. They're Neanderthals. If I go in alone, I can convince Cerberus to show me around. Can you guys get me a bag into the bathroom window when I need it? I'm gonna need some firepower!"

"Ray, I don't like this! How far are you willing to take the club slut thing, as there are certain things we can't come back from."

"I'm willing to do whatever it takes to get Tali back in one piece. I'm also willing to listen to and work around your boundaries!"

Letting out a shaky breath, he grabs my face gazing into my eyes.

"I can't... I don't..."

I reach up to cup his face. "Hey, just say it, okay?"

"I think I can handle some mild touching, possibly a kiss, definitely nothing sexual. I don't think I can come back from that. It will rip me apart!"

"Okay."

"Okay?"

"Yeah, I'm not gonna lose you to get Tali back. I will make it work and get her back while not stepping over your boundaries. I will work it out. I need you guys as backup and maybe to make a diversion down the line!"

After discussing the details of my plan, we head back to the pool. "Carmen, do you have an armoury of sorts? If not, I can get what we need, but it will take a few hours; we'll need more... tools."

Carmen nods towards Viking. He gets up from his seat. "I can show you."

I turn to Steel. "Gorgeous, can you get what we need? I need to talk to Carmen."

Steel nods and leaves with the guys. "Dice, before you go, can you get an earpiece or something so I can keep in touch?"

"If you go with Viking, it's all in the armoury. He knows where everything is!" Carmen adds.

Dice nods at Carmen and follows after the boys. "What do you need, Ray?"

After going through what I need, I follow her to her room "Okay, Carmen do you worst!" After twenty minutes, my hair's pinned up in curls. Hopefully, I can slide my helmet on and take the pins out when I get there. She applies bright red lipstick, a smoky eye and contours my face enough to make me look like a different person.

I need an outfit. "Do you have anything… slutty?"

Carmen hands me large silver hoops, leather hot pants and a basque. I put the basque over my black vest to cover my back tattoo. I leave my boots on. "Perfect!" Carmen forces a smile at me.

"Trust me, Carmen. I'm gonna get her back or die trying!"

"I do trust you, Ray, but please both come back. I can't lose you, too, okay?"

"You won't lose either of us, Carmen. I promise I will get her back, whatever it takes!"

I walk out to the patio. "Holy shit!" Dice shouts out as all the guys spin around.

"Fuck's sake!" Steel shakes his head, sweeping me into his arms and kissing the breath out of me. Thank heavens for lip stain, as this guy would be permanently covered in my lipstick. I bet he would even make that look fucking sexy. He drops me back to my feet.

"We all know what we need to do?" Nodding, everyone turns to leave.

"Ray, take this, please!" Carmen says, handing me a Hellcat and a box of ammo.

"It should slide in your boot along with your knives! Be safe, okay, and bring her back to me!"

"I will, I promise. Viking, you keep her safe, okay?" Nodding at me, he hugs Carmen and kisses her head.

"Be safe, okay, and make 'em pay!" He nods as he squeezes Carmen tighter.

"Will do, Brother! Let's roll out, guys." Sliding my jacket on and heading to the bikes, we set off.

Pulling up down the road from the clubhouse, it's not as big as ours. It's not fenced in, or on its own land. It's part of a truck stop, which works in our favour. As I slide off my bike, the guys can be close without drawing suspicion. I remove my ring and zip it in the pocket of my jacket, handing them to Steel. "Look after these for me, baby. I'm gonna need them back when this is all over!"

"Don't do anything stupid, woman, you hear me?"

I wink at him. "You know me, sexy, if I can't be good, I'll be careful!"

Shaking his head at me and pulling me into a bruising kiss, he says, "Come back to me, okay?"

"Always!" Removing the clips from my hair and tousling my fingers through it to leave it wavy and down my back, I remove my boot and slide the gun to one side. It hurts, it's crushing the side of my foot and ankle, but I can put up with it. Opening the duffel bag, I take a smaller bag out of it, placing in it a couple of smoke bombs, a few grenades, my Glock 19s, a box of ammo, some mini bolt cutters, a hammer, and a hatchet, all while sliding my Emerson Combat Karambit and my CRKT Tecpatl into the side of my boots.

I place the earpiece and test it. "Can you hear me?"

"Yeah, all clear," Dice returns.

"You got this, baby, just take your time and be careful and keep us in the loop!"

I kiss him again, just in case this is the last one I get. "Don't kiss me like you're not coming back!"

"Hey, I'm coming back! Hades himself doesn't want me hanging around. He will soon kick my arse back here!"

He smiles, but it doesn't reach his eyes. As I turn, he slaps me on the arse. "Go get 'em, tiger!"

I turn, wink, and strut across the truck stop, pushing my way into the clubhouse. It stinks of sex and stale fags, and stale beer. I think I can smell piss and sweat too.

"Fucking foul!" I mutter under my breath as I walk straight to the bar. I see Cerberus in an alcove opposite, so I purposely don't look. Instead, I sidle up to a slightly overweight guy in his fifties at the bar. "So, who's a lady gotta blow to get a drink round here?"

He barks a laugh. "I will raise my hand to that. sugar tits." Smiling, I slide my hand over his arm. His badge says 'Road Captain' on it, and his name, 'Mayhem.'

"I didn't say I was a lady, just asking a question, hot stuff!"

He barks out another laugh. "Why don't you slide over on my lap, sugar tits, and see what comes up?"

"Too late, old man, it's already standing to attention!" It's my turn to laugh, and I make it a good one so I get noticed. Sliding up onto the bar, I push my foot between his legs, sliding his stool back slightly as I slide in front of him and reach over the bar to grab the bottle of tequila. Sliding it straight to my lips, I make it look like I take a massive chug, but I don't swallow any and don't let it past my lips. Leaning over to Mayhem and licking the bottle's rim, I hand it to him, smiling. He slides his hand up my thigh and takes a drink. Placing the bottle back on the bar, he leans forward, cups my arse, and slides me into his lap so I'm straddling him. "Oh shit!" I gasp and fan my face with my hand. "That's the biggest dick I've felt in so long!"

I shuffle my arse against him and he groans, tipping his head back. "Keep that up, sugar tits, and I'll be coming in my jeans like a twelve-year-old boy!"

"Now that I would like to see! Wanna take me somewhere and show me what you can do with that trouser snake? I bet you're the biggest in here. Come on, Daddy, what do you say?"

"Daddy, huh? I think I like that!" He grabs my hair and pulls it back as he licks my neck, sending a shiver of repulsion through my body. "Ah, you like that sugar tits?"

I moan to cover the urge to vomit. I bat my eyelashes at him, and there's a cough behind us. "Mayhem! You're needed elsewhere. I will look after your… friend!"

"What the…?" He turns his head and his face pales "Yeah, boss, sure thing!" He grimaces at me. "Sorry, sugar tits, you're really not my type!" He picks me up and sits me on the bar before sliding off his stool. Standing up, he adjusts his junk.

"You should maybe tell your dick that. I don't think it got the memo!"

He just glares at me as he walks off. I slide off the bar and go to walk in the opposite direction.

Cerberus grabs my wrist. "Where do you think you're going, little lady?"

"Bathroom."

"Corridor, third door on the left!" He points over to the corridor beside the bar as I go to walk away. He pulls me back.

"Why don't you come and have a drink with me after? What's your poison?"

"I'm good, thanks!" As I go to leave, I smile as I feel his grip tighten on my wrist. The thing about men is if you show you don't want them, they want you all the more, proving the little show with Mayhem worked. Now I have his full attention. I need to make him work for it. If I'm too easy, he will get bored, but if I'm too difficult, he will also get bored, there's a fine line, and I need to straddle it. "What can you offer me that

Mayhem can't? When I walked in here, I looked for the most powerful-looking man!"

"Ah, well, that's where you fucked up, little lady. I am the president of this club!"

"President? Well, fuck me in the arse with a dildo!" I bark out a laugh. I spin on my heels and head to the bathroom. As I walk into the corridor, there's a storeroom behind the bar. There's a guy sitting in the doorway on a stool with a gun in his lap. "Well, hello there, handsome. How the devil are you?"

"What the fuck are you doing down here? It's off-limits!"

"Ladies room, need to powder my nose!" As I wink at him and pull the little bag out of my shorts pocket shaking it. "Care to join? You look like you could be fun!"

"What kind of fun are you looking for, princess?"

"The kind that's more trouble than fun!" I flash him a wink and slip over to the bathroom door. "You know where I will be." I walk into the bathroom. I whisper, "Guys, I'm in the bathroom. There's a guard in the store room. I can't see anyone in there, but there's a hatch in the floor, so I need to get the guard out of the way."

"Incoming!" I hear back from Dice, as there's a tap on the window. I slide it open and take the bag from Steel. His face is stone, eyes of ice, the swirling grey ones, frozen. I can see he's not happy with what he's heard, but he's not saying anything. I poke my head out the window and slap a kiss on his lips, winking at him.

"You're the only guy for me, gorgeous. Don't you ever forget that!" He smiles as I slide the window shut and stash the bag. I slide up onto the counter. Fuck, this place is grim. There's a tap on the door as it cracks open. I smile as the guard pokes his head in.

"Well, shit, princess. You waiting for me?"

"I sure am, sugar!" I prep him a line up on my thigh and roll a $20 bill, handing it to him and winking. "Help yourself, sugar." He slides his hand up my thigh and I tip my head back and moan.

He licks around the line and grins up at me. "Fuck, you're sexy as fuck!"

"Take your line like a good boy. I wanna snort mine off your dick!"

"Shit, princess!" He leans down with the bill and snorts the whole fucking line. His mouth springs open, and his eyes bulge as he grabs at his face and his throat as he gasps and goes purple. I put my boot to his chest and shove him back as he stumbles into a cubicle and sits on the disgusting toilet. He's clawing at his throat.

"I have the antidote here. Tell me where the girl is, and I will let you live!" His eyes dart to the door. "Is she under that storeroom?" His eyes go wide, and he nods. "Let me help you."

He nods again as he goes blue. His eyes bulge, his mouth foams, and blood starts leaking from his nose and ears. He slumps back into the wall. "Game over, motherfucker!" I whisper, and I hear a chuckle back through my earpiece, patting the dead guy down. I find a bunch of keys, snatching them up and grab the bag. I crack the door open, looking both ways down the corridor.

I slip out and over to the store room, slipping the door shut behind me, hoping that will draw less attention than the lack of guard. I walk into the room, sliding the bolt back on the hatch in the floor. There are some steps leading down. I go down the steps. I pull the hatch shut behind me. The smell hits me, damp and dirty, sweat and piss. As I creep down the wooden steps, I can see six cots with bodies on four of them. I whisper, "Tali, it's Ray!"

One of the bodies shoots up. "Ray?" She coughs out a sob. "I knew you'd come."

"Shh, we still need to get you out of here." Walking over to her, she hugs me, and I check her over a split lip and a few bruises. She points to her ankle. I slip into the bag and grab the bolt cutters, snipping the chain. I move over to the other beds and find three other girls dirty and bruised. I snip their chains too.

"I'm gonna get you all out of here. I need you to be quiet. I need you all to do what I say you got it?"

They all nod. Reaching into my boot, I give Tali her mum's gun, and she smiles. I wink at her and lead the way. I fling the duffle over my back like a backpack, arming myself with a Glock and a grenade. As I creep up the stairs, I hear mumbling outside the door. Rushing the girls out, I close the hatch and slide the lock back in place. Raising my fingers to my lips, telling them to be silent, I shove them unceremoniously behind some stacks of crates and we wait.

"Where the fuck's Joker?" I hear from the hallway as Cerberus flings the door open. He scans the room, checking the hatch is bolted. "If he's fucking that slut in the shitter, I'm gonna lose my shit. Find him!"

As he slams the door and walks back down the hallway, glancing around, there's a small window the girls can fit through, but I know I won't. I crack the window open. "Be silent. Tali, you go first. The guys are gonna come get you, go with them, okay? I will make my way back to you." Tali nods. "Guys, change of plan. Four girls are coming out the storeroom window on the opposite side of the bathroom. I need you to get them. I can't fit through the window. I will make my own way back, okay?"

I hear grumbles and shuffling as I start stuffing Tali out the window. It's a tight fit, but she makes it with a slight thump on the other side. I throw the next girl through as I hear the guys come around the corner, and Tali throws herself at Steel, sobbing. "I've got you, kiddo!" He strokes her hair back and hugs her close.

I throw the third girl out as I hear talking from the hallway again. I grab the last girl by her hand and drag her behind the crate. "Get them out of here!" I bark at the boys. "Go, leave my keys on the bike. I will get us out!"

"I'm not leaving you!" Steel grimaces through my earpiece.

"Steel, please get them back to the villa. I will meet you there!"

"Fuck!" He gasps as they take off running.

I turn to the girl when we move. "Grab the back of my shorts, stay with me, do not let go for anything, stay close, okay? This is gonna be messy. If I tell you to run, run and don't look fucking back, you got me?" She nods, trying to hold in her tears. I cup her face. "I'm gonna do everything I can, okay?" She nods.

The door flings open, and Cerberus and another guy stride in. "Check the cellar!" he barks as the guy opens the latch and slides in. I run out, slamming the latch shut, sliding the bolt in and kicking out Cerberus's legs from under him. He hits the deck, my element of surprise knocking the wind out of him as I dart out of the door. The girl follows me. I turn right and run to the bathroom. Grabbing her, I shove her out the window as I'm half out. "You fucking whore!"

I'm grabbed and dragged back. "Run!" She takes off sprinting.

I hear Dice over the earpiece. "Shit, I'm going back for the girl!" I hear the roar of his bike and trust that he will get to her as I'm thrown on the floor. I hear the screech of tyres. "Get on! I've got her, Ray!"

Cerberus is towering over me. I cower away from him "Please, please don't hit me. I'm sorry, I'm sorry!" He laughs in my face as he grabs me by the hair.

"You're gonna fucking pay for this, you slut."

"I know, I'm sorry. I didn't have a choice. It was…" I trail off.

"It was what? It was who? Who the fuck are you working for, bitch?" He kicks me in the ribs, and I feel a twang, a sharp pain. Fuck, I think he's broken a rib. I gasp and beg some more just for safe measure. "Please, you don't understand!" I clutch my ribs and double over. "Please let me tell you, it's…"

"Fuck spit it out!" He spits in my face while gripping my hair. Thing is, he's totally underestimated me. While he's getting in my face, I've slid my other arm that's not holding my ribs into my boot and slid out my Emerson Combat Karambit, gripping it tight in my hand. I smash it upward through his neck, then remove it and stab his cheek. He gasps as he grabs for his neck, but I'm stabbing over and over again. He crumples to his knees, still trying to hold his neck while he bleeds out, and I stab again and again for good measure. The blood is sliding all over me, and I kick my leg out and shove him away from me as he convulses on the floor.

I try to climb out the window, but all the blood… I'm too slimy, too slippery. I'm covered head to toe, so I decide the only way is out the front door. Reaching into my bag, I grab both grenades, ripping the pins out and grasping the triggers taking a deep breath.

"I'm heading out the front door any minute, guys. Get away from here. I won't be far behind you… hopefully!"

"Fuck, Ray, what you gonna do?" Dice chimes in.

"Just get them girls to Carmen's. I will meet you there, Steel. Make sure they're safe, okay?"

"Okay, beautiful, just come home to me, okay?"

"On it, baby!" As I step out into the corridor, I'm met with a young prospect with a look of sheer horror on his face. "Turn the fuck around, dipshit. Don't make any sudden moves, or I will blow us all sky-high. You hear me, motherfucker?"

He nods, raises his hands, and backs down the corridor into the bar. Things quieten. As I walk in, there's a clatter as a few of the guys jump off their stools, knocking them over. "No fucker move, or I will blow us fucking up. Go on, underestimate me if you dare. Cerberus just did, and he's dead on the bathroom floor in a pile of his own blood. Joker's toast, too, so step fucking back, arseholes!"

As I head towards the door, Mayhem bares his teeth at me. "You won't get away with this, you fucking whore!"

I laugh at him. "I'm the motherfucking Reaper, shithead! See you in Hell!" As I back out the door, I fling both grenades into the middle of the room at them and run like fuck. I'm about five to ten metres away as the blast goes off, throwing me onto the cement. My ears ring as I climb to my feet and try to shake it off. I stagger a little as I try to gather my bearings. I look around at the clubhouse. I've taken the bar out totally, and only about a third of the building still stands. I can hear a couple of guys coughing and groaning. Taking the gun out of the back of my shorts, I shoot the grey figures standing in the smoke, dropping them like flies. I must take out five of them before turning on my heel and running for my bike.

As I get further away from the blast sight my ears steady in their ringing. "Ray, Ray! Ray! Fucking answer me, Ray!"

"I'm okay. I'm okay, I'm coming!" Fuck, my head is pounding, my rib is killing, my knees are skinned and so are my palms. I slide onto my bike, throw my helmet on and fire it up, chasing down the road after the guys. They're only about fifteen to twenty minutes ahead of me. I can feel the blood drying and cracking against my skin as I pull up at Carmen's. They're all waiting out the front for me.

The three girls are huddled together, and Tali is wedged between Carmen and Viking. I slide off my bike. Tali runs at me, throwing her arms around me. "I knew you'd come, I knew it!" Looking down at her and pulling her tighter against me, I kiss the top of her head. "I will always come for you!" She shudders against me, and I just hold her wincing as she squeezes, but I don't let go.

"Tali?" Steel says in the softest voice I've ever heard him use. "We need to get Ray inside, cleaned up and looked at! We need to look over you girls too, okay?" She nods at Steel, releasing her hold on me.

"I will take the girls to my room to shower and change, we will meet you by the pool!"

"Good girl!"

She hugs Steel as she passes him. "Thank you for coming for me!"

"Anytime, kiddo!" She walks off grabbing the girls and heading inside.

Steel sweeps me into his arms. "Fuck, I thought I lost you when we heard the explosion!"

"Nah, that was just me covering my bases. We need to keep an ear to the ground after the explosion. I took out five more guys, but I need to keep an eye on those who are left. If there are any left." The guys all nod.

Carmen steps up and snatches me from Steel. "Hermana, perra loca!" "*Sister, crazy bitch!*" She huffs at me shaking her head. "How can I ever repay you?"

"No payment needed, you're family!"

She grins at me.

"I really need to get Cerberus off me. That guy is in places he really shouldn't be!" I pull at my bra and make a gagging noise.

"Come on. I've got you!" Steel drags me towards the guest rooms and into the shower. Shoving me unceremoniously into the shower against the wall, fully clothed, and then turning the water on, he strips his clothes off and hustles in after me, pinning me against the wall, dick hard against my stomach. He grinds into me. "Why does seeing you covered in blood get my dick so hard?"

I slide my hand around his length. "Because you're my own special kind of pervert!"

"Ah, you get me!"

"You're right, I do." As I twist my hand, dipping it down and back up again, his head flops forward, resting on mine.

"You're fucking crazy. I thought I'd lost you!"

"Never. I'm too good at what I do!"

"And what's that exactly?"

I wink. "Well, at this moment, I'm hoping that's you!"

Smiling down at me, he slowly tugs my clothes off, dropping them into the bottom of the shower, leaving me in my boots. Sliding his hand between my legs, he leans in and kisses me. I moan into his mouth. "So fucking wet. I hope that's for me and only me."

"Always, only for you, now, and for always!" Sliding his hand out of me and around my leg, he lifts it to his waist and plunges inside me, slamming my back against the wall, almost like he's punishing me for the things I had said to the scum on the mission. I will take it like the good girl that I am and take all he has to give, as I hated every second. I've never been big on affection or touching, but this man here shattered my defences, broke through my walls and rebuilt them around us both, arming us with the best defence we could ever need: each other.

I don't know when it happened, but I know I can never live without him. He's the one I breathe for now. Slamming me against the tiles again, he pushes his way in and out of me, making me quiver and moan. I grip around him while he holds my thigh in place and slams into me repeatedly. It's delicious, the pain and the pleasure the perfect balance.

We're like the day and the night, the sun and the moon. You can't have one without the other. He slams into me again. I quiver, and he bites down on my neck, thrusting in again as my orgasm thunders inside me, flushing through me, my core sending heat waves through my whole body. Every place our bodies touch sears with intensity.

I stare into his eyes and hold his gaze as I convulse around his thick, pulsing dick while he fills me with burning ribbons of come. After what seems like a lifetime of eye contact and panting, we both sag against each other as he lets my leg slowly make its way to the floor.

I wobble slightly in my heels, but he has me moulded to his body against the wall. "Fuck, I love you! You and your crazy."

"Hey, your crazy matches my crazy!"
"It sure does, beautiful. You're perfect!"
I kiss him till I have no breath left.

"We should go and sort out this mess."

I laugh, gesturing to my thighs. "This mess?"

Laughing, he slides his hand between my thighs, sliding his come back up my legs and dipping his come-coated fingers back in my pussy, making me groan from the sensitivity after my orgasm. I grab his wrist. "Be very careful. Right now, I can walk away. Carry on like that, and you'll be lucky to see outside this time next week!"

He slings his fingers back in and out of me, then around my clit. "Punishment accepted!" Grinning into the kiss, he brings me to the edge again, then throws me over it till I can't hold my own weight on my legs. Fucking traitors.

He grins at my neck. "I'm never gonna get tired of hearing you come and scream my name!" But then he steps back, leaving me panting and cold. "If I don't leave you now, I never will. Get ready, wife, meet you out by the pool!" And with that, he stalks out of the bathroom.

"Wanker!" I yell after him just because I can. I hear him chuckle as he throws his clothes back on and heads out the door. Washing myself off and scrubbing my hair to remove the blood and drowning my boots, I head back out to the pool. Someone has left my jeans from before, a fresh pair of pants and a vest top on the bed. I leave my boots to dry and head towards the pool. The guys and Carmen are already out there.

"Where are the girls?" I ask them.

"Still getting sorted. They'll come out here when they're done." Reaching Steel, my jacket's over the back of the chair. I grab it and fish my rings out, slipping them back on.

"Holy shit, Ray!" Carmen gasps, grasping my hand and dragging it straight to her eyes glaring up at Steel. "Is that a … black diamond?" Looking closer, she turns my hand over. "Diamonds and a platinum band?"

He just nods.

"Shit, this must have cost a small country!"

He just grins waggling his eyebrows. "Wouldn't you like to know!"

I slide myself over his body, straddling him in the chair and pulling my hand free of Carmen's. "Nope, I wouldn't!" And I kiss him breathlessly. There's a cough behind us as the girls reach us.

"Hey!" I smile at them all as I slide around to face them still in Steel's lap. His arms reach around and hug me to his body, holding me close. We have laid some chairs in between Carmen and Dice, and Tali takes the one next to her mum. The two girls who had escaped with Tali are holding hands, and one has hold of the other's arm, too. They drag the next two seats, and the one who had stayed with me's lips started to quiver. She hugs herself as she shakes. The tears start, and I stand.

Dice does, too, placing a firm hand on her shoulder. "Hey, it's okay. You're gonna be okay!" She looks at him through tear-stained lashes. After a few minutes, she calms down, and Dice steers her towards the seat next to him. She shuffles it closer to him, resting her hands in her lap and gazing at them.

"So, you're safe now, but I need to know your names and where you're from so we can get you back to your families, okay?"

The two clutching each other nod, but the one next to Dice looks into his eyes, and he nods to her. "It's okay." She shakes her head and turns, facing her hands again.

"How about you guys? You got a good home to go back to?" They both nod. "Okay, write the details down. I will contact your families and let them know you're safe! We'll get you some food and a good night's sleep, and tomorrow we will take you back to wherever you want to go, okay?!"

The girls look at each other and one says. "Really? We can go just like that?"

"Yep, just like that!"

They both look at each other again, then back at me. "We can just go home?"

"Yep! I was there to rescue Tali. You girls just got lucky, you don't owe us anything, but we're gonna have to take you on the bikes, so you need to get some food and sleep, and when you're feeling a little better in the morning, we will take you home, okay?"

"You promise?" the other one says.

"Promise!" I smile.

"You can trust Ray. She always keeps her promises, don't you?" Tali looks at them nodding.

"Sure do, kiddo!" I wink at her and she gives me the biggest smile as she tucks herself into her mum.

Viking comes from the villa, walking straight up to Tali, draping his arms over her shoulders, and hugging her from the back of the chair. He places a kiss on her head. "You okay, kiddo?" She looks up at him with total adoration as she smiles and nods, cuddling into his arms. Clearly, they have gotten close with the amount of time he's spending here with her mum. The next thing we know, there's a commotion shouting from what sounds like the gates, and then Carmen's phone is ringing.

"Go ahead... Name... Yes... the pool!" Hanging up the phone, she smirks as the doors fly open and Roach storms through them. Tali's up out of her chair and across the tiled floor before anyone can do anything. She throws herself into Roach's arms.

He lifts her up off the floor. "Fuck, you're okay." He nuzzles his face into her hair and just holds her there, her legs dangling in front of him.

We all glance around smirking as Carmen shakes her head. "Suppose we should have called him!"

"So they're a thing now, huh?" I quiz.

"Apparently, they're getting married when they're older. After what went down at the wedding and how you and Steel are, they believe they're meant to be!" Carmen shrugs like she can't bring herself to be mad at them.

Roach slowly lowers Catalina to her feet, glaring over her shoulder at me. "Do you ever answer your phone, Ray? I've been calling for hours, and when I couldn't leave any more messages for you and Catalina, I had to come!" Gripping her to him again, he kisses her head and she sags into him.

Steel pushes to his feet, about to give Roach a telling off for speaking to me that way, but I know how

I'd feel, so I can't find it in me to give a shit. Me and Roach are close. I should have thought to at least call.

I turn and shove the note pad at the girls.

"Food will be out shortly" Carmen gestures to Roach and Tali to come and join us as the girls write their details down. They are called Sophie and Olivia. The girl with Dice refuses to give her name and just sits with Dice, barely moving when the food comes out.

I step away to call the girls' parents, checking how long it's gonna take to take them back. One's an hour away, the other an hour and twenty. Once I head back to the table, Dice's trying to get the girl to eat, but she's just staring at me. The others have cleared their plates and are yawning.

Carmen glides from her seat. "Sophie, Olivia, why don't you come with Catalina and me and we can get you settled and get some rest? Would you prefer separate bedrooms, or would you like to share?"

"Could we share please?" Sophie asks.

Carmen nods, walking away towards the villa, looking back over her shoulder. "Viking, Sweetheart, could you show the gentlemen to the guest rooms, and we can meet back here later once we've all cleaned up and rested?"

Everyone gets up. Dice starts to follow after Viking, and the girl's eyes follow him.

She goes to follow him but I shake my head at her and she sits back down. "Do you have anywhere you want to go? Do you have someone I can call? Somewhere you want to go?"

Looking at the floor, she shakes her head.

"If you talk to me, I can help you."

"How old are you?"

"Nineteen."

"Okay, so here's what's gonna happen. You're gonna go get some rest, then tomorrow we're gonna take the girls home, and you need to decide what you want to do. Do you want to go home? Do you want us to take you somewhere for a fresh start? Or do you want to come with us till we can figure something out? The choice is yours, but you need to decide in the morning." She looks around, then back at me. "I don't think you understand. You're free to do what you choose. You don't owe us anything, let's get you a room, and you can get some rest. Do you want to be on your own or with the other girls?"

"On my own."

I nod and walk her to the room. "Do you want some food?"

She shakes her head. "I'm tired."

I back out of the room. "See you in the morning." She nods as I close the door. "Shit!"

As the alarm rings, there's a groan from beside me, which makes me smile. Leaning over, I kiss him. "Morning, gorgeous!"

He groans again, pulling me against his body, grinding his hard-on against my arse cheeks, and gripping tightly. He moans into my neck, and shivers go down my spine.

"Baby, don't, we don't have time, and you know those noises drive me insane!" It's the chuckle that does it. He knows they go through my body, vibrating along every nerve ending before ending up pulsing between my thighs. Flipping him over onto his back and me straddling him, his eyes go wide with shock, and I grin down at him. He smiles, closing his eyes again, "We don't have long, baby, so be a good boy and hang on to something. It's gonna be hard and fast!" His eyes fly open as I slam myself down, impaling myself on him, groaning with the delicious full feeling of being stretched to my limit by my beautifully feral husband before grinding myself into him and starting off as though I've grown up my whole life in the goddamned rodeo. One arm flies up to hold himself against the headboard as the other grabs onto my hip.

My hands glide down his chest as I dig my nails into his abs as I ride faster and harder.

He gasps. "Fuck!" The hand on my hip tightens, and his arm that's up slams against the headboard harder to stop me from smashing him into it. I'm like a runaway train. I can feel my skin electrifying, and the heat rising from my centre drives me on.

I feel his thighs tense. "Baby!" He gasps as I grind harder, faster, not letting up for a second.

Gazing into his eyes and licking my lips, I say, "Come for me, beautiful!" I smile down at him as his breath stutters, and he groans out his release. As soon as I feel the first streams of come hit my insides, I plough over the edge after him, not relenting till I orgasm and squeeze his dick for everything I can.

"Fucking hell!" he mutters as I slide off him. He's panting as he leaves one hand on the headboard, the other rests over his eyes; kissing the back of his hand, I move off the bed, grab my clothes and head for the bathroom.

"Fuck, you look perfect with my come sliding down your thighs!"

I throw my clothes into the bathroom and turn to face him as he gazes out from underneath his arm. I slide my hand down my stomach between my legs and rub him around me with two fingers. He groans. I raise my fingers to my lips and plunge them into my mouth, groaning myself. "Tastes perfect too!" I step back and kick the door shut.

I hear another groan followed by, "Motherfucker!"

I chuckle as I throw myself in the shower. Once I'm dressed, I head out of the bathroom. Steel's still on the bed where I left him. "You good, baby? I need you by the pool ready to eat in thirty minutes, so we can get on the road!"

"K."

"You okay?"

"Just need a minute. I think my wife's trying to kill me off."

"Really? You want me to sort that bitch out?"

"Nah, I'm good. I'm thinking it's a great way to go, anyway. Just waiting for the feeling to come back in my legs!" He waves his hand around as if he's trying to wave me off. I chuckle and head out the door.

"Love ya!" I grin.

I get a thumbs-up, and I bark out a laugh as I head out the door. I wake the girls first. Tali sorts their clothes while they grab a shower. I tell the girl to wait with Tali and Carmen. I will be back for her, but she doesn't say a word. I give Carmen the heads up as to what's gonna happen, and she doesn't seem to like being bossed around.

"Ray, I'm the head of the Castillo Cartel. I am a ruthless woman in my own right, and I can look after myself."

"I know, but you're gonna do as you're told, Carmen, so help me, Hades, I will spank you if you don't listen to me. I will never forgive myself if anything happens to either of you, so suck it up, buttercup, and do as you're fucking told for once!"

She growls at me under her breath. "If you were anyone else, I would string you up and gut you like a pig!"

"And if you were anyone else, you would already be over my knee!" I cock an eyebrow at her and pop my hip, throwing my hand on it. "Are we gonna have a problem?"

"You're a sick bitch when you want to be, Ray!"

"I will take that as a no, we don't." The girls come out for breakfast, and we all gather around the table to eat, waking up the guys before me and Steel leave with Sophie and Olivia. I give them all jobs to do to be ready for when we get back.

Arriving back at the villa after being on the road for the last few hours, I grab Dice to one side.

"Everything set?" He nods. I give Carmen the wink and she nods to Tali. We all take our positions. Carmen goes out to the gates and calls a meeting with the entire staff, about eighteen of them all together.

While Carmen faces the house, they all gather around her in an arch as soon as they're there, we all dive into action. I don't trust any of these motherfuckers since Tali got taken, so Dice went to the nearest town and grabbed some equipment, mics, tiny cameras and hard drives. He heads to Carmen's office, downloads everything from her laptop, and swaps the hard drive.

He empties her safes and grabs the paperwork she's requested, stuffing it all into his backpack. He empties her drawers of all the personal documents she keeps locked away and grabs anything of a sensitive nature. While he's doing that, he taps into her camera feed. Tali's grabbing bare essentials as we're taking them to the MC with us. Over my dead body am I leaving them here. The rest of us have swarmed the building and have been given cameras and mics to put in each room, covering blind spots so that Carmen's security won't know they're there. We're now going to cover them all, as I know her staff will be fully aware of the gaps and will use them as necessary. Well, not on my watch, dickwads.

I'm gonna find the rat before either of them sets foot back here. Once we've finished, we all head out to the bikes. Carmen then informs the staff to lock this place down and await further instructions.

I grab the girl. "You're riding with me." She nods and climbs on. Roach has Tali, and I give him a nod.

"Stay close, be safe!" He nods and they slam their visors down. Carmen dives on behind Viking, and we peel out of there, leaving the staff gaping by the gates, confused as to what just happened.

Pulling up to the clubhouse, Ares is standing waiting with his arms crossed over his chest. "And just like that, Bedlam returns. I was just thinking it has been too quiet around here. How's my favourite sister-in-law?"

I bark a laugh at him. "Ah, Boyband, you missed me?"

"Like a hole in the head!"

"You'd miss your gob!"

"Touché!"

I walk over to him and throw my arms around him and as he swings his arms around me he whispers into my ear. "Everything good?"

"For now."

He takes a step back and nods. "Still good for tonight?"

"Yeah, got some shit to sort first, but I'll be there."

"Never a dull moment, hey?"

"Never!" I laugh as I head back to Steel.

He leans down and kisses my cheek, and whispers into my ear. "I think they should stay with us."

"You sure?" He nods and heads to our place.

"Tali, Carmen, we will set you up with us!" I nod to the girl. "You too." She looks at all the guys and then falls in behind us as we head off. Viking grabs Tali's and Carmen's bags and follows behind us.

"This is nice!" Tali whistles as we walk in.

"Do you have enough room?" Carmen looks at the doors and sees only three.

I laugh. "Plenty, mi casa es tu casa."

"*Plenty, my house is your house.*"

Steel points to our door. "That's our room, bathroom." He nods to the middle door." He walks through the third door.

"Carmen, make yourself at home. There's fresh bedding and towels in the drawers." He walks to the next door. "Here, kiddo, this should be fine for you. Do you need anything?"

She shakes her head. "Thanks, Steel, this is lovely!"

Walking to the last door, to the slightly bigger room of the three, he gestures. "You can stay here as long as you like, okay?" She nods and walks into the room. They are painted and clean with the basics, but they aren't anything special. There's just a bed, a chest of drawers, and a mirror in them all, no pictures or homely touches, not like the rest of the house, but all the beds and bedding are new, so they should be comfortable for however long this lasts.

I give them a grand tour then grab the truck keys from the bowl. "Carmen, write a list of what you need and your sizes. Me and the girls are going shopping, unless you wanna come?"

A high-pitched squeal comes from Tali. "You're taking us shopping?"

"Don't get too excited, we're only going to Walmart, maybe Target too!"

Carmen grins, grabs the pen and paper off the table, and then hands me the list.

"Want anything, baby?"

He pulls me in for a kiss. "I'm good, beautiful, be safe!"

I nod, walking to the back of the sofa where Viking is sprawled. I kiss him on the head. "Keep an eye on her!" I nod at Carmen. He gives me a nod, and then I clip him around the ear.

"Fuck's that for?"

"Boots! Off my motherfucking coffee table, asshole!" Smirking, he slides them off and throws them near the door. "Fucking brothers! Animals, the lot of you!" I shake my head as I place them next to the door and head out.

As we get to the store I lay out some ground rules. "Rule one, you get a trolley each. Rule two, fill said trolley with shit you want. Rule three, try it on if you're not sure after the time limit. Rule four, you have thirty minutes." I check my watch. "Meet you near the changing rooms... Go!" Tali runs towards the clothing, and the girl just looks at me. "Go have fun. Grab what you need clothing-wise, shoes, underwear, PJs, anything, okay? It's on me. I will pay for whatever you grab, okay?" She nods, wide-eyed, but takes off after Tali.

I wander over to the electronics counter and grab three burner phones, then I head to the clothing aisles myself, grabbing the list from my pocket for Carmen and filling my trolley. I might also have got myself some cute underwear and some vest tops with skulls on and some swimmers.

I plan on taking them to the falls in a couple of days. I also grab some beach towels, beach balls, and crap like that. Once the girls have got full trolleys nearly an hour later, I take them to get girly shit, shampoo and nail varnish, make-up and crap like that, then we grab pizza and snacks and head back to the truck with a shit tonne of bags.

"So, have you decided on a name yet?"

"I can pick a new one?"

"You can if you want."

She contemplates for a while before saying. "Skye! … Skye… Yeah, Skye!"

"You sure?" Nodding, she gives me a god-honest genuine smile. "Well, okay, then! Skye, welcome to the fucked up family that's all ours. You're welcome as long as you want to stay!"

Rooting into the bag in the front seat, I launch two of the phone boxes into the back with the girls. Tali squeals. "You got us phones?"

"They're just basic ones, but they'll keep you going for a bit. Tali, will you text my phone from them both so I have the numbers and you both have mine? You can sort the rest out later, okay?"

As the girls sit in the back playing with the phones, I pull up outside the shop I need.

"You guys wanna wait in the car, or do you wanna go get a drink in the coffee shop over the road?"

Tali's brow frowns, but she nods to Skye. "Skye, you wanna drink?" I toss them some cash and tell them to wait for me there and go nowhere else. I will grab them when I'm finished.

The bell on the door rings as I enter the shop. "Reaper?" Savage stands from behind the counter, looking almost surprised. "Everything ok?"

"Yeah, good, Savage, thanks. Is Tatts around?"

"He's with a customer, what do you need?"

"Thought I'd get a little something before tonight, has he got time?"

"Yeah, he should be free in about ten, fifteen minutes if you wanna wait. Fancy a brew or a cheeky piercing?"

"Piercing?" I cock my brow. I have quite a few in my ears, tragus, daith, conch, helix to name a few and my nose, tongue, lip, also my belly button. "Sure, how about… nipples? Both."

Savage raises a brow and takes a deep swallow. "Sure, I can do that!"

"Okay, let's do this." As I follow him out to the piercing room, I remove my jacket and vest top. I take off my bra, and as Savage turns around, he flushes.

"You good, Savage?"

"Erm, yeah, it's just a lot warmer in these rooms. Let me just turn the heating down a little!" He walks to the thermostat on the wall and jiggles it.

After cleaning the area and grabbing the jewellery, just plain bars for now, I was soon done. "What do ya think, Savage? They look cute?"

"Uh-huh!" He nods with his back to me and what looks like a slight adjustment of his dick before he leaves the room without another word.

A few minutes later, the door flings open. "Reaper, what the fuck you said to Savage? He said he had to go for… " His eyes dart from my face to my chest and back to my face. "Holy fuck! No wonder he had to go for a wander!"

"What the fuck? Tatts, you guys see tits and shit all day … " I gesture across my chest. "They're not the worst tits I've ever seen!"

Tatts starts shaking his head. "We're normally very… professional, Reaper, but let's just say Savage might have a little crush, so… "

"Oh!"

"Yeah, oh!" He laughs. "Okay, so what ya thinking?" After going through what I want and being careful not to catch my new jewellery, he finishes by cleaning off my new tattoo. "While I've got you here, shall I size up the stencil for tonight?"

"Sure!"

"The guys normally go for the right arm or back, but they're both out of the question. Can I take a look?" I turn around to face him and he runs his fingers over the back tattoo. "Fuck, Reaper, this is beautiful, up close, I mean… even the artwork in the skulls and roses is so detailed, but this is a work of art." He lingers for a few more minutes, checking every detail. He points. "Front of the right hip… yep, think it will work well there. What do ya say?"

"Whatever you think, Tatts. I'm in your capable hands." Nodding, he grabs some tracing paper as I slide my jeans down, and he draws out the size we need.

"I'll leave you to get dressed. See you tonight, Reaper. Welcome to the club!" He tips an imaginary hat at me and steps out of the room. Grabbing my stuff, I head back out. Savage still isn't back, probably for the best. I head to the coffee shop and grab the girls and some takeaway coffees and pastries for the others before heading back. As I pull into the parking lot, I lean on the horn. Some fucker needs to come grab these fucking bags.

Roach comes flying out of the clubhouse as Viking and Steel come down from the apartment. That should do it. I point to the back.

"Holy fucking shit, Ray, you buy the whole of Walmart?" Viking laughs.

"Oooh, I got you a little something too!" He grins at me as I shake my hand around in the bag before pulling it out and flipping him off! Steel barks out a laugh and taps him on the shoulder. "Come on. These bags aren't gonna shift themselves."

"Why is she so mean?" He whines at Steel, and he just laughs again.

As he loads his arms with bags I stuff a doughnut in his mouth. "Better?" He nods and groans around it as he heads up the stairs. Roach leans down and gives Tali the sweetest kiss on the cheek before whispering into her ear that he has to work as I'm getting my ink, so he will see her tomorrow for breakfast. So cute. Tali gives Roach her new number and we head upstairs after the guys.

"Where's Carmen?"

"She wants a bath. She's only just gone in," Viking replies, stuffing another bite of his doughnut in.

I grab the bags that are hers, and I also grabbed her a fluffy dressing gown, same as the girls', and the coffee and pastry. I knock on the door. I step in and drop her stuff to the side of the door, pointing at the bath.

"There's room for two if you want company!" I grin at her.

"Ray, I love you, but that might be a little far, even for our friendship!"

I bark out a laugh, doubling over and leaning on my knees. "Not me, knobhead, Viking!"

"Ah, that makes more sense, that would be great, actually, we haven't had much time together!"

"Leave the girls to me." I head out the door, yanking my thumb over my shoulder. "Viking, you're up!" Smirking at me, he laughs and heads into the bathroom.

Grabbing some of the bags, I say, "Come on, girls, let's go sort this shit out." They follow me down the corridor, where we sort through the bags, and I leave the girls to put it where they want it all.

Heading back out to Steel, he's stood at the kitchen counter. I slide my hands around his waist and run my hands up his taught chest, his muscles bunching and flexing under my fingers. I hug a little too tight and catch a nipple. I grit my teeth. Fuck, that hurt, but I don't want him to see till later, so I lean up and kiss the back of his neck. "I'm going for a shower, beautiful." I head out. When I get back to the living room, the girls are curled up on the sofa, and Steel's making them food.

I slide onto the sofa next to the girls and pause the TV, "We're gonna be late. We've got an MC thing. Tali, make sure you lock up after us and don't answer the door to anyone. Call us if you need anything, and I will come straight back or send Steel or one of my brothers!" I nod to Tali. "You know who to trust!" She returns my nod. "Skye, you okay?" She just nods. "You make yourself at home, okay? You can stay here as long as you like, and when you're ready to talk, we can sort stuff out, but you don't have to go anywhere unless you want to, okay?" She just nods in reply, and I give Tali a look that says see what you can find out, and she nods once in reply. Fuck, I love this kid!

As Viking and Carmen emerge from the bathroom, I smirk as she's all flustered and red-faced behind her beautiful caramel skin. "Bath a bit warm?"

"Yeah, something like that!" She nods as Viking leans down and kisses her neck. "I need to head over to the MC, got some shit to sort out. Babe, I will see you shortly, okay?"

He spins her in his arms and kisses the breath out of her while Tali makes gagging noises in the background, and I can't help laughing at the girls' faces.

Viking strides out of the place, playfully tapping Tali around the head while Carmen's left panting for breath. "Ese hombre será la muerte para mi!" *"That man will be the death of me!"*

I can't help but smile. "Come on, cartel queen, get ready. We need to go in ten minutes!" Carmen stomps into her room, and I smile at Tali. "They seem to be getting on like a house on fire!"

Smirking, Tali mocks, "I think she's in love, but she won't admit it!" We both laugh at that. Something tells me Tali knows exactly what she's talking about.

"Speaking of being in love, what about you and Roach?" She flushes and looks at her nails. They all of a sudden became far more interesting than anything else at that moment. I smirk at her. She's so cute. "He's a good lad, and if he hurts you, I will knock his teeth out. How about that? I can pretend it was an accident in the gym!"

She bursts out laughing. "No, don't do that, I kinda like his teeth!" She flushes a little more, looking up from her hands. "I kinda like the rest of him too!"

I shrug as I stand. "Well, you make sure you give him hell, keep him on his toes, okay?"

Steel laughs from the kitchen. "Ray certainly keeps me on my toes!"

I smile over at him. "You fucking love it!"

He barks out a laugh. "I fucking do, you're right!"

He brings the girls their food as Carmen comes out of her room, looking like a total fucking smoke show. "Damn, girl, you look hot, like a proper old lady!"

She chuckles at the title. "I'm definitely no one's old lady!" She's dressed in jeans and a plain white T-shirt, but she's paired it with a pair of her Louboutins. Her hair's down, but it looks rough-dried and not straightened, so it has more volume and a slight wave. She has on her signature red lipstick and a subtle smoky eye.,

"You look beautiful, Mum." Tali smiles at her.

"Right, come on, let's get this show on the road!" Steel calls from the door.

Walking through the MC door, the place erupts with cheers. As we walk towards the bar, Savage steps out, blocking my way. He's already drunk, and I smile up at him. "Hey Savage."

"Reaper!" He nods, he then gives me a devilish smirk and leans a little closer. "If you need a hand with the aftercare," he nods towards my tits, "I'm a very hands-on piercer!" He winks at me.

I smile up at him and place my left hand on his chest, leaning over to speak in his ear, keeping the smile on my face. "Wow, thanks, Savage, that's not at all inappropriate, you fuck knuckle!" I swing my right hand back, clenching it to a fist, and dick punch the fucking douche canoe.

There's a grunt. He drops to his knees like a lead weight. Looking up at me, he grunts out, "Yup, totally deserved that!"

I smile down at him and pat him on the head. "You won't make that mistake again, dickhead!"

I stride past him to the bar. As I look back, I see Steel stride over to Savage with a massive smile on his face. He looks down at him, then just laughs and follows after me.

Viking strides over and grabs Carmen's hand, dragging her after us and putting his whole hand in Savage's face, pushing him back so he falls backwards. "Fucking twat!" He shakes his head as he reaches us.

There's a tap on a glass as Ares shouts, "Listen up, motherfuckers, we know why we're here now. Let's get started!" He stalks over to me, handing me a bottle of tequila as Tatts drags a table over to the middle of the room. Wiping it down and laying a mat on it, and tapping for me to hop up, I slide off my boots and jeans, and all the guys start wolf whistling as Steel's gaze murders every single one of them multiple times in various bloody ways, which makes me laugh.

I have on a pair of bikini bottoms that tie at the side, so I slide onto the table, take a massive swig of tequila then lie back. Tatts undoes the string on the right, folds them back, and preps the area, slapping on the stencil and getting to it. Most people watch and chat around me for a while, then get bored and head to sit down or play pool or darts while they wait.

After my Reapers tattoo is finished, I have to sit on the bar and drink till I either finish the bottle or fall off. Needless to say, I'm rather pissed by the time I've finished the bottle and barely upright.

Swaying as I sit there, Steel slides between my legs and slides his hand into my hair, pulling my head back and biting down on my neck before licking across it painfully slow. I slide slightly forward and grind myself into him.

"Fuck, baby, don't do that, you're shit-faced, and I know as soon as I get you in bed, you're gonna pass the fuck out and sleep like the dead!"

I grin at him and slur, "I fucking love you, you know that!"

He grins. "I love it when you get all squishy when you're pissed!"

"I fucking love your dimples. They should be illegal. I think if you popped those dimples at me and asked me to murder anyone, I just would!"

"Ah, baby, you say the sweetest things."

"I know, right!" I grin back at him as he shakes his head at me.

"Come on. Bed, now!"

I two-finger salute him. "Aye, aye, Captain!"

Shaking his head, he laughs again, throwing me over his shoulder and stalking across the clubhouse. "We're out, guys!"

There are shouts of byes and laughter as I'm just dangling there down Steel's back. I think I manage a thumbs-up as we leave. Carmen and Viking follow us out, and we head back to the apartment.

"You need a hand with… that buddy?" I hear Viking say, chuckling behind us.

Steel reaches into his pocket and slides the key out tossing it over his shoulder. "You could get the door for me!"

As he strides up the steps, I can feel myself giving into the darkness. I want to show Steel his presents, so I have to stay awake. He pushes through the bedroom door and lowers me onto the bed. "Presents," I mumble.

"You want presents?"

"No," I mumble back. I'm struggling to keep my eyes open. He chuckles and slides off my boots, sliding my jeans down carefully so he doesn't drag them across the new ink. He slides my T-shirt off and sits me up to reach my bra, flicking it open. I wince as my nipples crash into him.

"Shit, babe, did I catch your tat?" Blinking up at him, I smile, and he lays me down, removing my bra and gasping. "Holy shit, beautiful, are these for me?" I smile again, feeling the heat rising as he slides his hand up to cup my right breast to get a closer look. I raise my hand and point to my left breast. He sits back and looks. He can see the swirling black text that says …

Steel

… as near to my heart as I can get it. "Shit, babe… they're beautiful, and my name… that's the most perfect thing I've ever seen. How long before I take them for a full test drive?" He waggles his eyes at me, and I only manage a goofy smile back. "How the fuck am I meant to sleep now with all that going on?" He scrubs a hand down his face. "I'm gonna go grab a quick shower. Probably a cold one!" I feel him move off the bed, but that's the last thing I hear.

Ray

I step out of the bedroom. Scar had been helping me get ready for tonight. It's Pa Bernie's job for the judge. We decided to go ahead with it, as the information we could get may still be useful. It's a no-brainer, really!

"Fucking hell!" Steel breathes out from behind the kitchen counter. "You should come with a health warning, baby!"

I smile over at him. "You're just biased." He grins at me, and my swinging brick stutters in my chest. Fuck, I adore this man. Taking in his handsome face, the scar that runs down it giving him an edge that makes my thighs clench. His dimples wreck me every time, then his scent, that smell that's all encapsulating. But the spell is broken when there's a cough from the living room.

"Really uncomfortable over here with the amount of eye fucking going on. Just saying."

I turn to Pa Bernie and laugh. "Sorry, Pa B. I just can't help myself."

He waves his hand in my direction. "Yeah, yeah, just do it on your own time, you're on the clock now!"

I laugh again as I walk to the kitchen counter. I'm wearing a red dress, tight clinging, with a slit right up the right leg. The plunging neckline leaves little to the imagination, but it has sleeves and a full back, covering all my tattoos. My hair hangs over my shoulder in soft flowing curls, and my make-up is subtle and understated.

I tighten the knife holster on my left thigh, slide my favourite knife into it, my Emerson Karambit, and slip the Hellcat gun into my clutch. I slide my brass knuckles on my right hand, which look like rings, and Bernie hands me the necklace I'm to wear. It has a mic in it so Dice can listen in. I hand Steel my rings. "Save them for me, baby, till I get back!"

Tali and Skye huddle on the sofa, cooing at my pretty dress, and I wink over at them. "Red's the best colour… hides the blood!"

They bark out a laugh. Skye's starting to relax but still hasn't told us anything about herself. I slide on the shoes Steel bought me as a wedding present, and he lets out a slow whistle. "Damn, baby, don't be too long, okay!" He adjusts his dick.

I toss him a wink as we walk out. "Don't wait up!"

Priest drives us to the judge's office. He's going to drop us off at the event so we can pass him the gizmo.

I step out of the town car at the judge's office and slide in my earpiece. "Big Daddy, can you hear me?" I ask Dice through the mic in the necklace.

"Roger that, Black Widow." He half laughs.

"Which twat picked these stupid names?" I can just hear Dice laughing through the earpiece.

"Will you two quit it? We're supposed to be professional!" Bernie curses under his breath.

"Roger that, Poppa Bear," Dice breathes out.

I smirk as Pa Bernie takes my arm and leads me to the front entrance. Pa Bernie's security and I'm an escort, apparently! We sign in and head up to the judge's chambers, climbing the stairs and straightening my dress.

"You know what to do?" I nod as we reach Judge Metcalf's chambers. Pa Bernie knocks, and we are called in. Behind the desk stands a slim, short, balding man, approximately about five foot seven. His dark brown hair is slicked back with product, which you can see through his scalp. He's pasty, with flushed cheeks. His eyes are dull and brown, and there is a sheen over his forehead. He's dressed in an expensive charcoal three-piece suit, his jacket's open, and I can see the pocket watch hanging from his waistcoat, with a white shirt and red tie and pocket square. Bernie strides to the desk, arm outstretched.

"Marcus, Your Honour, I will be your security for this evening. Judge Metcalf, this is the escort we vetted for you, Celeste."

I lean in and take his hand as he kisses the back. The slimy motherfucker. I smile sweetly. "It's a pleasure. How should I address you this evening, sir?"

"Celeste, if you would call me Joseph, it will seem less of a business transaction and more a pleasure… " He smiles smarmily at me as if he thinks he's getting any pleasure at the end of this. Over my dead body, dickwad! He rakes his gaze over every inch of my exposed skin, then barks out. " ...and Marcus, refer to me as Judge Metcalf!"

"As you wish." Pa Bernie nods.

"Can I get you a drink, Celeste?"

"That would be wonderful, Joseph. Thank you." Smarmy fucker. I sickly smile at him as he pours himself a large scotch and a smaller one for me.

"May I speak with you outside for a moment, Judge Metcalf?"

He nods towards the door. "Of course, Marcus, please, step outside."

I slide my fingers along his nameplate, making appreciative noises. As I slide my hand along his leather inlaid desk, I sip at my drink as they leave the room. Throwing the rest of the drink in the potted plant in the corner, I shove my hand in my bra and pull out the device Dice has given me, grimacing as I catch my new jewellery. Fucker. I open his laptop and slide in the USB connector. "I'm in, Big Daddy. Fuck my life!" I grumble out.

"Okay, type in this password as I say it, okay?"

"On it!"

"M. K. 4. 2. 7. R. U. S. N. 2. 4. 9. 3. 7. G. Q."

"I'm in!"

"Black Widow, the lights on the device should all be red. Once each light is green, that section has been copied. They all need to turn green. Let me know when that's done, okay?"

"Will do!"

"Say it!"

"Fuck's sake, will do, Big Daddy. I fucking hate you. If you weren't my brother, I would castrate you!"

That just makes him chuckle through the earpiece.

"Motherfucker!"

"Halfway!" I breathe out after a few more minutes. "Two lights left." The door handle twitches.

"Just one more thing, Judge Metcalf," I hear Bernie say. Shit, the judge is itching to get back in. I slide the laptop almost closed in case they come back in, and I perch on the desk between the door and the laptop. I slide my dress over my left leg, covering all my tattoos, and cross my bare right leg over the top, so the judge will have a view of my whole bare leg right up to almost my underwear.

I lean back on the desk with my right hand, and I'm gripping the glass in my left. I peer over my shoulder. "One light left." I can hear mumbling voices now, and it sounds like the judge is getting impatient. I look back at the device. It's all green. I snatch it out of the laptop, pushing it closed.

"Done," I breathe out as the door swings open, and I give the judge my winning smile. "Well, don't you look a sight for sore eyes?" I smile wildly at him. I can see Pa rolling his eyes behind him. Fucking dick bag. This is gonna be a long, long fucking night, and I'm certain I'm not getting paid enough for this shit.

Pa rounds the judge, reaching out a hand to help me stand from the desk. Really I'm just handing over the device so he can hand it to Priest, who's driving the town car. Placing my glass down and picking up my clutch, I rise to my full height towering over the judge.

I must be six foot two in my heels, at least. He reaches out his arm to me. "Shall we go, my dear?" I smile politely, linking my arm through his. The judge is bent as fuck, and it's my job to get him to say something he shouldn't or do something he shouldn't. I'm supposed to be a big temptation, something we can use against him to get him in our pockets. He's as straight as they come on paper, but he's in someone's pocket, most definitely!

I stroke my hand down his arm as we head out of the building. "Oooh, Joseph, you must work out a lot to keep as trim as you are. You do look fabulous in that suit."

Pa opens the door for us, and we slide into the car. "Sir, miss." Priest nods as Pa climbs into the front passenger seat, and we head off to the gala. Pulling up, Pa Bernie opens the judge's car door, letting him out before they both come around to collect me.

Pa opens the door as I slide out to take the cockwomble's arm and give him a little peck on the cheek. "Thank you, Joseph, how chivalrous of you, darling!"

"Oooh, I like that!" he purrs. "Call me darling!"

Nodding, I smile again. "Of course, darling!"

A grin spreads across his face as we reach the bottom of the steps. There are paparazzi cordoned off to one side, separating them from us as we walk along the red carpet. I ascend the stairs, and twat takes my left hand in his left and slides his right hand to the small of my back, slowly creeping it to my arse cheek. I smile at him. *I swear to motherfucking Hades; I'm gonna rip his fucking arm off and beat him with the soggy end.*

My inner monologue is having a fucking field day with this cunt knuckle.

As we enter the ballroom, I reach for a glass of champagne, grabbing one for the judge. My clutch is burrowed under my arm, his hand still on my arse cheek.

"Here, darling." I thrust the glass at him so he has to remove his hand from my butt cheek. A sudden flush of cold hits it at the lack of contact, and it feels like the best feeling in the world. It is very short-lived as he passes the glass to his left hand. *Motherfucking dickwad.* I smile at him again as he returns his hand to my arse. Pa follows behind us, looking ever professional as I glance over my shoulder. I can see him smirk, and I give him the death glare as he straightens his face. *I'm gonna motherfucking murder some twat. I swear to Hades, I will actually do it.* I breathe out as there's a group of gentlemen. *Twat waffles.*

Joseph is leading us towards them, and he leans over to my ear, "I need you to be extremely attentive around these gentlemen."

I smile and nod.

"Gentlemen, how wonderful to see you all," Joseph coos.

"Allow me to introduce you to my better half, Celeste. Sweetheart, these are my work colleagues and golfing partners."

"Gentlemen, it's a pleasure, so you're all the reason my darling spends so much time away from me golfing. It's a pleasure to meet my competition."

One portly gentleman takes my hand, and while he's kissing the back of it, I'm sure he fucking licks me, honest to Hades, actually fucking licks me.

"Delectable," he mumbles. *Him, it's him I'm going to murder.*

Another takes my hand and raises it to his lips, but instead of kissing it, he smells me. "Devine."

I smile at them all in turn, run my hand up Joseph's chest, and fiddle with his lapel as they chat. A handsome younger guy steps up to us. "Uncle Joseph, would you mind if I took your date for a spin around the dance floor?" He nods without a backward glance and wafts his arm in the young man's direction, as if dismissing me. *Him. I'm gonna motherfucking kill him next.* "I'm Darnel," he says as he takes my hand, leading me to the dance floor.

"Celeste." I politely smile.

"Whatever he's paying you, it's not enough," he whispers in my ear.

"What makes you think he's paying me?" I smile sweetly.

"Have you seen yourself? It's totally obvious he's paying you. No one in their right mind who looks like you would be here with him otherwise."

"Not a fan, I take it?"

"What can I say? He's family, but just be careful. He doesn't like the word no, and tends to disregard it altogether."

"Duly noted, appreciate it." He nods, and we dance in silence for a little while, eventually making small talk as we waltz or whatever poncey shit we are doing before leading me back to the leech's den.

"Sweetheart, I missed you." Joseph leans up to kiss my cheek and gropes my arse again. He stinks of scotch, and his cheeks are even redder now. Clearly, he has a drinking problem. They are all starting to slur their words a little, tossing scotch back like it's going out of fashion. I glance back at Pa and nod.

I think now's a good time to see if I can get something to slip. "Darling," I purr in his ear, sliding my hand up his chest under his tie and sliding a finger in between the buttons, rubbing my finger along his moist hairy chest. *Ew, gross barf.* "I'm going to slip to the ladies' room." I kiss him on the cheek and linger a little longer than I should. *I'm gonna need to bleach every inch of myself and get my husband to fuck me senseless for a goddamned week to get the feel of this slimy bastard off me.* As I walk away, I sway my hips and glance back seductively over my shoulder and bite my lip.

"Fuck, Black Widow, this is making me wanna barf. I don't know how you're not," Dice grumbles in my ear.

"I've thrown up in my own mouth at least twelve times already, Big Daddy," I whisper, and he barks out a laugh down my earpiece, making me jump slightly. "Fucker!" I gasp at him, only making him laugh again.

"Incoming!" Pa's voice comes through.

"Okay, give us a little space. Make sure you're recording. I'm about to get what we need." I slow my pace as I reach the ladies' room door. As I step inside, I hold the door open a little longer than normal. As I let it go, Joseph steps in. I turn with a gasp.

"Joseph, darling, this is the ladies' room. The men's room is further down the corridor." He steps towards me, glazed over eyes, a sheen of sweat on his brow, his tie loosened, and his waistcoat now open. There is a slight bulge in his trousers as he grabs his dick through them, then tugs at it.

"You know how powerful I am. I can end you, so here's what's going to happen. You're going to get down on your knees and give me what I'm paying you for!" His hand grabs the back of my neck, and I have to still myself and play the part. *Oh, you're gonna be so fucking sorry once I get what I need.*

"Joseph!" I gasp. "I'm an escort, not a prostitute. How dare you!"

He pushes me back against the wall. "You're a whore, and you'll do what I pay you for!" Yanking on my hair, I wince.

"Black Widow, hold out, don't kill the bastard before we get what we need, okay?"

"Fucker!" I mumble under my breath. "Joseph, you're hurting me. Please let go of my hair, please."

"On your knees, whore, and take what I'm about to give you!" He's yanking my hair down and fumbling with his zipper.

"Please, please don't do this. I'm not a hooker. This isn't what I'm paid for. I'm here to escort you to this event, nothing more."

"Well, I'm gonna escort my dick in and out of your mouth till I come, and you're gonna swallow what I give you. Then after this event, you're coming back to the hotel, and you will do as you're told! Like the little bitch that you are!"

He gives up fumbling with his zipper long enough to slap me across the face. *Keep going, motherfucker. You're signing your own death warrant.* Yanking my hair back again to try and get me on my knees, he drags his zipper down and pulls out his half-hard dick.

"Get it in your mouth, whore."

"Keep it together, Black Widow," Dice reasons.

"Please don't do this," I beg him, but the feral look on his face tells me he's too far gone. He's not gonna stop till he's raping me, or he would if I wasn't me. "Are you going to rape me, Joseph?" I ask, as this will be a very compelling argument if I can get him to admit it.

"No!" he snarls at me. "Not here!" He grins down at me, grabbing my face.

"Judge Metcalf, Joseph, you're hurting me. You've forced me to my knees, you have me held by my hair, I'm crying on the bathroom floor in front of you, and you're trying to force your penis in my mouth. Please don't do this. I don't want you to go too far and rape me. I don't want to lose my virginity this way, please."

"You're a virgin?" He gasps and smiles. It's a nasty, vile, disgusting smile, and then his eyes glaze.

Dice snarls out, "Fuck it, Black Widow. Kill the son of a bitch."

Pa yells out, "Hold out, Black Widow!"

"Fuck sucking my dick. Take your fucking dress off now. I'm gonna fuck you on this floor like the slut you are."

"Please? I've just told you I'm a virgin. Don't do this!"

"I'm gonna fuck you every way I can because you're a virgin slut, and I'm gonna make you fucking bleed like a little bitch." He slaps me again, and I fall back on the floor as he dives on top of me, groping at my breasts. *Ow, motherfucker, they're still sore!*

"Please, please, someone help me!"

"Poppa Bear, we have enough!" Dice snarls over the earpiece.

The door opens, and Pa slips in. "Well, well, what do we have here?"

"Get outside and watch the door. Do what I tell you. We're role-playing. I'm gonna fuck her, and she's gonna scream blue murder while I pin her down. Either watch the door or grab her fucking arms. I will double your pay."

"Double, you say?"

"Just fucking do it now."

I thrash around. Well, I use that term loosely as a good stiff wind would blow this prick over. I don't think he could fight his way out of a wet paper bag, and we need to make it look good.

"All good, Black Widow. Take him out," Dice spits in the earpiece.

I rear up from underneath him, grabbing him by the throat and slamming him back into the wall. He gasps in surprise, his eyes darting from me to Pa and back again. As I relax my grip, I slam his head back into the wall again.

"You fucked up, darling!" I smirk at him, and he starts to claw at my hands and grabs at my wrist.

"Stop her," he chokes out, looking over at Pa.

My pa, who's checking his fingernails and leaning on the sink, says, "Sorry, boss… I'm on a break."

His eyes bulge as he's gasping, trying to draw air in. I lean in and whisper, "You shouldn't have underestimated me, motherfucker. This is gonna be fun." His eyes start to flutter, and he's verging on passing the fuck out. I drop him to the floor like a rag doll, and I kick him in the ribs once, twice, three times for good measure. "Fucking arsehole." I spit on him as Pa hauls him up. My cheek is red from where he hit me, and my hair's a little messy, but I think I can pull it off as we go to drag him out of the door while he gasps for breath.

"Guys, hang fire. Two black SUVs are pulling up… shit, eight guys, armed, full tactical gear. Get out of there!"

"Shit!" I murmur. "Poppa Bear, you need to take him out the back. I will cover you if they come for him. We need to get him out. Saving him will actually put him in our pocket more."

Pa nods. "Shit, okay, let's go!"

Slapping him round the face to bring him back to us, I say, "Come on, motherfucker." He starts to focus. I slap him hard, and his gaze spins to me, and full-on panic sets in. "Darling, I've got a proposition for you." He glances back between Pa and me, tears streaming down his face. "Please don't kill me?"

"There are eight men here to kill you. I can save you, but then you'll be in my pocket, and you'll do what I say when I say it, do you understand!"

"You're just an escort!" He looks confused at me, causing a laugh to erupt out of me, more of a maniacal laugh by this point.

"You fucked with the wrong girl this time! You're gonna be my little bitch now."

"Celeste, please."

"Oh, you can call me Black Widow. I'm about to become your saviour and also your motherfucking worst nightmare. Good luck with that!" I laugh out at him, grabbing the scruff of his neck. "Follow me, stay close, do not do anything stupid, or I will shoot you myself." I snatch up my clutch and grab the gun, pointing it at him. "Escape route three!" I nod to Pa, and he shoves Joseph through the door. We head up to the fifth floor. We've had the blueprints for this job for weeks.

I know the layout like the back of my hand: fifth floor, room 515. The Juliet balcony is directly opposite a larger balcony across the alleyway. Smashing the door in and yanking the balcony doors open, I point to the balcony. It's a floor below, so it should be easy enough to jump onto. "Poppa Bear, you go first, then I will send Joseph across."

Pa grabs him. "Fuck around, and she will gut you and leave you for dead!"

Joseph nods. It's then that the smell hits me. "Motherfucker pissed himself," I bark out.

"Fuck!" Bernie recoils in disgust.

"Go, we need to get out of here!" Pa Bernie makes the jump easily, and I shove Joseph over the balcony to stand on the ledge on the other side.

There's a bellow from the door. "In here!"

I shove Joseph over the end, and he grabs for the rail of the balcony, falling to the alley side rather than the balcony side, but Pa has grabbed for him and is dragging him over. I throw my shoes at Bernie. "I'll buy you some time, get that fucker out of here, meet you at rendezvous two!"

I launch back into the room. "Go!" I bellow.

The guy who was gobbling off steps towards me, and I lunge for him, punching him straight in the throat. As he gasps and clutches his neck, I kick his knee back, causing him to stumble.

As he rights himself, I kick him in the balls. Not as hard as I would have done with my shoes on, but it still drops him to his knees. I punch him in the temple, and he sways, trying to stand back up.

I take off towards the balcony as another guy barrels in after me. I jump up, poised, ready to thrust myself into the air. As I leave the balcony, the guy leans over, grabbing the bottom of my dress in his meaty fist.

I end up swinging back towards the balcony, lifting my arms to protect my face as I slam upside down on the railings.

There's an immediate ripping noise.

"In here!" The meathead who has my dress in his vice grip screams again. I hadn't given much thought to how I would die, but hanging there upside down by the fabric of my dress, one wrong move and I was a goner.

I thought I would die in some fucked up bloody gun battle somewhere, me against a hundred men, after killing ninety-eight of them. My injuries would be too bloody, but not before taking out the last two before perishing myself. Still, after Steel, I imagined it would be an orgasm that would take me out. What can I say? The man's talented. I did not imagine my death as me slipping out of a dress and plummeting five stories, face-first into an alleyway that probably stinks of piss and puke.

I kick my leg out and catch him in the face. He's trying to haul me up but has his elbows overextended over the railings hanging onto the fabric of the dress. There's another ripping noise, and I drop a bit more. "Fuck, in here!" he bellows again.

I need to get away. I bend my arms and legs, and I push off the balcony with all my strength and shoot forward, lunging out across the alleyway as a bloodcurdling scream comes from behind me, ripped out of the guy as he tumbles over the edge with me. He lets go of me to grab for the railings, but he's too slow to process what is happening.

As I fall, I wish I had more time in this life, more time with Steel, my brothers, my pas, my sisters, my family and most of all, more time as myself, the real me, instead of the half version I had been until I got here. I mourn the person I am now. I mourn the marriage I'm losing, the man I will no longer see. I mourn the children I will never have, the life I will never get to live, and as I plummet to my death, beyond anything else I wish.

To Be Continued…

Acknowledgements

For those of you who have made it this far in the series, thank you for taking a chance on an unknown author releasing this, the second book in my debut series. I've poured my swinging brick and little black soul into this series, and my swinging brick thanks you from the bottom of it for your support. I couldn't have done it without you all,

My mum and son,
My boozy book club Bestie,
My queen.
My besties,
The girls at United.

My new author/bookish besties for being there through my rants and the chaos.

I LOVE YOU ALL!!

To anyone who's read my book, liked a post, shared a video, no matter how small you think the gesture, I appreciate you all!

There are four books in this series, so if you loved this as much as I loved writing it and can't wait to see if Ray makes it out alive? Stand by and get ready to ride this rollercoaster with me. I promise it won't be dull! This is only the beginning!

Buckle up, buttercup, it's only gonna get bumpier!

♥

Books by Harley Raige

The Reapers MC, Ravenswood Series

Reaper Restrained 1 Aug 23
Reaper Released 1 Oct 23
Reaper Razed TBA
Reaper's Revenge TBA

Printed in Great Britain
by Amazon